RT BOOK REVIEWS PRAISES
NEW YORK TIMES BESTSELLING AUTHOR
MADELINE BAKER!

CHASE THE LIGHTNING

"Madeline Baker offers time-travel fans an innovative treat."

UNFORGETTABLE

"Madeline Baker continues to delight fans with her passionate Western adventures that thrill and captivate."

SPIRIT'S SONG

"Madeline Baker consistently delivers winning, heartwrenching, passionate romances and *Spirit's Song* is no exception."

UNDER A PRAIRIE MOON

"Madeline Baker writes of a ghost, a curse, and a second chance with such power and passion readers cannot help but be mesmerized."

CHASE THE WIND

"This sequel to *Apache Runaway* is pure magic and packed with action, adventure, and passion. Madeline Baker fans, get ready to laugh and cry from beginning to the surprising ending."

FORBIDDEN DESIRE

Shunkaha Luta closed his eyes as he tasted the inner sweetness of Brianna's mouth. His blood was singing loud and hot in his veins; his nostrils filled with the scent of her hair, and with the intoxicating scent of woman. Never had he wanted a woman more, and yet, despite her full breasts and soft curves, she was not a woman, but a child, untouched and innocent. Her arms twined around his neck and he felt her straining toward him, felt his skin turn to flame wherever her body brushed his.

"Ishna Wi," he said thickly. "You must tell me to stop before it is too late."

She did not understand. He read the confusion in her eyes, knew she yearned for him to give her that which she desired but did not fully understand.

Clenching his jaw, he put his hands on her shoulders and held her away from him. If only she were not a maiden. If only she were not so young. If only he did not want her so desperately. . . .

Other books by Madeline Baker:

CHASE THE LIGHTNING
UNFORGETTABLE
SPIRIT'S SONG
UNDER A PRAIRIE MOON
LOVE FOREVERMORE
LOVE IN THE WIND
FEATHER IN THE WIND
CHASE THE WIND
THE ANGEL & THE
  OUTLAW
RENEGADE HEART
LAKOTA RENEGADE
APACHE RUNAWAY
BENEATH A MIDNIGHT
  MOON

CHEYENNE SURRENDER
WARRIOR'S LADY
THE SPIRIT PATH
MIDNIGHT FIRE
COMANCHE FLAME
PRAIRIE HEAT
A WHISPER IN THE WIND
FORBIDDEN FIRES
LACEY'S WAY
RECKLESS DESIRE
RECKLESS LOVE
RECKLESS HEART
RECKLESS EMBRACE

Writing as Amanda Ashley:

MIDNIGHT EMBRACE
AFTER TWILIGHT (Anthology)
THE CAPTIVE
SHADES OF GRAY
A DARKER DREAM
SUNLIGHT, MOONLIGHT
DEEPER THAN THE NIGHT
EMBRACE THE NIGHT

First Love, Wild Love

MADELINE BAKER

First Love, Wild Love

Montlake
Romance

Published by Montlake Romance
P.O. Box 400818
Las Vegas, NV 89140

ISBN-13: 9781477831137
ISBN-10: 1477831134

To Mary Herzberg
best friend, critic and adviser

Gert Clements
and her entourage, and

Gina Hovda
songwriter/poet
for making my Tuesday mornings fun, and

To Nancy Smith
even though she moved so far away

Chapter One

It was late January and the Lakota were starving. His mother had taken *Wanagi Tacaka*, the Spirit Path, only the month before, too weak from lack of food to fight off the white man's coughing sickness. His sister, Tasina, had died in the night, and even now her spirit was wending its way to *Wanagi Yatu*, the Place of Souls.

He had no other living kin, and so he had been the one to prepare his sister's body for burial. He had dressed her wasted body in her finest doeskin tunic and ceremonial moccasins. With loving hands, he had braided her favorite red ribbon into her long black hair, had placed her favorite shell necklace around her slender throat. Lastly, he had placed her sewing kit at her side. He had gazed at her for one timeless moment, remembering the day she had been born, the way she had followed at his heels when she was a spindly-legged child, her liquid brown eyes openly adoring, her hand ever seeking his.

His eyes were damp with tears as he wrapped her frail body in a robe. Over that he placed a tanned deer hide, tying the whole securely with rawhide thongs to form a solid bundle. He had erected her burial scaffold on the same snow-covered hill where their mother's body lay, careful to make the scaffold high enough and strong enough so that predators could not desecrate the remains.

And now he stood at the foot of his sister's final resting place, his arms dripping blood where he had gashed his flesh to express his grief and sorrow at her loss.

"Wakan Tanka," he murmured, lifting his face toward the

cloud-draped sky, "please accept the soul of this fine young woman into your keeping."

Lifting his knife, he raked the finely honed blade across his naked chest. He welcomed the pain that trailed in the wake of the blade, rivaling the hurt and anger that warred in his heart. His mother and sister were dead, and his hatred for the whites burned hotter and stronger than ever. The Agency had promised beef and blankets and medicine to see the Lakota through the long hard winter. As always, they had delivered only empty words. And now the People were starving. Their lodges were filled with the piteous sound of children weeping as hunger clawed at their empty bellies, with the high-pitched keening wail of women as they grieved for their departed loved ones. Only a few warriors remained, and they lacked the stamina to fight. Their chief, White Hawk, had lost the will to go on.

The way of peace had failed, he thought bitterly, and now his sweet little sister was dead before she had really lived. It was more than he could bear.

He felt a twinge of homesickness as he remembered days gone by. The People had rarely known hunger in the old days. They had flourished in the Black Hills. Deer, elk, beaver, duck, the buffalo and the wolf, kit foxes, raccoons, badgers and squirrels, prairie dogs, the bear, all could be found in the wooded hills of the Pa Sapa. The People had harvested wild potatoes and onions, turnips and artichokes, strawberries and cherries, plums and June berries. But here, on the reservation, under the heavy thumb of the white man, the People wasted away.

He shivered as a cold north wind blew across the face of the land. Once, the People had spent their winters camped in the wooded hollows near the Pa Sapa where there was an abundance of wood to warm their lodges. They had eaten dried meat and pemmican, rose berries and acorns; if food supplies ran low, the men went hunting. Winter was when the women sewed new moccasins or made new clothing for their family from the hides they had tanned during the summer; the men fashioned new bows and arrows or repaired old weapons. Winter was a time for resting, for storytelling, for sledding on bowed buffalo ribs or sheets of rawhide.

He had heard rumors that some of the Oglala and Hunkpapa had not surrendered; that they still lived in the Black Hills, fighting for their land and their way of life. For a moment, he considered leaving the reservation to find his kinsmen. It would be good to fight the *wasicu,* good to draw the blood of the enemy, to hold a rifle in his hands once more. *It is better to die on the battlefield than to live to be old* was a well-known saying among the Lakota. But he could not turn his back on his people, not now, when they were slowly starving to death, when one man with courage might make a difference.

Turning, he left the burial site and returned to his lodge. It was cold and empty now that his mother and sister had followed his father into the world of spirits. He gazed, unseeing, into the sparse gray ashes of last night's fire. Had his mother and sister and father been reunited in the Land of Many Lodges? It was said that in the Place of Souls were pitched the tipis of all one's ancestors, that the departed lived in lush green valleys filled with all the good things nature had to offer. Buffalo and other animals were said to roam the Afterworld, where all things that had ever existed were believed to live again for eternity.

Face grim, he wiped the blood from his arms and chest, then donned a heavy buckskin shirt. It was the last thing his mother had made for him. The sleeves were long, fringed at the seam. An intricate design had been fashioned across the back, worked in dyed porcupine quills. It was a fine garment, made with loving hands.

Picking up his knife, he left his lodge. Restless, his heart filled with grief, he walked among the lodges of his people. Only a handful of men were outside. A few nodded as he passed by, their eyes dull and empty of hope. He heard the cries of children as they begged for food that wasn't there, heard the high-pitched keening of a squaw and knew that someone had died.

His mouth thinned in determination. No longer would he sit patiently in his lodge, waiting for the Agency to deliver the food and clothing that were promised but never delivered. His people were hungry *now*.

Returning to his lodge, he swung aboard his horse and guided it away from the scattered lodges of the Sioux. Once there had been hundreds of tipis. Now there were only a few. Once, he had owned a hundred fine ponies. Now he had only one. It was a bitter thing, not having a horse to kill so that his sister might ride in comfort to the Afterworld. Once all this land had belonged to the Lakota and their allies, the Cheyenne and the Arapahoe. Now the white man had come, claiming the land of the Spotted Eagle as his own, putting up fences of wood and spiked wire, grazing their fat red-and-white cattle where the humpbacked buffalo had once roamed in numbers too great to count. It was the spotted cattle of the white man that filled his mind now. If the Agency would not supply the meat they had promised, then he would steal it from the *wasicu*, for he could no longer bear to hear the hungry cries of his people.

The land was quiet, seemingly devoid of life. Dark clouds scudded across the sky, driven by an icy wind. The trees stood stark and bare, the hills were streaked with snow. He huddled deeper into his shirt and urged his gaunt pony into the face of the wind.

It took the better part of the day to reach the outskirts of the ranch that sprawled over hundreds of acres that had once known only the footsteps of the People. The whites claimed to own the land, but such a concept was inconceivable to the Indian. The land was free, like the wind and the water. The earth was the mother of all life. Man borrowed that which was needed to sustain life, but he did not own it. The Indian saw only today, lived only for today. He trusted the earth to provide for tomorrow.

The *wasicu* kept his cattle close to home during the winter, supplementing the sparse graze with hay. He guided his pony toward a few head of cattle that were bunched near a small knoll. He had fashioned a crude lance from a stout limb; his knife was secured to the head of the lance.

A squeeze of his legs put his horse into a lope and he went after a fat spotted cow. The cow turned and ran, but she was no match for his horse, and he chased her down as he would have chased a buffalo, a wild cry of triumph erupting from his throat as his lance brought the cow down.

Reining his horse to a halt, he jerked the lance free. Removing his knife from the shaft, he began to skin the beast, his mouth watering at the prospect of fresh meat. *Woman's work*, he thought with wry amusement, and felt a catch in his throat. His women were dead.

He lit a small fire and roasted a good-sized chunk of meat, wolfing it down before it was even half cooked, licking the rich red blood from his fingertips, savoring the taste of the meat, which was not so sweet as the flesh of *pte* but was very good to a man who had not had meat of any kind in over a month.

When he had eaten his fill, he wrapped the remainder of the meat in the cow hide, draped it over his horse's withers, and vaulted onto his back. There would be meat in the lodges of the Lakota this night, he thought triumphantly, and for many nights to come.

He was riding away from the scene of the kill when a pair of cowhands topped the rise.

"I'll be damned!" the taller of the two white men exclaimed. "Will you look at that? That redskin's butchered one of our cows!"

"Let's get him," the second man said, drawing his rifle from his saddle scabbard.

"No killing," the first cowboy admonished with regret. "The boss wouldn't like it."

The second man nodded, and the two cowhands spurred their mounts down the hill.

The warrior urged his horse into a gallop, but the animal was heavily burdened and could not outdistance the pursuing riders.

The Indian cursed his lack of a weapon as one of the white men began firing at him. A bullet slammed into his back, driving the breath from his body, and he toppled from his horse, spiraling down, down, into a world of darkness.

Chapter Two

Brianna Beaudine brushed a wisp of sweat-dampened hair from her forehead. It was unusually hot, even for July, and her dress was damp with perspiration. Her back ached from hours of weeding her Aunt Harriett's vegetable garden. She had made her way through twelve rows and had another twelve to go before she was through. Her hands were red and sore; there was an ugly blister on the heel of her left hand, another on her right thumb.

Sullen-faced, she looked past the garden to the line of clothes flapping in the mild summer breeze. When she finished weeding the garden, she would have to take the clothes from the line. Then it would be time to milk the cow, feed the pigs and the chickens, and set the table for dinner. And those were just her daytime chores.

Brianna let out a long sigh. It wasn't the work itself she hated. She loved the land, loved tilling the soil and planting and watching things grow. More than anything else, she longed for a home of her own, for a husband who would cherish her, for a child to love as she had once been loved.

Instead, she must live here, toiling for her aunt and uncle. And here she would remain until her uncle found her a suitable husband, or until she got so fed up that she ran away. She considered it often, but somehow she could never bring herself to leave. This was the only real home she had ever known. Her parents had never owned a house, never stayed long in any one place. Her father had been an itinerant preacher and had traveled the length and breadth of New England, preaching the word of God to any and all who would listen. Brianna had idolized her father, certain he had been ordained by God to spread the Word, but she had still yearned for a home of her own, for a chance to go to school, to make friends. She had often gazed longingly at the neat red brick homes they passed, wishing her family would settle down in some quiet town. But they never did. And then her parents had been killed.

Brianna remembered that night well. They had been on their way to some small New York town where her father was scheduled to preach when they were caught in a violent summer storm. Lightning had spooked the carriage horse and it had bolted, overturning the carriage. Brianna's mother and father had been killed instantly, and she had been sent to live with her father's brother.

Two large tears welled in Brianna's brilliant blue eyes and she dashed them away. Crying was childish and a waste of time and energy. But, oh, how she hated it here! Her aunt and uncle made her work like a field hand, never expressing a word of thanks, never complimenting her on a task well done. Instead, they were constantly reminding her that if she lived to be a hundred years old, she would never be able to repay them for taking her in and giving her a place to live and three meals a day.

Brianna made a sound of derision. A place to live, indeed! She slept in a tiny attic room on a hard narrow cot. The room was cold in the winter, as warm as an oven in summer. In truth, she thought it looked more like a jail cell than a room. There were no curtains at the small circular window, not so much as a rag rug or a picture to brighten her dismal surroundings. There was only a bed to sleep in, a chipped white enamel chamber pot, and a battered trunk to hold her few belongings.

The rest of the house was luxurious by Western standards. The kitchen was spacious and cluttered with every gadget imaginable. The wood stove was the best that money could buy; the pantry was well stocked with jars of vegetables and fruit that Brianna had put up. The dining room featured a large mahogany table and six matching chairs, a sideboard, and a small crystal chandelier that Harriett Beaudine had brought all the way from Pennsylvania. The bedroom was quite large, with a big brass bed, an oak commode, highboy, and wardrobe. Pink damask draperies hung at the single window; there was a matching pink counterpane on the bed. A gaudy Chinese carpet covered most of the floor. The parlor was dominated by a large fireplace built of native stone. An upright piano occupied one corner of the room. Brianna loved the piano, but she was not permitted to touch it. She was, in fact, only permitted in the parlor on rare occasions, like when the Reverend Jackson came to call. It made her aunt and uncle feel very righteous, showing the minister what wonderful people they were by providing a home for Henry's niece. The rest of the time, Brianna was expected to stay in her room, or in the kitchen, out of the way.

She wiped a sleeve across her brow, hating the ugly dress she had to wear. It was a size too large because her aunt didn't believe a young lady should flaunt her body. The dress had long sleeves and a high neck. Brown in color, it was unrelieved by ribbon or lace. Her other work dress was exactly the same, except that it was dark blue. Her only other dress was a severe black wool that she wore to church on Sundays. Its only redeeming features were that it was the right size and had a bit of dainty white lace at the collar and cuffs.

With a heavy sigh, Brianna went back to work, carefully pulling the weeds from the rows of peas and beans and squash and lettuce. It was such a long, boring job, one that would have to be done again and again before all the crops were harvested.

By the time she finished weeding the garden, she was certain her back would break in two. She began to hum one of the hymns they sang at church as she took down the laundry,

hoping it might make the task go by quicker. She had a pleasant voice, and the preacher had asked if she might sing in
the church choir, perhaps even offer a solo, but Aunt Harriett wouldn't hear of such a thing. Singing in church might
put foolish notions of pride into Brianna's head.

As she dropped the last article of clothing into the wicker
basket at her feet, Brianna sent a long look toward the
house. Her aunt and uncle had gone into town and wouldn't
be back until dark. If she hurried, she could sneak in a quick
swim in the lake and still get all her chores done before they
returned home.

The thought of floating in the cool, clear water was stronger than the threat of punishment if she got caught, and she
kicked off her shoes and stockings, then ran lightly across
the fields. The lake was one of her favorite places. Located
near the crest of the hill that separated her uncle's land from
the forest beyond, it was surrounded by shrubs and wild
blackberry bushes. Tall, lacy cottonwoods provided shade
even on the hottest days.

As she neared the lake, the sound of a man's voice drew
her attention and she glided past the shimmering pool, her
curiosity drawing her toward the sound.

The ground past the lake was flat and studded with pines
for about twenty feet and then it sloped downward, the hill
on the far side being long and steep and heavy with timber.
Reaching the crest, she came to an abrupt halt, then ducked
out of sight behind a tall oak tree.

A handful of men were cutting trees at the foot of the
hill. The men wore heavy iron shackles on their hands and
feet. Two other men, mounted and armed with rifles, rode
up and down the line of prisoners, shouting orders and
whipping the men who did not respond quickly enough.

Slowly, Brianna edged a little further down the hill for a
closer look. The men on the road gang were all young, in
their twenties and early thirties. They were shirtless, their

sun-browned torsos gleaming with sweat. She knew she should return home immediately. This was no place for a girl. Her ears burned with the vile language the two mounted men hurled at the prisoners, and her stomach felt queasy as one of the guards struck a prisoner and drew blood.

But she stayed rooted to the spot. She had never seen a convict before, never seen a man without a shirt. Slowly, her gaze wandered down the line of shackled men, coming to rest on the man at the far end of the line. He was taller than the others, with straight black hair, copper-colored skin, and angry black eyes. A long red welt ran the length of his chest.

Brianna gasped as she realized he was an Indian. She had never seen an Indian before and she could not help staring at him. He wore a pair of grimy buckskin pants that were fringed on the outer seams, a clout, and moccasins. His arms were long, his biceps bulging as he swung an ax at a large pine tree. His movements were graceful, filled with power, and she felt her mouth go dry as she watched the rhythmic play of muscles in his arms and back and shoulders.

She flinched as the whip danced over the Indian's broad back. His dark eyes burned with anger and pain as the lash drew blood, but he made no sound.

She sat there for half an hour, unable to take her eyes from the Indian. The two mounted men whipped him more often than the other prisoners, their voices chastising him for working too slow, calling him a "lazy, no-account buck" even though he worked as hard and as fast as any of the other men.

Another twenty minutes passed by, and the prisoners were allowed a break for lunch. Brianna shook her head, her heart filling with pity, when the road boss refused to let the Indian have anything to eat or drink. He did not object to their ill treatment. Instead, he hunkered down on his heels and stared up at the tree-studded slope, his face impassive, his dark eyes smoldering with impotent fury.

Brianna froze, her heart hammering in her breast as his

eyes met hers. Scrambling to her feet, she darted up the hill toward home.

Her uncle mentioned the road gang at dinner that night. The Reverend Jackson was dining with them, as he did at least one night a week. Brianna welcomed the minister's company. He always had a kind word for her, a warm smile, as though he knew how desperately she craved such things.

"Have you heard about the new road they're building between here and Jefferson?" Uncle Henry asked the Reverend Jackson. "Gonna shave thirty miles off the trip."

"Is that so?" the minister replied.

Henry Beaudine nodded.

Matthew Jackson frowned. "Tell me, how are they going to get through the Ridge?"

"Gonna blast their way through," Henry Beaudine answered, slapping his thigh for emphasis. "It'll take a while to get the road finished, of course. First they've got to cut their way through those trees, then level the ground."

Harriett Beaudine threw a stern look in Brianna's direction. "Sit up, girl," she admonished sharply.

Brianna quickly sat up straight, her cheeks flushing a bright pink. Aunt Harriett was always picking on her when they had company, always trying to make her look bad, chastising her for her poor posture, criticizing the way she held her fork, the way she used her napkin.

"They'd get that road done a sight quicker if they had more men on that road gang," Henry Beaudine was saying. "They've only got five men to do a twenty-man job."

"Personally, I do not care to have those despicable men so close to our place," Harriett Beaudine remarked sourly. "They are nothing but scum."

"We are all God's children, and all the same in His sight," Matthew Jackson said quietly, "regardless of our circumstances."

"Yes, of course," Harriett Beaudine said quickly. "I feel sorry for the poor unfortunate men, but you must admit it gives one cause for alarm, especially when we have an impressionable young girl to consider."

Matthew Jackson nodded, his eyes moving to Brianna's face. She was a lovely girl. In spite of the fact that Harriett Beaudine refused to let Brianna wear decent clothes or arrange her hair in a more becoming style, the girl possessed an air of quiet beauty and femininity that promised to grow still stronger as she matured. He had spent many a sleepless night contemplating her natural beauty and grace, and many a morning on his knees seeking forgiveness for his carnal thoughts.

Harriett Beaudine stood up. "Come, gentlemen," she said, placing her napkin on the table. "Let us go into the parlor for tea. Brianna, clear the table and see to the dishes."

"Yes, ma'am," Brianna answered, her tone bordering on insolence.

Harriett Beaudine shot the girl a quelling glance. The little chit had been getting a mite too uppity of late. Perhaps it was time to give her the whipping she so richly deserved, time to remind her of her place.

Brianna's face paled as she recognized the ominous expression in her aunt's pale green eyes. It was a look she had seen before, one that she dreaded, and she knew she was going to get a whipping if she didn't keep a tight rein on her tongue.

Oh, how she hated it here! If only she had the nerve to run away. But she had no money, no friends, and no place to go. But someday, she vowed, someday she would get away from her aunt. Please, God, she prayed, let someday come soon.

Chapter Three

Shunkaha Luta sat huddled against the tree, his hands shackled behind his back, the shackles on his feet chained to those of the man next to him. All around him he could hear the sounds of men snoring, but he could not sleep. His thoughts were troubled, filled with concern for his people. It was July now, the Month of the Cherry Ripening Moon, the month when the seven tribes of the Lakota nation met in the Black Hills for the annual Sun Dance ceremony. He had been away from the lodges of his people for six months.

Six months, he mused bitterly. After he had been shot and captured by the two cowboys, he had been taken to the white man who owned the ranch. The white man had eyed him curiously.

"You speak English?" the old man had asked, but Shunkaha Luta had refused to answer.

"In the old days, I'd have strung you up," the white man had remarked, "but we're more civilized now. We'll let the law decide what to do with you."

Shunkaha Luta grimaced. The white man's law had decided that the penalty for stealing one cow was worth two years of his life at hard labor. He had spent a month in prison while the wound in his back healed, his soul slowly dying, withering like a flower deprived of the sun as each day behind bars seemed darker and longer than the last. He had spent his time remembering his youth, remembering the values he had been taught by his grandfather. Bravery, generosity, wisdom, and fortitude, these were the virtues a warrior was expected to seek.

Bravery was the attribute most warriors sought above all else. To have courage, to have a strong heart, was of extreme importance. Honors went to those who proved themselves in battle, who took chances and courted danger, who defended themselves against overwhelming odds. Bravery was a virtue that women sought as well, and was lauded as it was among men. Bravery was impressed on the mind from childhood. It was in the stories the old ones told around the campfires at night, in the rules for behavior that the parents handed down, in the games the children played. Bravery was not just an ideal, it was a way of being, of acting, of doing. Young boys were encouraged to behave fearlessly, to laugh in the face of danger. Counting coup was one way to achieve war honors. It took great courage to get close enough to one's enemy to touch him, and whether the enemy was slain or only wounded was not important. To touch an opponent and risk death at his hand was far more courageous than shooting him from a distance. A man could boast of his coups, so long as he did not exaggerate.

Fortitude was also a virtue widely admired, for it meant that a man could endure physical discomfort and pain, as well as the ability to remain stoic during times of emotional stress. Warriors on war missions or hunting expeditions were expected to suffer wounds unflinchingly, to accept long periods of hunger and exposure without complaint.

Generosity was as much a necessity as a virtue. To accumulate wealth for its own sake was disgraceful. Gift-giving was a way of life. Men returning from a hunt shared the kill; men returning from a raiding party shared whatever goods and horses they had stolen. Feasts and celebrations were given on important occasions. Everyone was invited and gifts were exchanged.

Wisdom was to be sought, and was highly prized. A man who was wise was asked to advise others, to help settle arguments, to teach the young. Such men often became shamans.

Shunkaha Luta gazed into the darkness, aware of a coyote gliding soundlessly through the shadows of the night, and then he gazed up at the stars. Fortitude was the virtue he now stood most in need of. Living in chains, treated like a beast, whipped and abused by his enemies, he had called on every ounce of self-control he possessed. True, being on the road gang was better than languishing behind bars. Here, at least, he could breathe the cool clean air, see the mountains, smell the sweet fragrance of earth and trees. And yet, in some ways, it was harder than being locked in a cell. To see the hills and not be able to run their wooded slopes, to breathe the sweet fragrance of the earth while chains rattled at his feet, seemed the worst torture of all.

He stared at the heavy irons on his hands and feet. When his captors had first locked the cumbersome shackles in place, he had struggled as wildly as a wolf caught in a trap. Even knowing he could not break free, he had struggled against the chains until his wrists and ankles were raw and bleeding. Now, six months later, their weight was as familiar as the color of his skin.

One of the prisoners cried out in his sleep, and Shunkaha Luta turned his gaze toward the convicts. The other prisoners ignored him, distrusting him because he was an Indian, hating him because he refused to grovel, refused to be less than a man. They sold their pride to avoid the whip, cowered at any threat. Shunkaha Luta would not. Could not. His pride was all he had left and he guarded it jealously.

With a sigh, he closed his eyes and the image of the young white girl he had seen on the hillside earlier that day danced across his mind. He had caught only a glimpse of long sun-gold braids and then she was gone, but her memory had stayed with him all through the long hours of the afternoon. Who was she? Where had she come from?

Her image was still in his mind when, at long last, he fell asleep.

*   *   *

He woke with the dawn, a sense of dread welling up inside
him at the thought of yet another day in bondage. The time
passed so slowly. How would he endure another year and a
half in chains? The two white men in charge of the road gang
harassed him constantly, taunting him, making endless jibes
about the color of his skin, exchanging foolish jokes and lewd
remarks about Indians, and Indian women in particular.

In the beginning, he had lashed out, wanting nothing
more than to kill the two *wasicu* who treated him with such
contempt. But his outbursts had resulted in cruel beatings
and whippings and days without food and water, until the
futility of fighting back overcame his need for vengeance.
His back was scarred from the many whippings he had received; he no longer reacted to their childish taunts, but inside he was seething with rage. He no longer spoke, no
longer fought back verbally or physically, but neither did he
grovel before them. His silence, his unwillingness to bend,
to give in, irritated the white men. He knew that was the
reason they continued to torment him, knew he had only to
pretend he was cowed and they would let up on him. But he
could not do it. Instead, he labored day after endless day, his
need for vengeance growing like a worm in his belly, eating
at his soul, until he sometimes thought he might die with
the need to strike out, to spill the blood of his enemies.

There had been days when they worked him long after
the other prisoners had settled down for the night, days
when his hands bled and his back and shoulders screamed
for relief, days when they refused to let him rest, refused him
both food and water.

With time, his hands grew hard and calloused; the muscles in his arms, back, shoulders and legs grew stronger, more
powerful. There was no excess fat on him now, only taut
bronze flesh stretched over corded muscle. He bore their
abuse stoically, the patience that had been instilled in him

as a young warrior still strong. Someday, he vowed, someday
he would have the revenge he so desired.

But it would not be today.

Brianna tried to keep a cheerful thought as she carefully
ironed Aunt Harriett's navy blue go-to-meeting dress, but
she was so weary. She had always hated ironing more than
anything else, and now she had to do every single item over
again because her aunt had been displeased with the way
Brianna had ironed one of Uncle Henry's work shirts. If
only it wasn't so hot! If only she could go for a swim in the
lake. Thinking of the lake brought the Indian to mind, and
she wondered if he was still there and what he was doing.
Did he hate felling trees as much as she hated ironing?

She could hear Aunt Harriett chatting with Margie
Croft. Margie and her husband, Luke, owned Crofts' General Store in the nearby town of Winslow.

Brianna slammed the iron on the board, her movements
quick and angry as she pressed the wrinkles from one of
Uncle Henry's shirts. Aunt Harriett always had time to visit
with her friends, Brianna thought sullenly, because Brianna
did most of the housework and all the washing, ironing,
mending, and gardening. About the only thing Aunt Harriett ever did was cook dinner, and that only when she was
in the mood "to be creative" in the kitchen.

It took two hours to finish the ironing, and when she was
done, Brianna went into the parlor to see what her aunt wanted
her to do next.

Margie Croft smiled at Brianna as the girl entered the parlor. Brianna Beaudine was a lovely child, with a sweet disposition and a gentle nature, and Margie had often thought the
girl deserved a better life than the one she had with Harriett
Beaudine.

"Good afternoon, Brianna," Margie Croft said pleasantly.
"We haven't seen you in town much of late."

"No, ma'am," Brianna answered.

"You should try to get in more often, dear. There's a church social this coming Saturday. Luke and I are going to chaperone. Could we pick you up? Say about seven?"

Brianna looked at her aunt, not daring to answer.

"If Brianna decides to go, her uncle will take her," Harriett Beaudine said. She frowned at her niece over the rim of her blue china tea cup. "We'll discuss it later. Why don't you take Chauncey to the lake and give him a bath? I think you have done most of the inside chores for today."

"Yes, ma'am," Brianna answered meekly. She dropped a quick curtsey in Mrs. Croft's direction, pasted a stiff smile on her face, and left the room.

Oh, wouldn't it be heavenly to go to a church social! To dance and laugh with people her own age. To wear a pretty dress and listen to the music, perhaps meet a handsome young man who would fall in love with her and give her a home of her own.

Instead, she had to bathe Chauncey. She hated her aunt's dog. It was a huge beast, with long hair that had to be painstakingly brushed after she bathed him. But, Brianna thought with a smile, it would give her a chance to go for a swim.

Removing her shoes and stockings outside where her aunt couldn't see and object, Brianna called the dog and skipped off toward the lake. Chauncey trotted at her side, his long pink tongue lolling out of the side of his mouth. He was, Brianna thought, quite the ugliest dog she had ever seen.

By the time she had bathed Chauncey, she was soaked to the skin, but she didn't care. The water was wonderfully cool, and after tying Chauncey to a tree where he couldn't roll in the dirt, she slipped out of her clothes and went for a leisurely swim. How pleasant to float on your back with nothing to do, to be able to take time out just to daydream, to study the vast blue vault of the sky, or watch a blackbird drink from the edge of the quiet pool.

Some time later, she stepped from the lake and quickly pulled on her ugly brown dress, rebraided her hair. Chauncey was asleep, his forelegs twitching as he dreamed of chasing rabbits and squirrels. After a moment's hesitation, Brianna made her way toward the hill, slipping from tree to tree so she wouldn't be seen as she edged down the slope.

She spotted the Indian immediately. He was wrestling with the stump of a tree, trying to dislodge its tenacious bond with the earth. His broad shoulders and long arms were taut with the strain, every muscle bulging and well-defined. Sweat coursed down his broad back, and Brianna found it suddenly hard to breathe as she watched him. He closed his eyes in concentration as he summoned every ounce of strength he possessed and focused it on the stump. She marveled at the beauty of his profile; held her breath as he gave a mighty shove, felt like cheering as the tree stump toppled sideways to the ground, its roots splayed like tentacles.

For a moment, the Indian stood there, breathing heavily, his arms dangling at his sides, his legs slightly spread. How magnificent he looked, Brianna thought, with his bronze body sheened with perspiration, his sides heaving from the strain. He reminded her of a wild stallion that had been caught and hobbled but would never be tamed.

One of the road bosses called for a rest break and passed among the prisoners carrying a bucket of water. Brianna frowned when the road boss passed by the Indian without giving him a chance to drink. Why did they treat him so abominably? He worked as hard as, if not harder than, the others.

She sat there for almost an hour, forgetful of the time. He was such a joy to watch. His every movement was graceful, beautiful to behold. She marveled at his easy strength, at the sight of so much naked male flesh, so many rippling muscles. Just looking at him filled her with feelings she had never known and could not identify; strangely pleasant sensations that fluttered in the pit of her stomach and made her heart beat fast.

She saw him gaze into the distance, saw the longing that flared in his fathomless black eyes as he stared at the faraway mountains. Intuitively, she knew he was thinking of home.

A short time later, the second road boss herded the other prisoners farther up the road until they disappeared from sight around a bend. The first road boss fastened a short length of chain to the iron cuff around the Indian's left ankle, then secured the other end to one of the heavy, iron-rimmed wagon wheels. Moving out of the Indian's reach, the road boss tossed a hand saw onto the ground at the prisoner's feet.

"Get to work on that wood pile," the boss ordered curtly. He gestured at a large stack of logs. "I want the whole pile cut into neat three-foot lengths by the time I get back, or you'll go to bed hungry again tonight. You savvy?"

The Indian did not reply, only glared at the white man for a long moment before he stooped and picked up the saw. Fleetingly, he thought of removing the wheel from the wagon and trying to make a run for it, but it was a foolish idea. How far could he get with his feet shackled while dragging a wheel that weighed close to a hundred pounds? He worked with steady precision, glad to be alone.

Watching him, Brianna found herself again admiring his easy strength and economy of movement, the play of corded muscle and sinew beneath his smooth, copper-hued skin. Twice, he paused, his eyes lingering on the water bucket that hung from the tailgate just out of reach.

Before she quite knew what she was doing, Brianna slipped out of her hiding place and ran down the hill.

Shunkaha Luta came to an abrupt halt, the saw in his hand forgotten as the girl with the sun-gold hair darted across the road toward the wagon. He watched through narrowed eyes as she scooped a dipper full of water from the bucket and started toward him.

Brianna's footsteps slowed as she felt the full force of the Indian's gaze upon her face. Pausing in mid-stride, she held the dipper out toward him. "Water," she said. "Would you like a drink?"

Shunkaha Luta nodded warily. Was she teasing him? Playing a childish prank?

Brianna took a step forward and then stopped again. Seen up close, the Indian was much taller and broader than she had thought and she was suddenly afraid of him. "You won't hurt me, will you?"

The Indian shook his head and Brianna wondered if he could speak. She had never heard him say anything, but he obviously understood English. Still, she remained where she was, wondering how she could hand him the dipper without getting any closer. Her eyes met his and she felt a quick heat suffuse her from head to foot. Almost, she changed her mind, but then she saw him swallow, saw his tongue slide over his lips, which were dry and cracked, and she knew she could not refuse to let him quench his thirst.

Shunkaha Luta did not move as the girl slowly closed the remaining distance between them. He sensed she was afraid of him, knew she would have turned and fled except that her pity for him was stronger than her fear.

Her hand was shaking as she held the dipper out to him. Slowly, so as not to startle her, he reached out and took the dipper from her hand, emptying the ladle of its contents in two long swallows. He closed his eyes with pleasure as the cool water bathed his throat and dry lips.

"Would you like more?" Brianna asked, her eyes intent on his face. How handsome he was! His eyes were black as midnight. His brows were thick and straight, his jaw strong and square, his cheekbones high. And his mouth . . . she felt her stomach flutter queerly as he licked the last drops of water from his lips. "More?" she asked again, and her voice came out in a high-pitched squeak.

Shunkaha Luta nodded as he handed her the dipper. His fingertips brushed her hand and for the space of a heartbeat they stared at each other. Brianna was the first to look away. Her whole hand seemed to be on fire from his touch and she was hardly aware of walking toward the bucket and refilling the dipper.

She offered him the ladle a second time, her mind whirling with his nearness, her eyes never leaving his face. How could a man be so beautiful?

"*Le mita pila,*" he said, his voice low and resonant. "My thanks."

"You're welcome," Brianna replied softly. She continued to gaze up at him, her cheeks flushed, her heart beating a wild tattoo.

Abruptly, she turned on her heel and hurried toward the wagon, frightened by the strange emotions running rampant through her heart. Dropping the dipper into the bucket, she ran up the hill without a backward glance.

Chauncey's tail thumped the ground as she fell to her knees beneath the tree, her hand pressed over her heart. What was happening to her? Why did she feel so strange? She glanced up at the sun, then groaned in despair. She had been gone for over an hour and Chauncey wasn't even groomed yet. Aunt Harriett would be furious.

Working quickly, she began to brush the dog's thick coat, tears of frustration welling in her eyes when the beast refused to stand still.

Aunt Harriett was waiting for her on the back porch, her face stern, her eyes angry. "Where have you been, young lady?" she demanded crossly.

"At the lake," Brianna answered.

Aunt Harriett looked pointedly at her watch. "It does not take an hour and a half to bathe Chauncey," she said in an icy tone.

"I . . . I fell asleep."

Harriett Beaudine fixed her niece with a hard stare. "I have not been pleased with your attitude or your performance of late," she declared. "If you do not mend your ways, young lady, I shall be forced to punish you."

The cold hand of fear wrapped itself around Brianna's insides. She had been whipped several times before; once when she had broken her aunt's favorite teacup, once for scorching one of Uncle Henry's shirts, twice for being impudent. The memory of those beatings was enough to bring a cold sweat to her brow.

"I'll do better," Brianna promised quickly.

"See that you do. Hurry now, it is time to set the table for dinner."

"Yes, ma'am."

Brianna was especially cautious at dinner that evening. She sat up straight, used her napkin often, took tiny bites, chewed her food thoroughly, and kept her eyes on her plate. Aunt Harriett was just itching for an excuse to whip her, she thought with dismay. She would have to tread with care in the future.

Shunkaha Luta stared up at the vast vault of the midnight sky, too weary to sleep. Instead, he thought of the girl with the golden hair. He had glimpsed her up on the hill almost every day for over two weeks. He wondered what she found so fascinating about watching a man in chains toiling in the hot sun. Surely a beautiful young girl had better things to do than hide behind a tree spying on a bunch of shackled men.

And yet, unaccountably, it pleased him to know she was there. She was the first white person to show him any degree of kindness, the first white woman he had ever seen up close, and he was enchanted by her fair hair and brilliant sky-blue eyes. It had taken courage for her to help him. Likely she would have incurred scorn and derision from her friends and family for giving water to an Indian; perhaps she would have been punished. Yes, there was steel beneath the velvet skin and soft-spoken words. And he admired that most of all.

Brianna hastened through her afternoon chores, then ran to the hill. She could spare only a few minutes today, but she had to see him, had to know he was still there. She could not explain how or why he had become so important to her, only that he had.

From her vantage point behind a tree, Brianna watched him labor in the hot sun. She saw the lash bite into his back, saw him wince though he never uttered a word of protest or a cry of pain. She saw the hatred in his eyes when he looked at the two white men who tormented him, and she wondered how he had learned to keep such a tight rein on his temper. It finally dawned on her that the road bosses abused him more than the other convicts not only because he was an Indian, but because they feared him. Like her, they sensed the power sleeping beneath his passive facade.

Occasionally, Brianna saw him glance up the hill. Was he thinking of her, looking for her? Were his dreams haunted with her image as hers were haunted with his?

Nightly, his swarthy countenance rose up before her, his eyes dark and strangely compelling, calling to her in ways she did not understand. She woke from such dreams feeling slightly breathless. Often her skin was damp with sweat, her face flushed as though with a fever, and she felt curiously empty inside. One night she had slipped from bed and touched a match to the candle on her bedside table. Then she had stood before the small cracked mirror that hung on the wall, studying her face, wishing she were prettier, older, wiser in the ways of men. Suddenly feeling guilty, she had blown out the candle and crawled back into bed, only to lay awake for hours, thinking of the Indian.

She stayed in her hiding place a moment longer, hating to

leave, yet not daring to remain. Still, the knowledge that he was still nearby filled her with a sense of peace.

On Saturday, her aunt and uncle made their weekly trip into town for supplies. As usual, they did not invite Brianna to accompany them. Once, being left behind had filled Brianna with feelings of anger and regret. But no more. As soon as they were out of sight, she raced to the hill. There had been a time when she had spent every moment she could spare at the lake, or curled up in her secret corner of the loft with a book, but neither cool water nor the written word held any appeal for her now. Not when she could see the Indian.

She heard the sound of the whip as she crested the hill.

"Not him," she murmured. "Please, not him."

The words were a prayer for mercy, a softly uttered plea that died on her lips as she crept down the brush-covered slope, darting from tree to tree until she could see him clearly.

The Indian's arms were shackled to a stout limb high above his head. His feet barely touched the ground. The road boss Brianna had nicknamed Black Hat was whipping the Indian with steady precision, the rawhide lash rising and falling in a neat arc to land with cruel force upon the Indian's tawny flesh. His whole back seemed covered with blood, and Brianna felt suddenly sick to her stomach.

Unable to watch any more, Brianna covered her face with her hands as the whip fell again, the sound of the lash insidious and cruel as it slithered through the air to slice through cringing flesh. She shuddered with each blow, her eyes filling with tears. How could he survive such a beating? How could anyone endure such pain? She had received many whippings from her aunt, but they were as nothing compared to this. A sob rose in her throat as the whip cracked through the air again and yet again. And then there was silence.

Taking a deep breath, Brianna spread her fingers and

peered down the hill. The Indian's head had fallen forward. His long body was limp and she knew he would have collapsed but for the heavy iron shackles that bound his arms to the tree.

When the road boss Brianna had nicknamed Toad because of the large wart on his chin started to release the prisoner, Black Hat shook his head.

"Leave him," Black Hat said curtly. "Maybe it'll teach him a lesson he won't soon forget."

Toad nodded. Swinging aboard their horses, the two men marched the rest of the prisoners down the road and around the bend that was too narrow to allow them to move their wagon closer to the day's work site.

Shunkaha Luta let out a low groan. His whole body felt as though it was on fire and he felt himself teetering on the edge of unconsciousness. He had been stupid, he mused bleakly, so stupid. For months, he had endured the cruelty and mockery of the two white men, knowing that to fight back was to invite just such a whipping. For months he had curbed his tongue. Until today . . . He closed his eyes, leaning toward the darkness that hovered all around him.

Brianna stayed in her hiding place until she was certain the men were out of sight around the bend, then she hastened down the hill, unmindful of the prickly brush that snagged her dress and scratched her face.

"Indian?" she whispered, her head tilted up so she could see his face.

The sound of her voice drew him back from the edge of oblivion. Slowly, he opened his eyes to find Brianna standing before him. He gazed at her through a red haze of pain. Was she real, or only an elusive figment of his imagination come to haunt him?

"Indian?"

He licked dry lips, unable to speak for the terrible pain in his back and shoulders and the awful dryness in his throat.

But Brianna understood. Quickly, she went to the wagon and filled the dipper with water. Standing on tiptoe, she lifted the big wooden ladle to his mouth so he could drink, felt tears sting her eyes at the look of gratitude he gave her. How could she ever have been afraid of him?

She filled the dipper again and yet again, and he emptied it each time, the cold water reviving him. She was real, this golden-haired angel of mercy who had appeared out of nowhere to offer him that which he desired most.

"Ishna Wi," he murmured hoarsely.

Brianna cocked her head to one side. "Ishna Wi?"

Shunkaha Luta smiled weakly. "Sun Woman," he explained, for thus had he named her in his dreams.

"Ishna Wi," Brianna murmured. "I like that." Biting down on her lower lip, she stepped around behind him, felt the nausea rise in her throat as she got a closer look at his mutilated flesh. There was hardly an inch of his broad, muscular back that wasn't torn or bleeding or crisscrossed with ugly red welts.

She longed to reach out, to lay a comforting hand on his shoulder, to stroke his arm, to feel his flesh beneath her hand. Instead, she withdrew a kerchief from her skirt pocket and started to wipe the blood from his back.

"*Heyah!*" he admonished softly, flinching as the cloth touched his torn flesh. "No. You must not."

With a nod, Brianna drew her hand away. He was right, of course. If she tended his wounds, they would know someone had been there to see him. She moved to stand in front of him again. "Why did they beat you?"

"I hit the *wasicu* called Hart."

"Why?"

Shunkaha Luta shook his head ruefully. "It was a foolish thing to do. They have called me names and mocked me since the day I came here. I thought I had learned to accept it. But today . . ." He shrugged, then grimaced as the movement pulled on his lacerated back. "Today, when they began to mock me, I could not ignore them. And when the man called Hart called my mother a foul name, I hit him." Shunkaha Luta smiled. "It felt so good, I hit him again. And then again."

"Was it worth it?"

Shunkaha Luta grinned wryly. "I thought so at the time."

"And now?"

He considered her question seriously for a moment before he answered. He thought of the pain he was suffering, the renewed agony every time the whip cut into his back, and then he remembered how it had felt to strike the road boss, to lash out at his enemy, to feel Hart's blood on his hands. "I have no regrets."

"Is there anything I can do to make you more comfortable?" Brianna asked. "Anything at all?"

Slowly, he shook his head, his eyes never leaving her face. What did she look like beneath that shapeless dress, he wondered, and chided himself for such a thought. She was only a child, after all, and he was a grown man. His gaze moved to the two long braids that fell over her shoulders. He had never seen hair that color before, as gold and bright as the sun, and he wished suddenly that his hands were free so that he might unloose her braids and run his fingers through her hair. Could it possibly be as soft as it appeared? Again, he chided himself for entertaining such thoughts.

"Are you hungry?" Brianna asked.

Shunkaha Luta shook his head. His back was a constant throbbing pain that overshadowed everything else. And now his arms began to ache from being stretched over his head for so long.

"I'd help you if I could," Brianna said, close to tears. "I wish there was something I could do for you."

"You are here, Ishna Wi," he murmured thickly. "That is enough."

His words flooded her being with warmth. How wonderful, to be appreciated, to know that her mere presence made a difference.

Shunkaha Luta shifted his weight from one foot to the other, wincing as the slight movement sent new waves of pain darting across his back and shoulders.

Brianna bit back the urge to cry as she saw the agony mirrored in the Indian's dark eyes. "I've been here every day," she told him, her heart aching for his pain.

Shunkaha Luta nodded. "I have sensed your presence even when I could not see you."

"Really?"

He nodded again. "Why do you come here?"

Brianna shrugged. "I don't know. I . . . I just want to be near you."

Shunkaha Luta gazed into Brianna's clear blue eyes, the pain in his back and arms and shoulders momentarily forgotten. He was a man who lived close to the earth, who believed in all the ancient traditions and beliefs of his people. Since childhood, he had hated everything that the whites stood for, hated what they had done to his people. He had sworn to kill every white man who crossed his path, and when his mother and sister died, he had slashed his flesh in grief, vowing again that he would fight the *wasicu* to the last breath in his body. And now this beautiful child with hair the color of the sun had come to him, offering him water when he would have given his soul to *Kaga,* the devil spirit, for just one drink, her very presence cheering him, lifting him from the black despair that had covered him like a death shroud.

Brianna returned his gaze, her whole heart and soul drawn toward him though she could not say why. She felt a curious attachment to him, a bond being forged between them that she was powerless to explain. How long they stood thus, gazing into each other's eyes, she did not know, but a sudden sound made her jump. Fearful of discovery, she turned and ran up the hill, her heart pounding with fear at the thought of being seen where she had no right to be.

Shunkaha Luta lifted his eyes toward heaven, his heart deeply troubled by the feelings the young white girl aroused in him.

"*Wakan Tanka, unshimalam ye oyate*," he murmured. "Great Spirit, have mercy on me."

The road boss left Shunkaha Luta in shackles overnight. His back was a swollen mass of torn flesh and ugly red welts. Hart had tossed a bucket of salt water over his back the night before, roughly wiped away the blood, then doused the raw wounds with whiskey. Shunkaha Luta had nearly passed out from the pain as the fiery liquor seared his lacerated flesh, and even his determination not to show pain before his enemy could not stifle the groan that had risen in his throat. Hart had laughed as the Indian shuddered convulsively, and then doused the wounds with whiskey a second time out of pure cussedness.

"Wouldn't want to see them stripes get infected," Hart had drawled.

Now it was late afternoon and Shunkaha Luta's arms were still shackled over his head. Blood trickled from his wrists as the iron cuffs cut into his flesh. Sweat trickled down his arms and back and chest. Flies came to torment him. Thirst plagued him, worse than the hunger that gnawed at his belly.

Closing his eyes, he imagined the many ways he would torture his captors if he ever got the chance. Ah, how he would laugh with pleasure as he peeled the skin from their bodies, or watched them squirm as he covered their faces with honey and let the ants feed on their flesh . . . only it was his flesh that was wracked with pain, his arms that cried for relief from their imprisonment, his leg muscles that screamed to be released from their punishing stance.

In an effort to forget the pain, he summoned Ishna Wi's image to mind, concentrating on the brilliant blue of her eyes, the quiet beauty of her face, the radiance of her smile, the sun-gold mass of her hair. Was she up the hill even now, he wondered. Would she dare come to him again today?

He sensed her presence even before he opened his eyes and saw her standing before him.

Brianna smiled shyly as she lifted the dipper to his lips. It pleased her beyond words to ease his thirst, to be able to lessen his discomfort.

"I brought food," she said, holding up a thick slice of roast beef. "Are you hungry?"

He nodded, his pride warring with his hunger as she tore the meat into strips and fed it to him. The meat was rare and tender, better than anything he had tasted in six months. She offered him a piece of cheese, more water, a slice of bread.

When the food was gone, she took a deep breath, then stepped around to look at his back. Never had she seen anything so awful, but there was no sign of infection and she murmured a silent prayer of thanks.

"Is it bad?" he asked when she came around to face him again.

"Yes," Brianna said, "but I don't think it's infected. I hope not."

He smiled at her, touched by the compassion he read in her eyes and heard in her voice. What a sweet creature she was.

Brianna smiled back, wishing she had a pretty dress to wear for him, that her aunt would allow her to put a bit of rouge on her cheeks and lips, never realizing that her own natural beauty far surpassed anything she might create artificially.

"How are you called, Ishna Wi?"

"Brianna," she answered. "But I think I like Ishna Wi better."

"I am called Shunkaha Luta," he told her, pleased beyond measure that she approved of his name for her.

Brianna repeated the Indian's name, liking the way it rolled off her tongue, the way it sounded in her ears. "What does it mean?"

"Red Wolf," he replied. "How old are you, Ishna Wi?"

"Seventeen."

She was older than he had guessed, but still too young for him, he thought sadly, for he was nearly twice her age.

"How old are you?" Brianna asked.

"I have seen thirty summers."

Thirty, Brianna mused. Once she had thought of that as old, but no more. There was nothing old about Shunkaha Luta, nothing at all. He was the most virile, attractive man she had ever seen.

She hated to leave him there, hated to go back to the house, but she had been away too long already.

"I'll be back tomorrow," she promised. "Watch for me."

Shunkaha Luta nodded, his eyes following her until she was out of sight.

Brianna felt a moment of apprehension as she reached the top of the hill the following afternoon. The road gang was working around the bend in the road; she could hear the sound of their axes striking wood, could hear Black Hat and Toad filling the air with curses as they drove the men to work harder, faster. But where was the Indian?

Moving slowly down the hill, she wondered if he had died. Or if they had killed him out of hand because he was unable to work. Where was he?

She moved cautiously toward the wagon, refusing to believe he was gone. And then she saw him. He was sitting with his back against one of the big iron-rimmed wagon wheels, his hands shackled above his head. Someone had placed a bowl of water beside him and she thought how cruel that was, to leave the bowl where he could see it when he couldn't reach it. Surely heathen savages could not be as cruel as the two men who supervised the road gang, she thought angrily.

Shunkaha Luta opened his eyes at the sound of Brianna's footsteps, a now familiar warmth flooding his veins as she came toward him. Just looking at her made him feel better, stronger.

"I was afraid they'd sent you away, or . . . or killed you," Brianna said, kneeling beside him.

"Death would be welcome," Shunkaha Luta remarked. Indeed, he would have welcomed anything that would free him from the life he now lived.

"Don't say that," Brianna admonished. "Here," she said, offering him the dipper. "You'll feel better after you've had something to drink."

He swallowed the water, his eyes on her face. All day he had sat in the sun, yearning for a drink, the water in the bowl mocking his thirst.

"I've brought you something to eat," Brianna said, unwrapping a parcel of food.

"Why do you do this?" he asked, puzzled by her kindness. "Why do you not hate me? I am Indian. You are white."

Brianna shrugged as she offered him a slice of roast chicken. "Why should I hate you? You've never done anything to me."

"My people and your people are at war," Shunkaha Luta said flatly. "Is that not reason enough?"

"We're not at war, you and I," Brianna replied.

Shunkaha Luta smiled at her. "You are wise, Ishna Wi, wise beyond your years."

"No, I'm not. It's just that I . . ." She lowered her head, her cheeks turning crimson.

"What is it?" he asked.

"I can't stand to see you in pain," she answered quietly, so quietly he could scarcely hear her words.

"You have a kind heart, little one," he said. "I hope your loved ones treasure you."

Brianna laughed bitterly. Oh, they treasured her, all right, but not because she had a kind heart. They valued her strong back and her capable hands, and nothing else. She was not a person to her aunt and uncle, merely a servant who exchanged labor for room and board. They didn't care how she felt or what she thought or what she dreamed of; they were only concerned with how much work she could do.

They both heard the sound of hoofbeats at the same time. Brianna scrambled to her feet. Grabbing the cloth that had covered the chicken, she fled toward the hill in panic, reaching the foot of the heavily wooded slope as Black Hat rounded the bend in the road.

"Hey!" the road boss hollered. "You, girl, what the hell are you doing here?"

Brianna halted in her tracks, willing her heart to stop pounding as she turned to face the man who had whipped Shunkaha Luta. He was a tall man, with light brown hair and dark brown eyes. She guessed him to be in his late twenties.

"I live up the hill," Brianna said, forcing her voice to remain calm. "I was going for a walk when I saw the Indian and I came to get a better look. I've never seen an Indian before."

Jim McClain removed his hat and wiped the sweat band with his bandana as he studied the girl. She was a pretty little thing, he thought, soft and sweet and innocent.

"You'd best stay away from here, missy," he admonished. "I'm sure your folks wouldn't cotton to the idea of your hanging around scum like this."

"No, they wouldn't," Brianna agreed quickly. "You won't tell them?"

Her fear, all too plain in her face and voice, did not go unnoticed by Jim McClain. "Trust me," he said, grinning at her. "I won't say a word." His eyes moved to her mouth. "It'll cost you, though."

"What do you mean?"

Jim McClain dismounted and walked toward her. "I'll let you buy my silence with a kiss."

"A kiss?"

"You know, a kiss."

"I've never kissed a man," Brianna said, backing away from him.

"Never?"

Brianna shook her head. She knew suddenly how a rabbit felt when faced by a fox.

"Well, I'd sure like to be the first," McClain drawled.

"I'm sorry, I can't!" Brianna cried, and dashed up the hill as fast as her legs could carry her. She would as soon kiss a snake as kiss a man who could so callously whip another and then ride off without a backward glance.

She could hear the road boss laughing at her headlong flight as she crested the hill and ran for home.

Chapter Four

It was raining. Brianna sat in her room staring out the window as the summer storm ravaged the landscape. Usually she loved the rain, the thunder and the lightning, the sound of the raindrops splashing on the roof and against the windows. Rain meant fewer chores, giving her a chance to read or sleep or to just sit and daydream. Today it meant she could not see Shunkaha Luta, even from a distance.

She jumped as thunder rumbled overhead, as loud and sharp as a pistol shot. Crossing one knee over the other, she propped her elbow on her thigh and rested her cheek in the palm of her hand. Gradually, the sound of the rain lulled her to sleep. And in her dream Shunkaha Luta came to her. He was tall and strong and handsome. His dark eyes were free of pain and unhappiness; no shackles hindered his steps or restricted the movement of his hands. He smiled at her, his teeth very white against his swarthy skin. Whispering her name, he took her in his arms and kissed her gently . . .

"Brianna. Brianna!"

She woke with a start, expecting to find the Indian waiting for her. Instead, she looked up into her aunt's cold gray eyes and stern countenance.

"It is time to set the table for supper," Harriett Beaudine said gruffly. She lifted a hand to her hair, which was dark gray and habitually worn in a severe knot at the nape of her neck. "Straighten your dress and wash your face. Your uncle has brought a guest home."

"Yes, ma'am," Brianna replied meekly.

Brianna felt her heart catch in her throat when her aunt

called the men into the dining room for supper. Uncle Henry's guest was none other than the road boss, Jim McClain. Brianna bobbed a curtsey when she was introduced to McClain, her eyes silently beseeching him not to mention the fact that they had met before.

"Pleased to meet you, Miss Beaudine," McClain said politely. He was dressed in brown twill pants and a plaid shirt open at the throat. The toes of his black boots were splattered with mud.

Brianna did not miss the laughter in his eyes. The expression on his face seemed to say, "Don't worry, your secret is safe with me."

Uncle Henry smiled at McClain as they all sat down at the table. "I found this young man slogging around in the mud looking for his horses," Beaudine said, grinning.

"Thunder spooked our mounts," McClain explained. His words were directed at Harriett Beaudine, but he had eyes only for Brianna. "I found them near your barn."

Henry Beaudine chuckled. "Inviting him in for a hot meal seemed like the neighborly thing to do."

"Of course," Harriett Beaudine replied, but she fixed her husband with a cold frown, letting him know she considered the boss of the road gang only slightly better than the convicts he supervised.

Henry Beaudine frowned back at his wife. He liked Jim McClain and if Harriett didn't, then that was just too damn bad. He had suffered through many a meal entertaining *her* friends; for once, she could entertain one of his.

Brianna did not miss the vitriolic glances that passed between her aunt and uncle, but McClain seemed totally unaware of the tension at the table. He smiled at Brianna, making her nervous and fidgety.

Henry Beaudine monopolized most of the conversation, asking questions about the road and how soon it would be completed, asking, curiously, if the prisoners gave McClain and his partner much trouble.

McClain shrugged. "Most of the men on the road gang are short-timers. They don't cause us any trouble because they're afraid of picking up extra time for bad behavior. But we've got an Indian down there who's full of sand. He's an ornery bas—" McClain glanced at Brianna and his face reddened. "An ornery cuss. He attacked my partner the other day and we had to discipline him."

"Of course," Henry Beaudine said, nodding. "You've got to maintain order."

Brianna opened her mouth, wanting to cry out that Shunkaha Luta had been taunted and harassed until he had lost control of his temper, just as any man would. She wanted to say that the beating he had received was far worse than he could possibly have deserved. Instead, she shut her mouth and looked down at her plate, realizing that defending Shunkaha Luta wouldn't help the Indian and would bring her nothing but trouble.

McClain hung around after supper. At Henry Beaudine's invitation, he sat in the parlor and smoked one of Henry's cigars while Harriett Beaudine pleaded a headache and went to bed, leaving Brianna to clear the table and wash and dry the dishes.

In the parlor, Henry Beaudine offered Jim McClain a glass of whiskey. For a moment, the two men sat in companionable silence, enjoying the purely masculine pleasures of smoking and drinking.

"Miss Beaudine is a very attractive young woman," McClain remarked at length. "I . . . I know I've only just met her, but I was wondering if you'd mind if I came calling on her?"

Henry Beaudine pondered that for a long while and then he nodded. "I expect it would be all right."

McClain could not suppress a grin. "Thank you, sir. Would tomorrow night be too soon?"

Henry Beaudine laughed as he slapped the younger man on the shoulder. "I reckon not," he said exuberantly. "I wouldn't want to stand in the way of young love."

Brianna was stunned when her uncle told her the news. "He wants to call on me," she said, frowning. "Why?"

"He seems to find you attractive," Henry Beaudine replied tersely. "Hell, girl, you should thank your lucky stars this young fella's come along. You don't want to be an old maid, do you?"

Brianna stared at her uncle. He was short and stocky, with thick gray hair and sharp blue eyes. She had tried to love him, had tried to win his approval, but he had never displayed any sign of affection for her.

"Do you?" Henry Beaudine repeated.

"No, sir," Brianna answered, her mind reeling. Surely her uncle was not suggesting she set her cap for Jim McClain! Why, she'd rather spend the rest of her life here on the farm than marry a man like McClain. But she did not say so to her uncle. She thought of Shunkaha Luta, so tall and strong, at peace with himself in spite of the dreadful circumstances that surrounded him. She knew, somehow, that he would never be cruel to another human being. And yet, as much as she cared for him, she knew she could never be his. He was a heathen, an Indian, as far from her reach as the stars in the sky. But he was the kind of man she wanted for a husband. Someone kind; never a man like McClain.

Harriett Beaudine was less than enthusiastic at the thought of the road boss courting Brianna. She did not consider Mc-Clain a suitable match for her niece, but, more than that, she was in no hurry to see Brianna married off. The girl was a hard worker, and having her in the house relieved Harriett of all the household chores she found tedious and unpleasant, giving her time to visit with her neighbors, to while away a few pleasant hours in town, or to merely sit in a comfortable chair and do nothing at all.

But Henry Beaudine was pleased with McClain, and pleased that the man found Brianna attractive. Henry had always wanted a son, and he thought Jim McClain might just fit the bill.

And Henry Beaudine's word was law.

Shunkaha Luta huddled against the sodden hillside, his expression bleak. He was cold and wet clear through. The thin blanket wrapped around his shoulders provided little warmth and scant protection against the wind and the rain.

As always, his thoughts turned to Brianna. He closed his eyes and pictured her sitting before a warm fire, her face and hair bathed in the glow of the flames. Was she thinking of him even now, missing him as he was missing her? He knew so little about her. All in all, they had probably spent less than two hours together, yet she filled his thoughts and glided through his dreams. Brianna. Child-woman. Ishna Wi of the sun-gold hair and sky-blue eyes.

He peered into the rain-drenched darkness as he heard McClain return to camp.

Roy Hart poked his head out of the back of the wagon. "Hey, where'd you find the horses?" he hollered.

"Little place up the hill," McClain replied, swinging from the back of his horse and tethering both mounts to the end of the wagon. "Family called Beaudine lives up there. Nice people. Got a pretty niece name of Brianna." McClain smiled broadly. "I'm gonna call on her tomorrow night."

"No shit!" Hart exclaimed. And then he chuckled. No matter where they went, McClain found a woman.

Shunkaha Luta felt his anger rise as he watched McClain climb into the back of the wagon. Brianna. McClain was courting Brianna. Jealousy such as he had never known suffused him, heating his blood so that he no longer felt the cold. McClain was courting Brianna.

It rained all the next day as well. Shunkaha Luta chafed at the inactivity. He did not like felling trees, did not like building a road for the *wasicu*, but it was far better than squatting on his heels in the mud hour after hour. Still, the rain gave his back a chance to heal a little before he had to go back to work and he supposed he should be grateful for that.

After dinner, McClain saddled his horse and rode up the hill. Shunkaha Luta's eyes followed the road boss until he was out of sight.

Brianna sat on the sofa in the parlor, her hands primly folded in her lap. Jim McClain sat at the other end of the sofa, his hands resting on his knees. Tonight he wore a pair of dark gray pants, a white shirt, and a black string tie. They had been making small talk for the better part of an hour under the watchful eye of Brianna's aunt and uncle. Brianna had never been so ill at ease in her life. McClain kept staring at her in a way that made her feel dirty, and Uncle Henry kept smiling at them.

Later, Aunt Harriett served cake and coffee. Brianna nearly fainted in surprise. Imagine, her aunt playing the role of hostess. Usually it was Brianna who performed such services, passing out plates, refilling coffee cups, collecting the dishes, washing them up and putting them away. No doubt she would be the one to wash and dry the dishes later, but it was nice to have someone wait on her for a change.

As always, the men found time to talk about the new road. They were making real progress, McClain said. A good section of the trees had been cleared away now and the ground was reasonably level. Once a section of the hill had been disposed of, they would have almost half of the job completed.

"We'll be working on that hill tomorrow or the next day,"

McClain remarked between bites of cake. "It's a job well done, if I do say so myself."

"I don't see how you can take credit for it," Brianna declared. "You're not doing any of the work."

"Brianna!" Uncle Henry scowled at her, silently berating her for her rude remark.

"Well, it's true," she said stubbornly. "The prisoners are doing all the work, aren't they?"

"She's right," McClain said quickly. "The prisoners *are* doing the work." He smiled indulgently. "But you must realize the work wouldn't get done at all if me and my partner weren't there to supervise." He turned a charming smile on Harriett Beaudine. "That's mighty good cake, ma'am. Would it be rude of me to ask for seconds?"

"Gracious, no," Harriett Beaudine assured him. She took his plate, smiling down at him as she did so. Perhaps she had misjudged the boy.

"I'll get it," Brianna said. Rising, she took the plate from her aunt's hand and headed for the kitchen. "After all, I made it."

Henry Beaudine laughed out loud, ignoring his wife's chagrined expression. "I guess tonight we're giving credit where credit's due."

Chapter Five

The sound of an ax striking wood drew Brianna's attention and she left the ironing to peer out the back window, felt her heart skip a beat when she saw Shunkaha Luta. He was cutting down the big old oak that loomed menacingly over the side of the barn.

Grabbing a bowl of scraps that she had been saving for the chickens, she ran outside, her pulse racing with excitement. Two days had passed since she had seen him. It had been the longest two days of her life.

Her steps slowed as she saw Jim McClain squatting in the shade of the tool shed, a shotgun cradled in the crook of his arm.

McClain smiled as he saw Brianna coming toward him. Rising to his feet, he tipped his hat in her direction. "Mornin', Miss Beaudine," he drawled.

"Good morning. What are you doing here?"

McClain jerked his head in Shunkaha Luta's direction. "Your uncle mentioned that he had a tree that needing cuttin'. He said he'd been puttin' it off because his back was botherin' him, so I told him I'd take care of it."

"*You'd* take care of it?" Brianna repeated dryly.

"Indirectly." McClain grinned at her, thinking how pretty she looked with her cheeks flushed and her mouth pouting at him. He liked pretty women, and she was the prettiest he'd ever seen.

"If you'll excuse me, I've got to give these scraps to the chickens."

McClain nodded at her, his eyes sweeping over her in a

most impudent way. Pivoting on her heel, Brianna walked toward the barn where two dozen chickens were scratching in the dirt.

She called the chickens, tossing the scraps of potato skins and other vegetables on the ground, but all the while her eyes were on Shunkaha Luta. Though he had been working only a short time, he was already sweating. It was cruel, she thought, to make him work now, when the sun was high in the sky.

Throwing the last of the scraps to the chickens, she hurried back to the house and mixed up a pitcher of lemonade. The water from the well was cold, and she smiled as she thought how good it would taste to Shunkaha Luta as she filled two tall glasses.

Returning to the yard, she handed a glass to McClain, and then started toward Shunkaha Luta.

"Hey!" McClain called. "Where do you think you're goin' with that?"

"I'm going to give the Indian something to drink," Brianna answered calmly. "I'm sure he needs it more than you."

"He doesn't need it," McClain said curtly. "Drink it yourself, or, better yet, give it to me."

"I made it for him."

They glared at each other for a moment, then Brianna turned and walked toward Shunkaha Luta. Behind her, she heard McClain cock the shotgun.

"Here," Brianna said, handing the lemonade to Shunkaha Luta.

"*Le mita pila, Ishna Wi*," he murmured. His hand lingered on hers as he took the glass and she felt a sudden rush of heat as his eyes caressed her face. He drank slowly, wanting to keep Brianna close to him for as long as possible. She stood near him, never taking her eyes from his face, his nearness surrounding her, enveloping her like an invisible cocoon.

"Are they treating you all right?" she asked, her voice low so only he could hear.

"Well enough."

"Does your back still hurt?"

"A little." He took a step away from her and handed her the empty glass as McClain strode toward them.

"What's takin' so long?" the road boss demanded.

"Nothing," Brianna said. Turning, she took hold of Mc-Clain's arm and started toward the house.

"Was he botherin' you?" McClain demanded.

"Of course not." Brianna forced herself to smile at Mc-Clain. "Would you like some more lemonade?"

"What I'd like is a kiss," McClain replied. Coming to a halt, he pulled Brianna into his arms and kissed her, his mouth grinding against hers as his tongue sought to penetrate her lips.

Revulsion swamped Brianna and she twisted her head to the side to avoid his touch. "Leave me alone!"

"Just one little kiss," McClain insisted. "You owe me that."

"I don't owe you anything! Let me go!"

She gasped as she felt herself being pulled from McClain's grasp, cried, "Oh, no!" as Shunkaha Luta barreled into Mc-Clain. The road boss grunted with pain as his shoulder slammed into a fence post; then, as Shunkaha Luta drew back his fist, McClain rammed the butt of his shotgun into the Indian's belly. Shunkaha Luta dropped to his knees, his arms folded across his stomach as he fought the urge to vomit.

"What the hell's going on here?"

Brianna whirled around as she heard her uncle's voice.

"Nothing, Mr. Beaudine," McClain said quickly. "The redskin attacked me and I had to hit him. He'll be all right."

"Attacked you?" Henry Beaudine exclaimed. "Why?"

Jim McClain shrugged. "He's an Indian."

Henry Beaudine nodded. "Well, you'd best take him back down the hill. I don't want any trouble."

"There won't be any more trouble," McClain said. "I can promise you that."

"Well, if you're sure—"

"I'm sure." McClain glared at Shunkaha Luta, and then he glanced at Brianna, his eyes warning her not to say anything about what had happened between them.

Brianna nodded imperceptibly, knowing that Shunkaha Luta would suffer for it if she told her uncle that McClain had tried to kiss her.

Shunkaha Luta rose to his feet. There was the bitter taste of bile in his mouth, a dull ache in his belly that was as nothing compared to the rage in his heart.

Henry Beaudine glanced from McClain to Brianna. Then, with a shrug, he returned to the barn.

McClain jabbed his gun barrel into Shunkaha Luta's ribcage. "You ever lay a hand on me again, redskin, and I'll blow your head off. Now, get back to work."

Shunkaha Luta did not move. He stared at the road boss through eyes dark with fury as he fought down the urge to lash out at the white man who had dared touch Brianna. He wished fleetingly that he had not dropped the ax when he went after McClain. It would have made a formidable weapon.

From the corner of his eye, he could see Brianna watching him. Her face was pale, lined with fear, not for herself, but for him.

Slowly, he felt the tension drain out of him. Drawing himself to his full height, he threw McClain one last look of disdain and then went back to where he had left the ax. Picking it up, he began to swing it at the tree with all the strength he possessed.

"Impudent bastard," McClain muttered under his breath. He lowered the shotgun, wishing the Indian had given him an excuse to pull the trigger.

"Don't ever come calling on me again," Brianna said coldly. "I won't be home if you do."

"Don't fight me, Miss Beaudine," McClain warned. "I'm determined to have you. Besides, your uncle likes me, and I think you'll do whatever he says."

His words were like a slap in the face. And they were all too true. She *would* do whatever her uncle said. She had no choice. He was her guardian. In a day when women had little say in what they would do and whom they would marry, she had little recourse but to do what she was told or suffer the consequences.

Shoulders sagging with despair, Brianna hurried back to the house. Surely her uncle wouldn't expect her to marry McClain against her will. Even Uncle Henry couldn't be that unfeeling. She'd rather spend the rest of her life working for her aunt and uncle than be married to a bully like McClain. She had seen the expression on his face when he whipped Shunkaha. He had caused the Indian pain and he had liked it. A man who took pleasure in the misery of others was not the kind of man she wanted for the father of her children, nor one she would wish to spend the rest of her life with.

Going to the kitchen window, she watched Shunkaha Luta as he swung the ax again and again. She had the feeling that he was taking his anger out on the tree, that he might not have backed down if he had been alone with McClain.

She returned to the window often as she went about her household chores, and each time she saw him, her heart seemed lighter. He worked effortlessly, tirelessly, his arms swinging the ax with practiced ease, slowly cutting his way through the hard oak.

She was at the window when the tree fell. There was a sharp crack, a great whoosh as the oak toppled to the ground, its branches shuddering for a moment, as though in the throes of death.

Shunkaha Luta was breathing hard now. Dropping the ax, he wiped his forearm across his sweat-sheened face, then squatted on his heels in the shade of the fallen giant.

A few minutes later, Uncle Henry came in for the midday meal. "Brianna, go out and invite Mr. McClain to eat with us."

"Is that necessary?" Harriett Beaudine asked.

"Damn right," Henry Beaudine replied curtly. "I like the man." He glanced at Brianna and smiled. "And I've got a feeling we'll be seeing a lot of him in the future."

McClain smiled a knowing smile as Brianna invited him to sup with them. "Thank you, Miss Beaudine," he said insolently. "I'm obliged."

"It wasn't my idea," Brianna snapped.

"I'll be right along," McClain said, grinning. "I'll just chain up the Indian so he doesn't wander off."

Brianna said little during the meal, speaking only when she was spoken to. And all the while she was aware of McClain's eyes watching her. She was glad when the men left the table and went to sit out on the front porch.

Brianna was preparing a plate of food for Shunkaha Luta when her aunt entered the kitchen.

Harriett Beaudine frowned. "What are you doing? You can't still be hungry?"

"No, ma'am. I thought I'd take the Indian something to eat. He worked hard today."

"I'm sure Mr. McClain will look after him. The savage is not our responsibility."

"Mr. McClain is busy with Uncle Henry."

"Very well. But don't get close to that man."

"Yes, ma'am." Taking up the plate and a glass of lemonade, Brianna went out to Shunkaha, who was sitting with his back against the hitching rail. His left hand was shackled to the post; his feet, also. "I've brought you something to eat."

Shunkaha Luta nodded. He took the plate with his free hand and placed it on the ground beside him, drained the glass in one long swallow.

"Thank you for what you did," Brianna said. "Do you think he'll beat you for it?"

"Perhaps."

"I don't want you to be punished because of me."

"It does not matter, Ishna Wi."

"I've got to go," Brianna said. "Enjoy your meal."

Shunkaha Luta nodded. Once again he was in her debt.

Brianna sat on the porch, her hands fidgeting with the folds of her black wool dress. McClain had somehow managed to get himself invited to dinner and now he sat beside her, telling her about how he hoped to have his own spread someday.

But Brianna couldn't concentrate on what he was saying, nor did she have any interest in his future plans. She could think of nothing but Shunkaha Luta. She had watched McClain drop a rope around the Indian's neck and lead him away earlier in the day. Shunkaha Luta's hands had been shackled behind his back; the ever-present chains on his feet had hindered his stride. She had heard McClain laugh as he gave a jerk on the rope.

Now she could not help wondering what had happened to Shunkaha when they reached the road camp. Had McClain whipped him?

Jim McClain paused as he took a cigar from his shirt pocket. "Mind if I smoke?"

"No." Brianna licked her lips. "What happened to the Indian?"

McClain lifted an eyebrow. "What do you mean?"

"Did you beat him for attacking you?"

McClain studied Brianna's face thoughtfully as he drew on his cigar. She lowered her eyes to her lap, but not before he saw the worry reflected in her clear blue eyes.

"Did you?"

"What difference does it make what happens to that savage?" McClain asked brusquely.

She could feel his eyes watching her, waiting for her answer, and she felt suddenly vulnerable, like a rabbit caught in the open by a coyote.

McClain's eyes narrowed ominously and his hands curled into tight fists. "How many times have you been down the hill to see him?" he demanded roughly. "How many times?"

"Just that once," Brianna said. She did not meet his accusing stare.

"Like hell!"

"Please don't hurt him," Brianna begged. "He's done nothing to you."

McClain snorted. "You're too late, Miss Beaudine," he said venomously. "I beat the shit out of him when I got him back to camp."

"No!"

"Yes." McClain held out his hands, palms down. His knuckles were bruised and swollen. "I beat him with my bare hands."

"Why?"

"Why? Because the bastard attacked me, that's why."

"He was only trying to protect me," Brianna wailed softly, and then gasped at what her words implied.

McClain's smile was cold and cruel. "I wonder what your aunt would say if she knew you'd been sneaking down to visit that redskin."

Brianna felt her stomach muscles knot with dread. "You wouldn't tell her?"

McClain shrugged. He wanted to possess Brianna, to humble her, and he knew suddenly that he had found the way.

"Please, McClain, please don't say anything to my aunt." Brianna's voice was shaking with fear as she placed her hand on McClain's arm. "Please."

"I'll keep quiet on one condition," McClain said. "You meet me by the lake tomorrow night at midnight."

"Why?"

McClain dropped his hand to her thigh and gave it a squeeze. "I think you know why."

Brianna shook her head. "No, please."

"Yes, please," McClain mimicked. "You'll meet me there or I'll tell your aunt what you've been up to."

Slowly, Brianna nodded. She was afraid of McClain, afraid of the thinly veiled lust in his eyes. But she was more afraid of her aunt's temper, and of the thick razor strop that her aunt wielded with such zeal.

Chapter Six

Shunkaha Luta kept his face devoid of expression as he jammed the shovel into the damp earth. Each movement sent waves of pain rippling down his back, which was still covered with half-healed scabs and welts, but he worked steadily, knowing that to stop would bring the whip singing down over his lacerated back. The mere idea of another beating so soon after the last one caused his stomach to churn with revulsion. He could not face the whip again, could not accept the pain or the humiliation.

Worse than the ache in his back, worse than the beating McClain had doled out with his fists the night before, was the knowledge that McClain was courting Brianna. The thought cut into his heart like a knife. And even though he knew she could never be his, he could not abide the thought of another man looking at her, touching her.

Slowly his shovel ate away at the part of the hillside that spilled across the road, each shovelful of dirt undercutting the hill. He had cut about ten feet into the hill when he encountered a large rock. Tossing the shovel aside, he put his shoulder against the boulder and began to push, the muscles in his arms and back straining with a mighty effort until at last the rock was dislodged and a barrage of dirt cascaded down the hillside, completely blocking the road and momentarily separating him from the road boss and the other prisoners.

Cursing the chain that hobbled his stride, he began to run, his heart slamming against his chest as the powerful muscles in his legs carried him away from the road gang. From behind, he could hear McClain shouting, and he knew it would be only a matter of minutes before the road boss was in pursuit. Shunkaha Luta ran with all the speed at his command, his lungs on fire, his throat aching. He grunted as a sudden weight smashed into his right shoulder, heard the report of the rifle as blood spurted from the wound. And still he ran, his eyes darting from right to left as he sought a place to hide and found none. He heard hoofbeats closing in on him and uttered a hoarse cry as he plunged down a rocky, brush-covered slope. He groaned as he landed on his wounded shoulder, and then he rolled down the hill, crashing through shrubs and brush until he came to rest against the side of a rotting deadfall. Fighting for each breath, he crawled inside the hollow log, then lay there panting heavily.

He could hear McClain cursing loudly from the top of the hill, but the slope was covered with brush, blocking the white man's view of anything more than a few feet away.

McClain smiled as he saw the splotch of blood at the top of the hill. So, he hadn't missed. That would make things easier. A wounded man could not get far, and a wounded man in shackles would be a sitting duck.

McClain rubbed his jaw. The savage had been nothing but trouble since the first day. Now would be a good time to get rid of him once and for all. No one would blame him for killing a prisoner attempting to escape. Especially when that prisoner was an Indian.

Dismounting, he made his way down the hill, his eyes following the droplets of blood.

Shunkaha Luta peered warily from the log, his eyes following McClain's progress down the hill. When the road boss passed by his hiding place, he slithered out of the log and hurled himself at McClain, and the two of them tumbled down the hill. McClain was on top when they came to a halt. His hands closed around Shunkaha Luta's throat and he began to squeeze, his mouth twisted into a sneer as he slowly choked the life from the Indian.

The world was turning dark when Shunkaha Luta's hand closed on a rock. Summoning all the strength he had left, he brought the rock down on the back of the white man's head. McClain grunted softly as his body went limp.

Shunkaha Luta lay where he was, panting heavily, for several minutes. His back felt like it was on fire, and when he reached around to touch it, his fingers came away sticky with blood. His shoulder, too, was bleeding, sapping his strength, making him light-headed.

He wanted nothing more than to close his eyes and sleep, but he knew he could not stay where he was. The other road boss would be looking for him soon.

Sitting up, he pressed a handful of dirt over the wound in his shoulder. That done, he searched the dead man's pockets until he found the key to the shackles on his hands and feet. Then, drawing a deep breath, he stood up. The world reeled out of focus for a few moments and he struggled to stay conscious. Later, he would surrender to the pain; later he would rest, but for now he had to keep moving.

On his hands and knees, he climbed laboriously to the top of the hill. He had hoped to find McClain's horse, but the animal had apparently wandered back to camp. Pausing, he listened for some sound that would indicate the other road boss was coming, but he heard only the sighing of the wind and the faint song of a cricket. He wished suddenly that he had taken time to search for McClain's rifle, which had slid to the bottom of the hill during their scuffle.

Rising to his feet, he crossed the rough-hewn path and started up the opposite hill that led to the Beaudine place. Brianna had mentioned a lake at the top of the steep slope, and his body cried for water.

The sun was setting behind the distant mountains by the

time he reached the top of the hill, and there, shimmering like liquid silver, he saw the lake.

Breathing heavily, he staggered to the edge of the pool and dropped down on his belly. Burying his face in the water, he took several long swallows.

Exhaustion overcame him then, and with his last bit of strength he dragged himself toward a stand of tangled brush and timber. Covering himself with leaves and small branches, he curled up and was immediately asleep.

Brianna lay in her bed, staring at the ceiling, as the clock downstairs chimed eleven times. Soon, she thought, soon she would have to go to meet McClain. She thought of calling his bluff, of staying here, safe inside her room. Surely he wouldn't be cad enough to tell Aunt Harriett that she had been sneaking down to see Shunkaha Luta. Surely even a man like McClain wouldn't be that mean. But then she recalled the look in his eyes, and she knew he would have no qualms about revealing her secret. He was the kind of man who enjoyed the suffering of others.

The thought of Harriett Beaudine's rage when she discovered her niece was aiding an Indian caused a cold sweat to pop out across Brianna's forehead. Oh, Aunt Harriett would love nothing better than an excuse to whip her again. First there would be a lecture, of course, berating Brianna for her misplaced and misguided charity, and then a whipping. Always a whipping. And yet the alternative of meeting McClain was equally frightening. Once she agreed to meet McClain on the sly, she would be at his mercy. She was certain he would not settle for one meeting, or one kiss, and she knew if she met him once, he would have the means of blackmailing her again and again.

Her hand worried a corner of the bedclothes. The strap or McClain, she mused bleakly, which would it be?

When the clock struck the half-hour, she slipped quietly out of bed, dressed hastily, and tiptoed out of the house. If she did not meet McClain, he would surely tell her aunt about Shunkaha Luta, but, worse than that, McClain might punish Shunkaha because of her, and she could not bear to think of the Indian being whipped again, not when he had already suffered so much at McClain's hand. Not when she could prevent it.

The night was inky black. Low clouds covered the moon and stars, and Brianna felt a shiver of apprehension as she led her uncle's big roan gelding out of the barn and climbed aboard his bare back. Trees and shrubs that were familiar and beautiful during the day now seemed foreign and fraught with menace. Rocks and bushes took on the shapes of wild beasts; the quick call of an owl made her jump.

The cloud cover broke as she reached the lake and the moon cast a bright silvery glow over the surface of the water. At any other time, Brianna would have been enthralled by its beauty, but not now.

Her heart was hammering as she rode slowly around the lake. There was no sign of McClain and she wondered if she was early, or if he was late, or if, please God, he had changed his mind.

A faint breeze blew out of the north as she circled the lake a second time and she wished she had thought to bring a shawl.

She had reined the gelding to a halt, wondering how long she should wait for McClain, when a whispered voice sounded from nearby.

"Ishna Wi."

Brianna's eyes probed the darkness. "Shunkaha Luta, where are you?"

"Here."

She saw him then. He was barely visible behind a tangled

mass of brush and saplings. Dismounting, Brianna hurried toward him, her eyes growing wide when she saw the blood caked on his shoulder.

"You're hurt!"

Shunkaha Luta nodded.

"Is it bad?"

"I do not think so."

"How did you get away?"

"I was lucky."

"Lucky!" Brianna exclaimed, glancing at his shoulder. "You call that lucky?"

"*Nahan rei ni wayon heon*," he murmured laconically. "I am still alive."

Brianna cast an anxious glance over her shoulder. "You can't stay here. You've got to go."

Shunkaha Luta nodded. "Soon."

"No, now," Brianna insisted urgently. "Before—"

Shunkaha Luta frowned at the urgency in her voice. "Before what?"

Brianna sighed heavily. She did not want to tell Shunkaha she was meeting McClain, did not want him to think she liked the man enough to sneak out and meet him in the middle of the night, but that didn't matter now. Nothing mattered but getting Shunkaha Luta away before the road boss arrived.

"McClain is coming here," she said, her head lowered so the Indian could not see her face.

"Why?"

"It doesn't matter why," she replied evasively. "You've got to go."

"You came here to meet him?" Shunkaha Luta asked, not wanting to believe it.

"Yes, but not for the reason you think. There's no time to explain now. Just please go."

"McClain will not come here tonight."

Relief washed through Brianna. "You're sure?"

"I am sure."

"Thank God," she murmured, and felt a great weight lift from her shoulders. "They'll be looking for you soon. You've got to find a place to hide."

Shunkaha Luta nodded, his dark eyes searching the landscape. They would expect him to run away, toward the reservation or the Black Hills, they would not expect him to double back toward civilization. By the time they realized their mistake, he would be safely away.

"Here," Brianna said, leading the roan to Shunkaha Luta. "Get on. I've got an idea."

Gritting his teeth, Shunkaha Luta grasped the gelding's mane and pulled himself onto the animal's bare back. The strain on his wounded shoulder and back brought a grimace of pain to his face and a fine sheen of sweat to his brow.

He smiled weakly as he took the reins from Brianna's hand. "I, too, have an idea," he said. Though he doubted he would get very far in his present condition, one thing was certain: he would get farther on horseback than on foot.

"You'll never get away," Brianna said. "You're too weak to get very far, and you've got no food." Tears welled in her eyes. "And my uncle will beat me black and blue if you steal his horse."

"He will not know that you helped me."

"He'll find out. And even if he doesn't, he'll take it out on me."

The very real fright shining in her eyes touched the Indian's heart. "What is your idea?"

"You could hide in the loft in the barn until you're stronger," Brianna suggested. "No one ever goes up there except me. I could take care of your wound and bring you food and water until you're well enough to travel."

It was a mistake and he knew it. But she had been kind to him, brought him water when he needed it, offered him her sweet smile and kind words when everyone else showed him nothing but abuse. He could not steal her uncle's horse if it would cause her a moment's pain.

"I will do as you suggest," he agreed, and handed her the reins.

Getting him up the ladder to the loft was an ordeal. He was weak from loss of blood and in much pain, and he leaned heavily on her shoulder as they made their way up the ladder, but she soon had Shunkaha comfortably settled on an old quilt she had spread over a pile of soft, fragrant hay. She left him for a few minutes, then returned with bandages and ointment for his back and shoulders. Fortunately, her aunt and uncle were sound sleepers and had not heard her rummaging around in the kitchen. Shunkaha Luta winced as she removed his tattered, blood-stained shirt and tossed it aside. For a moment, she stared at the wound in revulsion; then, face grim with determination, she washed the wound, flooded it with a strong dose of carbolic, then gently spread a soothing coat of ointment over his lacerated back.

Shunkaha Luta felt the tension drain out of him as Brianna spread the healing salve over his back and shoulders. Her touch was soft, comforting, more healing to his soul than the salve which greatly reduced the pain in his body.

When she had finished her ministrations, Brianna opened a basket and offered Shunkaha Luta a plate of sliced ham, bread that had been baked that day, and a container of cold milk.

Shunkaha Luta ate greedily, feeling his strength return as he wolfed down every scrap of food. "*Le mita pila,*" he said sincerely. "My thanks."

He let out a contented sigh. His wounds no longer pained him and his stomach was full of good food for the first time in months. He gazed at Brianna with warm affection. "*Le mita cola,*" he murmured, his eyelids suddenly heavy. "My friend."

Brianna felt a wave of tenderness engulf her as the Indian's eyelids fluttered down and his head dropped to her shoulder. Very, very gently she placed her hand on the back of his head, her fingers threading through his hair. It was heavy and thick and straight; as black as ten feet down. His eyebrows were thick and straight, his jaw strong and square.

She studied his profile, marveling anew at how handsome he was. She had heard talk of Indians all her life. They were a savage and godless people, her neighbors said, unfit to live among civilized human beings. They were barbaric, mutilating their enemies, delighting in bloodshed and butchery. No one had ever told her they could be beautiful.

Her eyes lingered on his mouth. It was full and wide, the lips slightly parted. She stared at his mouth for a long time. It was well-shaped, sensual. She liked the color of his lips, the fact that the lower one was slightly larger than the upper one. She touched his lower lip for the merest fraction of a second, her fingertips as light as a snowflake drifting over a windowpane, and then she pressed her fingertips to her own lips.

She knew she should go, but she couldn't bring herself to leave him. Sitting there, cradling his head against her shoulder, made her feel very protective. Maternal, almost. She looked at his shoulder and wanted to cry; remembering the ugly welts on his back made her angry. He would be left with several scars, and she thought what a shame it was to mar such masculine perfection.

How had he endured so many months on a road gang? She could not imagine living in chains, being whipped daily, mocked and tormented. It seemed a cruel, inhuman form of punishment.

She sat there watching Shunkaha Luta sleep until dawn began to brighten the sky. Rising, she moved toward the ladder, looking back to make certain the Indian was hidden from any casual observer.

When Henry Beaudine entered the kitchen a few minutes later, he found Brianna frying up a mess of bacon and eggs.

It was mid-afternoon when Roy Hart showed up at the front door.

"Sorry to bother you, ma'am," Hart said, tipping his hat to Harriett Beaudine, "but one of our prisoners escaped last night. Killed my partner."

Brianna stared at Hart, not wanting to believe her ears. Shunkaha Luta had killed a man.

Harriett Beaudine's hand went to her throat. "Good heavens," she murmured, "you don't think he'll come here, do you?"

"No, ma'am," Hart replied, his eyes on Brianna's face. "I reckon he'll run as far away from here as he can get, but if you don't mind, I'd like to have a look around just to be on the safe side."

"Please do," Harriett Beaudine invited, stepping back so the road boss could enter the parlor.

While Hart and Aunt Harriett checked the house, Brianna hurried to the barn, ostensibly to throw some carrot scraps to Uncle Henry's horse. She was still there when Roy Hart entered the barn, Uncle Henry on his heels.

"What's going on here?" Henry Beaudine was saying. He glanced at Brianna and then over to Roy Hart.

Quickly, the road boss explained what had happened.

Henry Beaudine felt a sense of loss at the news of McClain's death. In the back of his mind, he had hoped Brianna would marry McClain; perhaps the two would stay on at the farm and McClain would take the place of the son Henry never had. But that was all over now, all because of some damn redskin.

Henry Beaudine turned to face Hart. "You say something?"

"I asked if I could take a look around in here?"

"Sure, sure, help yourself."

Roy Hart walked the length of the barn, peering into each stall, checking behind several bales of hay. His expression turned thoughtful as he saw the ladder to the loft. "What's up there?"

"Nothing much," Henry Beaudine answered with a shrug. "Some old furniture and a couple of trunks. My niece has a hideaway up there."

"Mind if I take a look?" Hart asked.

"Okay by me," Henry Beaudine said.

"I'll look," Brianna offered. She laid a restraining hand on Roy Hart's shoulder. "Please. I don't like for strangers to trample my things."

"Okay," Hart agreed. His hand dropped to the butt of the gun holstered on his right hip. "You sing out if he's up there."

Brianna nodded, her heart pounding in her throat as she climbed the ladder and pretended to look around. She gave Shunkaha Luta a reassuring smile, then turned and hurried back down the ladder.

"There's nothing up there," she told Roy Hart truthfully, "except what I put up there."

Hart nodded. "Yeah, well, I didn't figure he'd dare show his face around here, but I had to check to make sure. I imagine he's halfway back to the reservation by now. Either that, or he's lying dead somewhere out on the prairie feeding the buzzards. Either way, they'll find him sooner or later. Sorry to have troubled you, Mr. Beaudine."

"No trouble at all," Henry Beaudine replied, following Hart out of the barn toward the hitch rail. "How's that road coming?"

"Pretty slow," Hart answered, "but it should be about finished before the snow flies, leastwise finished enough so's it'll be passable."

"Good, good," Henry Beaudine said. "Sorry about your partner."

Hart nodded, his face grim. "I'd best get back," he said, swinging aboard his horse. "I left the prisoners shackled to a tree." He glanced over Beaudine's head to where Brianna stood near the barn door and wondered fleetingly if McClain had managed to get her in the sack. He tipped his hat in her direction, bid Henry Beaudine goodbye, and rode out of the yard.

Brianna heaved a sigh of relief as Roy Hart rode away. Shunkaha Luta was safe, and he was here, where she could see him and speak to him every day.

Shunkaha . . . he had killed a man. She could think of little else as she did her chores that evening.

Late that night, when she was certain her aunt and uncle were asleep, Brianna crept down the stairs to the kitchen to prepare the Indian something to eat. She placed the food in a wicker basket, along with a container of coffee and some bandages.

He killed a man. The thought filled her mind as she made her way through the dark barn and up the ladder to the loft. Shunkaha Luta was waiting for her.

She lit a small candle and placed it on the floor, smiled at him uncertainly. He had killed a man!

"You look much better," she said.

"I feel better, thanks to you."

His words were like liquid sunshine, filling her being with warmth. Surely this kind and gentle man could not be guilty of murder.

She sat beside him while he ate, content to be near him, pleased by his appetite. A healthy appetite was always a good sign, Aunt Harriett said, and the Indian certainly had a healthy appetite.

When he finished eating, Brianna removed the bandage from his shoulder. To her untrained eye, the wound looked ghastly, but she was relieved to see there was no pus oozing from the wound, no telltale streaks that hinted at infection. His back, too, seemed to be healing nicely. He was lucky, she thought, very lucky.

Vastly relieved, Brianna placed a fresh bandage over the wound in his arm, then sat back, suddenly shy. She had never been completely alone with a man at night. Even with Mc-Clain, she had not been truly alone, for her aunt and uncle had been in the parlor. This was very different, she thought. No one would hear her if she called for help. Shunkaha's scent filled her nostrils, the sight of his bare torso blocked everything else from her sight. He was probably cold, she thought, but she was the one who was shivering.

Her mouth was suddenly dry as she lifted her eyes to his face, only to find him gazing down at her, his dark eyes brimming with an emotion she did not understand.

"You are trembling, Ishna Wi," he said quietly. "Are you afraid of me now?"

"No, of course not." Her voice sounded strange in her ears. "Did you kill him?" The words came out of nowhere.

"Yes."

"Why?"

"To save my own life," Shunkaha Luta said, his voice hard and flat. "But I would gladly have killed him in cold blood, as I would gladly kill all the white men who invade our hunting grounds." He laid his hand over hers, the anger leaving his voice as he said softly, "But I would never hurt you, Golden Hair."

"I know," Brianna murmured. And she did know. She was not afraid of him, not now, not ever, but how else to describe these strange feelings? Her stomach felt as if it had captured a butterfly, her mouth was dry, her palms damp. Without quite knowing how it came about, she found herself wishing he would kiss her.

Shunkaha Luta knew he was staring at her, but he could not seem to draw his eyes from her face. Her braids were as bright as a flame, her skin translucent, her lips slightly parted, tempting him to kiss her, to taste the sweetness of her, but he did not. Her eyes were luminous in the flickering light of the candle, innocent, trusting. She was only a child, he reminded himself, a young girl who had risked much to help him.

"You had better go," he said thickly.

"Yes," Brianna agreed, rising to her feet.

Shunkaha Luta felt his breath catch in his throat as she stood before him. The candlelight shone behind her, making her long white cotton nightgown transparent, revealing long shapely legs, gently rounded hips, a narrow waist.

He groaned low in his throat as she left the loft, reminding himself again and again that she was just a child, an innocent young girl clothed in the soft flesh of womanhood, ignorant of the ways of men.

Sleep was a long time coming.

Chapter Seven

The next five days held a dreamlike quality for Brianna. She rose early to do her daily chores, sneaking a few moments with Shunkaha Luta after she fed the cow and the pigs and the chickens. His appetite seemed limitless. Only that morning her aunt had remarked on the sudden increase in the amount of food they had been consuming the last few days. Brianna had shrugged and said she was responsible, that she had been feeling hungry all the time lately. Aunt Harriett had looked at her strangely, but said no more.

Late at night, when Uncle Henry and Aunt Harriett were asleep, Brianna padded quietly out of the house to the loft to take the Indian something to eat, to spend a few quiet moments at his side, listening to the deep musical sound of his voice, basking in the friendliness and acceptance she saw in his beautiful black eyes. He was the first friend she'd ever had, and she felt she could tell him anything.

To Shunkaha Luta, she could complain about the hard work she was forced to do, she could lament the fact that her aunt and uncle did not love her no matter how much she tried to please them, she could weep softly when she spoke of her mother and father, dead these past six years.

All the hurt and loneliness that filled her heart melted away when Shunkaha held her in his arms, his hand, so big and strong, lightly stroking her hair and back, his deep voice soft with compassion as he promised her that someday she would know love and happiness, that *Wakan Tanka*, the Great Spirit of the Sioux, would not let her spend the rest of her life in misery and servitude.

Shunkaha Luta found surcease from his own unhappiness as well. He told her of his great sadness when his mother died, of feeling helpless and inadequate as he watched his younger sister waste away from hunger and malnutrition.

Brianna had wept as she listened to his story, for he was even more alone than she. He had lost not only his family and his home, but a way of life as well.

She stayed with him a little longer each night, his nearness warming her, his approval like a breath of fresh air after a storm. For six years she had known only hard work and rejection, but Shunkaha Luta had nothing but praise and admiration for her, and she basked in his approval.

They talked of many things. Brianna told him of going to school and how much she had liked it, and how Aunt Harriett had made her quit when she turned sixteen because she felt it was unseemly for a woman to have too much education. She told him of her childhood, of the happy times she had known with her parents, of the love and laughter and affection they had shared. It was hard to believe that Henry Beaudine was her father's brother, for Henry was as cold as ice, while Brianna's father had been warm and friendly, able to find good in everyone he met.

Shunkaha Luta told Brianna of living in the Black Hills, of fighting against the whites to hold onto their land. His people had surrendered, he said bitterly, but there were others who had not, other tribes that were still fighting for their old way of life. *Tashunke-Witke,* who was known as Crazy Horse to the whites, had not yet surrendered, nor had *Tatonka Iyotake,* Sitting Bull.

"Is that where you want to go when you leave here?" Brianna asked. "Back to the Black Hills to be with your people?"

"Yes. I want to fight again."

Brianna nodded, her heart aching at the thought of his going away.

"And what of you, Golden Hair?" Shunkaha asked. "What is it you desire of life?"

"I want a home of my own," Brianna said with conviction. "I want to get married and settle down and never move again. I want to have my own house, my own land. A place like this." She smiled wistfully. "My aunt hates it here. She's never forgiven my uncle for making her leave Pennsylvania to come out here, out to the wilderness, as she calls it. But I love it here. I think it's beautiful."

You are beautiful. The words formed in Shunkaha Luta's mind, but he dared not speak them aloud.

"Do many of the young *wasicu* court you?" he asked instead.

"*Wasicu?*"

"White men."

"No."

"No?" Shunkaha Luta exclaimed in disbelief. Were they all blind?

"There are only a few boys my age," Brianna replied, "and I don't care for any of them. They're all so silly."

"And you do not care for silly men?"

"No. I want a man who's strong and smart, someone who can take care of me." *Someone like you.*

"I hope you find him. You deserve all the good things that life has to offer."

"Thank you," Brianna murmured, feeling suddenly shy again.

Brianna's thoughts were full of the Indian as she helped her aunt prepare the evening meal the following night. Already she was thinking ahead to the time when she could sneak out to the barn and be with him again. A succulent ham was baking in the oven, and she was eager to take him a slice. She liked to watch Shunkaha eat, liked to see the enjoyment in his eyes as he wolfed down the food she brought him. She had practiced cooking since he came, and that afternoon she had baked a chocolate cake, ostensibly for Uncle Henry but in reality for Shunkaha Luta. He was fond of sweets, especially cake.

And yet, in the midst of Brianna's joy, there was sorrow. The Indian's wounds were healing rapidly. Soon he would leave to return to his own people, and she would never see him again. How empty her life would be when he was gone!

Dinner was a silent meal that night. Harriett Beaudine was not speaking to her husband, and Henry was not speaking to her. Neither spoke to Brianna. It wasn't uncommon. Harriett often imagined some slight and refused to speak to her husband until he had offered her an apology or brought her a gift that she deemed worthy enough of her forgiveness.

Personally, Brianna preferred the silence. It was so much more pleasant than their constant bickering. Sometimes, as now, she wondered why her aunt and uncle had gotten married in the first place. They did not seem happy together, they did not seem to enjoy any mutual interests, they rarely exchanged a kind word.

It was while Brianna was clearing the table that it happened. Somehow the delicate china teapot that Uncle Henry had given to Aunt Harriett for an anniversary present tumbled from her hands and hit the hardwood floor, shattering into a million sparkling pieces. Brianna looked up, stricken, to meet her aunt's merciless gaze.

"Get the strop," Harriett Beaudine ordered curtly.

"Please, Aunt Harriett. It was an accident."

"There are no such things as accidents," Harriett Beaudine retorted angrily.

Brianna sent a desperate look in her uncle's direction, hoping he would intercede in her behalf, as he sometimes did, but Henry Beaudine was in no mood to extend mercy to his niece. He was fed up with his wife, fed up with the farm, fed up with life in general. Muttering an oath under his breath, he snatched his hat from the hall tree and stalked out of the house, headed for town and a cold beer.

Brianna's whole body was shaking with dread as she went to the kitchen and took down the heavy leather strop that Uncle Henry used to hone his razor. Her mouth was as dry as the desert as she climbed the stairs to her room and lay face down on her narrow cot, her back bared to the waist.

Aunt Harriett's voice was cold and implacable as she took the strop from Brianna's hand. "You are an ungrateful child, willful and clumsy."

The strop came down on Brianna's tender flesh.

"I have done everything I can to give you a good home, and how do you repay me? By breaking an object I treasured with your clumsiness."

The strop came down again, harder this time. Brianna closed her eyes and bit down on her lower lip, her body writhing in pain as her aunt struck her again and again. Her aunt's words became a jumble of sound in her ears, their meaning lost as tears burned her eyes and ugly red welts were raised on her flesh until her back felt like it was on fire. *Brave Shunkaha Luta,* she thought as a scream erupted from her throat, *to endure such a whipping without uttering a sound.*

She was sobbing with pain and unhappiness when her aunt left the room, locking the door behind her. She wouldn't be able to see Shunkaha tonight, and that hurt more than anything else.

Shunkaha Luta stirred restlessly. Where was she? His stomach rumbled loudly, reminding him that he had not eaten since that morning, but more than food he longed to see Ishna Wi, hear her merry laughter, see her sweet smile. Rising, he walked across the loft to the window and peered into the night. The house was dark and quiet. Where was she?

Another hour passed and still she did not come. Impulsively, he climbed down the ladder and padded noiselessly through the barn. He was about to open one of the big double doors when Henry Beaudine entered the barn.

For a moment, the two men stared at each other. Shunkaha Luta cursed his lack of a weapon as the white man jerked a rifle from his saddle boot and eased back the hammer.

"Don't move!" Beaudine warned. His eyes narrowed as he stared at the man silhouetted in the darkness. "Damn," he muttered. "You're the redskin that escaped from the road gang, the one who killed McClain." He chuckled softly. "Wonder if there's a reward posted for you yet."

Shunkaha Luta did not move, nor did his gaze waver from the barrel of the rifle that was leveled squarely at his midsection. The white man's finger was steady on the trigger; the slightest pressure would send a bullet into Shunkaha's belly.

"Turn around," Beaudine ordered brusquely, "and don't try anything funny. There's no law against killing Injuns."

Shunkaha Luta hesitated, his eyes darting past the white man to the darkness beyond the barn door.

"Don't try it," Beaudine warned. "Now, turn around or I'll put a slug in your gut. That's a bad way to die, Injun. Could take days."

A muscle worked in Shunkaha's jaw as he slowly turned around. There was a sudden pain in the back of his head and then he was falling, falling, into nothingness . . .

"I'll feed the stock this morning," Henry Beaudine informed Brianna as she served him his breakfast.

Brianna looked at her uncle askance, her eyes mirroring her anxiety. "Have I done something wrong?"

"No." Henry Beaudine glanced at his wife as she took her place at the other end of the table. "Had me some excitement last night," he remarked.

Harriett Beaudine's eyes were frosty as she returned her husband's gaze. "Did you?" she said, her voice as cool as the expression in her eyes.

"Yes, ma'am," he said, smiling. "And it happened right here on my own place."

Harriett Beaudine felt her curiosity rise in spite of her resolve to remain disinterested in anything her husband might say, but Brianna felt her insides grow taut as she waited for her uncle to continue.

"Yep," Henry said, looking extraordinarily pleased with himself. "I caught me an Injun right out in the barn."

"An Indian!" Harriett exclaimed.

Henry Beaudine's expression turned smug. He had her attention now, by damn! "I caught that Injun that escaped from the road gang. You remember, the one Hart was here looking for."

"He was here? In our barn?" Harriett murmured.

Henry nodded. "I reckon he came to steal one of our horses."

"Where is he now?" Harriett asked, her hand over her heart. Imagine, an Indian skulking around the place in the dark. Why, they might all have been scalped in their beds.

"He's tied up in the barn," Henry Beaudine assured his wife. "There's nothing for you to be concerned about. I'll ride down and notify the road boss he's here after I feed the stock."

"Good," Harriett Beaudine said, letting out a sigh of relief. "I won't have a moment's peace until I know he's gone."

Brianna's heart was heavy in her breast as she picked at her breakfast. Shunkaha Luta was a prisoner again. Soon he would be back on the road gang, slaving in the hot sun. No, she couldn't let that happen. She knew how he hated being in captivity, knew how he longed to return to the Pa Sapa, the Black Hills.

She fought down the urge to cry as she cleared the table. Aunt Harriett must never suspect that the Indian meant anything to her.

Time and again as she washed the dishes, her eyes went to the barn. He was there, hungry, perhaps hurting. She watched

Uncle Henry ride away, and she began to wonder what excuse she could invent to go to the barn. But Aunt Harriett kept her busy inside the house all morning. And then she heard Uncle Henry return and she knew that any chance of helping Shunkaha Luta escape was gone.

Her uncle's face was red and angry when he entered the house.

"What is it, Henry?" Aunt Harriett asked.

"The road gang's gone. I talked to Heber, and he said some kind of sickness overtook the prisoners and they'd all been taken back to prison."

"What about the Indian? What are we going to do with him now?"

"I stopped off in Jefferson. The marshal's out of town, won't be back until tomorrow. I left word with Hadley to tell Pickett to get out here first thing in the morning and collect the Injun."

"He's going to stay here overnight?"

"Damn right! I'm not hauling him down to Jefferson." Henry Beaudine fixed Brianna with a stern look. "You stay away from the barn, missy. I don't want that savage looking at you. Understand?"

"Yes, sir," Brianna answered quickly.

With a nod, Henry Beaudine took off his coat and hat and went outside to hitch up the team. It was time to begin plowing the south field. Once again he felt a twinge of regret that his brother's only child had been a girl. She'd have been a sight more help if she'd been a boy, he thought sourly.

It seemed to Brianna that the day would never end. Every time she thought her work was finished, her aunt found a new task to keep her occupied. The silver needed polishing. The kitchen floor needed waxing. There was a large basket of mending that must be done. Company was coming for dinner the following night and the house must be cleaned from top to bottom, the furniture dusted, the rugs aired.

Brianna's back ached as never before as she moved from chore to chore. Her aunt had never whipped her with such force before, nor did the woman have any sympathy for her today. Surely God had been wise when He made her aunt barren.

Slowly, slowly, the hours passed until, at last, the sun began its descent and twilight covered the land. Soon, Brianna thought, soon she would go to him.

Shunkaha Luta groaned softly, his whole body aching. Inwardly he cursed *maya owicha paka*, the fates, for bringing Henry Beaudine into the barn just as he was about to go in search of Brianna. Her uncle had struck him across the back of the head with his rifle butt and then, to make certain his prisoner could not escape, had bound his hands together, secured the end of the rope to one of the cross-beams, and left him hanging there like a side of beef.

Closing his eyes, Shunkaha Luta lifted his voice toward heaven. "*Wakan Tanka, unshimalam ye oyate*," he murmured. "Great Spirit, have mercy on me."

Gradually, the interior of the barn grew dim and he knew that night was spreading her cloak across the face of *maka*, the earth. He had been two days without food now, and hunger clawed at his belly like a wild beast. His throat was dry, his arms and shoulders aching with the strain of bearing his weight. And soon, too soon, the white men would come for him.

He opened his eyes, his body growing tense, as the barn door slid open, admitting a draft of cold air. They were coming for him and there was no way to escape.

"Indian?"

"Ishna Wi?"

Brianna padded softly toward the sound of his voice. "Where are you?"

"Here."

Brianna lifted the candle higher, her eyes growing wide when she saw him hanging by his wrists from the cross-beam overhead. Moving quickly, she placed the candle on an upended barrel. Reaching into the basket of food she had brought for him, she withdrew a knife. Placing it between her teeth, she dragged a ladder across the floor, climbed nimbly to the top, and sawed through the heavy rope that bound Shunkaha Luta's hands. In moments, he was free.

"*Le mita pila, cola,*" he murmured as he massaged his bruised wrists.

"You're welcome. I've brought food and coffee."

"I have no time to eat," Shunkaha said as he followed her down the ladder. "I must go."

"Go?" But of course he must go, she thought bleakly. They were coming for him in the morning.

"I will not forget you, Ishna Wi," he said, cupping her chin in the palm of his hand. "You have been my good friend."

And you have been my only friend, Brianna thought wistfully. Two fat tears welled in her eyes and rolled down her cheeks. He was really going. She would never see him again, and when he went, all the kindness and affection she had known in the last six years would go with him and she would be alone again.

"I'll miss you," she said, her throat tight with unshed tears. "Be careful."

With a nod, Shunkaha Luta bent and placed a gentle kiss on her forehead. He did not want to leave her, yet he had no other choice. A last look, a lingering caress as his hand brushed her cheek, and then he started for the door.

"Indian, wait." Brianna ran after him. "Please wait."

Shunkaha Luta turned, his heart aching as he read the abject misery on her face, the sadness in her eyes. The night called to him, urging him to flee while there was time, but he could not leave her like this. She had cared for his wounds, provided him with food and shelter and comfort, and asked nothing in return.

"Do not weep, Ishna Wi," he murmured, enfolding her in his arms. "I cannot bear the sight of your tears."

Brianna closed her eyes, a sigh of contentment whispering through her lips as his arms went around her. He was so strong, and she felt so safe in his embrace. She placed her cheek against his chest. His skin was firm and warm, his hearbeat strong and steady beneath her cheek, and she wrapped her arms tightly around his waist. He was the only happiness she had known in the last six years. How could she let him go? She groaned as he drew her closer.

"What is it?" Shunkaha asked, drawing away from her, his brow furrowed with concern.

"My back," Brianna murmured, not meeting his eyes.

"What is wrong with it?"

"My aunt . . . ," Brianna said, still not meeting his gaze. "She . . . she whipped me."

Rage filled Shunkaha's soul at the thought of anyone daring to harm this precious child. "Shall I kill her for you?" he asked, thinking he would do it gladly.

Brianna laughed shakily, certain he was joking until she saw the fierce glint in his eyes. "No," she said quickly, afraid he might actually do her aunt harm. "But there is something you can do for me."

"Anything," Shunkaha Luta promised.

"Take me with you."

"Ishna Wi." He whispered her name as he gently drew her toward him once more, his lips moving in her hair. For one brief moment, he considered doing as she asked. The long journey to the Pa Sapa would not seem so long if she were at his side. He would delight in showing her the vast rolling plains, the beauty of the Black Hills, the wild flowers that bloomed along the Rosebud and the Little Big Horn. But even as he considered it, he knew it was impossible. She belonged here, with her own people, as he belonged with his.

"I would take you with me if I could," Shunkaha Luta said, "but it would not be wise."

"Please. My uncle will know that I helped you escape. They'll beat me again."

He was weakening—she could see the uncertainty mirrored in the depths of his eyes. Turning away from him, she unfastened her nightgown and let the garment slide down over her shoulders so he could see her back. "Please, Shunkaha," she begged.

He felt sick to his stomach as he gazed at her slender back, covered now with large red welts. What kind of woman was her aunt, to treat Brianna in such a manner? No Indian ever beat a child. Such a thing was unthinkable and brought instant disgrace.

Gently, Shunkaha drew Brianna's gown up around her shoulders, his hands lingering on her arms for just a moment before he let her go. Surely she would be better off with him than with a woman who beat her so cruelly.

Brianna felt her heart sing when she turned to face him. Even before he spoke the words, she knew she had won.

"You must have clothes," he said. "You cannot travel in that gown."

"You'll wait for me?"

"I will wait."

Brianna's feet fairly flew over the cold ground as she ran back to the house. In her room, she quickly changed out of her gown and into her brown dress. Grabbing the case from her pillow, she began to pack her few belongings: a change of undergarments, her blue dress, a hairbrush, a faded photograph of her mother and father. Downstairs, she grabbed several loaves of fresh-baked bread, a slab of bacon, some apples, a hunk of cheese, a small frying pan, an old enamel coffee pot, a box of matches, a couple of knives and forks, a towel, and a bar of soap.

She was about to leave the house when she saw her uncle's rifle hanging over the fireplace. After a moment's hesitation, she took that, too, along with a box of shells. The rifle was her uncle's pride and joy, and it pleased her to take it. She also took the knife he used for skinning fish and small game. It was an awesome weapon, with an eight-inch blade.

When she returned to the barn, Shunkaha Luta had two horses waiting. Her uncle's saddle, the only one on the place, was cinched on the roan; the second horse, a big buckskin gelding that Henry Beaudine used for plowing, stood beside the roan, a bridle over its head.

"Can you ride?" Shunkaha asked.

Brianna nodded. "Here," she said, handing him the knife and the rifle. "These are for you."

Shunkaha Luta took the weapons from her, his hands caressing the rifle's smooth walnut stock, the gleaming barrel. It was a fine weapon, much better than anything he had ever owned. He slid it into the saddle boot on the roan's saddle, tucked the sheathed knife into his belt. Taking Brianna's bundle, he tied the open end shut with a piece of twine, then slung it over the saddle horn.

And then he turned to face her, his hands resting lightly on her shoulders. "You are sure you want to do this? It is not too late to change your mind."

Brianna gazed into Shunkaha's eyes, knowing she wanted nothing more than to be with this man always. "I want to go with you."

With a nod, he placed his hands around her waist and lifted her onto the back of the roan, adjusting the stirrups to accommodate her legs. Then, with effortless grace, he swung aboard the buckskin's bare back and rode out of the barn. Brianna followed him, her eyes fixed on his back.

Brianna snuggled deeper into her coat as the wind hit her and she wished she had thought to steal one of her uncle's jackets for Shunkaha. Doubtless it would have been tight in the shoulders and too short in the sleeves, but at least it would have kept him warm. Shunkaha Luta held his horse to a walk as they made their way out of the yard. *Hanhepiwi,* the moon, was bright overhead, lighting their path as they rode by the lake and angled their horses down the hill.

Shunkaha Luta grinned ruefully as they reached the road he had helped clear. All his hard work had not been in vain, after all, he mused, and urged the powerful buckskin gelding into a lope. He glanced over his shoulder to make sure Brianna was behind him, felt his heart swell with affection when she smiled at him.

They rode all that night, each mile taking them farther from civilization and deeper into the unsettled wilderness that stretched for over two hundred miles between Jefferson and the Pa Sapa.

As they rode, Shunkaha Luta offered a silent prayer of thanks to Wakan Tanka for sending Ishna Wi to aid him in his hour of need. Truly, she must have been sent by the Great Spirit.

It was the dark hour before sunrise when Shunkaha Luta reined his lathered mount to a halt near the top of a tree-studded slope. He lifted a trail-weary Brianna from her horse and gently placed her on the ground, his arm curving around her waist to steady her as she swayed against him.

"We will rest now, Ishna Wi," he told her. "Only stay awake long enough for me to spread a blanket for you."

Brianna nodded, her eyes never leaving him as he removed the saddle blanket from the roan and spread it on the ground. Grateful, she curled up on the heavy saddle blanket and closed her eyes.

Shunkaha Luta felt a wave of tenderness as he gazed at

the golden-haired girl at his feet. She was already asleep, her cheek pillowed on her arm, her long tawny lashes like sun-kissed crescents on her cheeks. He gazed at her a moment longer, his own body weary from the long ride and the abuse he had received from her uncle, but he would not sleep yet. Tethering the horses to a nearby tree, he went back over their trail for several hundred yards, erasing all signs of their passing.

The sun was climbing above the distant mountains when he returned to Brianna. She was sleeping as he had left her. Quietly, he stretched out beside her, shivering as *Waziah's* breath blew across the land. His shoulder was still sore from McClain's bullet, the back of his head ached where Henry Beaudine had struck him, yet as he closed his eyes, he had never been more content, or felt more at peace.

Brianna woke slowly, aware of a great weight across her body. Opening her eyes, she stared for a long moment at the vast blue vault of the sky overhead and then, in a rush, she remembered where she was, and whom she was with. Turning her head, she saw Shunkaha Luta lying beside her. It was his arm that weighed heavily across her breasts, but it was a welcome burden and she never thought of moving it.

How handsome he was! There were no harsh lines around his eyes and mouth when he slept. His lips were full and slightly parted and she had a quick urge to kiss him while he slept, to taste his lips and see if they were hard and cold, or warm and soft. His hair was as black and shiny as polished ebony, tempting her touch. Timidly, she reached out and let her fingertips caress a thick lock where it fell across his shoulder.

Brianna's touch was as light as that of a butterfly landing on the petal of a rose, yet Shunkaha Luta woke instantly, one hand closing over hers in a grip of iron, the other reaching for his knife. Brianna gasped, frightened by the look in his eyes, startled by how swiftly he had reacted to her touch. Had she been an enemy, she knew she would have been dead.

And then she blushed from the roots of her hair to the soles of her feet. "I . . . I'm sorry," she stammered. "I didn't mean to wake you, I just—" She broke off in an agony of embarrassment. How could she say she had wanted to touch his hair? It sounded so silly.

Shunkaha's eyes seemed to look right through her and into her secret heart as he loosed his grip on her hand. "Did I hurt you?"

"No."

His eyes held hers a long moment. Almost, he was tempted to kiss her, to discover if she could possibly be as sweet as he imagined. And then he reminded himself that she was just a child.

"What did you bring to eat?" he asked, breaking the tension between them.

"You must be starved!" Brianna exclaimed. Jumping to her feet, she began to rummage around in her bag, glad to have something to do. In no time at all she had bacon sizzling in the pan and coffee perking in the pot.

Shunkaha Luta watched her, admiring the quick way she moved, her deftness with a knife as she sliced the bacon, the way she hummed softly as she worked. She had lived with her aunt's cruelty and indifference for the past six years, yet Brianna radiated sweetness and light. Truly, she was a remarkable child.

They ate bacon and bread and cheese for breakfast and washed it down with strong black coffee. Shunkaha saddled Brianna's horse while she cleaned up, and then they were riding toward the distant mountains.

Father Wi climbed higher in the sky, and Shunkaha Luta lifted his face to the sun, absorbing its warmth as it chased the cold from his bones. He was clad only in buckskin pants, clout, and moccasins. Somewhere he would have to find a shirt and jacket to turn away the chill of the night.

They rode all that day across gently rolling prairies. Once, far in the distance, Brianna saw a couple of white-tailed deer. Riding on, she saw a pair of eagles take wing. They were beautiful birds, so graceful as they wheeled and soared across the vast blue sky.

Shunkaha gazed at the eagles, his expression bleak. Once, this land had belonged to the Sioux and the Cheyenne. Once, vast herds of curly-haired buffalo had roamed the prairie, too numerous to count. The earth had vibrated with their passing, their cloven hooves had churned up great clouds of dust. But now the buffalo were gone and the prairie was quiet. So quiet.

Brianna glanced at Shunkaha Luta and frowned. Almost, she asked him what was wrong, but then she changed her mind. If he wanted her to know what he was thinking, he would tell her.

They paused now and then to rest the horses, and Brianna found herself awed by the vastness that surrounded them. As far as the eye could see there was nothing but earth and sky and the distant snow-capped mountains that never seemed to get any closer. Occasionally she saw a clump of wildflowers, perhaps a stand of cottonwoods near a winding stream, but those were rare. The vastness, the silence, the lack of humanity, made her feel small and insignificant and a trifle lonely even with Shunkaha beside her.

Late in the afternoon they came to a small box canyon. They rode single file through the sheer canyon walls, and Brianna could not help giving a little sigh of pleasure as they entered the canyon. It was quite the most beautiful place she had ever seen. She remembered reading about the Garden of Eden in Aunt Harriett's Bible, and she thought to herself that the canyon must look just like Eden. Trees grew in abundance, their leafy arms reaching toward Heaven in silent, never-ending supplication. A small waterfall emptied into a mirrorlike pool that was surrounded by wild-flowers and gray-green shrubbery and graceful pines. The grass was ankle-deep, thick and soft beneath her feet.

She glanced at Shunkaha, her eyes alight with the beauty of the place. The air was clear, fragrant with the scent of grass and earth and sweet-smelling pine. A black-eyed lizard sunned itself on a pile of boulders.

Shunkaha Luta smiled at Brianna. He, too, was charmed by the quiet beauty of the canyon. A red-tailed hawk soared in lazy grace, drifting aimlessly on the warm air currents. A fat gray rabbit darted from behind a bush and disappeared into a hole. A squirrel was perched on a tree limb, and from nearby came the angry twitter of a sparrow as it chased a jay away from its nest.

Brianna felt her cheeks grow warm as Shunkaha continued to look at her. If this was the Garden of Eden, then he was Adam and she was Eve . . . the thought made her heart do funny flip-flops in her breast.

She felt her heart quiver, felt her pulse begin to race as Shunkaha Luta walked toward her, but he only took the reins from her hand and began to unsaddle her horse. She watched him like one mesmerized, her eyes trapped by the graceful ebb and flow of his muscles as he moved, by the way the setting sun caressed the smooth bronze of his skin.

Turning, he removed the bridle from his own horse. And then he took her hand in his. "Come," he said. "Let us go exploring."

They walked hand in hand down the canyon, the only two people in all the world. Brianna saw the flowers and the trees, the rocks, the stream that got its start from the crystal pool, the high canyon walls, the darkening sky, but she was only truly aware of the tall man at her side. He was so near, and her hand was so small where it rested trustingly in his.

Her fingers tingled at his touch, and the heat from his hand seemed to travel up her arm and right to her heart.

She heard him talk, telling her about the different wild herbs and plants that grew in the canyon, but the words made no sense. She heard only the sound of his voice, deep and rich, as beautiful to the ear as his profile was to her eye.

He handed her a delicate pink flower and she sniffed its fragrance, but she did not smell the flower's perfume. Instead, her nostrils filled with the scent of man. It was most disconcerting. And satisfying.

She was hardly aware of returning to the place where they had left the horses. In a short time, their camp was set up. Shunkaha Luta gathered an armload of firewood, dug a shallow pit, and laid a fire while Brianna sorted through their supplies and began preparing dinner. Soon the smell of coffee drifted on the evening breeze, together with the tantalizing scent of frying bacon and potatoes.

They ate in companionable silence, shared a cup of hot black coffee. A shiver of pleasure skittered along Brianna's arm when Shunkaha's hand brushed hers, and she felt again that peculiar singing sensation in the pit of her stomach, a tremor of breathless excitement that washed over her whenever the Indian touched her.

She was aware of his eyes on her face as she washed their few dishes and utensils and put them away.

"It's cold," she said, suddenly feeling the need for conversation.

The Indian nodded and added more fuel to the fire. His skin glowed like burnished copper in the glow of the dancing flames, and Brianna's stomach did a somersault as he stretched his arms over his head, the movement making the muscles in his arms and chest grow taut. What a magnificent creature he was, so tall and strong. And male.

That night, with him lying beside her on the blanket, she

was acutely aware of his masculinity, and of her own femininity. She had never been overly curious about the difference between men and women. She had been born and raised by God-fearing Christian parents who had never discussed such things with her. Later, on her uncle's farm, she had seen the livestock mate and she knew that such couplings produced young. Her aunt had told her it was much the same with people.

Until now, Brianna had never thought much about marriage or children. She had never met a boy she liked, and she had especially never met a boy she would have considered doing *that* with. But now . . . she put such thoughts from her mind. Shunkaha Luta was her friend, and he thought of her as a child, nothing more. Still, she did not think she would find it disgusting to have him hold her and kiss her. She carefully kept her thoughts from straying any farther along that line.

In the morning, Shunkaha Luta told her they would spend a few days in the canyon. He had seen deer tracks near the pool earlier that morning, he said, and they would stay long enough to rest and hunt. A warm coat could be made from the deer hide; they could jerk the venison for their journey.

Brianna's heart was light as she prepared breakfast. She was free of her aunt's shrewish tongue, free of her uncle's domination. No more would she have to suffer their abuse and indifference. And *he* was here, her handsome, raven-haired Indian. He would protect her and provide for her, and she would care for him.

She watched as he honed the skinning knife on a flat stone, mesmerized by the play of muscles in his back. The ugly red welts had virtually disappeared, though the whipping had left many scars. He had never complained, not about the pain of the brutal whipping, nor of the wound in his shoulder. She wondered if the bullet wound still caused him pain. The area around the wound was turning greenish-purple; the scab was thick and ugly.

Shunkaha Luta ran his thumb along the edge of the blade. The metal was honed to a fine edge, sharp enough to slice through meat and muscle, strong enough to cut through enough small branches to make a shelter of sorts.

He spent the day building a crude three-sided shelter out of long, slender branches from the young trees that grew near the mouth of the canyon. Brianna made a thatched roof of leaves, and they smiled at each other often as they worked, pleased with their creation, and with the way they worked together, with never a cross word or an angry frown.

It was dusk when Brianna made her way to the small pool to bathe. Shunkaha had gone hunting, and she wondered if he would have any luck in finding a deer. Her mouth watered at the thought of fresh venison.

Stepping out of her ugly brown dress, she waded into the shallow water. Huddling there, she unbraided her hair and shook it loose, letting the heavy golden mass fall about her shoulders. Glancing around to make sure she was alone, she removed her chemise and drawers and then, feeling terribly wicked, she floated naked in the pool.

She was shivering when she stepped from the water. Drying herself with her dress, she knelt beside the pool and washed it, wishing she had something other than her shapeless blue dress to change into.

And that was how Shunkaha Luta found her.

He felt his heart slam against his chest as he saw Brianna kneeling beside the quiet blue-green pool. His breath caught in his throat as his eyes moved over her in slow fascination. The setting sun cast red-gold shadows over her creamy flesh; her hair cascaded down her slender back to her tiny waist, the shimmering tresses highlighted with streaks of flame. Her buttocks were softly rounded, wonderfully female, undeniably provocative.

A deep sigh escaped his lips, alerting Brianna to the fact that she was no longer alone. Startled, she jumped nimbly to her feet and whirled around, her cheeks flushing scarlet when she saw the Indian staring at her, his dark eyes smoldering as they traveled the length of her body.

Shunkaha Luta uttered a low cry of admiration mixed with despair. This was no child. This was a woman fully grown and of an age to please a man. How had he ever thought otherwise? Her breasts were high and full, her waist incredibly tiny, her hips softly rounded, her skin unblemished ivory perfection.

His physical reaction was immediate and obvious.

Brianna opened her mouth to speak, but no words came forth. Belatedly, she crossed her arms over her breasts, feeling her whole body burn with embarrassment as Shunkaha Luta's dark eyes moved over her from head to heel, his gaze alight with a bright inner fire she had never seen reflected in their depths before.

For an eternity they stood thus, neither one able to form a coherent thought. Shunkaha's blood was hammering in his ears, burning in his veins. She was more beautiful, more desirable, than he had ever imagined. Every instinct urged him to take her in his arms, to lower her to the ground and smother her with kisses, to bury himself in her womanly warmth and satisfy the awful ache in his loins by melding his body with hers.

His gaze lifted to her face. Her eyes were wide, filled with apprehension. Her mouth, as pink as the wild roses that grew along the banks of the Little Big Horn, were slightly parted. A muscle worked in Shunkaha Luta's jaw as he fought to regain control of his emotions. And then, summoning every ounce of willpower that he possessed, he turned on his heel and walked away. It was the hardest thing he had ever done.

Brianna went suddenly limp, as though she had been released from some magical spell when Shunkaha's eyes left hers. Her heart was hammering wildly, her knees were weak, her mouth as dry as dust. Quickly, clumsily, she pulled on her blue dress, draped the brown one over a rock to dry, deftly braided her damp hair. Why had Shunkaha Luta looked at her like that, his dark eyes hot and hungry? And why had she enjoyed it?

He was sitting cross-legged before the fire when she finally found the courage to return to their campsite. She saw that he had snared a rabbit; the meat was roasting on a spit over the fire, the juices sizzling as they splattered on the hot coals. He did not look up, nor acknowledge her presence in any way, yet they had never been more aware of each other.

It was a silent meal. For the first time, Brianna was ill at ease with the Indian, not knowing what to say, not certain what had happened between them at the pool, but knowing that nothing would ever be quite the same between them again. Her feelings were jumbled and confused, her emotions chaotic. One minute she felt light-hearted and happy, the next she was worried and afraid.

As soon as dinner was over, Shunkaha rose to his feet and left the fire. Brianna watched him walk down the canyon until he was out of sight. Was he angry with her?

She heated water for the dishes, washed them automatically, her thoughts on Shunkaha, always Shunkaha. She felt her cheeks grow hot as she remembered the way he had looked at her at the pool, the way his eyes had moved over her, lingering on her breasts before she thought to cover them. What had he been thinking?

You know what he was thinking, chided the voice of her conscience, and Brianna's cheeks grew hotter still. She *had* known what he was thinking. She had seen the telltale evidence of his desire, had felt her heart flutter wildly with the knowledge that he wanted her. The thought had been both frightening and exhilarating. She had felt a surge of disappointment when he turned and walked away. She had been so certain he was going to kiss her. She knew it was dreadfully wicked to wish for such a thing, but her whole body had ached for him in a way she did not quite understand.

Thinking of him now filled her with warmth and a quivery feeling in the pit of her stomach. He was so tall, so handsome. He had held her and comforted her, and she had felt at peace in his arms, safe, cherished.

The sound of his footsteps made her heart sing with excitement. A sudden shyness washed over her and she hurried into the shelter and crawled under the covers, unable to face him for fear he would read the wanting in her eyes, hear it in her voice.

The Indian did not share her blanket that night, nor did he sleep inside the shelter he had built. Instead, he remained near the fire, staring blankly at the flames. What was he thinking, Brianna wondered. What had happened to the easy camaraderie they had shared?

Shunkaha Luta gazed into the flickering flames, but it was not the fire he saw. Rather, it was Brianna standing near the quiet pool, her hair like a golden nimbus around her face, her alabaster body a study in feminine perfection. He felt his sleeping desire stir to life as he recalled the shape of her high pink-tipped breasts, her tiny waist, the swell of her hips, her long shapely legs.

He groaned low in his throat. He had never had time for a woman of his own. He had been too busy making war against the *wasicu,* his only purpose in life to fight off the white horde invading the Pa Sapa. He had thought of nothing else, wanted nothing else, only vengeance against those who killed the buffalo and slaughtered his people without mercy.

When his father's band had surrendered, Shunkaha had given up the war path to stay with his family. His father had been old and frail, his mother's health failing even then. His sister, Tasina, had been a young maiden of fourteen summers. He had spent almost a year on the reservation, where each day had been a struggle for survival, a struggle that only a handful of his people won. His father had died soon after the band surrendered. His mother had died eight months later, and then his sister had succumbed to *yunke-lo*, another victim of the white man's treachery.

Shunkaha's eyes moved toward the crude shelter where Brianna lay sleeping. In a fluid movement, he stood up and padded noiselessly toward the shelter. He paused in the doorway, his heart pounding, his blood running hot with desire as he gazed at her. He was not a stranger to women. There had been captive squaws among the Sioux who had traded their favors for food and clothing, and he had occasionally eased his hunger for a woman in their arms. But he had never known love or affection at a woman's hand until he met Brianna. She had nursed his wounds with gentle concern, had wept for his pain. Her tears had been unexpected and surprising, touching him deeply.

Brianna stirred in her sleep, and Shunkaha's breath stuck in his throat as he caught a glimpse of milky white flesh where her chemise ended, just above the swell of her breasts. He was breathing hard now, every instinct urging him to take her, to satisfy his desire and put an end to the awful hunger that gnawed at him day and night. It would be so easy to take her. Willing or not, it would be so easy to bend her to his will, to take by force that which he so desired.

His eyes traced her slender form beneath the blanket. Her waist was so tiny, her hips round and sweet, her legs long and coltish. All too clearly he remembered how she had looked at the pool, her sun-gold hair swirling about her shoulders, her eyes a vibrant blue, her body more beautiful than anything he had ever seen.

Slowly, his eyes moved back to her face and he saw that Brianna was awake and staring up at him.

"Is anything wrong?" she asked, and he heard the faint note of alarm in her voice.

"No, Ishna Wi," he answered thickly. "Go back to sleep."

She nodded drowsily, trustingly, her eyelids flickering down as sleep claimed her once more.

Shunkaha Luta muttered an oath as he turned on his heel and walked briskly toward the pool. Perhaps a cold swim would cool his heated flesh and take his mind from the golden-haired woman-child who fired his blood and enflamed his desire.

Chapter Eight

Brianna sat beneath a shady tree, smiling as she watched a sparrow dust its feathers. Early that morning, Shunkaha Luta had taken the rifle and left the canyon to go hunting. In his absence, Brianna had bathed in the pool, washed her hair, and then, feeling lazy and content, had settled beneath a gnarled oak to enjoy the beauty of the day and contemplate the future.

Two days had passed since Shunkaha had seen her kneeling beside the pool. He had seemed strangely preoccupied since then. Often she caught him staring at her, an odd look in his fathomless black eyes.

They were friends again. The uneasiness that had sprung up between them that night had disappeared, and Brianna wondered if she had imagined it. Never had she been happier than she was now, living with Shunkaha Luta. He was tall and strong and wonderful, and she felt completely safe, even here in the wilderness. She wondered if her aunt and uncle missed her at all and if they had searched for her. Probably, Uncle Henry would be more upset to discover his rifle was missing than his niece. And Aunt Harriett would miss her only because she would have to do her own chores from now on.

Brianna shook her head. It was too nice a day to think unpleasant thoughts. Better to think of Shunkaha Luta. She felt that odd little shiver in the pit of her stomach as she summoned his image to mind. She never tired of looking at him, never grew weary of hearing his voice. She had not known many men in her life, only a handful who lived and worked on the nearby farms. There had been boys her age in town, but her aunt had never let her associate with them except under strict supervision. And then there had been McClain. She grimaced at the thought of him, remembering how he had tried to kiss her and how repulsive it had been. Yes, she thought, Shunkaha Luta put them all to shame. Old or young, none of the men she had ever met could compare to her Indian . . . *her Indian.* She liked the sound of that. Her Indian. Her cheeks grew warm. What would it be like to be his woman? Would he do terrible things to her? When Brianna's cycle began, Aunt Harriett had explained the reason for it and had told Brianna, in no uncertain terms, that decent women did not engage in any form of sexual intimacy prior to marriage. A decent, God-fearing woman saved herself for her husband, and then she endured the intimacies of the marriage bed for the sake of bearing children. Without saying so, Aunt Harriett had let it be known that, since she was unable to have children, she no longer saw any reason to submit to Uncle Henry's love-making. There were women in town who catered to a man's baser desires, Aunt Harriett had remarked, thereby relieving decent women of *that* particular burden.

Brianna had listened to her aunt, dutifully voicing agreement with everything the woman had said, though she had secretly wondered if anything could be quite as awful as her aunt had described it. Surely if a woman loved a man, she would find pleasure in being held and kissed. Her mother and father had been warm, affectionate people. They had expressed their love for Brianna, complimenting her when she did well in school, hugging her, kissing her goodnight. Her mother had not been repulsed by her husband's touch, nor had Brianna's mother acted as though sharing her husband's bed had been an onerous chore and one to be avoided if at all possible. It was most confusing.

Brianna gazed down the canyon, her thoughts turned inward. She recalled the nights she had left her tiny room and made her way to the loft. There, in Shunkaha's arms, she had found solace for her troubled heart. On those days when everything went wrong, when her aunt upbraided her for every minor fault, when her uncle had been brusque and impatient, Brianna had looked forward to the few hours she could spend with Shunkaha. She could hide in his arms, shed her tears freely, tell him how miserable she was, how awful it was to be unloved. And he had understood. Even when he said nothing, she had seen the sympathy in his eyes, felt it in the way his arms tightened around her, in the soft stroke of his hand on her hair.

She knew, somehow she just knew, that her parents had shared that same special feeling of closeness. Was it love, or merely the ability to empathize with another human being? Why didn't Aunt Harriett feel the same toward Uncle Henry? Why had her aunt married her uncle if she couldn't stand his touch?

Brianna smiled a shy smile. She knew that Shunkaha Luta cared for her. Perhaps, if she tried to flirt with him, he would take her in his arms and kiss her.

Her heart skipped a beat as she heard the sound of hoofbeats echoing between the high canyon walls. Shunkaha had returned! She felt her heart race with anticipation at the prospect of seeing him again; knew that she would not find it unpleasant to be held in his arms, to feel his lips on hers . . .

She scrambled to her feet, eager to see him, and then froze, a hard knot of fear congealing in her belly as she stared at the riders coming toward her. It was not Shunkaha Luta.

The four men exchanged leering grins as they reined their horses to a halt a short distance from where Brianna was standing alone beneath a sun-kissed oak. The leader, a barrel-chested man with a bristly black beard and greasy black hair, leaned forward, his arms resting on the saddle horn.

"We smelled your coffee," he said. His close-set brown

eyes swept over Brianna and then perused the camp, noting
there was only one horse grazing nearby. "You all alone?"
Brianna shook her head, unable to speak past the lump in
her throat.

"She is alone," remarked a man Brianna recognized as an
Indian. "Let us take her and go before her man returns."

"Si," agreed a skinny Spaniard. "Es bonita."

The leader nodded. "Keller, take her."

Brianna began to tremble as an incredibly tall man slid
from the back of his horse and walked purposefully toward
her. "Come on, girly," he called as Brianna backed away
from him. "You might as well come along peaceful like.
There's no place for you to go."

Brianna screamed as the man's hamlike hand closed on her
forearm. With ease he tossed her over his shoulder, mounted
his horse, and dropped her, none too gently, in front of him.
She squirmed as his arm wrapped around her waist.

"Pablo," the leader called. "Get her horse."

This can't be happening, Brianna thought frantically. And
then she felt her captor's hand caress her upper arm, felt his
beard-roughened jaw against her cheek, and she knew the
nightmare was real.

They rode out of the canyon single file, with Keller and
Brianna bringing up the rear. The Indian stayed behind.

"To take care of your man," Keller whispered in Brianna's
ear.

"No," Brianna said in a choked voice. She shook her head
as she pictured Shunkaha riding into the canyon unawares,
being shot down in cold blood.

Keller laughed softly. "We don't want him to come looking for you and spoil our fun, now do we?"

"What do you mean?"

"We try all the girls before we sell them to the Comancheros," Keller explained, running a meaty hand along Brianna's thigh.

"Comancheros?"

"Yeah. They pay big money for fair-haired white women, and they don't mind if they're a little used, if you know what I mean."

"No, please," Brianna begged. "I've never . . . I don't—" She broke off in an agony of dread.

"Never!" Keller exclaimed. His smile was one of pure pleasure. "Well, I'll be damned!"

Shunkaha Luta paused at the canyon entrance, his instincts warning him that something was amiss. His eyes swept the canyon floor, immediately picking up fresh pony tracks. Four horses had entered the canyon. Four horses had left. But not the same four horses; one had been Brianna's big roan. Rifle in hand, Shunkaha dismounted to get a better look at the tracks, felt a sharp stinging blow across the back of his head as the sound of a gunshot echoed off the canyon walls. Dropping to his knees, he swung toward the sound of the report. An Indian was bearing down on him, a rifle in his hands, the shrill, ululating war cry of the Comanche on his lips.

"Ho, brother," Shunkaha Luta murmured as he sighted down the barrel of his Winchester and squeezed the trigger, "it is a good day to die."

Shunkaha's bullet caught the charging Comanche full in the face, killing him instantly.

Shunkaha Luta rose quickly to his feet. Jerking the deer carcass from across the buckskin's withers, he vaulted onto the animal's bare back. Lifting his rifle overhead, he shouted the Sioux kill cry as he urged his mount toward camp. Fear of what he might find sat like a stone in his belly. Would she be dead, or gone?

The sign of the intruders was easy to read. Four men had ridden into the canyon. Three had left, taking Brianna with them and leading her horse. The Indian had been left behind to make certain the other three weren't followed.

Shunkaha Luta reined the buckskin in a tight rearing turn and thundered back the way he had come, his narrowed eyes fixed on the ground. Four men had ridden into the canyon and laid hands on his woman, and for that they would die.

Brianna's mind and body were numb by the time her abductors stopped for the night. The sun was setting, and she shivered as a cool northeasterly wind blew across the prairie, chasing the sun's warmth from the face of the earth.

She had glanced over her shoulder repeatedly as they rode away from the canyon, hoping to see Shunkaha Luta riding toward her.

"You're wastin' your time," the man called Keller had told her more than once. "He's dead by now."

Brianna shuddered as Keller lifted her from his horse, then tied her hands and feet together. His fingers drifted over her breast as he stooped to whisper in her ear, assuring her he would be gentle when his time came.

Brianna stared at the ground, her mind refusing to accept what was going to happen, refusing to believe that Shunkaha was dead, that she would never see him again.

Around her, the three men laughed and joked as they unsaddled their horses, built a fire, threw a slab of meat into a cast iron skillet, brewed a pot of coffee.

The man called Pablo strolled toward her some time later, offering her something to eat, but the mere idea of food made Brianna nauseous and she turned away, cringing as his filthy hands moved through her hair. He was short and skinny, with close-set brown eyes and a thin moustache. His teeth were stained and yellow, his breath foul.

"Soon, *chica*," he murmured, giving her cheek a cruel pinch. "Soon."

The leader of the men sauntered over shortly after the Mexican moved away. He gestured at the plate of untouched food Pablo had left. "Better eat," he advised with a leer. "You'll need yer strength."

"Why are you doing this?" Brianna asked, blinking back her tears.

"Why?" The man looked at her as if she were slightly addled. "For the money, of course. Pretty little gal like yerself's worth a fair amount in cash or trade. Then, too, it's a good way for me and my boys to sample a wide variety of goods without having to pay fer it."

"Please let me go," Brianna begged.

The man laughed. "They all say please," he mused to himself as he turned away. "But they never say thank you."

Brianna was left alone while the men gathered around the fire to eat. They laughed and talked as they wolfed down a mixture of greasy bacon and red beans. Their language was vulgar and suggestive, liberally sprinkled with profanity, and Brianna cringed as she realized they were talking about her, about what they planned to do with her before they sold her to the Comancheros.

Brianna gazed into the distance. Had Shunkaha Luta returned to the canyon? Was he dead? Badly wounded? Two large tears welled in her eyes as she pictured Shunkaha lying dead in the canyon, his body left to rot in the sun . . .

"Yahoo!"

Brianna's head jerked around as Keller leaped to his feet, a card in his hand. He was grinning from ear to ear as he tossed the queen of hearts into the pile.

"I wouldn'ta minded going last," he drawled to his companions. "But first is gonna be a hell of a lot better."

Brianna screamed as he towered over her, his huge hands fumbling with his belt buckle, his eyes glazed with lust. As he bent toward her, she screamed again, her bound feet lashing out at his shins.

Keller swore a violent oath as her foot struck his knee. He

retaliated swiftly, his open palm striking her cheek so hard it made her eyes water and her ears ring.

"No, please," Brianna begged.

"We can do this two ways," Keller told her, his voice hard and flat, his face completely devoid of sympathy or compassion. "Just you and me, nice and private, or you can go on fightin', in which case I'll call Pablo and McGillis, over there, to hold you down. Either way suits me fine. I ain't had a woman in months."

Brianna gazed up at him, her eyes wide with fear. Slowly she shook her head, silently begging him to leave her alone.

"Which will it be, girly? I'm in no mood to wait."

"Just . . . just you." Brianna forced the words through teeth that were chattering with fear. She squeezed her eyes shut, willing herself to faint, as the big man began to unfasten his pants. This could not be happening! She had never known a man, but she had secretly yearned to be Shunkaha's woman, to have him initiate her into womanhood. He would be kind and gentle, patient and understanding . . .

She heard Keller grunt as he pulled off his boots and stripped off his pants and she began to struggle against the ropes that held her, but to no avail. This could not be happening. It was all a dream, a terrible dream. Tomorrow she would laugh.

She gasped as Keller grabbed hold of her dress and tossed the skirt up around her hips. She tried to pray for help as he yanked her undergarments down around her ankles, but she could not form the words. She clenched her teeth together, waiting for the inevitable to happen, hoping it would be quickly over. In the background she could hear the other two men egging Keller on, and she felt a sudden overwhelming sense of defeat. When Keller was through with her, there would be two more men to take his place.

"Oh, God," she murmured as Keller's hand squeezed her thigh, "please let me die."

Her whole body tensed as Keller lowered himself over her and began to kiss her. She gagged when she felt his tongue invade her mouth. Unmindful of the consequences that were sure to follow, she bit down on his tongue, felt a moment of victory when he yelped and drew away.

"Bitch!" he exclaimed, and slapped her, hard.

From far away she heard the sound of ribald laughter, heard McGillis and Pablo exchange amused remarks about the fact that one little *puta* could give a man like Keller so much trouble.

Keller heard them, too, and he swore under his breath as his sidekicks mocked him.

Brianna closed her eyes again as Keller reached for her. She heard Pablo shout something in Spanish, heard the crackle of flames as more wood was tossed on the fire. And then she heard three gunshots, the second and the third coming hard on the heels of the first, so that the three shots blended into one long, rolling report. She heard a loud groan near her ear, felt something warm and sticky splatter over her face and neck. And then there was only silence, louder than the sound of gunfire, and a great heaviness across her lower body.

Her heart was pounding like a drum as she slowly opened her eyes. A high-pitched scream of terror rose in her throat when she saw Keller sprawled across her thighs, but no sound emerged from her lips. Frozen with fear, she could only stare at the blood that soaked the ground and stained her legs. The blood of a dead man. For he was obviously dead. His eyes were wide and staring; blood trickled from the corner of his mouth.

And now another man stood before her, a man with swarthy skin and dark eyes filled with smoldering rage. There was no recognition when she looked at him, only gut-wrenching fear.

She began to scream hysterically as he rolled the dead

man from her thighs, then knelt beside her and gathered her into his arms.

"No! No!" Her hands clenched into fists and she pummeled his face and chest, her eyes filled with tears, her voice growing hoarse as she screamed for him to leave her alone.

Gently, yet firmly, Shunkaha Luta grasped Brianna's flailing fists in one of his hands. Sitting back on his heels, he drew her into his lap, cut the ropes that bound her hands and feet.

"Be still, Ishna Wi," he murmured, his voice low and soothing. "I am here now. No one will hurt you."

The sound of his voice calmed her and she stared at him, still not comprehending.

"Do not weep, *le mita chante*," he crooned, his hand lightly stroking her hair. "Do not weep, my heart. The men who took you from me are dead. They will not hurt you again."

"Shunkaha?" She blinked at him through her tears, the terror that had gripped her slipping away as the sound of his voice penetrated the stark horror that had engulfed her.

"I am here."

"Oh, Shunkaha," she sobbed, burying her face against the hollow of his shoulder. "I was so afraid."

Shunkaha Luta nodded. "I know, little one, I know."

Brianna's arms crept around his waist, clinging to him with all her strength. Shunkaha murmured to her in soft Lakota, his hand gently stroking her back, playing softly in the silkiness of her hair, until she fell asleep in his arms.

Tenderly, he lifted her and carried her away from the white man's camp. His horse was tethered several yards away in a grove of trees and he left Brianna there, sleeping on the soft grass. Returning to the white man's camp, he went through their gear, taking their foodstuffs, blankets, and cooking utensils. He went through their pockets, taking whatever cash he found. He knew the white man thought much of the bits of green paper and exchanged them for food and whiskey. Perhaps they would come in handy.

He found several boxes of ammunition of the same caliber as his rifle, and he took that, too, as well as a Navy Colt. Rummaging through the dead men's packs, he found a heavy buckskin shirt and sheepskin jacket.

When he had gathered everything he considered useful, he stuffed the items into a couple of war bags, tossed the blankets over his shoulder, and made his way back to Brianna. It never crossed his mind to bury the dead men. The wolves and the vultures would dispose of the remains, as befitting carion.

Brianna was still asleep, her cheek pillowed on her forearm. Gently, he washed the blood from her face, neck, and legs, drew her skirts down, then covered her with one of the heavy wool blankets. He felt a wave of tenderness flood his heart as he hunkered down on his heels beside her, and then the image of Keller bending over Brianna flashed through his mind and he smiled a feral smile as he killed the man again in his thoughts. It had been a good feeling, killing the three *wasicu* and the Comanche. He had gunned them down without a qualm, the way he would have killed a marauding animal, for that was what they were, animals, not men.

Wrapping a blanket around his shoulders, he stretched out next to Brianna. Her face followed him into his dreams.

The twittering of a bird aroused Brianna from sleep. Opening her eyes, she blinked at the sun shining overhead, then quickly sat up as she recalled the night before. Shunkaha had come for her, saving her from those awful men. But where was he now?

Scrambling to her feet, she opened her mouth to call his name, and then she saw him. He was standing several feet away, his back toward her, his arms stretched toward heaven, his head lifted to the rising sun. He wore only a clout, nothing more. His hair fell down his back, straight as a string, as black as pitch.

He stood there for a long time, and Brianna wondered what he was doing. She had often been told that the Indians were godless savages, so he could not be praying.

And then he was striding toward her, and she felt again that peculiar catch in her heart, that odd stirring in the pit of her stomach. How beautiful he was!

"Ishna Wi," he murmured. "Are you well?"

"I'm fine, thanks to you." She glanced around, but there was no sign of the dead men, and then she realized that Shunkaha had carried her away from the white man's camp so she would not have to see the bodies. She smiled up at him, touched by his thoughtfulness. "What were you doing over there?"

"I was praying."

"Really? My aunt told me the Indians had no God."

"We have many," Shunkaha Luta said, his voice solemn. "There is Waziah, White God of the North; Huntka of the reddening East; Wickmunke, the Rainbow God in the South; and the fearsome Thunderbird in the dark West. And there is Wakan Tanka, the Great Spirit, and Wanekia, the Life Giver."

"We have only one God," Brianna remarked.

"Perhaps they are all the same God," Shunkaha Luta suggested. "I have heard it said that the white man killed his God."

"Yes," Brianna said. "They crucified Him."

"It is what the white man is best at," Shunkaha said bitterly. "Killing."

"We're not all bad," Brianna said defensively.

Shunkaha's eyes softened as he took her face in his hands, his thumbs gently tracing the curve of her cheeks. "No race that produced a creature as lovely as my Ishna Wi could be all bad," he agreed.

"Indian," Brianna murmured breathlessly. "You make me feel so strange."

"Do I, *le mita chante?*"

Sweetness as she had never known flowed through her veins, filling her heart with such joy she thought it would burst. His gaze held her own captive and she wondered if he could see into her soul. Did he know the secret yearnings of her heart? Did he realize how desperately she longed for his kiss, how often she had dreamed of his touch? Did he know she often pretended they were man and wife, that she spent hours trying to imagine what it would be like to be his woman? His eyes were black and deep, like fathomless pools of ebony, holding the answer to all the mysteries of life.

She swayed toward him, her cheek resting on his chest, her body pressing against his, delighting in his hard-muscled strength, in the sound of his heart beating near her ear. His hands slid down her arms as his lips moved in her hair.

"Ishna Wi." His voice was husky, and she felt his hands tremble as they came to rest on her shoulders.

Brianna lifted her head, meeting his gaze, and it was suddenly hard to breathe. Her lips parted slightly, her tongue darting out to lick away the dryness.

Shunkaha let out a long breath and then, surrendering to an urge he could no longer deny, he kissed her. Brianna's eyelids fluttered down as his mouth closed over hers. His hands circled her waist possessively, protectively.

His kiss deepened and Brianna gave herself over to the sheer pleasure of it, all her senses reeling as sensation after sensation flooded her being with warmth. She felt her legs go weak and knew she would have fallen but for his arms tight around her. Her heart was pounding wildly, hammering so loudly in her ears she could hear nothing else. The tip of his tongue teased the sensitive skin on the inside of her lower lip and she shuddered with delight. *Oh, Indian, you make me feel so strange.*

Shunkaha Luta closed his eyes as he tasted the inner sweetness of Brianna's mouth. His blood was singing loud and hot in his veins; his nostrils filled with the scent of her hair, and with the intoxicating scent of woman. Never had he wanted a woman more, and yet, despite her full breasts and soft curves, she was not a woman, but a child, untouched and innocent. Her arms twined around his neck and he felt her straining toward him, felt his skin turn to flame wherever her body brushed his. Slowly his hands slid upward, his fingertips grazing her breasts. Fire shot through Brianna and she moaned deep in her throat, her hips thrusting forward. Shunkaha's response was immediate, and he felt her grow suddenly still as the evidence of his desire stirred to life.

"Ishna Wi," he said thickly. "You must tell me to stop before it is too late."

She did not understand. He read the confusion in her eyes, knew she yearned for him to give her that which she desired but did not fully understand.

Clenching his jaw, he put his hands on her shoulders and held her away from him. If only she were not a maiden. If only she were not so young. If only he did not want her so desperately.

"Shunkaha?" Her voice was shaky, her breathing irregular.

Shunkaha Luta let out a long shuddering sigh. "I think you should prepare the morning meal," he rasped, though food was the last thing he wanted. "I will saddle your horse."

Brianna stared after him as he turned and walked swiftly away. In wonder, she lifted her fingertips to her lips, a little awed by the powerful emotions his kiss had aroused in her. Was she bad, to feel this way? Surely her aunt would think so. Why, then, did she feel such elation?

She quickly prepared breakfast, though she wasn't sure she would be able to eat. Her stomach was still fluttering like a wild thing caught in a cage.

Shunkaha's eyes lingered on her face when he returned. Hunkering down on his heels near the fire, he took the plate she handed him, surprised to find that he was suddenly ravenous. Brianna, too, ate every bite, and then they smiled at each other across the fire.

Thirty minutes later, they were riding toward the canyon. Shunkaha was mounted on one of the dead men's horses, a big black gelding with a blaze face and a spotted rump. It was a beautiful animal, and Brianna thought it suited him perfectly.

When they reached the canyon, Shunkaha retrieved the deer he had killed. Scavengers had gnawed on the carcass, but there was plenty of meat left, and after he cut away the portion the animals had eaten, he cut the meat into long strips and hung it from a tree to dry. He spent several days tanning the hide, curing it until it was soft and pliable. Brianna watched, amazed, as the rough hide was transformed into a piece of material that felt like velvet.

Their comfort improved considerably with the addition of the food and utensils Shunkaha had looted from the gear of the white men. They had a good supply of canned goods now, enough blankets to make two comfortable beds, a variety of cooking utensils, a side of bacon, a sack of potatoes, some dried apples, a few spices.

Shunkaha had not touched her since that one soul-stirring kiss. He was careful to stay away from the pool when he knew she was there, careful to keep his distance inside the shelter at night. And yet they were ever aware of one another. Often, she pretended to be asleep so she could watch him pray, which he did each morning at dawn. She loved to watch him standing there, his arms stretched toward heaven, his magnificent body bathed in the dawn's clear golden rays. She often wondered what he prayed for, but she never asked. Prayer was a personal thing, between a man and his God. For herself, she prayed only that Shunkaha would always be there, that someday soon they would marry and have a home of their own. She wanted nothing more of life than that, the man she loved and a home of her own.

They had been back in the canyon just over a week when one night Brianna woke screaming from a nightmare. Shunkaha Luta was instantly by her side, his voice reaching out to her in the darkness as his arms drew her close.

"Hold me," Brianna sobbed. "Oh, please, hold me tight."

"I am here, *le mita chante*," he crooned, rocking her in his arms as if she were a small child. "I am here."

"It was awful," Brianna said, her words tumbling out in a rush. "Those men were chasing me, and no matter how fast I ran, I couldn't get away. And then they caught me, and two of them held me down while the big one did horrible things to me. I cried for you, but you never came. You never came."

"I will always come for you," Shunkaha promised. His lips brushed her hair, her forehead, the gentle curve of a tear-stained cheek. "Do not think of it any more, little one. It was only a bad dream."

Brianna sniffed, her eyes wide and trusting as she gazed into his face, barely visible in the shadows. Did he feel it, too, the intensity, the rightness, of the attraction between them? She wanted to feel his mouth on hers, to feel his hands moving over her, to taste him and touch him in return. To be his. Wholly his. Only his.

"I love you." She had not meant to say the words aloud, but they formed of their own volition, rising like a prayer in the darkness.

"Ishna Wi." His expression was filled with tenderness as he gazed into her eyes.

"You care for me a little, don't you?"

"More than a little, golden hair."

"Then . . . would you kiss me again?"

Shunkaha Luta swallowed hard. He loved her. Right or wrong, he loved her. But he did not want to defile her, nor did he wish to take advantage of her youthful innocence. He was a warrior, a man of honor. And a man of honor did not defile a maiden.

She was looking at him expectantly, her lips slightly parted, inviting. Just one more kiss, he thought. What could it hurt?

"Shunkaha?" She was watching his face intently, her eyes as blue and clear as a summer sky. Shyly she placed her hand on his cheek, let her fingers trace the outline of his cheekbone and the strong curve of his jaw.

Her touch, as gentle as that of a dewdrop kissing the grass, raced through him like a prairie fire. With a low groan, he grasped her shoulders, drew her hard against him, and kissed her, his mouth fierce and possessive. Brianna was startled by the suddenness of his kiss, unprepared for the roughness of it, and for the quick surge of heat that flooded her limbs and then centered deep in the core of her being.

His kiss was long and hard, filled with all the wanting, all the need, that he had held in check ever since the day he saw her kneeling beside the pool. His hands moved over her body, touching that which he had thought never to touch.

Brianna strained against him, surrendering to his kisses, thrilling to his caress, her whole being attuned to the whisper of his hands as he murmured soft love words to her in the Lakota tongue. She did not think to resist when he removed her dress and undergarments, only fretted anxiously as he discarded the barriers between them. He tossed his clout onto the pile of her clothing, and then he was lying naked beside her, his flesh against her flesh, and she thought she might die from the sheer wonder of it.

His hand cupped her breast and it seemed to swell as it filled his palm. His skin looked very dark against the creamy whiteness of her skin, and she noticed anew that he was dark bronze all over and not just where the sun had touched him.

He rose on one elbow, his long black hair falling across her shoulder, spreading like a dark stain over a lock of her own golden hair as he gazed at her through eyes as dark as hers were light.

We complement each other, Brianna thought absently, like night and day, winter and summer, fire and ice.

Shunkaha Luta offered her one last chance to change her mind. Lifting himself away from her, he asked, "Are you sure, Ishna Wi? If I take you now, you will be my woman according to the laws of my people. You will be my wife, and I will never let you go."

Brianna smiled up at him, loving him all the more for his tender concern. She let her eyes wander over him, frankly admiring his finely chiseled features, his strong sturdy neck, broad shoulders and chest. Her eyes lingered on his flat belly before skipping down to admire his long horseman's legs. And then, boldly, she let her gaze settle on that part of him that made him a man and she felt a tremor of excitement mingled with apprehension. It was evident that he wanted her, and wanted her badly, yet he had said he would stop if she but said the word.

Shunkaha did not move under her bold scrutiny. Only held himself away from her, waiting for the single word that would send him to heaven, or plummet him into hell. If her answer was no, did he truly have the strength to let her go, or would he shame them both by taking her by force? He felt her eyes rest on his maleness and he clenched his hands into tight fists, waiting, hoping she would not refuse him now.

But it never occurred to Brianna to say no. She wanted to belong to Shunkaha body and soul, and so she locked her hands behind his neck and drew him down toward her, her mouth slanting across his as her breasts flattened against his chest.

Shunkaha murmured her name as his knee parted her thighs, his lips gently kissing her eyes and nose and mouth. She gasped as she felt his manhood brush her thigh, her body instinctively tensing as he entered her. There was a brief stab of pain as he plunged deeper, and then only wondrous waves of delight as he moved inside her, his rhythmic movements whirling her into a vortex of pleasure, lifting her higher, higher, until, just when she thought she might perish, he brought her the fulfillment she so desperately desired.

Moments later she shuddered with ecstasy as his life spilled into her, filling her with warmth and peace and a sense of oneness unlike anything she had ever imagined. For a long while he did not move, and then he rolled onto his side, carrying her with him, their bodies still linked together.

And that was how they fell asleep.

Chapter Nine

Shunkaha Luta woke with the dawn to find Brianna's body nestled against his. Her hair, as bright as the morning sun, spread across his chest and arm like liquid gold. He lifted a lock of her hair between his thumb and forefinger and drew it across his mouth. It was incredibly soft, and he closed his eyes as he breathed in the scent of her silken tresses. Last night he had made her his woman for all time, and it had been unlike anything he had imagined, unlike anything he had ever experienced before. She had been shy yet bold, hesitant yet curious, modest yet passionate.

He had known other women in the past, had satisfied his carnal desires in their arms, but this was the first time he had truly made love to a woman, the first time he had been intimate with a woman who was more than just a warm body. Last night had been more than just a joining of their flesh. So much more. He felt a tenderness for Brianna, a protectiveness, that he had never felt for a woman. It filled him with a sense of awe, as well as a sense of responsibility. She was his woman now, his to provide for, his to defend, his to love . . .

He opened his eyes to find Brianna gazing at him through the thick veil of her lashes. Her cheeks blossomed with color as his gaze met hers.

"Did you sleep well?" Shunkaha asked.

Brianna nodded, conscious of her nudity beneath the blanket, of Shunkaha's hand cupping her breast, of the way their legs were twined together.

Shunkaha frowned at her silence, mistaking it for regret. "Are you sorry?" he asked gruffly.

"No," Brianna answered quickly. She would never be sorry. His lovemaking had been the most beautiful thing she had ever known. But it was all so new. She was embarrassed by her nudity, and by the way she had responded to his caresses. She wanted badly to bathe, but she was reluctant to leave the shelter of the blanket and have him see her unclothed in the full light of day.

Shunkaha studied the play of emotions on Brianna's face, smiled wryly as he realized that she was feeling a little shy.

"You would like to bathe." It was not a question.

Brianna nodded, grateful for his understanding.

"I, too, could use a bath," Shunkaha said. He threw the covers aside and rolled nimbly to his feet. "Come," he said, offering her his hand. "We will bathe together."

"Together?"

"You are my wife now," he reminded her. "You have no need to be modest or ashamed." His dark eyes moved over her body, as soft as a caress. "You are beautiful, Ishna Wi, the most beautiful woman I have ever seen."

"Have you seen very many?" Brianna asked, somewhat peevishly.

Shunkaha Luta grinned, amused by her jealousy. "No, not many."

"One other would be too many," Brianna muttered as she reached for his hand. She shivered with pleasure as his long brown fingers closed over hers, and then they were running toward the pool.

Brianna shrieked as Shunkaha lifted her in his arms and carried her into the water, squealed as the cold water closed over her.

"Beast!" she cried, splashing him vigorously.

Seconds later, they were engaged in a brisk water fight

that ended abruptly as Shunkaha Luta grabbed Brianna from behind, one long arm holding her hard against his chest while his free hand stroked her breasts and thighs. Brianna melted against him, her head lolling back against his shoulder, her legs suddenly weak.

"Ishna Wi," he murmured, his voice husky in her ear. "Truly you hold the sun, for I have only to touch you and my blood turns to fire."

She uttered a wordless sigh of contentment as she turned in his arms, her breasts pressing against his chest, her thighs seeking his, her face lifting for his kiss.

Shunkaha groaned low in his throat as he took her in his arms and carried her toward the shore. Near the water's edge, he laid her gently down, his big body covering hers as he rained feather-soft kisses on her mouth and nose and eyes, down the slender column of her throat to the swell of her breasts. And all the while he murmured to her, telling her she was beautiful, that he loved her, would always love her. Their bodies, still wet from the pool, writhed in delicious ecstasy as they came together, legs entwined, hands stroking and caressing. Brianna strained against Shunkaha, her hips rising upward to receive him, her nails raking his broad back as she cried his name, felt his warmth flow into her, filling her, making her complete.

Exhausted, they lay together, the cool water lapping around their legs, the sun warming Shunkaha's back. He lifted himself on his elbows so he could see her face, still flushed from his lovemaking, her eyes glowing like sapphires, her lips slightly swollen from his kisses.

Brianna flushed under his probing gaze. "Why are you looking at me like that?"

"I can think of nothing I would rather do than look at you, Golden Hair," he replied, and then he grinned. "Perhaps one thing."

When he started to rise, Brianna held him close. "No. Don't go yet."

Shunkaha quirked an eyebrow at her.

"I . . . you feel so good," Brianna remarked, blushing furiously.

Shunkaha Luta smiled, pleased beyond measure that she found pleasure in his possession of her.

It was a long time later when they parted. They washed again, took a leisurely swim, and then returned to camp.

The day passed blissfully. They ate breakfast, went for a long walk, made love beneath the shade of a gnarled pine, wrestled like two bear cubs, took a nap in each other's arms. And woke with a kiss, each hoping that all their days would be as wonderful.

The days passed swiftly by. Brianna went to sleep each night with a heart full of love for the man at her side. He treated her as though she were the most wonderful woman in the world. He never raised his voice, never grew impatient, never ridiculed her. She was constantly amazed at how much he knew, how easily he provided for their needs. She had watched him fashion a stout bow from a mulberry limb, create arrows from cane. He could tell her which animal had left which tracks, he knew where to hunt for wild onions and potatoes and sage, he taught her how to cure a hide.

Each day was an adventure, and each night a new lesson in love. She never tired of his caresses. He had only to touch her and she came alive, her heart fluttering with joy, her skin tingling and warm, her lips eager to receive his. He explored her body from head to heel, awakening the passion that slept within her. Sometimes, at first, she was embarrassed by the way her body responded to his touch, but Shunkaha assured her there was nothing to be ashamed of. They were married now, and there should be no secrets between them.

Gradually, Brianna's curiosity overcame her shyness and she began to explore Shunkaha's body, marveling anew at the sheer beauty of the man, the perfection of his face and form. She never tired of looking at him, enthralled by his strong, wonderfully handsome face, the symmetry of his physique.

As her modesty waned, she began to feel pride in the fact that Shunkaha found her desirable, that he wanted her body passionately, that he found pleasure in the touch of her hands. It gave her a sense of power, knowing that she could arouse him, that her kisses made him tremble with desire, and she began to grow more bold, openly flirting with him, exercising her feminine wiles, teasing him mercilessly until he took her in his arms and turned the tables on her, kissing and caressing until she was breathless, until she begged him to make her complete.

Like Adam and Eve in the Garden, they frolicked through the warm summer days, giving no thought to the future as they lived from sun to sun, taking each moment as it came.

They explored the canyon, walking barefoot through the grass, pausing to watch the antics of a chipmunk, or reclining on the grass to gaze at the sky. And, more often than not, they ended up making love beneath the bold blue sky, unable to keep their hands off each other, unable to be close without touching.

They swam in the pool each day. Brianna drew back, shocked, the first time Shunkaha took the soap from her hand and began to wash her breasts. Bathing was a private thing. But he quickly shushed her protests and she thought that she had never experienced anything quite so wonderful as having Shunkaha bathe her. And when he handed her the soap, she returned the favor. What a wondrous feeling, to rub her soapy hands along his chest and shoulders, down his long arms, across his broad, scarred back. How delightful to see his eyes grow smoky with passion, to feel his body tremble against hers. She had never known such joy, such total abandon, such blissful fulfillment.

They had been in the canyon for about six weeks when Shunkaha told her they would have to leave.

"Leave?" Brianna asked, not wanting to say goodbye to the place where they had known such happiness. "Why?"

"We are almost out of food, and there is not grass enough to feed the horses through the winter."

Brianna nodded. They had six horses now, the two they had taken from her uncle and the four that had belonged to the horrible men who had tried to abduct her. Glancing around, she saw that the grass was already turning yellow. The trees, so green when they had first arrived, were now taking on the bright red-gold hues of autumn.

"Where will we go?" she asked.

"To the Lakota."

"To the reservation?"

"No. I will never go back there. We will go to Crazy Horse."

Brianna felt the cold stirrings of fear at the mere mention of the name. Crazy Horse! He was making war on the whites, raiding and killing and leading the United States Army a merry chase.

She gazed at Shunkaha Luta. He was an Indian and she loved him dearly, but the thought of living with hundreds of Indians frightened her.

"You would wish to go somewhere else?" Shunkaha remarked.

"Yes."

"Where?"

She had no answer for that.

"We will go to the Lakota then," Shunkaha decided.

"I . . . I'm afraid."

"My people will not harm you."

"They won't like me, either," Brianna retorted. "They'll hate me because I'm white."

Shunkaha Luta let out a long breath. There was some truth to what Brianna said. In the past, the Sioux had accepted whites among them without rancor, but now, with more and more white men crowding the land, killing the buffalo, breaking the treaties, all whites were hated. And yet, where else could they go? He could not live among the *wasicu*. He had escaped from the road gang. He had killed a white man. They would be looking for him. Perhaps they were looking for Brianna as well.

"It will only be for the winter," Shunkaha said. "In the summer, perhaps we will return to this place."

Brianna nodded, but her heart was heavy. She did not want to live among savages, did not want to spend a long, cold winter with people who regarded her as the enemy.

"How soon will we have to leave?"

He had intended to leave the canyon in the morning, but seeing the distress on Brianna's face, and knowing how she loved their home, he relented. "We will stay two more days."

Two days, Brianna thought. It wasn't much, but she vowed to make the best of them.

Shunkaha held her close that night. Knowing that she was upset because they had to leave the canyon, he made love to her sweetly, telling her with his kisses and each gentle caress that he loved her, that he would take care of her, that she did not need the approval of others. He loved her and he hoped that would be enough, hoped that her love for him was strong enough to see them through the coming months.

Brianna clung to him fiercely. He was the only dependable thing in her life and she relied on him for everything: food, shelter, protection, companionship, love and laughter. Without him, she would be alone again, with no one to love and no one to love her.

For a moment, Brianna remained passive in his embrace, but as Shunkaha's hands began to play over her body, softly stroking her inner thigh, gently kneading her breast, she began to touch him in return, reveling in his muscular strength, in the smooth texture of his skin, in the way he groaned with pleasure as she boldly touched that part of him which made him a man.

She lifted her hips to meet him, shuddered with sheer delight as his flesh merged with hers, their bodies writhing in the age-old joy of mating as two became one in spirit and heart.

Brianna felt a sense of loss as they rode out of the canyon two days later. She had been happy there, truly happy.

She let her eyes linger on Shunkaha as they rode along. She was his woman now; his woman in every sense of the word. He had shown her what love was, what passion was. She had never dreamed such wonder existed. Why had her aunt thought of a man's touch as something to be endured, something to be avoided if possible? Surely there could be no greater joy than the love and fulfillment Brianna had found in her Indian's embrace. But then, perhaps what she shared with Shunkaha Luta was unique. Perhaps not every man and every woman had found what they had found.

The next few days were arduous and long. They spent hours in the saddle, slept under the stars at night. Winter was in the air; the days were cool, the nights cold. Their food supplies were nearly gone save for dried venison and coffee.

"I will go hunting tomorrow," Shunkaha remarked as he held Brianna close that night. "I grow weary of dried meat."

Brianna nodded drowsily. She could hear the wind sighing through the yellow grass, but, wrapped in Shunkaha's arms, she felt only warmth and a sense of peace.

Shunkaha Luta gazed at Brianna, his woman-child. She was a rare and delicate creature, so much a woman in his arms, yet still so trusting and childlike in other ways. He wanted only to love her, to protect her from harm, to let her see only the good things in life. And yet he knew that was

impossible. There could be no love without hate, no goodness without evil, no joy without sorrow.

He wrapped a lock of her hair around his hand. He was
taking her to his people, and he was afraid she would not be
welcome there. She was white, the enemy. Many would hate
her for the color of her skin alone. Too, his people were at
war, engaged in a long and bloody battle that they must ul-
timately lose. Perhaps he was making a grave mistake in
keeping her with him. And yet, how could he let her go?

"Ishna Wi." He murmured her name as he brushed a kiss
across her cheek.

Brianna made a sleepy sound as she snuggled closer to
him, her head nestling against his shoulder. She felt his lips
caress her cheek, felt his hand cup her breast, his touch
gentle, gradually moving down her belly and along the inside of her thigh. She uttered a little sigh of pleasure as his
hands lovingly aroused her, trembled with delight as he became a part of her, loving her so gently, so tenderly, that it
seemed more like a dream than reality . . .

Brianna hummed cheerfully as she cleaned up the breakfast
dishes. Shunkaha had gone hunting, leaving her to clean up
the camp and pack their gear. She was becoming quite pro-
ficient at making a respectable camp, and just as efficient at
loading things up. She had learned to cook over an open
campfire, to roll her blankets into a neat compact cylinder,
to skin the game Shunkaha provided. She was proud of her
newly acquired abilities, pleased that she could be a help to
him. She did not want to be a burden, did not want him to
be sorry he had chosen her for his woman.

Brianna glanced at the vast prairie that surrounded her,
wondering when Shunkaha would return, and then felt a
small knot of fear struggle to take root in her heart. The
plains spread endlessly before her, huge, uncharted, making
her feel small and helpless and alone. She had heard tales of

women who had gone mad, driven to insanity by the quiet, and by the miles and miles of rolling grassland that seemed to have no beginning and no end.

She was sipping a cup of lukewarm coffee when the riders appeared. One minute there was nothing to be seen but empty prairie, and the next a dozen riders appeared out of a shallow draw.

Brianna stared at them as they rode toward her. They were lawmen. Silver badges were pinned to their coats, and Brianna was filled with apprehension as they drew rein, boxing her neatly between them.

Adam Trent perused the campsite through cool gray eyes, quickly noting the horses grazing nearby, the bedrolls spread near the remains of a fire. He nodded imperceptibly as his gaze fastened on Brianna.

"Mornin', miss," he said, lifting his hand to his hat brim.

Brianna nodded, her hands clenched around the coffee cup, her heart beating a mile a minute. She had to get these men out of here before Shunkaha Luta returned. But how?

Adam Trent pulled a sheet of paper from his coat pocket, studied it for a moment before refolding it and putting it away. The girl standing before him fit the description on the flyer perfectly.

"Where is he, Miss Beaudine?" Trent asked. "The Indian who abducted you."

"He left early this morning to go hunting," Brianna answered. She pasted a smile on her face. "Could we go now, before he gets back?" She hated to desert Shunkaha, but it would be better than letting these men capture him.

"You needn't worry," Trent assured her. "Everything will be all right now." He glanced at his men, who sat their horses easily, waiting for his command. Only two were full-time deputies; the rest were volunteers. But they were all good men.

"My men and I are going to take cover in that draw," Trent

said. "We'll catch him when he shows up." He smiled at Brianna. "Don't worry, miss, we'll protect you."

"Thank you," Brianna said, hoping she sounded appreciative. Her first ploy had failed. Now all she could do was to try to warn Shunkaha about the lawmen.

To keep busy, she packed their gear, her eyes straying constantly toward the west as she searched for some sign of Shunkaha Luta's return.

An hour passed, and she had run out of things to occupy her hands. Now she sat on her saddle, nervously tapping her foot on the ground.

She stood up as she saw Shunkaha riding toward her, a deer carcass slung over the black's withers. Frightened as she was, she could not help noticing how wonderful he looked astride the big black gelding, how easily he rode, as though he were a part of the animal.

She glanced over her shoulder, wondering if the lawmen had seen him.

She was about to call out to Shunkaha, to tell him to make a run for it, when the lawmen exploded from the draw.

For a moment, time stood still. Brianna saw the look of surprise in Shunkaha's eyes as he stared at her, the look of accusation he threw at her, and she realized he thought she had betrayed him. Abruptly, he threw the carcass to the ground, wheeled the black around, and slammed his heels into the gelding's sides. The lawmen lined out after him in a dead run, their guns spitting fire and lead.

Brianna screamed as the black went down, throwing Shunkaha Luta over its head. The Indian rolled nimbly to his feet, but by then he was surrounded by a dozen armed men. She could only watch, helpless, as three deputies vaulted to the ground and quickly handcuffed Shunkaha's hands behind his back. She saw one of the men strike Shunkaha across the face when he tried to fight back, saw the blood ooze from his mouth.

Someone caught the black's reins as the horse scrambled to its feet. The horse was bleeding from its right shoulder where a bullet had nicked its flesh.

Two of the lawmen lifted a struggling Shunkaha onto the black's back. Shunkaha lashed out with his feet, catching one of the lawmen full in the chest and hurling him onto his back, but three others jumped into the fray and soon Shunkaha's feet were secured under the black's belly.

"Miss."

Brianna turned to find Trent standing beside her. "We're ready to go."

"Go?"

"We're taking you and the Indian to Bismarck. You can contact your uncle from there and make arrangements to go home."

"What will happen to the Indian?" She had to know.

Adam Trent shrugged. "I reckon he'll get what's coming to him, don't you worry about that." The lawman smiled reassuringly, supposing that Brianna was worried that the Indian might escape and come after her again. "I don't imagine he'll be allowed on the road gang again."

Brianna nodded. Shunkaha would die behind bars, she thought bleakly. They had spent only a short time together, but she knew he hated the thought of captivity.

Adam Trent saddled Brianna's horse and helped her mount the roan, and then they were riding toward their destination.

The next several days were unreal. They rode from sunup until dusk across a vast empty land. The long hours on horseback were hard on Brianna. Her back and legs ached constantly. Her shoulders grew weary, her back stiff. Shunkaha Luta rode with his head high and his shoulders back, his dark eyes focused on some distant point. Though his hands were cuffed behind his back, he rode easily, his long legs gripping the black's sides, his body moving with the rhythm of the horse. As always, she could not help but admire the way he looked, the way he moved, the quiet inner strength that was as much a part of him as the color of his skin.

The lawmen were a taciturn bunch of men, hard-eyed and trail weary. They treated Brianna with the utmost courtesy and respect, making certain she had enough to eat, privacy when she needed it, the smoothest stretch of ground for her bedroll at night. They were careful of their language in her presence. Adam Trent, especially, took care to see that she was comfortable. When he saw that she was tired or thirsty, he called a halt so she could rest or ease her thirst.

The lawmen were not so considerate of Shunkaha Luta. He was the enemy, an Indian, and not to be trusted. There were always two men guarding him, making sure he had no chance to escape. When they freed his hands so he could eat, a man always stood directly behind him, a rifle aimed at the back of his head. Otherwise, the Indian's hands were tightly cuffed behind his back.

Brianna yearned for a few minutes alone with Shunkaha, but such a thing was impossible. She studied his face daily, trying to determine what he was thinking and feeling, but his expression remained impassive, his eyes unfathomable. He never spoke, rarely looked in her direction, and she realized he had withdrawn into himself, shutting out the rest of the world, and her with it. It hurt to know he thought she had betrayed him. Though he seemed lost in a world of his own, she knew he was aware of what went on around him. She could feel his hatred flare whenever Trent spoke to her, could feel the almost palpable anger that swept over Shunkaha whenever Trent helped her mount her horse, or offered her a drink of water, or sat near her at the campfire.

When they arrived at Bismarck, three of the lawmen were assigned to escort Shunkaha to jail. He did not go peacefully. Inwardly Brianna screamed for him to go quietly, but he lashed out with his feet, striking one deputy in the groin and another full in the face. His actions proved futile. Three other lawmen rushed to the aid of their companions, and Brianna had to fight back her tears as the deputies rained blow after blow on the Indian until he was too bruised and battered to fight back.

"Sorry you had to see that, Miss Beaudine," Adam Trent remarked. "Would you like to get settled in at the hotel first, or send a wire to your uncle?"

"The hotel, please," Brianna said. She glanced down at her trail-stained dress. "I'd like to freshen up."

Trent nodded. He was quite taken with Brianna Beaudine, he admitted. She had not complained once on the trail. She seemed a well-bred young woman, modest and well-mannered, not overly talkative. She had not mentioned her ordeal at the Indian's hands, but that was to be expected. He wondered if the savage had violated her, but could not quite summon the nerve to ask. How did one inquire, politely, if a woman had been raped? In any case, it wouldn't change the way he felt about her.

Trent offered her his arm. "May I escort you to the hotel, Miss Beaudine?"

"Yes, thank you."

"I imagine you're quite anxious to return to your uncle."

"Yes, of course," Brianna lied.

"If he can't see his way clear to come after you, I'd be pleased to see you safely home."

Brianna looked up at Trent, suddenly aware that he was being more than polite. Was it possible he was attracted to her? But that was preposterous. They had only known each other a few days.

"Your job—" Brianna began.

"I've got some time off coming," Trent interjected. "I can't think of anything I'd rather do with my vacation than spend it accompanying a pretty young lady home."

"Yes, well . . . I . . . that is, I'll have to get in touch with my uncle first."

"Of course."

They were at the hotel now. Trent held the door open for her and followed her inside. Brianna had never been inside a hotel before and she was uncertain of how to go about obtaining a room, but Adam Trent took care of it for her, speaking to the clerk, signing her name in the register.

"Number six," Trent said, handing her the key. "I'll have the clerk send up some hot water so you can clean up."

"Thank you. You've been very kind."

"No trouble at all. I'll have one of my men bring your gear to the hotel after we stable the horses. Do you . . . uh, have you—?"

"Yes?"

"The room," Trent said. "If you can't pay for it, I'll take care of it for you."

"Thank you, but I have some money."

"What about dinner?"

"What about it?"

"Would you mind eating with me, say about seven?"

"All right."

Smiling broadly, Adam Trent touched his fingertips to his hat brim. "I'll see you at seven, then."

Brianna nodded, wondering if she should have refused him. She didn't want to get involved with Adam Trent, though he appeared to be a decent young man. Perhaps he would have been suspicious if she refused to see him again.

She forgot about the lawman as she stepped into her room. It was large and clean; the bed seemed immense when compared to her narrow cot. There were white lace curtains at the window, a dark blue quilt covered the bed, a patterned carpet covered most of the wooden floor. There was an oval mirror on one wall, an oak dresser across from the bed, a padded rocking chair in the corner.

Moments later, the clerk knocked on the door, bringing hot water for the tub.

Brianna took a long, leisurely bath. When one of the deputy's brought her saddlebags sometime later, she changed into her blue dress, washed the brown one, then sat on the edge of the bed to wait for Adam Trent. But it was Shunkaha Luta who filled her thoughts. Somehow, she had to find a way to get him out of jail . . .

Shunkaha Luta stood in the middle of the narrow cell, his eyes dark and defiant as he watched the marshal lock the cell door. He felt a moment of panic as he glanced at his surroundings. Irons bars closed him in on three sides, a wall of gray adobe completed his prison. The ceiling was low and flat and made of wood. There was a tiny, iron-barred window set high in the wall. A narrow iron cot was the only concession to comfort; a covered slop jar was shoved under the cot. The cell smelled faintly of old sweat and urine.

Shunkaha Luta watched the lawman until he left the cellblock, and then he began to pace the floor. They had exchanged his handcuffs for leg irons, and the familiar clanking sound of shackles ate at his nerves, yet he could not stop his restless pacing. Where was Brianna?

He padded back and forth for over an hour, the anger churning within him. They would not trust him on the road gang again, he mused bleakly, if he was lucky enough, or unlucky enough, to escape the hangman. He had killed a *wasicu*, and for that he would likely be hung. And he thought he might prefer that to spending the rest of his life behind bars, never to see the mountains again, never to be free of the shackles that gnawed at his pride. Never to hold Brianna again . . .

He dragged the cot under the window and stood on the iron frame so he could see outside, felt his heart go cold within him when he saw Brianna walking across the street with Adam Trent. The lawman was holding her arm, smiling down at her. And she was smiling back.

He stared at the two of them until they disappeared inside a building. Stepping from the cot, he hunkered down on his heels, his back against the wall, his teeth so tightly clenched it made his jaw ache. Brianna and the lawman. Was it possible? Jealousy cut into him like a knife, more painful than anything he had ever known.

Brianna did not object when Adam Trent took her arm as they crossed the street toward the restaurant. In truth, she was hardly aware of him, so concerned was she for Shunkaha Luta. She glanced down the street toward the jail, yearning to go to him, to see if he was all right.

The restaurant was small but nice. Red and white checked cloths covered the tables; matching curtains hung at the windows. Brianna sat with her hands folded in her lap while Trent ordered dinner, forced herself to listen attentively as he told her of his life, how he had been a lawman for ten years. He had a sister and three older brothers. His brothers were also in law enforcement, Trent said. Two were Texas Rangers, the third was a sheriff in Abilene. His sister was married to an attorney.

"You're a very law-abiding family," Brianna murmured, and wondered what Trent would say if he knew she was planning to break Shunkaha Luta out of jail that very night.

The meal passed pleasantly, though Brianna hardly tasted a thing. Just the thought of what she was planning to do already had her stomach in knots.

Trent seemed a little surprised when she told him she hadn't wired her uncle.

"I'll do it first thing in the morning," Brianna said. "I meant to take care of it this afternoon, but I . . . I fell asleep."

Trent nodded. "I understand. I guess you've had a pretty rough time of it the last couple months."

"Yes," Brianna said, knowing that was what he expected her to say. "I'd rather not talk about it."

Adam Trent smiled sympathetically. "Sure. Would you care for some dessert? Jilly makes a prime apple pie."

"No, thank you."

Later they walked down the main street, stopping now and then to look into this window or that. Brianna stared at the goods displayed without really seeing them, her thoughts on Shunkaha Luta. The prospect of seeing him again bolstered her courage as she thought about breaking him out of jail. Could she do it? Did she really have the nerve? But then she thought of Shunkaha and knew she would risk anything to free him.

She bid Adam Trent goodnight in the hotel lobby, then hurried to her room. Inside, she searched through the saddlebags until she found Shunkaha Luta's pistol. She checked to make sure it was loaded, then placed it on the dresser beside the bed. Next, she gathered their gear together and dropped it near the door. And then she sat down on the bed to wait.

Her plan was simple. She would wait until the hour after midnight, go to the jail, and demand that Shunkaha Luta be set free. She hoped that whoever was on duty would do as she wished, hoped that the threat of being shot would make them agreeable, because she wasn't certain she could shoot anyone, not even for Shunkaha.

The time passed very slowly. She heard the town clock strike ten, eleven, twelve. And then one. It was time to go.

Shunkaha Luta paced the cell, his legs weary, his ribs aching where the lawman had kicked him. All day and all night he had paced the hard stone floor, his anger refusing to allow him to relax for even a moment, his jealousy gnawing at his vitals as he pictured Brianna with the white man, smiling at him, laughing with him.

He stared into the darkness, a darkness as cold and bleak as his future, his heart aching with Brianna's betrayal. How quickly she had found herself another man to look after her! *"Ishna Wi."* He whispered her name, cursing himself for his weakness, for wanting her even now, when she had betrayed him for another.

"Hecheto aloe," he muttered bitterly. "It is finished."

Brianna made her way down the quiet street, keeping to the shadows, the gun hidden in the folds of her skirt. All the shops were dark and shuttered except for the saloon at the far end of town. Her heart was hammering wildly by the time she reached the jail. She glanced around to make sure she was alone before she opened the door and stepped inside.

A lamp burned low on the desk. A deputy was asleep in the chair, his booted feet propped on the scarred desk top, his chin resting on his chest.

Brianna paused, wondering whether she should wake him or not, when the deputy woke with a start. Seeing Brianna, he sprang to his feet.

"Can I help you, miss?" he asked politely.

"Yes," Brianna said, lifting the gun and aiming it at the deputy's chest. "You can unlock the cell and let the Indian out."

"Let him out?" Hap Wilson repeated, blinking at her. "I can't let him out."

"Well, you'd better," Brianna threatened. She thumbed back the hammer, willing her hands to remain steady.

The deputy's face went white. The gun looked very big in Brianna's small hand. Did she realize the slightest pressure on the trigger would cause the gun to fire?

"Take it easy, miss," he croaked, reaching for the ring of keys on the desk top. "I'll let him out."

Shunkaha Luta halted in mid stride as the door to the

cellblock swung open and the deputy came into view. He
frowned, wondering what had brought the white man into
see him at such an hour, and then grinned as he saw Brianna following the lawman, a gun held tight in her fist.

"Open it," Brianna demanded curtly.

Hap Wilson swallowed hard as he fitted the key into the
lock. How was he going to explain this to the sheriff? He'd
be the laughingstock of the town when people learned how
a little bit of a girl had taken a prisoner right out from under
his nose.

Shunkaha stepped out of the cell as soon as the door
swung open. Taking the gun from Brianna, he brought the
butt down across the back of the deputy's head, rendering
him unconscious, then dragged the lawman into the cell and
locked the door. He tried several keys on the shackles around
his ankles before he found the right one. Freed of the re-
stricting leg irons, he felt as if he could run on the wind.

"Let's go," he said urgently.

Brianna followed Shunkaha out of the jail, her whole being quivering with excitement. She had done it! She trailed
after Shunkaha as he made his way around the jailhouse,
following the back alley that paralleled the main street to
the livery barn. Their horses were in the corral, and
Shunkaha slipped between the bars, moving quietly between the horses until he came to the black. He quickly
fashioned a bridle from a length of rope he found over the
fence and led the horse from the corral. He found a bridle
for the roan in a keg of cast-off tack, boosted Brianna onto
the animal's bare back.

"Where are our supplies?"

"Behind the hotel. I left them there before I went to the
jail."

Shunkaha nodded. Vaulting lightly onto the black's back,
he rode toward the hotel with Brianna following close behind. At the rear of the hotel, he leaned over his horse's

neck, grabbed their saddlebags, and draped them over the black's withers. Then, with a smile at Brianna, he led the way out of town.

They rode all night. Brianna was too keyed up with her success at freeing Shunkaha to be tired, too thrilled at the prospect of being with her Indian again to care about anything else.

They were still riding when the sky began to turn from black to gray. They were heading southwest, Shunkaha had told her, toward the Pa Sapa. The Black Hills. Brianna shivered. That was Sioux country, and the Sioux were angry. In 1874, General George Armstrong Custer had despoiled sacred ground when he discovered gold at French Creek, and had incited a gold rush with the news. The federal government had attempted to keep the miners out of the Black Hills until an agreement could be reached with the Indians regarding the land, but the Sioux had refused to give up their sacred ground, and the government gave up its efforts to keep settlers out. And now it was war.

It was late afternoon before Shunkaha reined his weary mount to a halt. Brianna drew rein beside Shunkaha, her whole body aching from spending over twelve hours on horseback. She smiled weakly when Shunkaha vaulted to the ground and lifted her from her horse.

"We will rest awhile," he said.

Brianna nodded. Her eyelids felt like lead, her legs were shaky, and her back and shoulders ached dreadfully.

Shunkaha spread a blanket on the ground and Brianna sat down, grateful to be sitting on something that wasn't moving beneath her. Shunkaha sat behind her, his strong hands rubbing her back and shoulders and the nape of her neck, his fingers kneading away the soreness. She closed her eyes, surrendering to the pleasure of it, her head lolling forward as she slowly drifted to sleep.

With great tenderness, Shunkaha took her in his arms,

holding her close. She had not betrayed him, and he felt a rush of guilt for not having trusted her. Never again would he doubt her love or her loyalty.

"Forgive me, little one," he murmured, lowering her to the ground and drawing the blanket over them both. "I will never doubt you again."

It was nightfall when they awoke. Brianna smiled at Shunkaha, her heart in her eyes, the pulse in her throat beating a quick tattoo as his mouth closed over hers in a long kiss that gradually deepened until they were both breathless. No words were necessary as he began to undress her, his hands eager as they cast off her clothing to fondle the satiny skin beneath.

"I missed you," Brianna murmured as Shunkaha trailed kisses over her face and neck. "I was so afraid."

"Do not be afraid, Ishna Wi," he replied, his dark eyes gazing into hers. "I will never let anything happen to you."

Brianna nodded, her eyes glowing with passion as Shunkaha drew her close. How wonderful to be held in his arms again, to feel his hands lightly stroke her secret places, to hear his voice whisper to her in soft Lakota. Her own hands were busy, exploring taut muscle and smooth flesh, reveling in the sweet abrasion of skin sliding over skin.

Her touch fired Shunkaha's desire. He had thought her lost to him forever and now she was here, in his arms. He breathed deeply, inhaling the womanly fragrance of her skin and hair. His senses were filled with her and he groaned low in his throat, his wanting almost painful.

"I cannot wait longer," he said huskily, and rising, he made himself a part of her, his arms holding her so tight she could scarcely breathe.

Brianna shuddered with pleasure as he made her his own, her hands restlessly kneading his broad back and shoulders as their desire for one another soared higher and higher until they reached that one fleeting moment of perfection, then slowly spiraled back to earth, and reality.

Shunkaha Luta held Brianna close for a long while, his fingers threading through her hair as he gazed at the night sky. Once, the whole earth had belonged to the People. They had roamed the vast plains and prairies at will, living as Wakan Tanka had intended. Once, the buffalo had been as plentiful as the stars twinkling overhead. Now the shaggy beasts were few in number, and growing fewer each year as the white men hunted them relentlessly.

Shunkaha's gaze shifted to the face of his woman, sleeping peacefully in the crook of his arm. What would the future hold for the two of them? How would she fare with the Lakota? Would they accept her as one of them, or shun her because her skin was like cream and her hair as gold as the sun? He placed his hand over Brianna's flat belly. Had the seed he had planted in her womb taken root? What would the future hold for their children? Half-breeds often had a difficult time in life, never truly belonging in either world.

Brianna stirred beneath his hand, her eyelids fluttering open. She smiled at him, the love in her eyes chasing away all his doubts. Together they would overcome whatever obstacles the future held.

"It is time to go," Shunkaha said.

She did not argue. Rising quickly, she washed, then prepared breakfast while Shunkaha bridled the horses and rolled their blankets.

After a quick breakfast of boiled jerky and coffee, they were riding again. It was eerie, Brianna thought, riding through the night. The plains were quiet, dark, mysterious. Just before midnight, the wind began to blow, whispering secrets to the buffalo grass, teasing the leaves on the cottonwood trees.

Brianna shivered and drew her coat more closely around her. She looked over at Shunkaha, assuring herself that he was there. He rode tall and straight, his profile as clean-cut as the image on a coin, his dark hair blowing in the breeze. It occurred to her that this man was a warrior, a fighting man. Her people were at war with his people, and would likely consider her a traitor for loving him. The thought caused her a moment of pain, and then she shrugged it aside. Since her parents had died, she had known only unhappiness and cruelty from her people, while this man had shown her nothing but love and kindness.

Feeling her gaze, Shunkaha turned to face her. "What is it?"

Brianna shook her head. "Nothing."

"Something has troubled you," Shunkaha remarked, frowning.

"Yes."

"Can you not tell me?"

"It's silly," Brianna answered. "Foolish."

"There must be no secrets between us, Ishna Wi."

"I . . . it just occurred to me that you're a warrior, and I wondered if . . . I mean—" She broke off, not wanting to offend him.

"You wondered if I had killed any of your people."

"It doesn't matter," Brianna said quickly. "Really it doesn't."

Shunkaha Luta reined the black to a halt, and the roan stopped beside it.

"I have fought your people in the past," Shunkaha Luta said, his voice empty of emotion. "I have killed the soldiers who rode against us, and I have killed others who came into our land looking for gold." His eyes met hers. "There will be more battles in the days ahead, more killing."

Brianna chewed on her lower lip, her eyes intent on his face. The answer was what she had expected, and it left her with a choice to make. Shunkaha was watching her, waiting for her answer. Was she strong enough to turn her back on her people and be his wife? Could she live with him, knowing he had killed many whites, and would gladly kill more if he got the chance?

Shunkaha Luta felt a swift compassion for her. She was so young, so innocent. She had lived without affection in the past six years, but she had never known want, never experienced hunger, never seen the bloody horror of war. Was she strong enough to live as the Lakota lived? Was he asking too much of her?

"I will take you back to your uncle, if that is your wish," he said quietly.

"No!" Never that. How could she return to that empty life when she had known the wonders of Shunkaha's love? How could she go back to a life of misery and unhappiness when she had basked in his approval?

"Are you sure, Ishna Wi? Once we reach the lodges of my people, there will be no turning back."

Brianna felt a tug at her heart. Was he trying to discourage her? Perhaps he no longer wanted her with him.

She lowered her head, not wanting him to see her face, or the tears welling in her eyes. "Don't you want me any more?"

"Ishna Wi!" He was off his horse, pulling her into his arms. "I want only your happiness, little one. You are my woman, but I would not keep you here against your will, nor keep you from your people if you wish to return."

"I only want to be with you."

Gently, Shunkaha placed one strong brown finger beneath her chin and lifted her face. He brushed his lips tenderly across hers. "You are my wife, Ishna Wi," he murmured. "From this night forth, I will never willingly let you go."

"You are my husband," Brianna replied, her heart filled to overflowing. "From this night forth I will never willingly leave your side."

For a long moment they stood thus, gazing into each other's eyes, and forever after that night, Brianna felt as though she and Shunkaha were truly man and wife.

Chapter Ten

They traveled southwest for five days, crossing a corner of what Shunkaha called Maka Sicha, the Badlands. Brianna gazed in awe at fantastic rock formations and hills that were barren of life, breathed a sigh of relief when they left the area behind.

Several days later, they reached the Black Hills. It was a rugged land, a gradual uplift on the face of the earth that was broken by deep gorges, high ridges and buttes, and strangely shaped rock formations.

The Black Hills were not black at all, Brianna noted, but a dark green due to thick forests of yellow pine, white spruce, red cedar, white elm, aspen, poplar, birch, cottonwoods, and oak. Leaving the vast plains of North Dakota, Brianna was awed by the sight of so much timber.

They were nearing a wooded area near the foothills of the Pa Sapa when they saw the horsemen: twenty young warriors, armed and painted for war. The Indians rode toward Shunkaha Luta and Brianna at a gallop, a trilling war cry issuing from their lips as they quickly surrounded the intruders.

The warriors stared at Shunkaha Luta, recognizing him as one of them, and then at Brianna.

"*Hou, colapi,*" Shunkaha said, lifting his right hand in the traditional sign of peace. "Hello, friends."

"*Hohahe, cola,*" replied one of the warriors. "Welcome, friend. You are on Lakota land."

Shunkaha nodded. "I have come seeking refuge with my brothers."

The warrior nodded. "These are bad times for our people. Another warrior will be welcome. Even now, Tatonka Iyotake and Tashunke-Witke are preparing for war." The Indian glanced at Brianna speculatively. "Is the white woman your captive?"

Shunkaha Luta shook his head. "She is my wife."

The warrior nodded, his face disclosing a fleeting expression of disapproval.

"*Hoppo,*" the warrior said, wheeling his horse around. "Let us go."

It was with trepidation that Brianna entered the Indian village in a cleared space in the midst of a stand of cottonwoods. There were many lodges, too numerous to count, and many Indians. Her throat went dry as they rode into the village, instantly becoming a source of great excitement and curiosity. Men, women, and children gathered around them, black eyes glinting with disdain as they stared at Brianna's golden hair and fair skin.

"*Ishna wasicu,*" they muttered. "White woman."

The sea of people parted as a slightly built warrior made his way toward them.

It was Crazy Horse. Though Shunkaha had never met the great warrior before, he recognized the man immediately, for Crazy Horse was a man apart. His complexion was light, his hair almost sandy colored instead of black. As a child, he had been called Curly, an odd name for a boy in a world of straight-haired people. He had often been mistaken for a captive when he visited the trading posts with his family. In the mystic world of the Lakota, his peculiar physical traits presaged a life of distinction. He was dressed in a black wolfskin clout, fringed leggings, and moccasins. A red blanket covered his shoulders.

Shunkaha Luta held himself proudly erect, his face impassive, his eyes giving nothing away as the heart and soul of the Lakota people came to stand before him.

"Why have you come here?" Crazy Horse asked, his voice quiet, yet carrying a note of authority and command.

"I have come seeking refuge with the Oglala."

"You are one of us?"

"Yes. My father was Wanbli-Luta."

Crazy Horse nodded. The name of Red Eagle was well known among the Oglala. "Welcome, brother," he said. "I am Tashunke-Witke."

Shunkaha nodded. "I am Shunkaha Luta. And this is my wife, Ishna Wi."

Crazy Horse smiled at Brianna, his dark eyes lingering on her golden hair and light skin. "Truly, she is well named."

Shunkaha nodded. Lifting one leg over his horse's withers, he slid to the ground and helped Brianna from the back of the roan.

"You are in luck," Crazy Horse said. "Black Swan has divorced her husband this very day, and has not yet disposed of her lodge. Perhaps it will serve you."

"*Le mita pila,*" Shunkaha replied. "Tell Black Swan I would be honored to have her lodge, and in return I offer her one of my horses."

Crazy Horse nodded. "I will speak to her."

Moments later, Crazy Horse returned, followed by a middle-aged woman with graying black hair and a pock-marked face. Brianna stood quietly as Shunkaha Luta and the Indian woman talked together, then the woman stepped forward and took the roan gelding's reins from Shunkaha and walked away.

"My horse . . ." Brianna protested, staring after the woman.

"I offered her her choice, and she preferred the roan," Shunkaha explained. "I will get you another horse."

The lodge Crazy Horse directed them to was large and well cared for. There was a firepit in the center of the floor, two beds against the far wall, two willow back rests, one on either side of the fire. The tipi was lined on the inside to keep out drafts and dampness. Shunkaha explained that the warm air rising inside the tipi drew in the cold air from outside, which came in under the cover and went up behind the lining, creating a perfect draft for the fire and carrying the smoke out with it. The lining also served as insulation, keeping the lodge warm in winter and cool in the summer. Most importantly, the lining prevented shadows from being displayed on the outer cover, thereby offering safety as well as privacy. No enemy lurking on the outskirts of the camp could see a shadow to aim at.

That was all very interesting, Brianna thought to herself. But did she really want to live in a hide lodge?

"The tipi is yours," Shunkaha said, taking her hand in his. "Among my people, the lodge and its furnishings belong to the woman. You will have to learn to dismantle the lodge when we move, and to erect it when we reach a new camp."

"Aren't you going to help me?"

"Only the first few times. It is beneath the dignity of a warrior to help with the household chores."

Brianna nodded. Her uncle had never done any housework, either. Perhaps the whites and the Indians had more in common than she had supposed.

Shunkaha bent and kissed Brianna lightly on the cheek. "If I displease you as a husband, you have only to throw my belongings out of the lodge, and everyone will know we are no longer man and wife."

"Instant divorce," Brianna murmured, scandalized. Divorce was practically unheard of among her people. When a couple married, it was for life. Any salary a woman might earn, any property that came to her, automatically belonged to her husband. The children, as well. There was a saying that summed it up in a few words: "When a couple marry, the husband and wife become one, and that one is the husband." Apparently that was not true among the Lakota.

Shunkaha fixed Brianna with a stern glance. "Are you considering it already, Ishna Wi?"

"Of course not. But what if a man wants to divorce his wife?"

"When a man is displeased with his wife, he finds himself a giveaway stick, and at the next dance he throws it at some man who might take care of his woman for a while, at least protect her from enemies and provide her with meat if they are not interested in marrying. There is no permanent obligation between the two unless they wish it."

Brianna nodded, then gestured at the lining, which was painted with horses and buffalo. "Who did that?"

"Black Swan's former husband. It is a record of his victories in battle. You see the horse with the hand print on its rump? That means he killed a man in hand-to-hand fighting."

"Why did she divorce him?"

"He developed a taste for whiskey. It made him mean and lazy. She has gone back to her father's lodge."

"You mentioned something about moving," Brianna said, glancing around at her new home. "Where are we going?"

"My people move several times a year," Shunkaha said. "When winter comes, we will move to a wooded canyon in the Black Hills, perhaps. And when spring comes, we will follow the buffalo."

Brianna fought back her dismay. She had hoped to have a permanent home at last, a place to sink roots, a place to call her own. She brightened when she recalled that Shunkaha said they would only stay with the Lakota through the winter.

"Well," she said, "here we are. What now?"

"Today we will get settled. Tomorrow I must begin hunting so we will have food for the winter. And you must begin learning the Lakota language and the ways of my people."

"They don't like me," Brianna remarked sadly. "I saw how they looked at me, their eyes full of hate and distrust."

"They will learn to love you, as I have," Shunkaha assured her.

"I hope so."

The next few days passed quickly. Brianna did not leave the security of her lodge except to relieve herself or gather wood and water. Whenever she went out, she could feel the Indians staring at her. Shunkaha went hunting in the mornings, and when he returned, usually late in the afternoon, he showed her how to cook Lakota style. Most food was broiled or boiled. Some was baked in a hole in the ground. Before the white man came, boiling was done in a buffalo paunch, but now most Indian women had a large cast iron kettle. Brianna also learned how to jerk venison and buffalo. Jerky was a staple of Indian life; easy to prepare, it lasted indefinitely. Sometimes it was cooked, other times it was eaten off the rack. Pemmican was another Indian staple. It was made with jerky that had been cooked and pounded, then mixed with dried chokecherries and suet. It was quite tasty, and Brianna heard one of the women say that even the soldiers preferred Indian pemmican to hardtack and field rations. Many of the women had traded pemmican to obtain their cast iron kettles.

Living in a Lakota lodge was not as uncomfortable as Brianna had feared. It was snug and warm. Firewood was kept outside the door, along with the pots and pans and water skin. Willow and aspen made for a sweet-smelling fire.

The tipi was a temple as well as a home. The floor represented the earth, the walls represented the sky, and the poles were the link between the earth and the spirit world, the ties between man and Wakan Tanka. There was a little space of bare earth behind the firepit which was the family altar. It represented Mother Earth, and the Indian women often burned sweet grass, cedar, or sage as incense to the spirits.

Shunkaha instructed her on tipi etiquette. If a door was left open, friends felt free to walk in uninvited. If the door was closed, they called out or scratched on the door covering until invited inside. Two sticks crossed over the door meant the owner was away or desired to be left alone. The men usually sat on the north side of the lodge, and the women on the south. When entering a lodge, a man moved to the right to his designated place, and a woman to the left. When possible, it was polite to walk behind a seated person. If passing between someone and the fire, it was proper to ask their pardon. At a feast, the men were always served first. Guests were expected to eat everything put before them. To refuse would be an insult.

Brianna found the last bit of advice hard to accept. There were many items in the Lakota diet that she found repulsive. The Indians were partial to eating hearts and tongues and kidneys, as well as the liver. But she dutifully ate what was offered, swallowing the urge to vomit. It was important to be accepted, to make Shunkaha proud of her.

The Oglalas were polite to her. They included her in their feasts and ceremonies; the women invited her along when they went looking for vegetables or nuts, yet Brianna knew they considered her an outsider, an intruder. The enemy. It was only because they respected Shunkaha Luta that they accepted her at all.

The name of Shunkaha Luta was well known by the Lakota. He was a fearless fighter, an accomplished hunter and tracker. He never returned from a hunt empty-handed, and he was generous with the meat he brought to camp, unselfishly giving away portions to those in need.

They had been in the Indian village for about three weeks when the first snow fell. That night, Shunkaha filled the space between the lodge cover and the lining with prairie grass for added insulation. The lodge, heated by a small fire, was warm and cozy.

There were many days after that when it was too cold to go outside for more than a few minutes; days when it rained without respite, or snowed from dawn till dark. On those days, Brianna and Shunkaha passed the time in each other's arms. Brianna found herself falling deeper and deeper in love with the kind, soft-spoken man who was her husband. He never grew angry with her, never raised his voice. He answered her questions patiently, never ridiculing her, never making her feel ignorant because she did not understand his ways.

She was most curious about the Lakota religion, for it remained a mystery to her. The Lakota believed that the gods had no beginning and would have no end. Some came before others; some were related as parent and child, yet their gods had no mother and no father, for anything that is born must die. Since the gods were created and not born, they could not die. Mankind could not fully understand such things, Shunkaha explained, for they were part of the Great Mystery.

Wakan Tanka was the main force in the universe. Below *Wakan Tanka* came *Inyan*, the Rock; *Maka*, the Earth; *Skan*, the Sky; and *Wi*, the Sun. *Maka* was believed to be the mother of all living beings. *Skan* was the source of power and sat in judgment on all the gods and spirits; *Wi* was the defender of bravery, fortitude, generosity, and fidelity; *Inyan* was the protector of the household. There were four subordinate gods below these known as the Buffalo, the Bear, the Four Winds, and the Whirlwind.

There were evil gods as well. *Iya*, the chief of all evil, was personified by the cyclone. *Iktomi*, the first son of Rock, was known as the Trickster, and was a deposed god similar to Lucifer.

When the weather permitted, the Indians went visiting. Brianna didn't know which was worse, being a guest in a lodge where she felt unwanted or being the hostess in her own lodge. Most of the Lakota did not speak English, so she was excluded from most conversations, though she could pick up more and more words as time went by. She quickly learned that *ishna wasicu* meant white woman, *washtay* meant greetings, *amba* meant goodbye. The Lakota often used kinship terms, even when no actual relationship existed. Young people often called their elders "my father" or "my grandmother." Younger persons were referred to as "my brother" or "my cousin." It was most confusing.

Brianna spent several days making herself a dress out of a deer hide Shunkaha had brought her. He had showed her how to strip the hair from the hide, how to tan the skin until it was a soft, pliable, creamy white. While she worked on her dress, Shunkaha made a new bow to replace the one he had lost.

Brianna felt very domestic as she sat beside the fire, needle in hand, while Shunkaha worked on his weapons. The lodge was warm and cozy, filled with the scent of sweet sage. Rain made a soft tattoo on the lodge cover, there was an occasional hiss from the fire. She felt a thrill of contentment swell in her heart when his gaze lifted to meet hers. His eyes were dark and beautiful, and in them she read a promise of undying love.

Shunkaha did not say a word as he laid his bow aside. Rising to his feet, he crossed the short distance between them and took the dress from her hands. Then, sitting down beside her, he took her in his arms and began to kiss her, very gently, his lips bestowing kisses on her eyes and nose and throat, on her hands, the delicate skin along her inner wrists, up the length of her arms, over the swell of her breasts. Brianna's skin grew warm wherever he touched her, until she felt as if her whole body was on fire. As his passion grew more intense, he placed a hand behind her head, his fingers lacing through her hair, his mouth descending on hers in a fiercely possessive kiss that made Brianna's stomach quiver with delight.

She did not resist when he pressed her to the ground, his hand sliding under her skirt to caress her calf, the curve of her thigh. She watched his eyes as he undressed her, loving the way they burned with a deep inner glow, the way he regarded her, lovingly, adoringly. She was ready, impatient, when he stripped away his own clothing, revealing the hard muscular body she knew so well. And then he was molding himself to her, entering the warm feminine part of her that had been created for him and him alone.

And now nothing else existed in all the world, only the two of them now made one. There was no hatred in their world, no distinction between red and white, only the timeless magic of two bodies with one heart, one soul . . .

The days passed slowly, with storm following storm, and the snow drifts rising higher and higher. Brianna felt as though she were living in a cold white world and she sometimes wondered if the sky would ever be blue again. There were days when the wind buffeted the land, screaming like a keening Lakota squaw, nights when thunder rumbled through the heavens and shook the earth, when great spikes of lightning rent the blackened skies, and the rain beat upon the lodge with such fury she was amazed it didn't come crashing down around their heads.

And then, miraculously, it was spring, the Moon of Tender Grass. The snow disappeared, the sky was a sapphire blue, buttercups and poppies bloomed on the hillsides, together with larkspur and bluebells and wild orange geraniums.

The village was a flurry of activity now as the Lakota prepared to move to higher ground.

It was on a warm April afternoon when the runner from the Hunkpapa arrived. Later, Shunkaha told Brianna the bad news. Red Cloud had been called to Washington the autumn before. The Great White Father had decided to buy the Pa Sapa. Red Cloud had been stunned by the announcement, and when he refused to sell, he knew what the white man knew: there would be war.

But it would not be now. The Lakota pulled up stakes and traveled west, following the buffalo. White men poured into the Black Hills, seeking gold, but the Indians were not there. And there was peace in the Land of the Spotted Eagle.

Pte, the buffalo, was the Indian general store. From *pte* came fresh meat for daily cooking, dried meat and fat for pemmican; its hide was used for tipi coverings, clothing, leggings and moccasins, sleeping robes, war shields. Rawhide was transformed into boxes and ropes and other camp gear. The horn became spoons and ladles, bones and sinew were used for needle and thread. *Pte's* tail could be used for a fly whisk or a broom. Little wonder the Indians regarded the buffalo with such esteem; little wonder that they objected when the whites slaughtered the beast in large numbers, taking only the hide and leaving tons of meat to rot in the sun.

For Brianna, the days and nights were like nothing she had ever known. As she fell more and more in love with Shunkaha, she found herself growing more fond of the Lakota people, more tolerant of their customs, more understanding of their way of life. She was no longer regarded as an enemy, an outsider. She was Shunkaha Luta's wife, and her actions and her innate kindness had earned the respect of the Oglalas. She worked hard, her lodge was clean and well cared for, her man was happy. Daily her mastery of the Lakota tongue grew, as did her ability to cook and tan hides and make moccasins. Now, when the women went gathering wood or water, she was one of them, able to laugh at their jokes and converse with them in their own tongue. When Shunkaha Luta went hunting with the men, she passed the time sewing him a new shirt, or helped some of the older women gather nuts and berries. Cheerful and generous by nature, Brianna was respected by the women and admired by the men.

There were many feasts and ceremonies and dances. The
Night Dance was the most popular. Young women dressed
in their finest attire to attract the young men. This was the
only time men and women danced together. There were
Scalp Dances for warriors to celebrate victories. Here, the
men danced in the center, and the women danced quietly on
the outside. The men wore black paint to symbolize victory.

The Lakota were a musical people. Drums were the most
important instruments. Some were so big that four men
could sit around them comfortably. Flutes were considered
to be *Wakan* and full of power. Eagle-bone whistles were the
smallest and were used by warriors when performing the
Sun Dance. There were long tubular flutes that, if played in
accordance with instruction from the shaman, were believed to have influence over women. The big twisted flute,
carved with the body of a horse, was considered a powerful
instrument of love. Such flutes were expensive and when
supplied with the magic formula for love, could cost a man
as much as a fine horse.

That summer the Lakota gathered for the annual Sun
Dance. Brianna tried hard to understand the meaning of
this most sacred of all the Lakota ceremonies, but she could
not seem to grasp its significance. To her, the sight of men
and women offering their flesh and blood to *Wakan Tanka*
seemed inhuman and barbaric. What kind of god required
such pain and sacrifice? She shuddered with revulsion as she
saw young men hang suspended from the Sun Dance pole
while others offered pieces of their flesh to the Great Spirit.

Shunkaha Luta tried to explain it to her. Most often, he
said, a man participated in the Sun Dance to fulfill a vow he
had made to *Wakan Tanka*. Sometimes a man danced to
secure supernatural aid for a member of his family, or for
himself. The ceremony lasted twelve days. The first four
days were a festive time, a time to prepare the campsite and
visit with old friends. The next four days were spent in giv-

ing instruction to those who would participate in the dance. Warriors who desired to take part in the sacred ceremony were isolated in a special lodge with the medicine man. The last four days were Holy Days. A large circular dance arbor was built in the center of the camp. The Sacred Lodge where the participants met was placed to the east of the arbor. A warrior, known as The Hunter, sought for a cottonwood tree to be used as the hallowed Sun Dance pole. On the day of its discovery, the Buffalo Dance was held to propitiate the Buffalo and the Whirlwind, patrons of the household and lovemaking. A feast followed the dance.

On the second Holy Day, the chosen cottonwood tree was felled by the women. The pole was stripped of its bark to a point just below the fork, while the top leaves were left intact. Young men lifted the pole with carrying sticks, for the sacred tree must not be touched except by a shaman or by those who had participated in the Sun Dance previously. When the pole was placed in the center of the dance arbor, it was painted—the west side in red, the north in blue, the east in green, and the south in yellow. Several sacred bundles were placed in the fork of the tree, and then there was a War Dance.

And now it was the final day and the dancers were prepared for the ritual. The medicine man painted the hands and feet of the participants red, then painted blue stripes across their shoulders. Each dancer wore a long red kilt and arm bands of rabbit fur.

Brianna refused to watch as the shaman moved among the participants, slitting the flesh above their breasts and inserting wooden skewers. Some of the participants would hang from the Sun Dance pole, heavy rawhide thongs holding them above the ground. Others had skewers inserted in their backs and would dance around the pole dragging heavy buffalo skulls.

It was bloody and barbaric, and Brianna knew she would

faint or vomit if she stayed a moment longer. Unmindful of what the Indians would think, she left the dance arbor and made her way to a shady glen some distance from the celebration. Perhaps she had made a mistake in coming here. How could she ever hope to understand people who practiced such a heathen religion? How could she ever hope to understand Shunkaha?

Until today, she had readily accepted Shunkaha's beliefs. Though they were different from her own, they had not seemed barbaric. The fact that he believed in many gods had not offended her, for she believed that his gods and her God were one and the same. But today—today she had realized there was a vast gulf between what he believed and what she believed, a difference greater and wider than the difference in the color of their skin. Except for the love they shared, they had nothing in common. Nothing at all. For the first time, she realized that love alone might not be enough.

"Ishna Wi."

She had not heard his footsteps, but suddenly he was there, looking more Indian than ever before. He wore only a brief black wolfskin clout and calf-high moccasins. There was a bone-handled knife in his belt, a single white eagle feather braided into his long black hair, a slash of bright red paint across his chest.

Brianna gestured toward the Sun Dance arbor. "Did you . . . have you ever done that?"

Shunkaha Luta nodded, his dark eyes sad as he saw the growing revulsion in her eyes.

"I am Lakota," he said, his voice quietly proud. "I was taught from childhood in the ways of a warrior. When I was a young man, I went alone into the hills to seek a vision. After three days and three nights of fasting and prayer, a red wolf came to me. In the ways of our people, the wolf became my brother, and I took his name for my own. The following

summer I participated in the Sun Dance." He touched his
chest, drawing Brianna's attention toward two faint scars
she had never noticed before. "When the time comes, I will
ride to war alongside *Tashunke Witke.* I am Lakota, and I can
be no less than what I was meant to be."

Brianna nodded slowly, all her doubts and fears clearly
mirrored in the depths of her eyes. He was a stranger to her
now, this man who stood firm in the traditions of his people,
who practiced their religion, who believed a wolf could be
his brother.

She glanced toward the Sun Dance arbor again. Through
the trees, she could see the outline of a man hanging suspended from the tall Sun Dance pole. She could hear the
constant beat of the drums, hear the chant of the medicine
man, the high-pitched notes of an eagle-bone whistle that
the participants blew on when the pain grew severe. In her
mind's eye, she imagined Shunkaha hanging from the pole,
his face lifted toward the blazing summer sun, his chest
stained with blood, his body taut with pain.

And the awful gulf between them grew wider and deeper
and more difficult to cross.

"Did it hurt very much?" she asked, not looking at him.

"Yes."

"Would you do it again?"

"Yes."

Shunkaha watched Brianna's face, saw the anguish in her
eyes. Almost, he took her into his arms to kiss away her
fears, to assure her that their love was enough. Instead, he
turned on his heel and left her standing there, knowing she
must decide for herself which path she would follow.

Brianna stared after Shunkaha's retreating figure, her eyes
filling with tears. She loved him so much, but did she want
to spend the rest of her life living with a man whose beliefs
and religion were so vastly different from her own? Did she
want to bear his children and raise them as Shunkaha Luta

had been raised? Did she want to watch her son writhe in pain as he offered his flesh and blood to an alien god? Did she want her daughters to grow up in a house made of hide, to toil from dawn to dark, never to know the comforts and luxuries of the white man's world? Did she want to spend her life moving from one campsite to another, never knowing the security of one place?

Did she truly love Shunkaha enough to cut herself off from her own people forever?

It was not a decision to be made overnight.

Shunkaha treated Brianna politely in the days that followed, but he did not share her bed, never did he take her in his arms, and he spoke but rarely. He spent his days with the other warriors, stayed out late at the community campfire. Each day he hoped Brianna would come to him and tell him that she was his, body and soul, that his people would be her people, his gods her gods. And each night the gulf between them grew wider and more difficult to bridge.

Summer gave way to fall, and still no decision had been made. Brianna sank deeper and deeper into despair. Stay or go? If she stayed, she would have to embrace the Lakota way of life wholeheartedly. She would have to make his ways her ways, his gods her gods, his beliefs and traditions hers. She would have to spend her moon cycle in a special lodge with the other women who were having their menses, for the Indians looked with awe and fear upon a menstruating woman. Indeed, such women were thought to be possessed by a powerful and dangerous spirit . . . And if she left Shunkaha, she would have to return to her uncle, for she had nowhere else to go. She longed for someone to talk to, someone to advise her, but she had no one. And so she continued to postpone her decision, knowing that whatever she decided would determine her relationship with Shunkaha Luta from that time on.

And then *Waziah's* breath blew across the land once more, making travel impossible. Deep drifts of snow covered the plains, turning the whole world into a fairyland of white-laced trees and snow-covered hills.

There was a lessening of the tension between them now, and Brianna's decision was put off until spring, when the roads would be passable again.

It was during this waiting time that the Army sent an ultimatum to the Lakota and the Cheyenne that stated, in part, that any Indian who had not moved within the bounds of their reservations by the end of January would be deemed hostile and treated accordingly by the military. The order was dated December 3, 1875.

"The white man wants war," Shunkaha said upon hearing the news. "The nearest Lakota reservation is over three hundred miles away."

"What will happen?" Brianna asked.

"There will be war. Crazy Horse will not force his people to travel three hundred miles through the snow to reach the Agency where there is no food for them. Many Agency Indians have come here to fill their bellies with something besides empty promises. The white man wants war," Shunkaha said again, "and he shall have it."

"Surely your people know they can't win," Brianna remarked, the very idea of war filling her with fear for Shunkaha's life.

"This is a battle we will win," Shunkaha replied. "*Tatonka Iyotake* offered one hundred pieces of his flesh at the Sun Dance and was rewarded with a vision in which he saw hundreds of white men falling at his feet."

"You don't believe that!" Brianna exclaimed. "Why, it's nothing but superstitious nonsense."

"Crazy Horse believes it," Shunkaha said quietly. "Our brothers, the Cheyenne, believe it. They have gone to join Sitting Bull at his winter camp on Beaver Creek. Sitting Bull has

sent runners to every band still living free and invited them to
join him for one last fight with the soldiers."

"But you don't have to go," Brianna cried.

"I have given my word that I will fight beside Crazy Horse."

Brianna stared at him, the full implication of his words
hitting her like a physical blow. He was going to follow
Crazy Horse to Sitting Bull's camp. He was going to fight.
How had he put it? One last fight with the soldiers. She did
not want to be a part of it, did not want him to be a part of
it. She knew, as he knew, that the Indians would lose. The
whites had more men, more weapons, more of everything. In
the end, the Lakota and the Cheyenne would find themselves on reservations, just like the Comanche and the Paw-
nee and the Kiowa.

Shunkaha's dark eyes lingered on Brianna's face. The past
weeks had been hard on him, living with her but not touching her, wanting her but not wanted by her. Was it possible
he had misjudged her? Perhaps she was not as courageous as
he had supposed. Perhaps she did not love him enough to
embrace his way of life. And yet, if they were to be together,
she must accept him for what he was, live how and where he
lived. There was no other way.

It was during that winter that Brianna began to understand why the Indians hated the white man, for she spent
hours listening as the old men told tales of long ago. The
Lakota had no written language and therefore no records
except for the stories and traditions that were told and re-
told each winter.

It was in a hide tipi on a cold winter night that Brianna
learned the tale of Colonel John M. Chivington, who attacked a peaceful band of Cheyenne at Sand Creek on No-
vember 24, 1864. The chief of the tribe, Black Kettle, raised
an American flag over his camp and sent an envoy to meet
the troops to assure them that the Cheyenne were friendly.
But these attempts at friendship meant nothing to Chiving-

ton and his volunteers. Six hundred troopers fought approximately two hundred warriors. The whites, equipped with howitzers, easily slaughtered the Cheyenne. A few Indians escaped the initial charge, but most were pursued and killed, women and children included. Chivington and his men returned to Denver with over one hundred scalps.

The old men spoke of the Washita, and how Custer had attacked a band of Cheyenne camped in the valley of the Washita River. They spoke of broken treaties, of promises made and never fulfilled, and Brianna could hear the anger in their voices, the bitterness, the sense of betrayal.

Slowly, the winter dragged on, and the time Brianna was dreading grew closer at hand.

And then it was spring once more, and time to move to Sitting Bull's camp.

Chapter Eleven

Brianna sat outside her lodge, watching the warriors ride in and out of the village. They were camped along the Big Bend of the Rosebud River, and the war camp was in a constant state of turmoil. Warriors were sent to trading posts and agencies to barter for guns and ammunition. Other braves went out in search of fresh war ponies. And still others carried the words of *Tatanka Iyotake*: "It is war; come to the Rosebud." Old men went out in search of robes and blankets, squaws seemed to be always cooking, for there were many people to feed.

Brianna saw little of Shunkaha Luta. He, too, was caught up in the excitement that ran through the camp like chain lightning, infecting everyone it touched. Once, she saw Sitting Bull. He was a short man, powerfully built, with a large head and a broad flat face that betrayed little expression. His hair was turning gray. When she heard him speak, she knew why the Indians were willing to follow him, for he was a powerful orator.

And so it would be war, as Sitting Bull had predicted, and Crazy Horse would lead them.

In mid May, the Lakota and the Cheyenne went out to meet General George "Three Stars" Crook. Brianna stood outside her lodge, her eyes fixed on Shunkaha Luta, her heart as cold as yesterday's ashes. He was going to fight, and nothing she could say would change his mind. He sat astride the big black gelding, looking every inch a warrior from the feather in his hair to the moccasins on his feet. In one hand he carried a rifle, in the other a feathered lance. He was shirtless, his bronze torso streaked with paint, his muscles rippling under the smooth, tawny skin that she knew as well as she knew her own.

He was going to fight.

Crazy Horse rode up to Shunkaha and they exchanged a few words. Brianna glanced from Shunkaha Luta to Crazy Horse. The Oglala war chief's body was painted with white spots. A red lightning bolt ran down one cheek. Except for moccasins and breechcloth, he rode naked.

Shunkaha had told her that when Crazy Horse was a young boy of twelve or thirteen, he had spent three days on a hilltop without food or sleep. In time, weak and dizzy, he thought he saw a horse coming toward him. There was a warrior on the horse's back. The warrior carried no scalps, and his unbound hair hung below his waist. The warrior's body was decorated with hail spots, and a streak of lightning curved from his forehead to his chin. Bullets and arrows attacked the phantom warrior, but did not touch him. A storm raged, yet he passed through it unharmed. People reached out to him, but he rode through them with a red-backed hawk flying above his head.

When Crazy Horse became a warrior, he took on the characteristics of the warrior he had seen in his vision. Shunkaha told her that Crazy Horse never took scalps because the warrior in his vision had none.

And now more and more warriors had gathered around, their rifles raised in the air, their voices lifted with the Lakota war cry, *hoka-hey!* and the Lakota kill cry, *huhn!*

Dust swirled around the hooves of the Indian ponies as they pranced with excitement, their tails tied up for war, their manes decorated with feathers. Many of the horses had handprints painted on their rumps, indicating that the rider had killed a man in hand-to-hand combat. Other animals carried a lightning streak or a thunder stripe, which were symbols of war. Still others had lines drawn across their noses, two or three or four, depending on how many coup a warrior had counted.

Dogs entered the melee, barking wildly as they dodged between the horses. Little boys picked up the kill cry, their voices loud and shrill, their eyes wide with envy as they saw their fathers and brothers preparing for battle. It was the dream of every young Lakota boy to be a warrior, to fight the enemy and gain honors on the field of battle.

If the women were worried or apprehensive, it did not show on their faces as they waved farewell to their men. Their eyes were filled with pride, their voices carrying on the breeze as they called after their men, encouraging them to fight like warriors, to count many coup.

Crazy Horse lifted his rifle over his head and wheeled his mount in a tight rearing turn. "*Hoppo!*" he cried in a loud voice. "Let us go!"

Shunkaha Luta was one of the last warriors to ride out of the village. For an instant, just before he followed Crazy Horse and the others, his eyes met Brianna's and all the love he felt for her shone clearly in their depths. And then he was gone.

That look haunted Brianna all that day. Once, Shunkaha had offered to take her home and she had assured him that she would never willingly leave him, that she wanted only to be where he was. She knew now, as she watched him ride off to battle, perhaps never to see him again, that she still felt the same. She had let her foolish fears ruin their last few months together. She had slept in a cold and lonely bed when she might have been resting in his arms. And now she had let him go off to war without telling him that she loved him. If he died, she knew she would suffer guilt and remorse the rest of her life. If only she had kissed him goodbye. If only she had told him she loved him, would always love him.

At loose ends, she wandered through the village, aware of the stares of the Indian women, aware of their inner turmoil. They weren't really so very different from herself. They looked after their children, wept when they were sad, made love to their husbands, revered their old ones, worshiped their gods, laughed and danced, mourned for their dead. They were an honorable people, living in the traditions of their fathers, hoping and dreaming that things would be better for their children.

She saw the worry lurking behind their eyes as they waited for their husbands and brothers and fathers to return from the battlefield, saw the lines of anxiety in their faces, heard it in their voices. Watching them, she felt a bond of unity with these women, and with all women the world over who had spent the long lonely hours waiting for a loved one to return from battle.

Retracing her steps to her own lodge, Brianna curled up on her bed and willed Time to move faster. The waiting, the wondering, the not knowing, was almost more than she could bear. Was he all right? She imagined him wounded and bleeding, his face twisted in agony; pictured him dying, dead. *Oh, Lord, please bring him safely back to me.*

A triumphant cry drew her from the brink of sleep. Scrambling to her feet, Brianna hurried out of the lodge to see the war party swarming into camp. It had been a wild and bloody battle, as evidenced by the number of wounded Indians, and by the number of fresh scalps that fluttered from the lance tips of the Lakota warriors. The fight had been a victory for the Indians. Fifty of General George Crook's men had been killed or wounded, and Crook had fallen back to Goose Creek where he had left his supplies to lick his wounds and regroup his men.

Brianna was standing a few feet from her lodge when Shunkaha Luta rode up. He was grimy with dust and sweat, his dark eyes still alight with the excitement of the battle, the thrill of victory. He looked wild and savage and when he swung effortlessly from the back of the black, she noticed there was a fresh scalp dangling from the horse's mane. The sight of the bloody trophy made her stomach churn, and she pressed a hand over her mouth as she imagined Shunkaha killing a man, then cutting the hair from his head.

Shunkaha Luta stood before Brianna, hardly daring to breathe as he waited for her to make the first move. He had deliberately tied the scalp into the black's mane, knowing how it would affect her. The whites thought the taking of a scalp a cruel and barbaric practice, yet it was not a deliberate act of cruelty, but rather a part of the Lakota religion, a belief that the enemy would be less than a man in the Afterworld, less of a threat.

Would the sight of such a grisly trophy send her away? He had thought of nothing else on the journey back to camp, and yet, if she were to stay, she must know everything, accept him for who and what he was, and not for what she wished him to be. He was a warrior, a fighting man, and she must recognize that fact and accept it if they were to have a life together.

For a long moment Brianna gazed up at him and then, with a small cry, she hurled herself into his arms.

"Ishna Wi," Shunkaha Luta murmured thickly, his senses reeling at her nearness, his body aching with the need to possess her.

"Hold me," Brianna begged. "Hold me tight and don't ever let me go." She blinked back her tears as his arms tightened around her. "I've been such a fool."

Shunkaha Luta smiled as he lifted her into his arms and carried her downriver to a secluded spot well away from the camp. Brianna clung to him when he would have set her on her feet.

"I must wash," Shunkaha Luta said, chuckling softly.

Brianna nodded as she slowly slipped her arms from his neck, reluctant to be parted from him for even a moment. She watched as he pulled off his moccasins and stripped off his leggings and clout. Her eyes moved over him inch by inch, ascertaining for herself that he was truly unhurt.

Her nearness and the heat of her gaze sparked the expected result, and Brianna laughed softly as she saw the evidence of his rising desire.

"You dare laugh at me, woman?" Shunkaha Luta demanded, advancing toward her.

"No," Brianna said. Reaching out, she let her finger trace the paint smeared across his cheeks and chest. "I'm just so glad you're home safe."

Shunkaha Luta's eyes burned with a fierce intensity as he loosed the ties to her tunic and let the garment slide down around her ankles. "Come. Bathe with me."

She would have followed him anywhere, Brianna thought as she let him pull her into the river. The water was clear and cold, but Shunkaha's hands quickly warmed her as he washed her from head to foot; his hands, so big and brown, lingered on the slender curve of her neck, the sweet swell of her breast, then spanned her narrow waist and drew her close, crushing her breasts against his chest.

With a sigh, Brianna laid her head against his shoulder as waves of happiness rolled over her. He was here at last and she was in his arms again, where she had longed to be.

He whispered her name and she lifted her face to his, her whole being quivering with joy as she saw the love mirrored in his eyes.

In one fluid motion he lifted her in his arms and carried her from the water. Ashore, he sank down on the ground, still holding her in his arms, his mouth trailing tiny flames as he kissed each inch of her face, and all the while he was murmuring to her, the throaty Lakota words like the sweetest music she had ever heard.

Gently, he placed her on her back on the ground, then stretched out beside her, his eyes on her face, his hands wandering over her damp skin, familiarizing himself anew with her silken hills and valleys, until she was trembling beneath his touch.

She gazed into his eyes, those black depthless eyes that now smoldered with passion, and felt the heat of them clear to her toes.

Impatient, she twined her arms around his neck and drew him toward her, felt something warm and wonderful melt inside her as they became one. The months they had spent apart added a sense of urgency to their lovemaking, as did the distant knowledge that Shunkaha Luta could have been killed and this joyous reunion might never have been.

Oh, the incomparable pleasure of his touch as he made her his woman again! Her hands caressed the satin steel of his arms as he thrust into her, filling a need that was more than physical, more than mere passion. It was a reaffirmation of their love, a renewed pledge of the vows between them.

Brianna sighed his name as his life spilled into her, filling her with sunshine, making her complete.

Later, Shunkaha Luta held Brianna close, his hand lightly stroking her hair. Two wars had been won this day, he mused, and each victory was sweeter for the battle fought and won.

Brianna assumed that the Indian victory meant the end of the fighting. Sitting Bull's vision had been fulfilled and now the Lakota could return to the Black Hills and live in peace.

But it was not to be. Sitting Bull boldly proclaimed that the fight against "Three Stars" Crook was not the fight foretold in his vision. He had seen hundreds of white soldiers dead at his feet, he declared, and not the few bluecoats that had been slain at the Rosebud. There was yet another battle to be fought and won.

Crazy Horse believed in the words of the Hunkpapa medicine man, and so it was that the war camp prepared to move, their destination the valley of the Little Big Horn.

Brianna could not help being caught up in the excitement of the move, for she had never seen anything like it. She stared in wonder at the beauty around her as they made their way through the northern foothills of the Wolf Mountains. The grass was as high as her pony's belly. There were groves of yellow-green cottonwoods and clear mountain streams and slender-trunked birch trees. And far in the distance could be seen the Shining Mountains that the whites called the Big Horns, their snow-capped peaks rising in stately splendor against the cloudless blue sky.

Crazy Horse rode at the head of the long Sioux caravan, along with Dull Knife and Two Moons, chiefs of the Cheyenne. The warriors rode next in line, mounted on their finest ponies. Following the warriors came the women and children and the pack horses, and, lastly, came the vast Indian pony herds.

It was a long, noisy parade that stretched for three miles from end to end.

Brianna's heart was light as they traveled along, for the terrible gulf between herself and Shunkaha Luta had been bridged at last, the gulf between them spanned by a night of lovemaking such as Brianna had never known. Shunkaha had possessed her fiercely, passionately, masterfully, vowing he would never let her go. And Brianna had gloried in his touch, reveling in his strength, in the way he subdued her so skillfully, and then carried her to such heights as she had never dreamed of.

To please him, Brianna discarded her civilized dress the following morning and donned a doeskin tunic she had fashioned from a deer hide that had been tanned to a rich, velvety softness. Long fringe dangled from the sleeves; the bodice was adorned with many brightly colored porcupine quills. Her hair was pulled away from her face, tied back with a length of red ribbon. She had tossed away her shoes and stockings and wore a pair of soft moccasins. They were, she thought, a vast improvement over her stiff leather shoes. Now, riding toward the Big Horn Mountains, she felt very loved and very Indian.

She was unprepared for the sight that awaited her as they topped a tree-studded rise and saw the Little Big Horn River spread below. Hundreds and hundreds of lodges were situated in the valley, housing more Indians than Brianna had ever dreamed existed.

"Never have so many of the People been gathered together in one place," Shunkaha remarked, reining his horse up beside her. He gestured upstream. "There are the Hunkpapa, and there the Blackfoot Sioux and the Santee." His arm swung downward toward the Yellowstone. "There are the Minneconjou, and beyond them, the Sans Arc and the Cheyenne."

"There must be thousands," Brianna murmured.

Shunkaha Luta grinned. "More than four thousand men of fighting age," he said proudly. "Perhaps two thousand of them are seasoned warriors."

Brianna nodded. Perhaps the Indians *could* win. "Who are they going to fight?"

"Yellow Hair," Shunkaha Luta replied, his tone betraying his hatred for the man.

"Yellow Hair?"

"Custer," Shunkaha explained. "He is riding toward us even now."

George Armstrong Custer. The Boy General. The man who had slaughtered a peaceful band of Cheyenne Indians on the banks of the Washita in the dead of winter, then burned their lodges and belongings and slaughtered the horses.

"How do you know Custer is coming?" Brianna asked.

"Crazy Horse knows. 'Red Nose' Gibbon is coming from Fort Ellis, Terry is coming from Bismarck, and Custer is riding with him."

"When?"

"Soon."

"You're going to fight." It was not a question.

"Yes."

Brianna nodded. She had known what his answer would be, and she had resolved to accept it without an argument. But it was hard. So hard.

There was great excitement in the days ahead. Dances and war councils were held nightly. Men constantly coming and going, scouts arriving hourly with reports of the progress of the soldiers, and then the announcement that Custer was on his way.

Brianna wept as Shunkaha Luta held her in his arms that night, burdened by a terrible premonition that he would be killed and she would never see him again.

"What is wrong, *le mita chante?*" Shunkaha asked gently. "Why do you weep?"

"I'm afraid for you," Brianna answered. "Please don't go."

"Would you have me stay behind with the women and children?" Shunkaha asked with a wry grin. "Would you rather I was a *Winkte* than a warrior?"

Brianna shook her head vigorously. *Winktes* were men who were unable or unwilling to fulfill the traditional male roles as hunter and fighter. They wore women's clothing, pursued female occupations, lived in their own lodges at the edge of the camp circle. They were objects of disdain and derision, having "the heart of a woman" rather than "the heart of a warrior."

"I am a warrior," Shunkaha Luta said proudly. "You must not be afraid for me."

"I can't help it. I love you so much."

"Do you, *le mita chante?*" Shunkaha whispered.

"You know I do."

"Then show me," Shunkaha murmured huskily. "Show me now . . ."

Their lovemaking was bittersweet that night. Brianna

poured out her heart and soul, wanting Shunkaha to carry the memory of her love when he went to battle. She clung to him, drawing him closer, arching her hips to receive him, hoping that his seed might take root within her so that if, God forbid, he should be killed, she might have his child to cherish. Her hands caressed each inch of his flesh, memorizing the span of his shoulders, the length of his flanks, the warmth of his skin. Her eyes never left his face, for that, too, must be committed to memory, just in case.

Shunkaha Luta held Brianna all through the night, his arms folding her close, his lips repeatedly bestowing kisses on her eyelids, her nose, her mouth and throat. He did not have any sense of impending doom, but he knew it was possible he would not return from the battle. Custer was a fighter. The Seventh was a fighting regiment; they had many battle honors, many victories, to their credit.

He did not sleep that night. Long after Brianna had drifted off, he remained awake, watching her sleep, needing to feel her there beside him. She whimpered, as though plagued by a bad dream, and his arm tightened around her as he murmured to her, assuring her that all was well.

His hand slid down her shoulder to cup her breast. Many warriors did not sleep with their women the night before a battle, believing that intercourse drained a man's strength, but he needed to feel Brianna close to him, to draw on her love, to taste her sweetness one last time, just in case . . .

It was late afternoon on June 25th when Custer rode down the slope across from the Little Big Horn where Medicine Tail Creek entered the stream. Had he managed to cross the river, the outcome of the battle might have been different. But before he could reach the lodges at the lower end of the Little Big Horn, hundreds of Gall's Hunkpapa Sioux swarmed in front of him, and before the Seventh could retreat, half of Custer's men lay dead or wounded on the slope. And then

Crazy Horse and his Oglalas appeared on Yellow Hair's left flank. Custer retreated up the slope with the remainder of his command, fighting valiantly all the way, until they were crushed beneath an angry red wave. In less than an hour, George Armstrong Custer and all his men were dead.

Brianna learned the details of the fight long after it was over. Standing beside her lodge, she saw the warriors returning, the look of victory shining in their eyes as they uttered the victory cry. Yellow Hair and all his men were dead! Sitting Bull's prophecy had been a true one.

Brianna waited for Shunkaha to return, and when he didn't, she assumed he was with the warriors who were still trying to flush Major Marcus Reno and his men out of the trenches they had dug on a distant hill. That fight continued until nightfall, and then the Indians returned to camp.

And still there was no sign of Shunkaha.

Brianna wandered through the mass of celebrating Indians, her eyes searching for Shunkaha Luta. Over and over again she asked if anyone knew where he was, and always the answer was the same: no one had seen Shunkaha Luta since the fight at the Little Big Horn.

She wandered through the village for over two hours, her heart growing cold with the certainty that he was dead.

It was after midnight when she went to Crazy Horse, but the Lakota chief had not seen Shunkaha.

"We fought side by side for a short time," the warrior recalled, "but then we were separated. I have not seen him since."

"I think he must be dead," Brianna said, barely able to speak past the lump in her throat.

"Our dead have all been brought into the village," Crazy Horse told her. "He was not among them."

"Then where can he be?" Brianna cried, her voice filled with anguish.

Crazy Horse shook his head. "I do not know, Ishna Wi. If he does not return by tomorrow, I will take you into my lodge, or have you safely returned to your own people, whichever you prefer." He placed a sympathetic hand on her shoulder, gave it a gentle squeeze. "Go back to your lodge now. I will try to find out what happened to him." He smiled at her as he read the question in her eyes. "I will come and tell you if I learn anything," he promised. "Go now."

"*Le mita pila*," Brianna murmured. "My thanks."

She was heavy-hearted as she made her way back to their lodge. Small groups of warriors could still be seen gathered near the campfire, boasting of the coup they had counted during the battle, bragging of the men they had killed, bragging about Crazy Horse, the most powerful war leader the Lakota nation had ever known.

Slipping into her lodge, Brianna curled up on her sleeping robes, her hand softly stroking the robe where Shunkaha usually slept. Where could he be? Why didn't he come to her?

In the morning, the Indians launched a fresh attack on Major Reno's command. The assault lasted into the afternoon, and even while the warriors were fighting, the women were dismantling the lodges. Scouts had sighted Terry and Gibbon riding toward the valley of the Little Big Horn and the Indians were preparing to move out. Sitting Bull's vision had been fulfilled. It was time to go.

Brianna fought down the urge to panic as she watched the Indians begin to leave the valley headed for their summer hunting grounds.

She was standing outside her lodge, feeling lost and alone, when Crazy Horse came to see her. She had only to look at his face to know he brought bad news.

"Is he dead?" she asked quietly.

Crazy Horse shrugged. "It is as though he vanished from the face of the earth. No one has seen him. I am sorry, Ishna Wi. We must assume he was killed."

Brianna nodded, unable to speak, unable to cry, as a terrible numbness crept into her heart.

"You must decide what you wish to do. We are leaving here. Will you come with us? My woman will make you welcome in our lodge."

"I don't know." She knew she could not stay here alone, yet she was reluctant to leave. This was the last place she had seen Shunkaha.

"If you wish to return to your own people, Terry's troops will take you back."

"Yes," Brianna agreed at length. "I think that is what I must do." How could she go back to her aunt and uncle? How could she face them after what she had done? They would never understand her love for an Indian man. And yet, where else could she go?

She watched Crazy Horse walk away and then, sick at heart, she returned to the lodge she had shared with Shunkaha Luta.

We must assume he was killed.

She glanced around the lodge, no longer a home now that he was gone, but merely a dwelling made of wooden poles and buffalo hides. Her eyes lingered on the knife she used for skinning. Almost without conscious thought she picked up the knife. The haft was made of bone, the blade was long and sharp.

We must assume he was killed.

She groaned softly as she drew the blade across her left forearm, the pain in her heart far worse than that wrought by the blade.

Twice more she slashed her flesh, her tears flowing as freely as the blood on her arms as she mourned her husband's death in the Lakota way. And then she began to laugh soundlessly. She had not wanted to live among Shunkaha's people, she had scorned their barbaric ways, and yet she could think of no better way to express her grief than to follow the Lakota custom of bloodletting.

She knew now why the Indian women mutilated their

flesh, why their voices were lifted to the skies when a loved one was killed. She was part of their sisterhood now.

It was late afternoon when Crazy Horse escorted Brianna to the foot of the hill where Major Reno's battle-weary men were dug in. She had changed into her blue dress, packed her few belongings in one of Shunkaha's saddlebags before leaving her lodge for the last time.

Crazy Horse helped her mount the roan, then swung aboard his own pony. Lifting his lance high above his head, he shook it at the white men who were watching from the top of the hill. Then he smiled at Brianna. "May *Wakan Tanka* bless you with a long and happy life, Ishna Wi," he called, and rode down the valley at a gallop. A shrill war cry trailed behind him.

The soldiers were as hospitable as possible under the circumstances. They assumed Brianna had been a captive of the Sioux, and she let them think so because it was easier to explain than her love for a Lakota warrior.

From the bluffs, Brianna could see the long lines of the Indians heading southeast where they would scatter to the four winds, each tribe going back to its own hunting grounds for the remainder of the summer. And in the distance she could see the long blue line of the United States Infantry coming toward them, commanded by "Red Nose" Gibbon and General Alfred Terry. The men in Major Reno's command stood up and cheered; many of them wept openly, and who could blame them? They had stared death in the face for two nerve-wracking days and now their salvation was at hand.

Later that afternoon, Brianna sat astride her horse in the midst of the battlefield, surrounded by soldiers. George Armstrong Custer, his brothers, Tom and Boston, and his nephew, Autie Reed, lay dead upon a grassy slope, together with the troops of the Seventh Cavalry, their broken bodies obscene in the warm summer sunlight that bathed the grassy banks of the Little Big Horn. The Indians had carried away their dead before they left the valley; the white men would be buried where they had fallen.

An awed silence hung over the Little Big Horn. The men talked quietly, reverently, in the face of so much death. It was a scene that would be forever burned into Brianna's memory: the hundreds of bodies, many of them mutilated and scalped, stripped of their clothing and weapons. The smell of blood and death. The hum of insects.

The battle at the Little Big Horn was the main topic of conversation on the long trek back to Bismarck. Over and over again, the men asked the same questions. Why had Custer disregarded his orders? Why hadn't he waited for Gibbon and Terry? Why had he left the Gatling guns behind? Why hadn't he listened to Bloody Knife when the Arikara scout told him there were thousands of Indians camped along the Little Big Horn? Questions, questions, but the man with the answers lay dead upon the sun-bleached slope of the Greasy Grass.

Brianna was too wrapped up in her own personal grief to mourn for those she didn't know. Shunkaha Luta was dead and she felt as though her heart and soul had died with him. At night, she had only to close her eyes to summon his face to mind: the fathomless black eyes, the high cheekbones and strong jaw, the mouth that was full-lipped and sensuous.

During the day, she relived the time they had spent together, regretting the days she had foolishly wasted while wondering whether she belonged with him or not. Now he was gone, and she knew she would never belong to anyone else the way she had belonged to her Indian.

When they reached Bismarck, the Army went on to the fort and Brianna rode into town. She had some money, but it would not last long. Sooner or later, she would have to look for a job, or go back to Uncle Henry.

She had tethered her horse to a hitchrail and was walking toward the hotel when Adam Trent fell into step beside her. "Afternoon, Miss Beaudine," he said. His voice was cool and businesslike, but his eyes were warm and friendly.

"Mr. Trent," Brianna murmured. She came to a halt outside the door of the telegraph office, her heart racing with apprehension. Did he mean to arrest her for helping Shunkaha escape?

"Where is he this time?" Trent asked flatly.

"He's dead."

Trent cocked his head to one side, his expression skeptical.

"He was killed at the Little Big Horn," Brianna said, fighting the urge to cry.

Adam Trent grunted softly. "What was he to you, exactly?"

"My husband," Brianna answered proudly.

"Husband! No preacher in his right mind would marry a white woman to an Indian."

"We were married according to the laws of the Lakota."

"You helped him escape, didn't you?"

"Did I?"

"I'm asking the questions here. Hap Wilson doesn't remember what happened that night. Somebody hit him over the head and he was unconscious for several days. When he came to, he couldn't remember a thing."

"That's too bad," Brianna remarked, not meeting Adam Trent's eyes.

"Yeah. Well, I guess it doesn't really matter, now that the Indian's dead." Trent grinned wryly. "Beyond the long arm of the law, so to speak."

Brianna glared at him. She did not find his attempt at humor the least bit amusing.

"I'm sorry," Trent apologized. "Listen, let's start over again, shall we?" He smiled at her, his gray eyes twinkling.

"All right," Brianna agreed. She had no friends and she needed one desperately. And Adam Trent was a nice man, one she knew could be trusted.

"It's almost time for dinner," Trent remarked, checking his pocket watch. "Would you join me?"

Brianna glanced down at her blue dress, stained with the dust and grime of many days on the trail. "I don't think so."

Adam Trent smiled wryly, quickly understanding her dilemna. "I could buy you some new duds," he offered. "You could think of it as a loan, if you like."

"No need. I have a little money." She did not mention that Shunkaha had stolen it.

Trent nodded. "I have some business to take care of," he said, slipping his watch into his pocket. "How about if I pick you up at the hotel in about an hour?"

"Could we make it two hours?" Brianna asked. "I need to shop and bathe and do my hair."

Adam Trent smiled indulgently. He didn't spend much time with women and he tended to forget that it took them longer to get ready. "Sure. See you at seven."

Brianna secured a room for herself at the hotel, dropped her saddlebags on the floor beside the bed. She sat there for a long while, staring into space, more depressed than she had ever been in her life. Shunkaha was gone and she would never see him again.

It was an effort to leave the hotel. She seemed to have lost interest in how she looked or what she wore. Once, being able to shop for her own clothes would have filled her with excitement, for it was something she had never done. But now it no longer seemed important. What difference did it make how she looked if Shunkaha could not see her? Still, Adam Trent had been kind to her and she couldn't embarrass him by going out in public clad in her horrid blue dress and moccasins.

She purchased a simple frock of blue-sprigged muslin, undergarments, shoes and stockings, a white grosgrain ribbon for her hair.

Now, dressed and with her hair freshly washed and brushed and tied back with the ribbon, she stood before the mirror, studying herself with a critical eye. Why, she was almost pretty, she thought with surprise. The dress fit as though it had been made for her, emphasizing her breasts and trim waist, complementing the color of her hair and eyes. She was pleased that the first article of clothing she had chosen on her own had turned out so well, but her pleasure was quickly dimmed when she remembered that Shunkaha Luta was not there to share the moment with her.

She tucked ten dollars into her skirt pocket, shoved the rest of the currency into the bottom of her saddlebag. She had been astonished by the amount of money she had found in Shunkaha Luta's war bag. Apparently the men who had tried to kidnap her had been successful in their chosen line of work.

Later, sitting across from Trent in the town's finest restaurant, she felt terribly shy. She had no experience with men other than Shunkaha Luta and her brief encounter with McClain, and she felt a trifle uncomfortable. What were Trent's motives? Why was he so nice to her?

Unbidden came the memory of Jim McClain. He had seemed like a nice young man, if one didn't know of his darker side. But he had wanted only one thing from her. Was it possible that Adam Trent was cut from the same cloth?

They chatted amiably for several minutes and Brianna studied Adam Trent. He was a handsome man, though not so handsome as Shunkaha. His hair was dark brown and waved over his forehead. He wore long sideburns but no moustache. His features were clean-cut, but it was his eyes that were the most arresting of all. They were a deep gray, open and friendly.

They ate in companionable silence, and then, over dessert, Brianna asked the question that had been plaguing her all evening. She had little practice in the art of flirting or playing the coquette, and the question came candidly and unexpectly.

"Why are you taking such good care of me, Mr. Trent? We hardly know each other."

Trent looked a bit startled for a moment, and then he shrugged. "You're alone. Far from home. And I find you quite the most beautiful woman I've ever met." His eyes smiled into hers. "And I'd like to get to know you better. Much better."

Brianna's cheeks turned bright red at his bold words and admiring gaze.

Adam Trent grinned. "I can't remember the last time I saw a woman blush. It's quite becoming."

Brianna's cheeks grew even redder. "Please, Mr. Trent," she implored, "you must not say such things."

"Why not? They're true. I thought about you a lot after you left. I trailed you for a while, but then I lost your tracks. Even so, I couldn't stop thinking about you." He leaned forward and placed his hand over hers. "And please call me Adam."

Brianna met his gaze squarely, then dropped her eyes to the table where his hand covered hers. His hand was large, with long fingers and neatly manicured nails. It looked strong resting over hers. The skin was deeply tanned, reminding her of another hand.

With a sigh, she lifted her head and met Adam Trent's eyes. "I'm very flattered . . . Adam," she said honestly. "But you're wasting your time."

"Don't turn me down before I've had a chance to plead my case," Trent admonished, giving her hand a gentle squeeze. "I just want to be your friend. Nothing more."

Brianna looked skeptical. "Nothing more?"

Adam Trent grinned, liking her more by the minute.

"Nothing more," he said sincerely. "For now. I'd just like a chance to get to know you better."

"I don't know," Brianna answered tremulously. "I . . . I don't think I'm ready to try again."

"You loved him, the Indian, didn't you?"

"Yes. I don't think I'll ever love anyone quite that much again." Her eyes grew moist. "Perhaps I'll never love anyone again."

"You will, in time," Trent said quietly. "And I want to be there when you're ready."

Chapter Twelve

He woke to a great thirst and a searing pain in his right side. The sun was blindingly bright when he opened his eyes and he blinked against the harsh glare, his thoughts fuzzy and disoriented.

He made a feeble attempt to stand up, grunted as pain lanced through his lower right side. His hand went to the wound automatically and he felt a wet stickiness against his palm. Blood. Closing his eyes, he sank back down on the ground, his hand pressed hard against his side.

Gradually, the pain receded, leaving his mind clear. There had been a great battle. In his mind's eye he saw it all again: the soldiers sweeping toward them, certain of victory, then turning and fleeing for their lives as they retreated up the grassy slope, pursued by two thousand Lakota and Cheyenne warriors drunk on the taste of blood and imminent victory. He had seen Crazy Horse and Gall and Bob-Tail-Horse, heard their rallying cries as they charged up the hill. *"Hoppo! Let's go! It is a good day to die!"*

But it was the white men who were dying. The Indians fought savagely, avenging old wrongs, old hurts, taking a life for every treaty broken, every lie, every buffalo the white man had slaughtered, every acre of land the *wasicu* had stolen. Onward they came, certain of victory. Hadn't Sitting Bull predicted a mighty victory? Were not Crazy Horse and Gall leading the fight? How could they lose?

He had been in the thick of the fight when he had been shot. The bullet had passed through his right side, just below his ribcage. Despite the wound, he had chased one of

Yellow Hair's soldiers, following the white man into the hills away from the fighting. *Coward,* he had thought derisively. *Running away from the battle to hide in hopes of saving his own miserable life.* The white man had managed to squeeze off a round before Shunkaha's arrow found him. The bullet, meant for Shunkaha, had struck his horse instead. The animal had fallen heavily, throwing the Indian clear as it fell. He had landed on his wounded side, rolled down the rocky slope, pitched into a narrow defile, struck his head on a rock and passed out.

He had vague recollections of the sounds of battle fading away, of the agonized cries of wounded men and horses, the distant echo of drums, the night-long shouts and cries of victory that told him the Indians had indeed won the fight.

He had been sinking deeper and deeper into the blackness that hovered around him when Brianna's image had flashed before his eyes. She had been calling his name, her lovely blue eyes awash with tears of sorrow . . .

Brianna. He opened his eyes to find that the sun was setting in a blaze of crimson and orange. He pushed himself to his feet, swayed unsteadily as the world spun out of focus. His legs felt like rubber, his mouth was dry, his head was light from loss of blood and lack of food.

It took every ounce of strength he possessed to climb out of the gully and when he reached the top, he dropped to his hands and knees, his head hanging, his sides heaving from the effort. When his breathing returned to normal, he lifted his gaze to the valley below. The Lakota and their allies were gone, the grass had been fired, and the valley of the Little Big Horn lay silent as death, washed in the bloody glow of the setting sun.

His first thought was of Brianna. Where had she gone? Lurching to his feet, he stumbled down the hill and began walking toward the place where her lodge had stood. Nothing remained now but a blackened patch of ground and the faint outline of the lodge.

Where would she go?

It was an effort to think, to concentrate. The left side of his head was sore and swollen, caked with dried blood, and his whole body ached from tumbling into the gully.

Where would she go?

On trembling legs, he made his way to the river. Dropping to his belly beside the stream, he buried his face in the water, then took several long swallows, letting the cold water bathe his throat and quench his thirst.

Crazy Horse, he thought. *Crazy Horse would know where she has gone.*

Chapter Thirteen

Brianna smiled at Adam Trent as he poured her a glass of cold lemonade. It was a bright sunny afternoon in late July, and they were picnicking in the shade of a tall tree beside a sleepy stream. A few scattered clouds drifted lazily across the sky, as fat and fluffy as powder-puffs.

Since her arrival in Bismarck, she had spent most of her time with Adam, letting him squire her about town. He showed her the sights, took her to dinner each night, accompanied her to church on Sunday morning, entertained her with tales of outlaws he had captured. He was good company, easy to talk to, an interested listener.

Brianna welcomed his presence, for he helped fill the days and take her mind from Shunkaha Luta. She wept whenever she thought of her Indian lying dead in the valley of the Little Big Horn. What good was living when he was gone? What difference did it make if the sun was warm and the days bright and beautiful? He was gone and she would never see him again.

When she was with Adam, she forced herself to smile, to laugh, to pretend all was well. Alone in her hotel room, she sat on the edge of the bed, staring blankly at the wall while she relived every moment she had shared with Shunkaha Luta.

Adam Trent paused in his tale of arresting a particularly nasty character, aware that Brianna was no longer listening. He had taken a long-overdue vacation so he could spend time with her, wanting to get to know her better, daily falling more and more in love, even though he knew she did not feel the same about him. Looking at her now, he saw that her eyes were soft and dreamy and he knew she was thinking about that Indian again. How long did she intend to grieve for that damned redskin, he wondered irritably. How could she have fallen in love with the man in the first place? Brianna Beaudine was a sweet, sensitive young woman. How could she have given her heart to a heathen savage?

Trent frowned as he tried to recall what the Indian had been like. Tall, muscular, with black hair and dark eyes, a haughty demeanor. The man had remained impassive on the long ride to Bismarck after his capture, had fought like one possessed when they reached the jail, had endured a brutal beating without uttering a sound. Trent had detected no softness in the man, no trace of warmth. Why had Brianna been so drawn to him? And why couldn't she forget him now that he was dead?

Smiling, he reached out to tug at her skirt. "Hey," he called softly. "Remember me?"

"I'm sorry, Adam," Brianna said quietly. "I guess I was daydreaming."

"About him?" There was a faint note of bitterness in Trent's voice.

"Yes."

"He's dead," Trent stated flatly. "Dead and gone. You've got to get on with your own life, Brianna. You can't grieve forever."

"I'm not grieving, not really. I'm . . . remembering."

"Dammit, I . . ." Trent broke off at the expression of dismay in Brianna's eyes. Clenching his hands at his sides, he stood up and walked downstream, his mouth set in a hard line. Sometimes he wanted to strangle her, to shake her so hard that it would knock all thoughts of that damned redskin out of her mind. He'd spent his whole life looking for a woman like Brianna, and now that he'd found her, she was in love with a ghost! He almost wished the Indian was still alive. A man of flesh could be faced and defeated, but a memory . . . how did a man go about fighting a memory?

Brianna let out a long sigh. She hadn't meant to hurt Adam, but she couldn't help how she felt. She had loved Shunkaha with all her heart, and she would never love anyone that way again. Their time together had been short, so dreadfully short, and yet he had touched every fiber of her being, infiltrated her senses, completely captured her heart, so that there was no room for anyone else, not even a man as decent as Adam Trent. For a time, Shunkaha Luta had been her whole life. He had been father, mother, friend, and lover. Adam seemed to think that, because Shunkaha had been an Indian, Brianna's love for him could not have been real. But it was the most real thing in her life.

She smoothed her skirt, then folded her hands in her lap as she heard Trent's footsteps.

"I'm sorry," Adam said. He sat beside her, his hands shoved into his pockets.

"Perhaps we shouldn't see each other any more," Brianna suggested.

"Is that what you want?"

"No. I enjoy the time we spend together. It's just that we always seem to end up talking about the same thing, and then you get angry. I can't help how I feel. I loved Shunkaha. I always will."

Trent nodded, his eyes studying her profile, the way her golden hair shimmered in the sunlight. "He must have been quite a guy," he muttered enviously.

"He was. He was strong and reliable, and he loved me. I felt safe with him."

"And how do you feel about me?"

"I'd love you if I could," Brianna said fervently. "I think you're a wonderful man. Perhaps, if I had met you first . . ." She shrugged. "Who knows?"

"I'm a patient man. I still think you'll fall in love again, and I want to be there when the time comes."

Brianna smiled wistfully, but said nothing. Maybe Adam was right. Maybe, in time, she would be ready to love again.

"My vacation's over day after tomorrow, and I probably won't see you for a while."

"Oh?"

"I'm going after the Morrow gang. They robbed a bank over in Holt County a couple days ago. I've got a pretty good idea of where they'll go to ground, and I aim to be there."

"That sounds dangerous."

Trent shrugged. "Could be, but I've got two dozen men to back me up."

"I . . . I'll miss you."

Trent felt his heart quicken. "Will you, Brianna?"

She nodded. It was true; she would miss him. He was the only friend she had.

"That's the best news I've had in days," Trent exclaimed jubilantly. Catching her hands in his, he stood up and pulled her to her feet, then twirled her around until she was dizzy and breathless. "I love you, Brianna," he said, his heart in his voice. "I love you very much."

Brianna didn't resist when he kissed her. His mouth was cool and firm, gentle but insistent. It was a pleasant kiss, but it stirred no emotion within her breast, sparked no flame. Trent didn't seem to notice.

Adam took her to dinner the following evening. He insisted she order the most expensive meal the restaurant had to offer, and ordered a bottle of champagne with dinner. Brianna had never tasted champagne before, and after the first few swallows, she found she rather liked the bubbly wine. It relaxed her, making the present seem wonderful and the past and future unimportant.

Adam complimented her gown, her coiffure, the color of her eyes, the beauty of her smile. He gazed into her face all during dinner, smiling at her as if she were the most fascinating and desirable woman in all the world. They talked of his family, and Brianna felt a sense of envy. How wonderful, to belong to a close-knit family, to know there were people who loved you and cared for you, who were there when you needed them. He told her of how they all got together at Christmas, his brothers always teasing him because he still hadn't found the "right" woman and settled down.

"Maybe I'll surprise them this year," he said, and Brianna looked away, unable to face the hope shining in his eyes.

Later, walking home, he placed her hand on his arm, then covered her hand with his own. It was a beautiful, star-studded night, warm and clear, fragrant with the aroma of honeysuckle. There was no one else on the street and they strolled along as if they were the only two people in the world.

There was a narrow alley between the hotel and the newspaper office, and when they reached it, Adam drew Brianna into the shadows and kissed her, his mouth coaxing, demanding a response. His arms were loose around her waist, gradually growing tighter as his kiss deepened, until her breasts were flattened against his chest.

Brianna kissed him back, enjoying the warmth of his arms. It felt good to be held, to know that someone cared. She felt so alone. Shunkaha was dead, and her aunt and uncle did not love her.

Adam was murmuring in her ear, whispering that he adored her. His hands stroked her back, slid down her sides, his thumbs stroking her breasts.

His touch on such an intimate part of her body snapped her out of her dreamy state and she pulled away, her expression reflecting her indignation. No one but Shunkaha had ever touched her like that.

"Brianna, I'm sorry," Trent said hoarsely. "Forgive me. It's just that I love you so much, want you . . . I'm sorry."

"It's all right," Brianna murmured.

"Come on," Trent said, reaching for her hand. "I'll walk you to your room."

Brianna's thoughts were chaotic as they entered the hotel lobby and climbed the staircase. Shunkaha was dead. Adam Trent said he loved her, but he was leaving town tomorrow and might be gone for weeks, perhaps months. She was alone in a strange town, with no one to care for her. She had money, enough to get by on for quite some time, but no friends. There were very few decent women in town, and the ones Brianna had seen did not appear friendly. Trent loved her. He would continue to court her, always hoping she would learn to care for him, when she knew it would never happen. She liked him, felt a warm affection for him, but she would never love him. Better to end it now than let it go on.

By the time they reached her room, she had made a decision. She was going home, back to her aunt and uncle.

She did not mention her decision to Adam for fear he would try to talk her out of it.

Trent gave Brianna's hand a squeeze. "I'll miss you. Think of me a little while I'm gone."

"I will. Promise me you'll be careful."

"I promise." Bending, he kissed her tenderly. "I'll be the most careful lawman this territory has ever seen."

Brianna watched him walk down the hallway, her thoughts leaping forward to tomorrow. The thought of going home kept her awake all that night, and she was at the stage depot early the following morning, only to discover that the next stage going in her direction wouldn't arrive for three weeks.

She thought the days would never pass but on a sunny morning in mid August she climbed aboard the Overland stage that would take her to Winslow.

Making herself as comfortable as possible on the hard leather seat, she leaned back and closed her eyes. Home. It would be good to see the ranch again, to swim in the lake, to work the land and see things grow. She wondered if her aunt and uncle had missed her at all, if they would be pleased to have her back again. She frowned as she considered the possibility that they might not take her back. She had run off with an Indian, after all. They had never been fond of her. Perhaps now they would disown her completely.

It did not make her journey any more bearable, and yet, in spite of it all, she was glad to be going home.

Chapter Fourteen

The soft sound of a drum penetrated the mists of darkness that surrounded him, carrying him back in time. Pain lanced through him, and in his mind he thought he was a young man again, enduring the agony and the ecstasy of *Wiwanyank Wacipi,* the Sun Dance. Once again he was standing before Tokala, the medicine man, his body rigid, his muscles tense, as the shaman made two incisions in his chest and inserted the rawhide thongs that would connect him to the sacred medicine pole. He stared at the long rawhide thongs—twin umbilical cords that stretched like a lifeline between himself and the pole. He would dance back and forth, back and forth, until his flesh gave way, releasing him from the pole, expelling him into a new life as a mother expelled her child from her womb.

When all the other participants were ready, the drums sounded and the dancers began to dance, their footsteps muffled in the dust as they shuffled back and forth, back and forth, pulling against the thongs.

After a while, he forgot everyone else. Eyes focused on the sun, he danced forward and back to the beat of the drum. Then, as now, he had been lost in a world of pain until there was nothing else in the world but the warm blood trickling down his chest and the pain that enfolded him like a cocoon, closing him in and shutting out everything else. Once, in a lucid moment, he saw his father standing nearby. Wanbli Luta's face was grave, but Shunkaha had seen the look of pride in his father's eyes. Slowly, Wanbli Luta had lifted a hand to his scarred chest. *Be brave, my son,* his eyes seemed to say. *I, too, have endured the pain of the Sun Dance. Only endure to the end and you will reap the reward.*

Shunkaha had nodded imperceptibly. Closing his eyes, he danced with renewed vigor and gradually the pain ebbed and he felt as if his spirit had left his body. Weightless, he floated through a vast land until he came to an incredibly clear stream flanked by silver cottonwoods and slender aspens. Kneeling on the grassy bank, he gazed into the still water, but instead of seeing his reflection, he saw a red wolf gazing back at him.

"*Hou, cola,*" the wolf said, his voice like the rushing of many waters. "*I will be your guide from this time forward. Listen to my words, follow in my path, and you will never go wrong. Never go wrong . . . Never go wrong . . .*"

The wolf's voice had trailed off, the image had faded into nothingness, and when he opened his eyes he was lying in his mother's lodge . . .

Shunkaha's eyelids flickered open. He was inside a Lakota lodge, lying beneath a buffalo robe. An aged figure knelt beside him, and for a moment he thought it was his father come back from the dead, but then he recognized the old man as one of the medicine men who had been at the Little Big Horn.

Unaware that his patient had regained consciousness, the shaman began to chant softly. In his right hand he held an eagle feather which he drew through the fire, drawing the smoke toward Shunkaha Luta, the words of the healing chant rising and falling like a feather on the wind.

A woman appeared in Shunkaha's field of vision. She was in her early thirties, with waist-length black hair and almond-shaped eyes the color of ebony. Gently, she lifted Shunkaha's head and held a waterskin to his lips. Two long swallows, and he was too weak to accept more. The questions he wanted to ask were forgotten as the pain closed in on him again, and he retreated into the waiting darkness, seeking oblivion.

When next he woke, the woman was sitting beside him. She held an infant to her breast. The firelight played across the woman's face as she gazed at the babe in her arms.

Shunkaha did not move, but watched, transfixed, as she nursed the child. She was a beautiful woman. Her skin was smooth and unblemished, rosy in the glow of the fire. Her hair fell like a dark mantle about her shoulders. Her nose was small and straight, her lips full. With great tenderness, the woman lifted the infant from her breast and placed it to her shoulder to gently pat its back.

Shunkaha smiled faintly as their eyes met over the child's head.

"*Hou*, Shunkaha Luta," the woman murmured in greeting. "Welcome back from the Land of Shadows."

"You know me?"

"I remember you from the valley of the Greasy Grass. You disappeared the day that Yellow Hair was killed. We thought you were dead."

"Only walking in darkness. How did I get here?"

"A warrior of the Shyela found you lying half-dead near Bear Butte. He recognized you and brought you to us."

"How long have I been here?"

"The sun has crossed the sky five times."

Shunkaha shook his head. He remembered nothing of what had happened after he left the valley of the Little Big Horn.

He spent the next few days regaining his strength. He seemed to be hungry all the time. The woman, whose name was Soft Wind, prepared great quantities of food, pleased by his appetite. She was ever there, to offer him a dipper of cool water, a cup of warm broth, a handful of ripe berries. She wiped the sweat from his brow, kneaded the stiffness from his back and shoulders, efficiently saw to his personal needs. He chafed at being bedridden, his temper growing shorter with each passing day, but Soft Wind remained patient and

cheerful, ignoring his sour expression and irritability, refusing to let him out of bed until she felt he was strong enough
to be up and around.

As his strength returned, he began to take short walks
through the village, venturing a little farther each day. He
asked each warrior he met for news of Brianna, but no one
had seen her since they left the Greasy Grass. Crazy Horse
had sent her away with the soldiers and that was all anyone
could tell him.

Where would she go? He knew she had no family other
than her aunt and uncle. Would she have returned to them?
It seemed unlikely since she had been so unhappy there, so
eager to leave, and yet, where else could she have gone?

Crazy Horse, he thought impatiently. *Perhaps Crazy Horse
would know where she had gone.* But he was not yet strong
enough to go in search of Crazy Horse, who was camped
somewhere along the Powder River.

He was lying in his sleeping robes, thinking of Brianna,
the night Soft Wind came to him. She knelt at his bedside,
her long black hair spilling over her shoulders and covering
her breasts like a curtain of midnight silk.

She gazed into his eyes, silently offering herself to him,
and Shunkaha Luta let out a long sigh. It was not uncommon for a woman whose husband had died or who was divorced to offer herself to a man. Intimacy with an unmarried
maiden was unthinkable, but there was no disgrace in lying
with a woman who had lost her companion.

"Soft Wind." He murmured her name, wishing she had
not come to him. He did not want to offend her, did not
wish to shame her by turning her away, but he had no desire
for any woman but Brianna, only Brianna.

"Do I not please you?" Soft Wind asked.

"Yes, very much, but I do not yet have the strength to
please *you.*"

She placed her hand on his chest, let it slide slowly downward to where the blanket covered his loins. "Perhaps I could increase your vigor."

Gently, Shunkaha took her hand and gave it a squeeze. "In a few days, perhaps."

"I will be here when you need me," Soft Wind answered. She lowered her eyes, hiding her disappointment. "You have but to come to my bed."

Shunkaha Luta nodded, knowing he would never accept her invitation.

There was a community dance the following night, and Soft Wind chose Shunkaha to be her partner not once, but several times. Dancing across from her, he felt a twinge of genuine regret that he could not love her. She was of the blood. Her traditions and memories were his, her dark eyes were openly adoring when she gazed at him. It would be so easy to accept the love she was offering him, to hunt and fight with the warriors, to sleep beneath Soft Wind's blankets at night. But he could not forget Brianna, could not erase her golden image from his mind, or her love from his heart.

He grew increasingly restless and discontented as the days went by, and when a dozen of the young warriors decided to go raiding, he asked to go along.

Soft Wind regarded him through fathomless black eyes when she learned he was leaving.

"You must be feeling stronger," she remarked candidly.

"A little," he agreed. "I think a few days with the men will do me good."

"Not as much good as a night with me," she replied provocatively. She placed her hand on his arm, her dark eyes filled with warmth and concern. "Be careful, and come back soon."

"Soon," he answered.

They raided far to the northeast, attacking several small Army patrols, routing the soldiers and stealing their horses, guns, and supplies. Shunkaha Luta felt alive again, reborn.

It was good to fight the *wasicu,* to see the fear on their pale faces as the warriors swarmed through their midsts, to hear their cries of pain, to feel the hot blood of the enemy on his hands.

In the evening, after a day of fighting, they sat around a small campfire roasting meat and swapping stories of other fights, other victories. It was here that Shunkaha Luta learned the details of Custer's defeat. The combined forces of the Cheyenne and the Lakota had cut through the Seventh like an invincible red scythe, annihilating Custer's men. There had been Indian losses as well, men Shunkaha had known: Black Cloud, Whirlwind, Swift Cloud, and Lame White Man of the Cheyenne, White Buffalo, Two Bears, Standing Elk, Long Robe, Elk Bear, High Horse and White Eagle of the Lakota. Lame White Man, a Southern Cheyenne chief, had been shot and scalped by a Lakota warrior who had mistaken him for a Ree or a Crow. Dust and gunsmoke had obscured the battlefield, one of the warriors remarked, making it difficult to distinguish friend from foe.

After leaving the battlefield, the Indians went up the Little Big Horn, down the Rosebud to the Tongue, and east to the Powder. Before the two tribes separated, they held a parade. Pretending to be soldiers, several warriors had donned uniforms of the Seventh Cavalry, save for boots and pants, which they disliked. Mounted on the big gray horses they had captured, the warriors rode in a line. One warrior carried a guidon; another blew on a bugle.

Shunkaha grinned as he imagined what the parade must have looked like.

They had been raiding for over a week when they came upon a buffalo hunter and three skinners. The white men were through killing for the day. The hunter was sitting on a pile of rocks, smoking a long black cigar, while the skinners stripped the hides from the fresh carcasses. Several vultures hovered overhead, waiting for the men to quit the kill so they could move in.

Shunkaha Luta felt the familiar hatred creep into his soul as he watched the *wasicu* skin the buffalo. They took only the hides and the tongues, leaving thousands of pounds of fresh meat to rot in the hot prairie sun. He thought of his mother and sister, starving to death because they had no food, thought of the tribes wasting away on reservations, languishing for want of fresh meat, and his anger grew until there was no room in his mind for anything else.

He heard the voices of the other warriors, heard their anger, and then, as one, the warriors raced toward the hunters, the wild war cry of the Lakota lifting from their throats.

The white men glanced up, startled, as a dozen paint-streaked warriors thundered toward them. The hunter grabbed his big Sharps .50 buffalo gun, but before he could raise it to fire, a pair of arrows thudded into his chest. The skinners tossed their knives into the dirt and made a run for their rifles, but they were too slow.

In seconds, the four white men were dead. Four warriors leaped from their horses and lifted the scalps of the white men. Three other braves began to butcher one of the buffalo carcasses. They would eat well this night, and have plenty of meat on the long journey home. Two warriors were chosen to take the hides and the horses of the white men back to the village, along with as much meat as they could carry. The warriors thought it was a good joke. For once, the white man had provided the Lakota with food, horses, and scalps, instead of robbing them of what little they had.

It was late afternoon several days later when they saw the stagecoach far in the distance. Some of the warriors, anxious to return home, suggested they let the coach go in peace. But the others objected. There were horses and guns to be had for the taking.

"We will leave it to you, Shunkaha Luta," one of the warriors decided. "How say you? Do we fight, or let them go?"

"Fight!" Shunkaha declared. When had the white man ever let the Lakota go in peace? Lifting his rifle above his head, he drummed his heels into his horse's flanks and galloped after the coach.

The three passengers inside the Overland Stage exchanged frantic looks as the ululating war cry of the Lakota rang out loud and clear. One of the men stuck his head out the window, his face turning chalk white as he saw almost a dozen Indians bearing down on them.

"Indians!" he hollered, and slid to the floor, his arms over his head. The second man was a priest and he quickly crossed himself, then clutched his Bible to his chest, bowed his head, and began to pray. "Holy Mary, Mother of God, pray for us sinners now, and at the hour of our death . . ."

The coach rocked violently from side to side as the driver whipped the horses, cursing at them for more speed. The sharp crack of a rifle sounded overhead as the Overland guard began to return the Indians' fire.

Brianna knew a moment of gut-wrenching fear as the warriors surrounded the coach. She heard the driver cry out in pain as an arrow struck him in the side, heard the guard shout a vile oath as one of the warriors vaulted from the back of his horse onto the seat. She heard the guard's cry of pain as the warrior drove a knife into his chest, heard the Indians shriek with triumph as they drew the team to a halt.

The man huddled on the floor began to babble, "We're going to be killed, we're going to be killed," as the door was jerked open and three warriors peered into the coach.

Brianna heard the priest ask God for forgiveness and she murmured her own quiet prayer as she was grabbed by the hair and dragged out of the coach.

Moments later, she stood between the other two passengers, her eyes wide with fright as she waited to be killed. She felt suddenly numb, as though she were lost in a nightmare from which there was no escape. Time slowed and seemed almost to stop and she saw everything very clearly. The sky was a bright hard blue, the earth was reddish-brown, the paint on the Indians' faces was black. She could hear the man on her left sobbing helplessly; the priest stood quietly, resigned to his fate. She saw two of the warriors cutting the team from the traces while two others searched through the baggage on top of the coach, tossing the items they fancied to the ground in a jumbled pile of bright cloth.

Too soon, the Indians had taken everything they deemed to be of value, and Brianna knew that death was only a moment away.

A tall warrior, his face streaked with paint and sweat, strode toward the passengers, a rifle in his hands. Heart pounding with fear, her mouth as dry as dust, Brianna closed her eyes, waiting for the gunshot that would send her into eternity. Perhaps she would find Shunkaha there . . .

Time lost all meaning as she waited for death. Gradually, above the fierce pounding of her heart, she heard voices. Indian voices, arguing. And then she heard his voice, a voice she had not thought to hear again this side of heaven. Hardly daring to hope, yet wanting desperately to believe, she opened her eyes and saw Shunkaha Luta walking toward her. She tried to speak his name, but the world went suddenly dark and she felt herself spiraling down, down, into nothingness . . .

"Ishna Wi. Ishna Wi." His voice, calling her name. But it couldn't be his voice because he was dead.

"Ishna Wi." Was she dead, too?

Slowly, she opened her eyes. He was bending over her, his dark eyes filled with anxiety, his face wiped clean of the hideous war paint.

"You're here," Brianna said, her voice filled with wonder. "What happened? Where am I?"

"You fainted, and you are here, in my arms, where you belong."

Tears of relief welled in her eyes. "I thought you were dead."

Shunkaha Luta shook his head as he gathered her close, his lips brushing her hair.

Brianna peered over his shoulder. "Where are the others?"

"They have gone home."

"Did they . . . ?"

"No. The white men are walking back the way they came."

"You told the warriors not to kill them, didn't you?" Brianna asked. "Because of me."

Shunkaha nodded. He would not have cared if the Lakota killed two white men, or two thousand, but he did not want Brianna to think badly of him. It had been hard, convincing the warriors to spare the two white men, but it had been worth the effort to see the gratitude in her eyes.

"Do you feel well enough to travel?" Shunkaha asked.

"Yes." She smiled at him, her face radiant. "I think I could fly."

"Come, then," he said, rising to his feet and drawing her up after him. "Let us go."

She did not ask where, nor did she care. It was enough that he was alive, that they were together again. He lifted her to the back of his horse, a big gray stallion, swung effortlessly up behind her, his arm sliding around her waist to draw her close.

Brianna settled back against his chest, thrilling to the warmth of his thighs cradling her hips, relishing the kiss of the wind against her face as they raced across the sun-bleached grassland. Shunkaha's arm was like a steel band, holding her tight. She felt his lips against her neck, felt the rising evidence of his desire as her buttocks brushed against him.

He was here, he was alive. She closed her eyes as his lips moved in her hair, her heart beating a wild tattoo as she contemplated the night ahead. It had been so long since he made love to her, and she was so eager. The mere anticipation of his touch brought a flush to her cheeks and heat to her loins.

Shunkaha drew his horse to a halt as soon as the shadows grew long. The other warriors were not far ahead, but he was in no hurry to catch up with them. Brianna was here, and they needed to be alone.

He felt her shiver with anticipation as he lifted her from his horse, and he groaned low in his throat as he pulled her into his arms. Brianna gazed up at him, her eyes shining with love, her lips slightly parted. His nearness left her breathless, and then he was kissing her, his mouth hungry, his tongue like a flame, sending sparks of desire to every part of her body. Her arms went around his neck, pulled him closer, closer. Overcome with their need, they sank to the ground, their hands and lips more eloquent than words as they expressed their love for one another.

He was all the more precious now that he had returned to her, and she let her eyes wander over every inch of his body, reacquainting herself with the planes and contours of his hard muscular chest and shoulders and thighs, letting her hands renew their love affair with the one man who was right for her, the one man who filled every need, satisfied every desire.

Heart to heart, soul to soul, they pleasured each other all through the night. Her breath mingled with his as his flesh merged with hers, until they were no longer two, but one.

They caught up with the other warriors the following afternoon, and four days later, they reached the Lakota village.

Brianna's eyes wandered over the campsite. It was nowhere near as large as the war camp along the Little Big Horn had been. She counted fewer than twenty lodges.

Shunkaha drew rein before a small lodge. Dismounting, he helped Brianna to the ground. Taking her by the hand, he led her into the tipi.

Brianna frowned as her eyes grew accustomed to the dwelling's dim interior and she saw a woman kneeling beside the firepit, a baby nuzzling at her breast.

"Ishna Wi, this is Soft Wind," Shunkaha said by way of introduction. "Soft Wind, this is my woman."

The two women exchanged curious glances. Soft Wind felt a rush of jealousy for the woman of Shunkaha Luta. He had not mentioned the fact that he had a woman. Secretly, she had hoped to be his wife. She needed a man in her lodge; her son needed a father.

Brianna offered Soft Wind a thin smile. Who was this woman? Why had Shunkaha come to her lodge?

Shunkaha Luta's gaze moved from the face of one woman to the other. He would have to have been dead not to sense the animosity between them, and he realized he had made a grave mistake in bringing Brianna to Soft Wind's lodge.

"Sit," Soft Wind invited after an awkward pause. Her gesture included Brianna, but her eyes were for Shunkaha alone.

"Perhaps we should find other lodgings," Shunkaha remarked.

"No," Soft Wind said quickly. "You are welcome in my lodge." She spared a glance for Brianna. "Both of you," she added grudgingly.

Shunkaha Luta smiled at Soft Wind. It would have been rude to decline her invitation, and he could not be rude to her. She had cared for him and fed him. The least he could do was accept her hospitality until he could manage a lodge of his own. Until then, he would hunt for Soft Wind so that she would have food and hides to see her through the coming winter.

Life in Soft Wind's lodge was strained, to say the least.

Brianna felt ill at ease living in another woman's home. Ill at ease and in the way. Soft Wind refused to let Brianna help with the chores, insisting that Brianna was a guest, yet making Brianna feel that she was not a guest at all, but an unwelcome intruder. She did not miss the way Soft Wind's eyes lingered on Shunkaha's face, the many excuses she found to touch him. Shunkaha advised Brianna to make the best of it. They would not have to share Soft Wind's lodge forever, he assured her. It was only natural that he should want to stay, Brianna thought irritably. Soft Wind waited on him hand and foot, making certain there was food when he was hungry, that his pipe was ready when he wished to smoke, that he had the softest robes for his bed, the best place beside the fire. She praised his hunting skills when he brought home a deer, listened with rapt attention whenever he spoke. But worst of all was the fact that Brianna never saw Shunkaha alone. It was Soft Wind's lodge, and she was always there.

Things came to a head one night in late August. The men had returned from a successful hunt and the Lakota had a feast to celebrate. Brianna was fascinated by the singing and dancing that went on far into the night. She watched as warriors strutted in the center of the circle, recounting the thrill of the hunt, the excitement of the kill. They told of other hunts as well, of battles fought and won, of coup counted in battle, of scalps taken and hard-fought victories, of Black Kettle and White Antelope and Custer and Crazy Horse, of treachery and deceit.

And then came the time for social dancing. Some dances were for married couples only, some for the maidens and unmarried warriors. Shunkaha asked Brianna if she would like to join the dance, but she declined, preferring to remain in the shadows.

She was about to offer Shunkaha something to eat when Soft Wind tapped him on the shoulder, inviting him to dance. Shunkaha glanced at Brianna, shrugged as if it were a matter of no consequence before rising to his feet and following Soft Wind to the dance circle.

For a moment, Brianna sat where she was, staring at her husband as he danced with another woman. A beautiful woman. A woman who made no secret of the fact that she found Shunkaha desirable. A sharp stab of jealousy such as she had never known pierced Brianna's heart. They looked well together, with the firelight throwing shadows across their copper-hued faces and the glow of the fire highlighting their long black hair. Soft Wind spoke to Shunkaha and he laughed softly, his teeth very white against his swarthy skin. He was handsome, so handsome, and the Lakota woman was so beautiful. Was he regretting his decision to bring Brianna here? Was he wishing that he and Soft Wind could sneak off to her lodge to be alone?

The dance ended, and when Shunkaha started back toward Brianna, Soft Wind took hold of his arm and led him into the shadows.

Brianna remained where she was, as though rooted to the spot, her mind in turmoil, her heart filled with a sense of rage and betrayal.

Almost before she realized what she was doing, she stood up and followed them, her footsteps as light as a feather floating across the sky. She came to an abrupt halt as she saw Shunkaha and Soft Wind silhouetted in the velvet darkness of the night. They were standing very close. Shunkaha was leaning against a tree and Soft Wind was gazing into his eyes.

"I would make you a good wife," Soft Wind was saying, her voice low and soft, like silk ruffled by a summer breeze. "I know we would be good together."

Shunkaha started to speak, but Soft Wind placed her hand over his mouth. "I would not mind being a second wife," she assured him as she placed her free hand on his chest. "I could give you sons. Many sons." She thrust her hips forward provocatively, brushing against his manhood. "Lakota sons."

Brianna stared at the two of them for a long moment, her heart shattering within her breast, and then she stepped out of the shadows.

"You can be his first wife," she said curtly, her voice as cold as ice. "I am going back to my own people."

She did not wait to see what effect her words had on Shunkaha. Turning on her heel, she fled into the sheltering darkness, her eyes burning with tears, her heart churning with pain and despair.

She ran through the night with no destination in mind, knowing only that she had to get as far away from Soft Wind and Shunkaha Luta as possible. She ran until she was breathless, her lungs filled with fire, her legs like rubber, and then she sank down on the ground, her hand pressed to her side.

She had thought herself a woman grown, capable of handling her emotions, until she met Soft Wind. The Lakota woman was beautiful, mature, serene. She shared a common background with Shunkaha Luta, understood him in ways Brianna never would. She had often heard them reminiscing about the past, recalling people and places Brianna had never heard of. Soft Wind and Shunkaha. They had the same blood, the same heritage, the same customs and beliefs.

She heard nothing to indicate he had followed her. One minute she was alone, and the next he was kneeling beside her.

"Ishna Wi."

"Go away."

"Let me explain."

"There's nothing to explain."

"No?"

"No. Soft Wind loves you and you obviously care for her."
Brianna shrugged. "I hope you'll be very happy together."

Shunkaha Luta uttered a wordless sound of disgust. "You speak foolishness."

"Do I? I heard what she said. She practically begged you to marry her."

"But I did not accept."

"Why not?" Brianna flung the words at him, wishing she could hurt him as she had been hurt. "She's crazy about you. I saw the way she looked at you tonight. The way she looks at you every night. I've seen how she caters to your every wish, how she smiles at you. Oh, just go to her and leave me alone!"

"Ishna Wi, look at me."

"No."

He did not ask again. Instead, he cupped her chin in the palm of his hand and gently forced her to face him. "You have no reason to be jealous of Soft Wind."

"I'm not jealous," Brianna retorted, but she was lying and they both knew it.

"If I tell you there is no reason for your jealousy, will you not believe me?"

"No."

"Why not?"

"Because she's so beautiful. And because she's Indian, like you. You have so much more in common with her than with me . . ." Suddenly all her fears and unhappiness erupted in a flood of tears. "Oh, Shunkaha," she sobbed, "I'm so afraid of losing you."

"Do not be afraid, *le mita chante*. You have nothing to fear."

"I can't help it. Tell me the truth. Wouldn't you rather have a Lakota woman for your wife, for the mother of your children?" She lowered her eyes to the ground. "She said she would give you sons. Lakota sons."

Shunkaha stroked her hair, understanding only a little the jealousy that ate at her, the insecurity that unleashed a fresh flow of tears.

Again he lifted her chin, his eyes meeting hers, holding her gaze captive. "I want only you, Golden Hair. Only you."

"Truly?"

"Truly." With great tenderness, he took her in his arms and kissed her, and the passion between them bloomed like flowers in the spring. Their lips met hungrily, and Brianna pressed herself against Shunkaha, lifting his hands to her breasts, groaning with pleasure as his fingers kneaded her soft flesh.

"Ishna Wi," Shunkaha chided gently. "We have all night."

"I can't wait," she answered shamelessly. "Don't make me wait. It's been so long."

Shunkaha grinned into the darkness as her hands crept over his body, exploring between his thighs. His response was immediate, and he murmured, "You will not have to wait long," as he lifted her skirt and buried himself in her soft womanly warmth, their bodies fitting together perfectly, like a hand in a glove.

He made love to her all night long, telling her with his hands and lips and each gentle caress that she was his woman, the only woman in his life. And with his lips on hers and his hands working their sweet magic, how could she doubt him?

Brianna's cheeks turned bright pink as they entered Soft Wind's lodge the following morning, but she did not look away. Instead, she held her head high and met the Indian woman's curious gaze with what she hoped was a look of mature self-assurance.

Entering the lodge behind Brianna, Shunkaha Luta placed his arm around her shoulders and gave her a squeeze.

"It is time we had our own lodge," Shunkaha told Soft

Wind. "We are grateful for your hospitality, but we need a place where we can be alone." Shunkaha grinned. "Winter is coming, and we cannot spend all our nights in the woods." Soft Wind nodded stiffly. "I understand."

"I will continue to provide you with meat," Shunkaha said. "And protection."

"I am grateful."

Brianna was smiling when they left Soft Wind's lodge. At last, she would have Shunkaha Luta all to herself. She would cook for him and care for him and spoil him in ways Soft Wind had never thought of.

Shunkaha spent the rest of the day gathering hides from members of the tribe, promising meat and favors in exchange. It took twenty hides to make a tipi, and when they had the number required, Soft Wind showed Brianna how to sew them together. The other women of the tribe came to help, laughing and talking as they sat in a large circle. Brianna was glad for their help. Sewing twenty hides together was a prodigious task, one that would have taken her many days to accomplish.

Shunkaha and a dozen men spent most of the day felling trees for lodge poles, stripping away the branches and bark, and by nightfall the lodge was complete.

The interior of the tipi was bare save for their sleeping robes and few personal possessions, and lacked the little touches that had made their first lodge homey and comfortable. Still, Brianna felt a sense of ownership as she looked around. The lodge and all its belongings belonged to her. A man owned only his clothing and weapons.

Shunkaha Luta entered the lodge, his eyes lighting with desire as they came to rest on Brianna's face.

"Welcome home," Brianna murmured, and walked into his arms, her lips parting to receive his kiss, her eyelids fluttering down as his arms closed around her. For now, she needed nothing else.

* * *

The next day, Shunkaha went on a raid with several other warriors and returned with a good supply of blankets, cooking utensils, hides and horses. And now, by Indian standards, they were wealthy, for they had a place to live, clothes to wear, horses to trade, and food to eat. Indeed, life *was* good.

In mid-September, however, a weary Indian known as Buffalo Horn rode into the village with bad news. Earlier that month Captain Anson Miles and one hundred and fifty handpicked troops had struck Buffalo Horn's village near Slim Buttes, killing a few Indians and scattering the rest. The Lakota murmured among themselves. Slim Buttes was the first act of retaliation after the Little Big Horn, but it would not be the last. "Three Stars" was campaigning near Goose Creek; Terry and Gibbon were moving north of the Yellowstone. A band of about thirty Cheyenne had been ambushed by four hundred troops of General Merritt's Fifth Cavalry above the Red Cloud Agency.

Buffalo Horn stayed in the village only long enough to eat and obtain a fresh horse, and then he rode on to warn the other tribes that the soldiers did not intend to let Yellow Hair's death go unavenged.

As late summer gave way to fall, Brianna began to suspect that she was pregnant, and when she began to be ill in the morning, she was certain of it.

Shunkaha Luta was exultant at the prospect of being a father. He took Brianna in his arms and kissed her with much tenderness when she told him the news.

Brianna was also thrilled with the idea of having a child, but as the days passed and her nausea showed no signs of decreasing, she began to be discouraged. Would she spend the rest of her pregnancy vomiting every time she smelled roasting meat or saw a slice of raw venison?

Shunkaha was sympathetic and supportive. He knew that women were often ill at the beginning of a pregnancy; his mother had experienced the sickness in the morning when she carried Tasina. Still, it was hard to sit by Brianna, to see her retching uncontrollably, and know there was nothing he could do to ease her discomfort. The fact that she never complained only made it harder for him to bear.

He curtailed his activities with the other men to stay at her side, telling her often that he loved her, that she was beautiful. He helped her with the chores even though it was considered unmanly for a warrior to gather wood or draw water from the river. He told her stories of his people, hoping to take her mind from the nausea that plagued her.

It was on a cool morning in mid-October that he took her away from the village, hoping a change of scene and a few hours away from the ever-present smell of roasting meat would help her to feel better. They walked deep into the forest until they reached a small crystal pool, and there, in a clearing beneath a sun-dappled willow, he took her in his arms and held her close, his hand lightly stroking her hair, his lips dropping butterfly kisses on her face.

Brianna sighed as she rested her head on Shunkaha's chest. It was pretty in the forest. The trees were dressed in leaves of brilliant orange and red, the grass was soft, the air was sweet and clean. The village, with all its noise and confusion and smells, seemed far away.

She glanced up, her eyes lingering on Shunkaha's face. What a wonderful man he was, so thoughtful, so kind. How could anyone think of him as a savage?

Her heart fluttered with eager anticipation as he lowered his head and kissed her. His mouth was soft and warm, demanding nothing in return, wanting only to give her pleasure, to reassure her of his love. She closed her eyes, basking in his touch, in the sweet familiar warmth that spread through her limbs as his lips moved over hers.

She opened her mouth as his tongue teased her lips, shuddering as her stomach knotted with pleasure. Her hand delved inside his shirt to lie against his chest. She could feel his heart beating beneath her palm, felt it begin to beat faster as she stroked his chest, her hand slowly sliding downward.

"Ishna Wi." He murmured her name as his arm tightened around her. "Do you know what you are doing, *le mita chante?*"

"Oh, yes," she replied, suddenly breathless. "Do you mind?"

"Should we?"

She opened her eyes to find him gazing down at her, a troubled expression on his face. "Don't you want to?"

"That is a foolish question and you know it," Shunkaha said. "But I do not wish to hurt you, or the child."

"It will be all right," Brianna assured him, and felt her whole body tremble in anticipation as he began to undress her, his mouth trailing kisses on her shoulders and breasts as he removed her dress, his hands sliding over her waist and down her thighs.

Soon they were lying side by side in the soft green grass. Brianna uttered a little gasp of surprise as Shunkaha entered her and then rolled over, carrying her with him, so that she was straddling his thighs.

He grinned at her startled expression, laughed softly as she moaned with pleasure when he moved deep within her.

"I do not want to hurt the baby," he explained, then sucked in a deep breath as she bent toward him, her breasts stroking his chest.

"I appreciate your concern," Brianna murmured, scarcely able to breathe for the sensations rocketing through her.

"Any time," Shunkaha said, his voice husky, and then there was no need for talk as he began the slow rhythm that carried them both over the rainbow and into paradise.

Brianna frowned in her sleep, the sound of gunfire intruding in her dreams and bringing her to quick awareness. She sat up, her eyes darting about until she saw Shunkaha Luta standing behind her, his face a mask of fearful anger.

"What is it?" Brianna asked, scrambling to her feet.

"Soldiers," Shunkaha answered curtly. "They are attacking the village." He fixed Brianna with a hard stare. "Stay here. Do not move from this place until I return."

"Where are you going?"

"To fight."

"With what? You have no weapons." She grabbed his arm as he started to leave. "Shunkaha, don't go! Don't leave me here alone. Think of the baby. What if the soldiers come here?"

"They will not harm you, Ishna Wi," he said quietly. "You are one of them."

His words cut across her heart like a knife. "Please," she begged, her voice hoarse with pain and fear. "Please don't leave me."

Shunkaha Luta regarded her quietly for a long moment, his mind in turmoil. He had no weapon with which to fight; indeed, from the sounds of the battle, it seemed the fighting was almost over. And while the soldiers would not kill Brianna, they might rape her. Men who had just engaged in a struggle for life and death often did things they regretted later, acts of violence they would be deeply ashamed of when their blood had cooled and sanity returned. Could he live with himself if he left her here, alone and unprotected, and she came to harm? Could he live with himself if he did not try to help his people?

There was a quick burst of rifle fire, and then an ominous stillness settled over the land.

"It is finished," Shunkaha said heavily. He did not look at Brianna. For the next two hours, he stood as one turned to stone, his eyes fixed in the direction of the village, his face a mask of impotent rage and pain.

Brianna did not approach him. Instead, she went to the pool and bathed, then slipped into her dress and sat on the ground behind her husband, her hands folded in her lap, while silent tears tracked her cheeks.

Occasional sounds drifted their way: a burst of obscene laughter, the sound of a single gunshot, an animal's squeal of pain, a woman's frightened scream.

After what seemed an eternity, Shunkaha Luta turned to face her. "I am going to the village," he said flatly. "Wait here."

Brianna nodded, not daring to argue.

Alone, she began to shiver despite the warmth of the day. In her heart, she knew the Lakota had lost their fight; that the men and women she had worked with and laughed with lay dead, brutally slain because their skin was red, because they had refused to surrender to the will of the white man. Because they had killed Custer. Would Shunkaha Luta hate her now? Would this latest cruelty inflicted on his people by those of her race turn him against her? Could she blame him if it did?

The hours dragged by. The sun hid its face behind the distant mountains, and a keening wind blew through the trees, rustling the leaves and stirring the dust. The shadows grew long and Brianna was beginning to wonder if Shunkaha had abandoned her when she saw him striding toward her. He was leading two horses and a pack mule heavily laden with robes and parfleches.

Brianna rose to her feet, her eyes searching his.

"They are dead," Shunkaha said, his voice hard and flat. "All of them."

"Soft Wind?"

"Yes."

"I'm sorry," Brianna said inadequately. "So sorry."

Shunkaha Luta nodded, the bile rising in his throat as he recalled the carnage that had been spread before him when he reached the village. The bodies of his people had been scattered on the ground. Some had been mutilated, others had been clumsily scalped. The soldiers had killed them all: men, women, and children. He had never seen such butchery.

He willed the grotesque images from his mind, swallowed the vomit that rose in his throat. He would not think of it now.

Wordlessly, he lifted Brianna onto the back of one of the horses. Hate and revenge would have to wait. For now, he had to care for Brianna, find a safe place for them to stay until she gave birth to their child.

Swinging aboard his own mount, he took up the reins of the pack mule and headed south, toward the Yellowstone.

Chapter Fifteen

Adam Trent loosed a long weary sigh as he stepped from his horse. Hard to believe he had been gone for almost three months, but then he had never dreamed that tracking the Morrow gang would prove to be such a monumental task. It had taken almost eight weeks to track the gang. And that had been the easy part. They had caught the Morrow gang out in the open and there had been a brief, bloody battle. Trent had lost four good men; Vince Morrow had lost six; the others had surrendered. But Vince Morrow had managed to escape. Trent had sent his deputies back to town with the captured outlaws while he trailed Morrow. He found his man in a two-bit saloon in Deadwood. Trent had relieved Morrow of his Colt, but Morrow had pulled a hideaway gun and Trent had killed him. And now, at last, he was home again. Some of his weariness left him as he contemplated a hot bath, a cold drink, and an evening with Brianna.

He had thought of her constantly on the long ride back to Bismarck, remembering her smile, the way she laughed, the way the sun caressed her hair.

Leaving his trail-weary mount at Grodin's Livery Barn, he walked down Main Street toward the sheriff's office to write his report. It took the better part of an hour to get it all down on paper.

Trent leaned back in his chair. Two of the deputies who had been killed had wives who would have to be visited even though they had already been notified of their husbands' deaths. It was the worst part of his job.

Muttering an oath, he signed his name to the report, then

went to his room at Ida Mae's Boardinghouse to get cleaned up. Forty minutes later, dressed in clean denim pants and a white shirt, he went to visit the widows. It was a job that never got easier, no matter how often he did it.

He was feeling rotten an hour later when he headed for the saloon. Lou McCraney's wife seemed to be handling her loss well, but Sam Whitney's wife had gone into hysterics at the mention of her husband's name and it had taken a quarter of an hour just to calm her down.

Trent swallowed the first glass of whiskey in a single gulp, lingered over a second one. Fingering his badge, he wondered again if it wasn't time to call it quits. It was a rough life, being a lawman, laying your life on the line day after day. Spending weeks away from home chasing outlaws, wrestling drunks, writing endless reports, upholding the law. A hard job, he mused, and usually a thankless one at that.

He thought of Lou McCraney's wife, six months pregnant with her third child. Why was it always the married men who got killed? Men with families.

He tossed off his drink and left the saloon, eager to see Brianna, needing to hear her voice, see her smile. It was a moment he had been looking forward to all day.

He was whistling softly when he entered the hotel. He took the steps two at a time, felt his heart beat fast as he knocked at her door. And then knocked again. He frowned when there was no answer.

Returning to the lobby, he stopped at the desk and asked the clerk if he knew where Miss Beaudine had gone.

"She checked out almost two months ago," the clerk said, checking the register.

"Checked out? Did she say where she was going?"

"Not as I recall." The clerk studied the worried expression on the sheriff's face, then snapped his fingers. "I believe she took the stage east," he drawled. "Toward Winslow."

"Thanks, Abe," Trent murmured. Disappointed, he left the hotel and made his way to the sheriff's office. So, he mused, she had gone home. He swore under his breath, hurt more than he cared to admit because she had left town without a word.

He was thumbing through a sheaf of wanteds an hour later when his deputy, Larry Cable, sauntered in.

"Hi, Sheriff," Larry said cheerfully. "Welcome home."

"Thanks," Trent replied listlessly. "Anything exciting happen while I was gone?"

"Hap Wilson broke his leg rescuing Janie's cat from a tree," Cable said, chuckling. "Oh, and one of Overland's coaches was attacked by Injuns. I wish the Army would round up those damned savages once and for all."

Adam Trent felt the short hair rise along the back of his neck. "Which coach was it?"

"I don't remember. Happened two, three weeks after you left town."

"Did anyone go looking for the stage?"

"Overland sent a man out. They found the bodies of the driver and the guard."

"No passengers?"

Larry Cable shook his head.

Trent thrust the wanted posters into Cable's hands. "Finish these. I'll be back in a few minutes."

It took twenty-four hours for the answer to his wire to arrive. It was the longest twenty-four hours of his life. He knew, deep down he knew even before he read it, what the answer would be. Brianna had never arrived in Winslow.

Twenty minutes later he was riding out of town following Overland's eastbound route.

He was on a fool's errand, and he knew it, but he had to see for himself. He found the burnt-out shell of the coach three days later. Sifting through the charred remains, he found several arrows which he identified as Sioux, but nothing else. Time and the elements had erased whatever tracks the Indians had left.

Swinging aboard his horse, he rode in ever-widening circles around the coach, hoping against hope that he might find some clue as to Brianna's fate.

An hour later, he came upon a shallow stream some fifteen miles from the coach. And there, wedged between two moss-covered rocks, he found what remained of two bodies. The tattered remnants of their clothing identified them as male.

Trent cursed under his breath. The man Overland had sent out must not have looked very hard or very long, he thought angrily. Probably took a quick glance at what was left of the coach and hightailed it back to town. And who the hell could blame him?

He stared at the remains, his eyes thoughtful. How had these men managed to escape from the stage? Dismounting, he took a closer look at the arrow embedded in the ribcage of one of the men. The arrow was Cheyenne.

Trent frowned. The Indians who had attacked the coach had been Sioux. He puzzled over the mystery as he dug a shallow grave and buried the bodies, marking the grave with a pile of rocks in case the families of the deceased wanted to retrieve the remains for a proper burial.

Remounting his horse, he sat staring into the distance. Where was Brianna? If he kept riding, would he find her body decaying on the prairie, or had the Indians taken her prisoner? Her image played across his mind: huge blue eyes, long blond hair, the smile of an angel. And then he thought of her living as a slave in some savage's lodge and he knew he couldn't go back without at least trying to find her.

The next two days were long. The weather was cold, the wind blew in icy gusts, and dark clouds gathered over the face of the land.

Trent was about to give up and turn for home when he

came across the Lakota village. His horse snorted and rolled its eyes as they approached the burned village. The smell of death was heavy in the air. Several large black vultures squawked noisily and took to the air at his approach.

The lawman felt his stomach churn as he dismounted and picked his way through the carnage. Predators and scavengers had been at the bodies; most were picked almost clean. He felt his anger rise as he passed several small skeletons. There was no reason to make war on women and children, he thought bitterly. Wasn't it enough that the Indians and the white men were trying to kill each other off without attacking harmless infants?

He walked through the entire camp, poked into every lodge that had not been totally destroyed, hoping to find some clue that Brianna had been there and escaped, but he found nothing, only ashes and bodies and bits of burned cloth.

Utterly discouraged, he swung aboard his horse and rode away from the village, eager to put some distance between himself and whatever ghosts lingered in the Indian camp.

There was nothing to do now but go back to town, he thought wearily. Any Indians who might have survived would be long gone, and Brianna with them if she still lived. If she had ever been at this village.

He swung aboard his horse, shivering as a light rain began to fall. He took one last look at the destroyed village, refusing to believe that Brianna had been killed.

She was alive and somehow, someday, he would find her again.

Chapter Sixteen

It was a country of ravines, buttes, canyons, and valleys, a wild untamed land that few white men had ever seen. White-throated swifts, rock wrens, and cliff swallows nested on the face of high white cliffs. Badgers, coyotes, wolves, elk, bear, and deer roamed the wooded canyons. There were prairie dogs and snakes, jackrabbits and cottontails, water, graze for the horses.

Brianna had never felt so alone, yet the loneliness had nothing to do with the lack of people in the area, but was born of the deep gulf that stretched between herself and Shunkaha Luta. He had withdrawn into himself, shutting her out. He rarely spoke, and when he looked at her, she saw only bitterness in his eyes, a haunting bitterness and a deep sadness. She knew he felt guilty because he was alive, because he had not been in the village when the soldiers had attacked, because he had not died in battle alongside his people.

He spent long hours away from her. Hunting, he said. And he always came back with meat. But she knew he was avoiding her. Several times she tried to speak to him, tried to persuade him to tell her what he was feeling, to tell her what she could do to help. But he refused to answer her.

The first few weeks slid by, and although Brianna was sick at heart over the breach between them, she was too busy to dwell on it. Shunkaha had salvaged a lodge and it took Brianna several days to repair it and make it livable. There was food to prepare, wood and water to gather, herbs and vegetables to dig. She tanned the hides Shunkaha brought her and spent long hours fashioning warm garments for the two of them. It seemed to Brianna that they had spent most of their life together setting up housekeeping only to have their efforts destroyed by one calamity or another.

Life soon settled into a routine of sorts. They had a snug lodge, clothes to last through the coming winter, a good supply of fresh meat, jerky, and *wasna*, or pemmican.

And now, with the hardest portion of setting up a new camp behind them, the rift between them loomed larger than ever. Shunkaha had not touched her since the Lakota village was destroyed, and she longed to be held in his arms, to feel the security of his strength, to hear his voice whispering that he loved her. But he did not seek her bed, and she lacked the courage to cross the distance between them.

Shunkaha Luta stirred restlessly, unable to sleep for the conflicting emotions that warred within him. He glanced at Brianna sleeping peacefully across the fire, and then slipped out of his blankets and left the lodge.

Outside, the night was cool and quiet. A million stars twinkled above, a quarter moon hung low in the midnight sky. Slowly, he began to walk along the narrow winding stream that watered the valley. He was treating Brianna unfairly, and he knew it. It was not her fault that his people were being slowly and methodically slaughtered or banished to the living hell of life on a reservation. It was not her fault the soldiers had attacked the village. It was not her fault that she was white, nor would he wish her to be anything but what she was. And yet . . . and yet some of his hatred for the *wasicu* had spilled over onto her. He had walked through the village, seen the carnage wrought by the soldiers, seen the mutilated bodies of men he had fought alongside, women he had spoken with, children whose laughter he had shared, and it had been as though his heart had turned to stone. *It is enough*, his soul had cried in anguish. *It is enough*.

Heavy-hearted, he had covered the bodies with blankets and hides, placing family members together, knowing that he, too, should have been lying there with the bodies of his people. He had lingered beside Soft Wind's corpse, remembering the night she had come to him, offering herself to him, needing his touch. She had come to him, willing and eager to please, and he had refused her. What would it have hurt, he wondered bitterly, if he had made love to her?

Love . . . it was a cruel and painful thing. Better not to love at all. He thought of his mother and father, his precious sister, Soft Wind—all dead. And each death had cut like a knife, gouging out a piece of his heart, a piece of his soul. He thought of Brianna, growing big with his child, and he knew if he lost her it would be more than he could bear. And so he had shut her out of his heart, refusing to touch her, refusing to speak to her unless it was absolutely necessary.

But his body betrayed him. He might tell himself he no longer loved her, he might pretend to scorn her because she was a white woman, but his body cried out for her touch, for the sweet taste of her kiss, for the comfort of her embrace.

And so he walked, hour after hour, tormented by the needless deaths of his people, by the loss of all those he held dear. Walked until his body was weary and cried out for rest. Only then did he return to his lodge and the blessed forgetfulness of sleep.

Brianna woke early. She had spent a troubled night, her pride warring with her need. Time and again she had started to reach out for Shunkaha, to beg him to tell her what was wrong between them, to plead for his love. If only he would talk to her, perhaps she could help. Perhaps, if he spoke of the pain he was feeling, it would be easier to bear.

She slid a glance at Shunkaha's back and saw that he was still asleep. Didn't he know she needed him, needed the strength of his arms now more than ever? She was carrying his child, and while the thought of having Shunkaha's baby filled her with delight, it was also frightening. She knew nothing of childbirth, nothing of caring for an infant. What if she did something wrong and inadvertently caused the child harm? She needed reassurance, she needed to know he still cared.

With a sigh, she left her bed and stepped out of the lodge. Perhaps a long walk would help her feel better. Wrapping her arms around her expanding girth, she followed the path of the stream, lost in thought. Things could not go on like this indefinitely. She would have to confront Shunkaha, force him to speak with her. And if he refused, then she would have to leave him.

She was about to turn back for home when a low growl sounded from behind a tangled clump of brush. Brianna took a step backward as a big black bear reared up on its hind legs, its pointed black snout sniffing the air.

Brianna felt herself go cold with fear as she began to back away. The movement excited the bear and it dropped down on all fours and pushed its way through the brush, lumbering toward her, its thick pink tongue lolling out the side of its mouth.

"Oh, God," Brianna murmured. "No, please, no."

She continued to back away, unable to take her eyes from the bear. It was so big. Its eyes were small and black, its teeth were yellow, its claws long enough, sharp enough, to tear her to shreds.

She was about to turn and run for her life when Shunkaha Luta's voice sounded from her left. "Do not move," he said quietly, and she obeyed without hesitation, though her heart was pounding like a runaway locomotive.

The bear continued toward Brianna, its rank breath carried to her by the faint breeze. She closed her eyes, her whole body rigid with fear.

The sound of a gunshot made her jump, and when she

opened her eyes, the bear lay dead at her feet, killed by a single well-placed shot.

Brianna felt the strength drain from her limbs as she stared at the bear, knew she would have fallen if Shunkaha had not stepped forward and slipped his arm around her waist.

"Fool," he scolded. "What were you doing so far from camp?" His fear had turned to anger now that she was safe. He shook her once, and then drew her close. "Why did you leave without waking me?"

"I needed some time alone," Brianna said. She began to shiver as she thought of what would have happened if Shunkaha had not come looking for her when he did.

"Shunkaha," she said softly. "Please don't hate me any more."

The hard shell around Shunkaha Luta's heart cracked as he buried his face in her hair. Dropping his rifle, he placed his hands on either side of her face and gazed deep into her eyes, felt the sweet pain of loving her mushroom in his heart.

"I do not hate you, le mita chante," he said fervently. "I could never hate you."

"But you've been so far away from me," Brianna said in bewilderment. "Why? Why have you shut me out now, when I need you so much?"

"I have been punishing myself for being alive," Shunkaha admitted. "If I had not been with you that morning, I would have died with the others. But I did not die."

"Shunkaha . . ."

He placed a hand over her mouth, stifling her words. "For a while I hated you because you were white. And when I stopped hating you, I knew I would not want to live if you were taken from me, and so I tried to stop loving you." He smiled ruefully. "Only those you love can hurt you, and I did not want to be hurt again."

He glanced at the bear, and then his eyes moved to Brianna's face. "You might have been killed," he said thickly, "and it would have been my fault for driving you away. If you had been killed, I would never have forgiven myself for all the time I wasted trying not to love you when I might have spent that time holding you in my arms." He lifted his hand, gently stroking her cheek with his fingertips, his dark eyes welling with love. "Forgive me, Ishna Wi. I have behaved badly."

Two fat tears rolled down Brianna's cheeks. Turning her head, she kissed the palm of his hand. "There's nothing to forgive," she murmured. "Only promise that you won't shut me out again. I can bear anything but your indifference."

Shunkaha Luta smiled as he drew her body against his and let her feel the evidence of his desire. "I was never indifferent toward you, Golden Hair," he assured her.

Brianna's arms slid around his neck as his head bent toward hers. Her eyelids fluttered down as he kissed her, the touch of his lips filling her with wonder and desire and a sense of coming home. At last, she was back where she belonged.

The days grew shorter, the nights longer and colder. Great storms made war in the heavens, and Brianna huddled in Shunkaha's arms, frightened by the rolling crashes of thunder that shook the earth, and by the jagged bolts of lightning that slashed through the clouds.

Winter had come with a vengeance. It rained for days on end, making it virtually impossible to leave the lodge. A great depression settled over Brianna as one storm followed another. She tried to keep occupied by sewing sacques and gowns for the baby, but she was haunted by a recurring nightmare in which her baby was born dead and she herself lay gasping for breath, calling for a doctor who would not come. Morbid thoughts seemed to hover around her continually, and she could not shake them off.

Shunkaha Luta was troubled by her lethargy, by the dark

shadows under her eyes. She rarely smiled now, and never laughed. When he asked her what was wrong, she refused to answer. Daily, she seemed to grow thinner, so that her round belly seemed even larger than it was.

It was on a cold and snowy night that she woke in tears, her nightmares so real that she was certain her child had been born, and born dead.

Shunkaha woke at her first cry, his eyes dark with concern as he gathered Brianna, sobbing, into his arms. "Ishna Wi, tell me what is troubling you," he begged. "I cannot help you if I do not know what is wrong."

Brianna shook her head. She couldn't tell him she was a coward, couldn't bear to see the disgust in his eyes when she told him she was afraid of something as simple and ordinary as childbirth. And how could she tell him about her nightmares? Surely he would think she was just being silly. But they were so real, so terrifyingly real.

"Do you not trust me, *le mita chante?*" Shunkaha queried softly.

"Of course I trust you," Brianna assured him.

"Then you must trust me to help you. It grieves my soul to see you this way."

With a sigh, Brianna buried her face in his shoulder. "I'm afraid," she whispered. "Afraid to have the baby. Afraid it will be born dead."

"Do not all women have such fears as their time draws near?"

"I don't know," Brianna said miserably. "I only know that I'm frightened. I keep having the same nightmare over and over again. I see our child's face so clearly. It's a boy, and he's so beautiful, so perfect. But he doesn't breathe, Shunkaha. He doesn't breathe!"

A cold chill slithered down Shunkaha's spine. His people believed in dreams, in visions, in spiritual manifestations.

Were Brianna's nightmares simply a normal part of her pregnancy, or was it a warning from *Wakan Tanka*?

"Do not weep, little one," he said softly. He cradled her in his arms and rocked her gently, his hand stroking her hair. "Do not weep. We have time before the child is born. I will take you home when the snow melts."

Brianna looked up at him, frowning. "Home?"

"Back to your aunt. She is a woman. She will care for you when the time comes."

"No! I will not leave you."

"It is for the best."

Brianna shook her head. "I won't go unless you stay with me."

"I cannot. Have you forgotten that the whites are hunting me?"

"Then I'm not going," Brianna stated firmly. "I want to be with you when the baby comes."

Shunkaha Luta shook his head. "I will take you home."

"Please don't leave me."

Shunkaha smiled as he placed his hand over her belly. "I will never leave you, little one. I will stay close by, and after the child is born, I will come and take you away."

Brianna remained thoughtful for a long while. She did not want to be separated from Shunkaha, not even for a day, but the thought of going home to have her baby eased her troubled mind. She would not be so afraid if there was a woman to help her. And there would be a doctor nearby in case anything went wrong. *Yes*, she thought, her spirits lifting, *we'll go home.*

"I don't mean to be so much trouble," Brianna murmured. She gazed up at him, her hand resting on his shoulder.

"You are no trouble," Shunkaha replied, lightly caressing her cheek. "You give me nothing but happiness."

"I want to give you a son," Brianna said. "A strong, healthy son."

"I would like that," Shunkaha said. "But a daughter would be welcome too." He bent his head and kissed her tenderly. "Sleep now, little one. Dream only happy dreams."

"I love you," Brianna murmured. And placing her head in his lap, she fell asleep.

But for Shunkaha Luta there was to be no sleep that night. He spent the long hours until dawn studying the face of the woman he loved, silently beseeching *Wakan Tanka* to bless Brianna and their unborn child with health and strength. He did not blame Brianna for being afraid. She was still young for her years, unaccustomed to living off the land.

He rose with the dawn and left the shelter of their lodge. Outside, the world was covered with a fresh blanket of white; overhead, the sky was a clear vibrant blue.

He stood quiet for a long moment; then, lifting his arms toward heaven, he began to pray.

"*Wakan Tanka,* whose voice I heard in the winds, whose breath gives life to our world, hear me. I come to You as one of Your many sons. I am small and weak. I need Your strength. I need Your wisdom. May I walk always in beauty. May my eyes ever behold the red and purple sunset. Make my hands respect the things that You have made, and make my ears sharp, that I may hear Your voice. Make me wise so that I may know the things You have taught Your children, the lessons You have hidden in every rock and leaf. Make me strong, not to be superior to my brothers, but to be able to fight my greatest enemy, myself. Make me ever ready to come to You with straight eyes, so that when life fades as the fading sunset, my spirit will come to You without shame. Bless my woman, and my unborn child, that they may know only beauty and the good things of life."

Lifting his eyes, he gazed into the depths of the sky, his soul reaching out to the Great Spirit for guidance, and it came into his heart that taking Brianna home was the right thing to do.

His heart was filled with peace when he returned to the lodge.

And for Brianna, there were no more bad dreams.

Chapter Seventeen

Brianna stared at the darkened house, her stomach in knots. She was glad to be home again, glad to be back to civilization, where people lived in houses and there was a doctor nearby.

"They must be asleep," she murmured.

Shunkaha grunted softly. The house was dark, the land quiet.

"Go," he said. "I will wait here until I know you are safely inside."

"I'll miss you," Brianna said. She swallowed the sob building in her throat.

"It will only be for a short time," Shunkaha reminded her. "And I will not be far away." He reined his horse closer to hers and placed his hand on her swollen belly. "Take care of yourself and the little one."

"I will."

He kissed her then, a soft gentle kiss, afraid if he kissed her with any degree of passion, he would never be able to let her go.

"I love you," Brianna said, and reined her horse toward the house.

Shunkaha Luta waited in the shadows, watching. He had been right to bring her here. He was not a midwife. He had no experience with childbirth. Yes, it was better this way.

Brianna had reached the house now. Dismounting, she tried the door, but it was locked. She knocked, and then knocked again, louder, but no one answered.

Shunkaha frowned. Putting his heels to his horse's flanks,

he rode to the barn and opened the door. Inside it was dark. And empty.

He walked to the house and peered in one of the windows, but could see nothing.

"I don't think anyone's home," Brianna said.

"I think they have gone," Shunkaha remarked. "The barn and corrals are empty; there is nothing growing in the garden."

"But they had nowhere else to go," Brianna said, frowning. "They would never leave."

Together they checked the back door and all the windows, but everything was locked up tight. Finally Shunkaha climbed the tree outside Brianna's bedroom and tried the window. It opened with a loud shriek, and he swung a leg over the sill and ducked inside. On silent feet, he padded downstairs and opened the front door.

"There is no one here," he told her.

"Did you look in my uncle's bedroom?"

"No, but the house is empty. Can you not feel it?"

It *did* feel empty, Brianna thought, and a quick tour of the house proved just that. The closets were bare, some of the furniture was missing, and a fine layer of dust covered everything.

"I wonder where they've gone," Brianna mused. She lighted a lamp and looked around again, as though she might find a clue as to her aunt and uncle's whereabouts.

"I will put our horses in the barn," Shunkaha said.

Brianna nodded. "I'll look in the kitchen and see if there's anything to eat."

The cupboards were empty; likewise the pantry. She was standing in the middle of the kitchen, her arms folded over her stomach, when Shunkaha entered the room.

"I couldn't find anything to eat," Brianna said.

"It does not matter."

"What are we going to do?"

Shunkaha Luta shrugged. "What do you want to do?"

"I think we should go into town tomorrow. Margie Croft will know where my aunt and uncle have gone and when they're coming back."

"I cannot go into the white man's town."

"Then I'll go, and you can wait here."

He did not like the idea of her going anywhere alone in her condition, but it was something that had to be done.

"My aunt and uncle took the good silver and the grandfather clock and a few odds and ends, but that's all." Brianna frowned as she sank down in one of the kitchen chairs. "They must be coming back. They wouldn't go off and leave everything else behind. It doesn't make sense."

"You look tired, Ishna Wi."

"I am."

"Come," he said, reaching for her hand. "Let us go to bed now. Tomorrow we will know more and we can decide what to do."

The following morning, Brianna searched through the old trunk in the attic and found a dress that she could alter to fit her. It was cut high in the waist, so it would disguise her expanding girth; the color was flattering even if the style was out of date.

It took most of the morning to alter the dress, and then she bathed and washed her hair. When at last she was dressed and ready to go, she stood before Shunkaha.

"How do I look?"

"Beautiful, as always. How long will you be gone?"

"I don't know. It takes about a half hour to get to town. I should be home before dark. You'll be here when I get back?"

"I will be here."

"I'll miss you," Brianna said, and standing on her tiptoes, she pressed a kiss to his lips. Her horse was waiting outside, and Shunkaha lifted her onto its back.

"Be careful, Ishna Wi."

"I'll be fine. Don't worry."

The ride to town was pleasant. It was good to pass familiar landmarks, to be back home again. The town was much the same as it had been when last she saw it.

Nearing Crofts' General Store, she noticed a new tea shop on the corner and smiled faintly, thinking that the East was getting ever closer.

Margie Croft was sweeping the veranda when Brianna rode up. She stared at the girl, her mouth dropping open in surprise.

"Land sakes, if it isn't Brianna Beaudine!" she exclaimed as Brianna dismounted and looped the reins over the hitchrail. "We thought you had been killed and scalped by savages."

"No," Brianna said, smiling at the older woman. "I'm fine."

"Well, I can see that," Margie Croft remarked, and then grinned. "You always were a pretty little thing. Where've you been all this time, child?"

"In Bismarck," Brianna said airily. There was no need to tell Margie Croft about Shunkaha, or Adam Trent, or anything else that had happened to her since she'd left Winslow.

Margie Croft put her broom aside and took Brianna's hand in hers. "Honey, whatever possessed you to run away like you did? Why, it just about broke your uncle's heart when you left."

"I wanted to see more of the world," Brianna lied.

"Well, honey, he grieved for you something awful."

Brianna doubted the truth of that, but asked, "Where is my uncle? The house is empty."

Margie Croft took a deep breath and released it in a long-drawn-out sigh. "Don't you know, child? Why, he passed away in August, not long after we got word that the stagecoach you'd been riding in had been attacked by Indians."

"Uncle Henry's dead?"

"I'm sorry, child, I thought you knew."

"No. I just got home last night. Where's Aunt Harriett?"

"She went back East immediately after the funeral. Said she couldn't stand to stay another day in this Godforsaken place." Margie Croft draped her arm around Brianna's shoulders and gave her a squeeze. "Come inside, Brianna. I'll fix you a cup of tea."

"Thank you," Brianna murmured. She followed Margie Croft through the store and into the back room.

"Sit down, honey," the older woman said, her voice soft and sympathetic.

Brianna sank down on the sagging couch in the corner. She couldn't believe her uncle was gone. He had been such a strong, robust man.

She accepted a cup of strong tea from Margie Croft and sipped it slowly. "Did my aunt say when she'd be coming back?"

"Oh, she's never coming back," Margie Croft said. "You know she always hated it here. Why, she could hardly wait for your uncle's funeral to be over so she could leave."

A sense of defeat settled over Brianna. She had counted on being able to come home, if only for a short while, and now she had no home. Uncle Henry was dead, and Aunt Harriett had gone back to her beloved East for good.

Brianna finished her tea without tasting it, then stood up. "I'd better go."

Margie Croft stood up and wiped her hands on her apron. "You go see Mort Bradley right away. He's been in a stew ever since your uncle died."

"Mort Bradley?" Brianna frowned. "Why would he want to see me?"

"To settle your uncle's affairs," Margie Croft explained. "Isn't that why you're here?"

"No."

Margie Croft patted Brianna on the back. "Well, you

hurry along now. You can catch him in his office this time of day."

Brianna stared at Mort Bradley, unable to comprehend all that he was saying. Henry Beaudine had left the house and property to her, along with a tidy nest egg.

"There's close to a hundred acres of land," Bradley informed her, checking through some papers. "And a thousand dollars in a savings account over at the Winslow Bank. Now, if you'll just sign here, and here," he said, handing her a quill pen, "and, oh, yes, here, too, I believe that about wraps it up."

Brianna signed her name, her mind reeling. The house was hers, all hers! The land she loved belonged to her, to do with as she pleased. Almost a hundred acres. She could swim in the lake to her heart's content, plant whatever she wished in the garden. She could sit in the parlor now. She could play the piano all day long if it suited her, perhaps even take lessons from old Mrs. McCarthy. She wouldn't have to sleep in the attic. The master bedroom was hers now, and she could paint the walls blue, buy a new spread for the bed, buy a whole new houseful of furniture if she so desired.

She was smiling when she left Mort Bradley's office. She had a home of her own, at last. It was hers, all hers, and no one could take it from her!

She was walking on air as she skipped up the stairs to Crofts' General Store. Humming softly, she purchased salt and sugar and flour, tinned fruit, a side of bacon, needles and thread, soap, towels, two new pillows, a blanket and a blue calico comforter. She picked out material for new kitchen curtains, several yards of gingham and cotton, a few pots and pans, a sack of coffee, and anything else that caught her fancy, including a variety of seeds, and a blue ceramic cat.

Leaving the General Store, she went to Drummond's Livery Barn and hired a rig to carry her supplies home.

Her heart was singing when she reached the outskirts of the ranch. My land, she thought exultantly. My land. She was frowning as she pulled up at the house. The garden she had sweated and slaved over was dry and dead, overrun with weeds and thistles. Untying her horse from the back of the hired hack, she turned it loose in the corral.

She felt Shunkaha's presence behind her even before he spoke. "Is everything all right?"

"Everything's wonderful!" Brianna exclaimed. She threw her arms around Shunkaha's neck and kissed him soundly. "You're looking at a woman of property."

Shunkaha frowned. "I do not understand."

The smile left Brianna's face. "My uncle died last summer. He left me the house and the land and a goodly sum of money. I guess he knew Aunt Harriett wouldn't want it, and he couldn't bear to see it sold to a stranger."

Shunkaha nodded, his expression impassive.

"Don't you understand what that means?" Brianna asked, disappointed in his lack of enthusiasm. "This place is ours. We have a home, a place for our son to grow up. We won't have to wander around like homeless beggars any longer."

"Is that what I am?" Shunkaha mused. "A homeless beggar?"

"I didn't mean that," Brianna said quickly.

"And yet," Shunkaha remarked slowly, "it is what I have become. I have no home. The white man has taken it."

"This is your home," Brianna said, frightened by the look in his eye and the defeated tone of his voice.

Shunkaha glanced around, then shook his head. "The Pa Sapa is my home."

Brianna gazed into Shunkaha's eyes. He was a stranger again, separated from her by customs and beliefs she would never fully understand.

She knew the Indians could not comprehend the idea of owning the earth. But surely, when he thought about it, he would realize how lucky they were. They had a place to live, a place no one could take away from them. It belonged to her; she had a deed in the Winslow bank vault that said so.

Unconsciously, she placed her hand on her stomach. Shunkaha's son rested there, beneath her hand. One day this place would be his.

With a heavy heart, she picked up one of the brown-wrapped parcels and carried it into the house.

After a moment, Shunkaha gathered the rest of the supplies and carried them into the kitchen. He stood in the doorway, watching as Brianna unwrapped her purchases and put them away.

"What can I do?" he asked.

"We need wood," Brianna answered.

Shunkaha Luta smiled bitterly. "I will cut some."

He found an ax in the barn and spent the next hour chopping wood, remembering all too clearly the many hours he had spent felling timber to clear a path for the white man's road.

Stacking the wood beside the house, he thought of Brianna. This was her land now, and he knew she would not want to leave it after their child was born. Like all whites, she felt the need to be rooted to one patch of ground, to spend summer and winter in the same place. Again he wondered how the whites dared to say they owned the earth.

He walked toward the back of the house. Peering in the kitchen window, he saw Brianna bustling about the kitchen. She had whipped up a batch of bread dough and it was rising on the top of the stove while she peeled potatoes. He could hear her singing softly as she worked, saw the pride in her eyes when she looked around the tidy room. They had been there only one day, but the kitchen already reflected her personality. There was a brightly colored cloth on the table, a jar of spring flowers resting on the windowsill; the blue ceramic cat rested on a shelf.

Turning, he left the house and began to run, his strides long and easy, quickly carrying him past the lake and up to the top of the ridge. Coming to a halt, he stared down at the road. It was finished now, and even as he watched, a shiny black carriage passed by, driven by a middle-aged man in a city suit and a black bowler hat.

Shunkaha grinned wryly. Once, he would have attacked the man, lifted his scalp, and taken his horses. He let out a long sigh as he raised his gaze to the distant mountains. Once all this land had belonged to the Lakota. Now it belonged to the whites. To Brianna.

The next few days passed quickly, for there was much to do. Brianna swept the floors, washed the windows and measured them for new curtains, polished the brass candlesticks, scrubbed the cast iron stove, eliminated the lacy cobwebs from the corners. She washed the kitchen walls, waxed the floors, and went through the closets, discarding whatever she deemed useless.

She sewed new curtains for the kitchen windows, went into town and bought a rooster and six hens so they could have fresh eggs and poultry. She also bought a pig, a cow, and a goat.

And then she began to work the garden. At first, Shunkaha refused to help her, declaring that it was woman's work and beneath the dignity of a warrior. He was a hunter, not a farmer. But when he saw how hard she worked uprooting the weeds and preparing the ground, he put his rifle aside and took the spade from her hand, insisting that such work was too strenuous for a woman in her condition. Brianna protested that she was fine, but in truth she was grateful that he refused to let her continue to work in the garden. She tired easily these days, and her back seemed to hurt all the time. She insisted on planting the seeds, though, and

Shunkaha deferred to her experience, for he knew nothing of gardening or growing things.

In the evening, while he worked on repairing a worn bridle or oiled the rifle, she sewed things for the baby, and then she made several roomy dresses for herself.

In spite of the long hours and hard work, Brianna did not sleep well at night. Shunkaha refused to sleep in the bed. Instead, he slept on a blanket on the floor. At first Brianna slept beside him, her head pillowed on his shoulder, but as her pregnancy progressed, the floor seemed to grow harder and harder and finally, at Shunkaha's insistence, she returned to the bed. After the hard wooden floor, the mattress felt like the softest of clouds. But she did not like sleeping alone. Nor did she like the strain between them. Time and again she started to ask Shunkaha if he intended to stay with her after the baby was born, and time and again she changed her mind, fearful of the answer. She made several remarks about the future, about what they would plant the following year, about adding a room for the baby, but Shunkaha merely listened and nodded, never saying anything, never indicating that he would be there to help.

It was on one such night, when sleep would not come and her heart was sorely troubled, that the burden of unhappiness overflowed and she began to weep softly, her tears muffled by her pillow.

She had thought Shunkaha sound asleep, but he was instantly at her side.

"What is it?" he asked. "Are you in pain?"

"Yes."

"Is it the baby?" he asked, worried now because the child was not yet due.

"No."

"What, then?"

Brianna took his hand and placed it over her heart. "I hurt

here," she said softly. "I fear you no longer love me, that you're planning to leave me when the baby is born."

Shunkaha Luta sat on the edge of the bed, his hand still resting over her heart. "I have thought of it."

"Please don't go," Brianna begged. "I could not bear to live without you."

Her words twined around his heart, and he drew her into his arms, his nostrils breathing in the sweet clean scent of her hair.

"I will always come back to you, *le mita chante*," he vowed. "No matter how far from you I might go, I will always come back."

"I need you, Shunkaha. Your child needs you."

"And I need you," Shunkaha Luta replied. "Like the air I breathe." He stroked her hair, his eyes drifting toward the window and the darkness beyond. "If I stay here, I will always have to be on guard," he said bitterly. "Even now, I dare not stray too far from this place lest someone recognize me."

"I think you're worrying needlessly. No one in town knows that you killed McClain. No one ever saw you up close when you were on the road gang, and your name was never mentioned."

"Perhaps you are right."

"Would you rather live on the reservation?" she asked. And if he said yes, what then? Could she leave this place, give birth to her child in a place rampant with hunger and disease? Could she tolerate such a life, even for the man she loved?

"No. I want to live as my people have always lived."

"But that's impossible."

"No one knows that better than I."

"Shunkaha . . ."

Gently he placed his hand over her mouth. "We will not speak of it now, little one, but live each day as it comes until the child is born."

He kissed her then, filling her with a sweet yearning, and the problems of tomorrow no longer seemed important. Indeed, nothing mattered but the taste of his lips and the touch of his hands, and the soft huskiness of his voice as he whispered his love . . .

Chapter Eighteen

A slow smile spread over Adam Trent's face as he read the wire in his hand a second time.

"Regarding your query of October 28, last—stop—be advised that Brianna Beaudine has arrived in Winslow—stop—has taken possession of her deceased uncle's farm—stop." It was signed by Jared Clark, the town marshal.

Adam Trent let out a long sigh of relief. So, she was alive and well. Thank God. He wondered by what miracle she had managed to escape from the Indians and how she had been fortunate enough to find her way back home. But that didn't matter; nothing mattered except that she was safe.

In his heart he had refused to believe that she might be dead, refused to think he might never see her again. And yet, after so many months had passed without a word, he had almost given up hope.

He folded the wire and placed it in his pocket next to his heart. She was alive.

Soon, he promised himself, as soon as he could arrange it, he would go to Winslow and be with her again. He would declare his love and ask her to marry him. Hopefully, she would accept. If not, he would woo her with flowers and candy and sweet words and whatever else it took to win her heart.

He began to pace the floor as his excitement grew. His deputy would be back from Fort Peck by the end of next month, and since everything was quiet here, he would take off on one of his routine runs to Jefferson with a brief layover in Winslow.

Reaching for his hat, he left the office to make his afternoon rounds, imagining how surprised Brianna would be when he showed up on her doorstep with a bouquet of flowers and a proposal.

Chapter Nineteen

The next several days passed peacefully. There were enough chores to keep Brianna and Shunkaha Luta busy from dawn till dark, and then they retired to the house for dinner, a bath, and a few quiet hours before the fire.

It was on one such cool summer evening that the Reverend Matthew Jackson came to call.

Brianna felt the color rise in her cheeks as she opened the door and saw the minister standing on the porch.

"Reverend!" she exclaimed, conscious of her swollen belly. "I . . . how nice to see you."

"Good evening, Miss Beaudine," Matthew Jackson replied formally. His eyes darted to her stomach and quickly slid away. So, it was true. The news that she had returned to Winslow, pregnant and alone, had rapidly spread through town. Several of his parishioners had gone out of their way to tell him. "I heard you were back, and I wanted to come by and bid you welcome home, and offer you my condolences on the loss of your uncle."

"Thank you," Brianna murmured.

"I would have come by sooner, but I've been away."

"Oh?"

"My father passed away and I went home to comfort my mother and attend the funeral."

"I'm sorry."

Matthew Jackson nodded. "Would you mind if I came in for a few moments?"

Brianna hesitated. Shunkaha Luta was in the parlor and

there was no way for him to leave the room without being seen. Not that she was ashamed of him, but he *was* wanted by the law for killing Jim McClain, and the fewer people who knew of his presence here, the better.

"Is something wrong?" Matthew Jackson asked.

"No, I . . . please come in."

Matthew Jackson removed his hat as he stepped into the parlor, his eyes growing wide as he saw Shunkaha Luta standing near the hearth. His mouth dropped open as he stared at the Indian dressed in buckskin leggings, breech-clout, shirt, and moccasins. His long black hair fell loose, held from his face by a strip of red cloth.

There was an awkward silence as the two men sized each other up. Matthew Jackson could not hide his shock at seeing an Indian in Brianna's parlor, but if seeing Shunkaha left him slightly dazed, her next words left him speechless.

"Reverend, this is my husband, Shunkaha Luta. Shunkaha, this is Reverend Jackson."

Shunkaha met the white man's gaze, his hands clenched at his sides. Whatever had possessed Brianna to invite the man into the house? It could cause nothing but trouble.

"Won't you sit down, Reverend?"

"What? Oh, yes, thank you." He sank down on the sofa and looked at Brianna. "Where . . . when . . ." He cleared his throat. "How long have you been married?"

"Over a year."

Matthew Jackson nodded absently. "Please don't misunderstand my question, but where did you find a minister who would marry the two of you?"

"We didn't." Brianna lifted her chin defiantly. "Shunkaha and I exchanged our own vows."

"I see."

"You don't approve?"

"Such a marriage is not legally binding," Matthew Jackson

remarked. "Nor is it recognized by the church. Surely you know that your child will be considered a bas—" He bit off the word and shot a wary look in Shunkaha's direction.

"A bastard." Shunkaha spoke the word through tight lips.

"Yes."

"I think you should go now," Shunkaha said. His face was a dark mask of anger, his eyes filled with rage. How dare this *wasicu* come here and insult his woman.

"Please," Matthew Jackson said, extending his hand in a gesture of conciliation. "Hear me out. I did not mean to offend you. But you must realize that your . . . alliance will never be accepted." He looked steadfastly at Brianna. "The townspeople will be shocked when they learn you've given yourself to an Indian. The women will shun you, and the men . . ." He glanced briefly at Shunkaha, wondering if he dared go on.

"And the men?" Brianna asked stiffly.

"I'm afraid they won't show you much respect."

"I don't care," Brianna retorted. "I love Shunkaha. I'm proud to be carrying his child. Let people talk. Nothing will change the way I feel."

Matthew Jackson's gaze drifted to the fire burning brightly in the hearth. He had always been fond of Brianna. He had known her for six years, and in all that time he had never known her to be happy. Her aunt and uncle had treated her shamefully, never allowing her to mingle with people her own age, keeping her so busy on the ranch that she never had time for fun, never had the opportunity to meet any of the fine young men who lived nearby. And now she was in love with an Indian. For the first time since he had known her, she looked happy. He had not missed the way her eyes glowed when she looked at her Indian, had not missed the pride in her voice when she introduced him as her husband.

Matthew Jackson cleared his throat, then stood up, hat in hand. What he was about to suggest was unheard of. Perhaps it would cost him his parish. But in his heart, he knew it was the right thing to do, for Brianna, for the child, and perhaps for the Indian as well.

"Miss Beaudine, have you ever considered being married in a legal ceremony?"

"Of course I have," Brianna answered quietly.

"Yes, well, I would be willing to perform the ceremony."

Brianna was suddenly speechless. She swung around to face Shunkaha, her face aglow. She had never mentioned her longing for a proper ceremony to Shunkaha, had never admitted to herself that it was important. But it was, and now she could make her dream reality, thanks to Matthew Jackson. God bless him. She would be Shunkaha's wife; her child would not bear the stigma of being a bastard.

Her smile faded as she saw the expression on Shunkaha Luta's face.

Matthew Jackson saw it, too. "Perhaps the two of you would like a few minutes alone to discuss it. If it's all right, I'll just step into the kitchen."

Brianna nodded. "Thank you, Reverend."

When they were alone, Brianna took Shunkaha's hand in hers. "Would you mind terribly if we were married by the reverend?"

"You are already my wife," Shunkaha answered. "I do not need this white man's ceremony, or his approval."

"I need it," Brianna said quietly.

"It is important to you, to be married in the white man's way?"

"Yes. And it will be important to our son as well. My people will not recognize our marriage. I do not want them to call our son a bastard, or ridicule him because we were not properly married. If we let Reverend Jackson perform this ceremony, we will have a piece of paper to prove we are husband and wife."

"The white man's papers are worthless," Shunkaha said

bitterly. "My people have many papers saying the Land of the Spotted Eagle belongs to us as long as the grass grows and the rivers flow." He shook his head, a wry smile twisting his lips. "The grass still grows and the rivers still flow, but the Pa Sapa no longer belongs to my people."

"Please, Shunkaha, this is very important to me."

He let out a long sigh. Brianna had asked little of him. How could he deny her this one thing when it was so important to her?

"Very well, Golden Hair, we will let the white man perform his ceremony. Tonight, if that is your desire."

Rising on her tiptoes, Brianna kissed him. "Thank you."

Moments later, Brianna stood at Shunkaha Luta's side and spoke the words that made her his lawfully wedded wife. They had no rings to exchange, but his promise to love and cherish her was more binding than any piece of metal, and a sweet warmth filled her bosom as the reverend pronounced them man and wife. Shunkaha Luta hesitated a moment when Matthew Jackson said he could kiss the bride and then, very tenderly, he took Brianna's face in his hands and pressed his lips to hers.

"Ohinniyan, wastelakapi," he murmured. "Forever, beloved."

Brianna's heart swelled, filling with such a strong sense of love for the man who was now her husband that she forgot they were not alone until Matthew Jackson cleared his throat, a little embarrassed to be intruding on such an intimate moment.

"I'll take care of the paperwork when I get back to town," he told Brianna when she tore her eyes away from Shunkaha's face. "And I'll bring your marriage license with me next time I come."

"Thank you, Reverend," Brianna said fervently. "You've been very kind. But then you've always treated me with kindness and respect. I want you to know how much I appreciated it, then and now."

Matthew Jackson took Brianna's hand in his and gave it a squeeze. "Be happy, child."

"I will be, thank you. Oh!" she exclaimed, embarrassed. "I haven't paid you."

Matthew Jackson chuckled softly. "There's no need."

"Are you sure?"

"Quite sure. Goodnight."

Brianna stood at the door until the reverend was gone, and then she went to stand beside her husband. "That wasn't so bad, was it?"

"No. How long have you known the white man?"

Brianna shrugged. "Five or six years. Why?"

"Is he in love with you?"

"In love with me? Why would you think such a thing?"

"Because of the way he looks at you."

"You're imagining things."

"Perhaps." Shunkaha Luta placed his hands on Brianna's shoulders. "*Mitawin,*" he murmured. "My woman." His hands slid down her arms and then up again and Brianna thrilled to his touch. She belonged to him now, for better or worse, in sickness and health, so long as they lived.

She lifted her face, closing her eyes as Shunkaha's mouth slanted over hers, his lips warm and achingly familiar. She felt her body respond to his kiss, felt her heart begin to pound as his kiss deepened and became more ardent, more demanding. Her stomach fluttered with desire and excitement. Soon, she thought, soon he would make her his, carrying her away to a place where there was no red and no white, but only a man and a woman.

Shunkaha slipped one arm around her waist and the other under her knees and then he was carrying her swiftly into the bedroom, placing her on the bed, stretching out beside her.

He kissed her face and throat, her arms and hands, her hair and nose and eyes, and all the while he was kissing her his hands were deftly unfastening her bodice, removing her skirt and petticoats, chemise and pantaloons, muttering under his breath that white women wore too much clothing, until she lay bare beneath him, her body quivering with pleasure.

She felt his hand on her swollen belly, opened her eyes to see him gazing down at her, his dark eyes warm with love, awed by the mystery that had turned his seed into a living being. Their child gave a lusty kick, and Shunkaha Luta chuckled.

"Our son is restless," he remarked. "Does he not hurt you?"

Brianna shook her head. "No. Each kick reminds me that he is strong and healthy, like his father."

"I am weak in your arms," Shunkaha replied. "My heart pounds like that of a frightened deer, and my body is no longer my own, but yours to do with as you please."

Brianna smiled, warmed by his words. "It would please me very much if you would kiss me again."

"All night long, if that is your desire."

"All night long, then," Brianna murmured. "Pleasure me all night long . . ."

News of Brianna's Indian husband spread quickly through Winslow. The majority of the people were shocked and disgusted at the mere idea of a white woman living with an Indian. Such a thing simply was not done. Indeed, there were numerous stories of women who had killed themselves rather than surrender their virtue to some savage. The idea that a decent, self-respecting white woman would willingly live with an Indian, let alone marry one, was unheard of.

Brianna knew there would be people who would shun her, who would never accept her marriage to an Indian, but she had been certain that Reverend Jackson had been exaggerating about how bad things would be until she went into town for supplies. Women crossed the street to avoid her;

men leered at her, their eyes filled with lusty speculation. A few made comments that caused her cheeks to bloom with indignation and her ears to burn with embarrassment.

She was on the verge of tears when she entered the General Store. She clenched her fists at her sides as Margie Croft came toward her, ready to turn and flee if the woman so much as looked at her the wrong way.

But Margie Croft was a good, decent, God-fearing Christian who held the unpopular opinion that all men (and women) were equal in the sight of their Maker. She gave Brianna a brilliant smile of welcome as she took her list, chatted about inconsequential things as she filled Brianna's order.

Brianna tried to hide her tears when she returned home, but Shunkaha Luta sensed that something was wrong. He remained silent until she had put their supplies away, and then he took her in his arms. "What is it, *mitawin*?

"Nothing." Her voice was thick with unshed tears and she refused to meet his eyes.

"Is it so bad you cannot tell me?"

"Oh, Shunkaha, Reverend Jackson was right! No one would speak to me, but they all looked at me as if I was dirty. I haven't done anything wrong! Why should they care if I married an Indian?"

Shunkaha Luta held her while she cried, his face a mask of bitter anger mingled with regret that her love for him should cause her even a moment's unhappiness. He had known her people would never accept him. The old hurts and the old hates ran too deep. But he could not understand how anyone could treat Brianna unkindly. She was the soul of goodness, the epitome of what a woman should be.

He held her until her tears subsided, and then he drew away, his eyes thoughtful. "Are you sure you want to stay here, Ishna Wi? Would it not be better to go back to the hills and live where there is no one to belittle our love?"

Brianna stubbornly shook her head. "This is my home. *Our* home. I'm not leaving. I won't let a bunch of narrow-minded ninnies drive me away."

He did not argue, knowing that anything he said would only make her more determined to stay.

"Anyway, not everyone is against us. Margie Croft and her husband are coming for dinner tomorrow night. They wanted to meet you."

Margie Croft felt a twinge of nervousness as she alighted from the carriage and walked up the porch steps. She had never seen an Indian in her life, and she wasn't sure she wanted to see one now. But Brianna needed to know that not everyone in town thought she was no better than a squaw. After all, the girl had done nothing wrong except fall in love, and if she wanted to marry an Indian, why, that was her business. Personally, Margie could not understand how anyone could love a savage. They were all barbarians, ruthless killers, and the West was a far more peaceful and safe place to live now that they were all confined to reservations.

"You sure this is a good idea?" Luke Croft asked his wife as they stood at the front door.

"I don't know, but it's too late to turn back now. Smile, Luke." Margie beamed as Brianna opened the door and invited them in. The two women embraced, Brianna took their coats, and then she was introducing them to Shunkaha Luta.

Margie Croft could not help staring at the man Brianna introduced as her husband. He was by far the most handsome man Margie had ever seen, and she had seen many in her day. He was tall, dark-skinned, ruggedly handsome, and blatantly male. The buckskin leggings and shirt he wore fit like a second skin, clearly defining his long legs and muscular arms.

He was not good at small talk, but sat quietly as Margie,

Luke, and Brianna reminisced about Henry Beaudine and
then chatted about the changes taking place in Winslow.
He said little during the meal that Brianna served, but Mar-
gie was quick to see that his eyes strayed often to Brianna.
He might be considered a savage by others of her race, but
Margie was touched by the depths of the love that shone in
Shunkaha's eyes when he looked at his wife, and she de-
cided that, Indian or not, he was a good man.

Later, she was impressed with his quiet manner, with the
respect he showed Brianna, the politeness of his answers
when her husband, Luke, questioned him about the Indian
way of life. It was obvious that Shunkaha Luta was not fond
of white people, but he treated them as welcome guests in
his wife's home, and when they left, Margie Croft could understand why Brianna loved him.

Shunkaha Luta slid out of bed, pulled on his leggings, and
left the house. Outside, it was cool and dark. A bright yellow moon hung low in the sky. A stalking moon, Shunkaha
thought, and remembered the many nights he and his
friends had crept through the darkness toward an enemy
camp, lying in wait for the moon to set and the sun to rise
before they attacked. Those had been the good days, when a
man's blood ran hot with the thrill of battle, when there
were honors to be won and coup to be counted, when the
buffalo were more numerous than the stars in the sky and
the red man lived as *Wakan Tanka* had intended.

Standing in the moon-dappled shadows, he gazed at the
house where Brianna lay sleeping, then let his eyes wander
to the barn and the corrals, to the garden that was bloom-
ing under Brianna's expert care, to the surrounding darkness, and the silhouette of the distant mountains. What was
he doing here, he mused, living in the square wooden house,
taking his meals at a table, sleeping on a soft mattress beneath eiderdown quilts? He had abandoned the floor because

it was too hard for Brianna and he could not bear to sleep apart from her. Why had he abandoned the ways of the People? Why . . .

His gaze returned to the dark house. Why, he mused. Why, indeed. Because of a golden-haired white woman who had stolen his heart and captured his soul, who ruled his life with velvet chains that he could not have broken even if he so desired. She had become a part of him, a vital, irreplaceable part, and he knew he would perish without her. Indeed, he had no desire to live if he could not share his life with her. He knew that, deep in her heart, Brianna lived with the fear that he would leave her when their child was born. In truth, he had often considered it, for the pull toward his homeland was strong, but he knew that he would never willingly be parted from her. Better to live summer and winter on a little patch of sun-baked ground with the woman he loved above all else than to roam the vast sun-kissed plains alone.

Chapter Twenty

The two men took Adam Trent completely by surprise. One minute he was riding along, his thoughts on Brianna, and the next he was lying in the dirt with a bullet in his back.

Eyes closed, he fought off the blackness that hovered around him as he listened to the two bushwhackers close in on him. From their conversation, he could tell they were both drunk, and pleased as punch with their kill.

Only their quarry wasn't dead. Not yet.

He waited until he heard the creak of saddle leather, indicating they were dismounting to rifle his pockets, and then he rolled over, palmed his gun, and shot them both where they stood.

The exertion sent him tumbling into a deep black void.

It was nearly night when he regained consciousness. His wound had stopped bleeding, and he stood up slowly, his hand pressed to his back. Damn, but it hurt like sin.

Moving like an old man, he walked toward the two would-be bushwhackers and flipped them over. He recognized them both. Jack Booker and Danny McGuff. Both were wanted in Texas for a wide variety of crimes, including robbery and murder.

Trent swore under his breath as he grabbed hold of his horse's reins and placed his left foot in the stirrup. Pain shot through his back and he groaned as he pulled himself onto the horse's back.

Lying across the animal's neck, he urged the horse forward

in the direction of Winslow, hoping he'd make it to town before he passed out again.

For the first time, it occurred to him that he might die. He wondered if Brianna would care . . .

Chapter Twenty-one

Shunkaha Luta urged his mount down the tree-studded hill, his dark eyes sweeping back and forth as he followed the well-worn game trail that led to a narrow stream flanked by tall willows and slender cottonwoods. He often rode into the hills that were a part of Brianna's land, needing to be out in the open, to ride beneath the bold blue sky, to breathe in the scent of earth and trees, to be away from the house, away from the walls that closed him in and made him feel trapped. But for Brianna, he would have left long ago.

It was near dusk when he drew rein downwind of the three does and two fawns who stood drinking at the water's edge. He had had his fill of chicken and pork and beef; this night they would dine on venison.

Lifting his rifle to his shoulder, he sighted down the barrel, his finger curling around the trigger as he drew a bead on the one doe who had no fawn at her side. He was about to squeeze off a shot when a big bay horse trotted up to the stream, spooking the deer, which quickly bounded out of range and out of sight.

Shunkaha frowned as he lowered his rifle and urged his horse down the slope and across the stream. The bay horse whinnied softly as Shunkaha rode up.

Dismounting, Shunkaha Luta took up the bay's reins and tethered both horses to a tree, noting as he did so that there was blood on the bay's saddle. On soundless feet, the Indian backtracked the bay, his rifle at the ready, his eyes wary.

He found the man lying face down in the dirt some three

hundred yards away. A dark brown bloodstain covered much of the man's shirt. His breathing was shallow and erratic.

When he was certain the man was unarmed, Shunkaha rolled the man over, swore softly as he recognized the white man who had arrested him and taken him to Bismarck. He stared at the unconscious *wasicu* for a long time, his hand caressing his rifle. It would be so easy to kill this man, this enemy. So easy, and no one would ever know.

He considered it for a long while, and then he hoisted the man onto his shoulder and carried him to the stream where the horses waited, disgusted with the weakness within himself that would not allow him to kill a man who could not defend himself.

Draping the lawman face down over the back of the bay, he lashed the man's hands and feet together, swung aboard his own mount, and started for home, knowing that only trouble would come of saving the man's life.

Brianna was standing near the stove, preparing the evening meal, when Shunkaha Luta rode up. As always, a familiar warmth filled her breast at seeing him again. But her smile of welcome wavered when she saw the body lying across the saddle of the big bay horse. Wiping her hands on her apron, she hurried outside.

"What happened?" she asked anxiously. "Is he dead? Did you . . . ?" She couldn't say the words.

"Hush, *mitawin*," Shunkaha said sternly. "He is not dead. Yet. He was unconscious when I found him."

Brianna drew a deep breath as Shunkaha lifted the injured man from the saddle and she saw his face for the first time.

"Adam Trent," she murmured. "Oh, my."

"You remember him, then?" Shunkaha Luta asked.

Brianna nodded. Remember, indeed, she thought guiltily. How could she forget the last night they had spent together in Bismarck? Adam had kissed her hungrily, vowed that he loved her, wanted her. Though he had never mentioned marriage, she knew he had hoped she would one day be his wife.

Sorely troubled, she followed Shunkaha into the bedroom, drew back the covers on the bed. Trent's face was almost as white as the pillowcase.

"The bullet is still in his back," Shunkaha Luta remarked, and Brianna nodded.

The next few moments were busy ones. Brianna collected scissors, disinfectant, bandages, a bowl of water, and a clean cloth while Shunkaha removed Trent's boots and blood-stained clothes, covered him with a sheet, and then sterilized the blade of a knife.

"Can you do it?" Shunkaha Luta asked. They stood on opposite sides of the bed, their eyes meeting over Trent's back.

"I can do it," Brianna assured him, but when she took the knife, her hands were shaking so violently she dared not attempt to remove the slug for fear of causing more damage.

Shunkaha Luta's hand was rock steady as he took the knife from her hand and deftly probed for the bullet lodged low in Adam Trent's back. Brianna swallowed the bitter bile that rose in her throat as the blade sank deeper into Trent's bloody flesh. Moments later, Shunkaha removed a small leaden chunk of metal from Trent's back. Brianna clamped her lips together as she washed away the blood, poured disinfectant over the wound, and then bandaged it securely.

"Will he live?"

Shunkaha Luta shrugged. "Only *Wakan Tanka* knows the future."

"I need to change the sheets."

Shunkaha Luta lifted Trent while Brianna removed the bloody sheets and replaced them with clean ones. He told himself not to be jealous as she drew a blanket over Trent, smoothed the hair from his face, sponged the sweat from his brow. But all the while he was remembering how it had been in Bismarck: himself in jail, staring through the bars, watching Brianna cross the street with Adam Trent, seeing the way the lawman held her arm and smiled down at her, the way she had smiled back.

He left the room abruptly, needing to get away before he said something he would regret. Brianna loved him; he had no reason to doubt it.

Brianna spent the night at the lawman's side, patiently replacing the blankets he threw aside when the fever came. She wiped his face and chest with a cool cloth, offered him water, spoke to him even though he could not hear her.

Shunkaha Luta stood in the doorway, his face impassive, his eyes dark with unbridled jealousy as he watched his woman care for another man. She was a tender-hearted woman, kind and sweet, and he knew she would have nursed anyone, red or white, with the same tender concern. And yet the fact that she had known Trent before gnawed at Shunkaha's vitals. He had seen the way the white man looked at her, touched her.

As dawn began to lighten the sky, Shunkaha insisted that Brianna get some sleep, if not for her own sake, then for the sake of their child.

"I'm fine," she argued. "Someone has to stay with Mr. Trent."

"I will stay with him," Shunkaha Luta said irritably. And lifting Brianna into his arms, he carried her up the stairs and deposited her firmly in her old bed. "Sleep now."

Brianna nodded, too weary to protest. She *was* tired. Her back ached, her feet ached, and her eyes felt gritty with the need for sleep. With a sigh, she turned on her side, her cheek resting in her palm. She was asleep before Shunkaha Luta left the room.

Adam Trent regained consciousness a layer at a time, aware of a great pain in his back. He heard footsteps, wrinkled his nose appreciatively as he smelled fresh coffee. Feigning sleep, he tried to remember where he was, but his mind drew a blank. He remembered killing the two men who had bushwhacked him, mounting his horse, and then nothing more. He was aware that he was lying face down on a bed, naked beneath a starched sheet. He opened his eyes a fraction of an inch, swore under his breath when he saw the Indian standing in front of the window.

Shunkaha Luta grunted softly. "So, white man, you have decided to live."

"So it seems." Trent opened his eyes fully and glanced around. "Where the hell am I?"

"In the house of my woman."

"How'd I get here?"

"I found you lying unconscious not far from here."

"I'm obliged."

"I do not want your thanks."

"What do you want?" Trent asked guardedly.

"I want you to get well and then go."

"I'll do my best."

Shunkaha Luta nodded, and then Brianna breezed into the room, her face beaming when she saw that Adam Trent had regained consciousness.

The lawman blinked at her several times, and then he stared at Shunkaha Luta.

The Indian smiled. "My woman," he said softly.

Adam Trent felt as though a lead weight had been dropped in the pit of his stomach as he recognized the Indian. "But she told me you were dead. Killed at the Little Big Horn with Custer."

"Only wounded," Shunkaha Luta replied.

A taut silence stretched between the two men as they glared at each other.

Brianna fidgeted for a moment, then said brightly, "Well, Mr. Trent, you're looking much better this afternoon. Would

you care for something to eat? Some broth, perhaps, and a
cup of coffee?"

"That'd be nice," Trent replied, his eyes still on Shunkaha
Luta.

"Shunkaha, will you help me in the kitchen, please?" Brianna asked, knowing it would not be wise to leave the two
men alone.

Shunkaha Luta nodded and followed Brianna out of the
room.

Later, when Shunkaha had gone out to tend the stock,
Brianna and Adam Trent had a few minutes alone. Brianna
felt her cheeks grow pink under Trent's probing gaze.

"Is it his?" Adam asked, gesturing at Brianna's protruding
belly.

"Yes." She smoothed a wrinkle from her skirt. "How did
you happen to be in Winslow?"

"I was on my way to see you when two men bushwhacked
me." Adam Trent laughed softly. "I finished them off before
they got to me."

"You might have been killed."

"Yeah. I guess I owe you my life."

"No," Brianna corrected softly. "You owe Shunkaha Luta
your life. He found you and brought you here. He dug the
bullet out of your back."

"Damn," Trent muttered. "You know I've got to arrest
him, Brianna. It's my job."

"Arrest him!" Brianna exclaimed. "After he saved your
life? How can you be so ungrateful?"

"I'm not ungrateful. I'm a lawman, and he's wanted by the
law."

"I don't want to discuss it," Brianna said tersely. "Tell me,
why were you coming to see me?"

"You must know. I love you, Brianna. I came to ask you to
marry me."

"I'm married to Shunkaha."

Trent made a gesture of dismissal with his hand. "An Indian ceremony isn't a marriage. I'll make you a good husband if you'll give me the chance."

"I have a good husband, Adam."

"I told you, an Indian marriage isn't—"

"We were married by a minister last month," Brianna interjected. "It's quite legal."

"Brianna—"

"Please, Adam, don't say any more. I love Shunkaha Luta. I'm carrying his child."

Brianna was quiet at dinner that night. Shunkaha Luta studied her surreptitiously, wondering what had upset her. She ate little, which was unusual now that she was pregnant. Lately he had taken to teasing her about the fact that she seemed to be hungry all the time.

"What is it?" he asked as they lingered over a last cup of coffee. "What is troubling you?"

"Nothing."

"We have no lies between us, Ishna Wi. Do not let this be the first."

"It's Adam. He wants to arrest you."

"He can try," Shunkaha remarked lightly.

"This is no laughing matter," Brianna admonished sharply. "He's a lawman. He knows you're wanted for killing McClain, and for escaping from jail . . ." Brianna's voice trailed off. She had helped Shunkaha escape. Didn't that make her an accessory or something? Would Adam arrest her as well?

Later, when Brianna had gone to bed in her little attic room, Shunkaha Luta went to see Adam Trent. The two men regarded each other for a long moment, and the lawman could not ignore the shiver of fear that wound through his vitals. He was helpless, unarmed, the enemy. Had Brianna

told the Indian what they had talked about earlier? Had the
Indian come to do away with him and thus settle the rivalry
between them once and for all?

"How are you feeling?" Shunkaha Luta asked.

"Fine," Adam Trent answered warily. "Brianna tells me I
owe you my life."

Shunkaha Luta shrugged. "She tells me you intend to arrest me."

Trent nodded. "It's my job."

Shunkaha Luta grinned coldly. "And if I do not wish to
go back to jail?" He nodded in Trent's direction. "You are
wounded. You have no weapons."

Trent said nothing, only gazed, unflinching, at the Indian, knowing that to show weakness now would be a grave
mistake.

"This is not about right or wrong," Shunkaha Luta remarked. "It is about Brianna. You want her, and I want her.
But she is my wife; she carries my child, and I will not let
her go."

Adam Trent had fought Indians in the past. He knew of
their love for the wild life, the free life. He looked at Shunkaha
Luta, and he wondered how long the Indian would be content
to dwell in a house, to spend summer and winter in the same
place year after year.

That was the question he put to Shunkaha. "How long?"
he asked. "How long will you be happy here? What will happen to Brianna when you get tired of living like a white man
and decide to go back to the blanket?"

It was a question Shunkaha Luta had often asked himself.
As much as he loved Brianna, as much as he had come to
cherish her, he could not help wondering if he would be able
to accept her way of life. Hearing Trent voice his own doubts
sparked his anger. What made it even worse was the knowledge that Adam Trent was the kind of man Brianna should

have fallen in love with in the first place, the kind of man who could give her the life she desired.

"You ask too many questions, white man," Shunkaha Luta retorted sharply.

"Questions you've asked yourself," Trent replied. "Admit it."

"She is my woman. I will kill you before I let her go."

Adam Trent nodded slowly. "I fear this will not be over between us until one of us *is* dead."

"We will not speak of killing now," Shunkaha Luta said. "The child is to be born in the Moon of Cherries Ripening, the month you call July. We will do nothing until then."

"Agreed."

"You will leave here as soon as you are able," Shunkaha Luta said.

"How do I know you won't take off?"

"I will not leave. You have my word." Shunkaha Luta smiled ruefully. "You do not think I would go before I have seen my son?"

"I guess not."

"But be warned, white man. I will not go to the white man's jail. And if you try to take me, I will kill you, or you will kill me. But I will not live behind iron bars. And I will not spare your life a second time."

Chapter Twenty-two

As June gave way to July, Brianna was infused with a sense of urgency. She cleaned the house like a demon, spent hours turning her ugly attic room into a nursery. Shunkaha Luta surprised her by making a cradle. Margie Croft came over one morning and painted the room a soft powder blue, insisting that Brianna go about her business elsewhere. "Climbing ladders and smelling paint fumes is no way for a pregnant woman to be spending her time," Margie had said in motherly fashion, and shooed Brianna out of the room.

Adam Trent had moved to town and was staying at Gordon's Boardinghouse. Shunkaha Luta had not told her what had transpired between himself and Trent, and Brianna did not ask, certain that whatever had happened was something she would rather not know.

Shunkaha Luta treated her as though she were made of fragile porcelain and might shatter at any moment. He did all the chores now, ignoring Brianna when she teased him about doing woman's work.

The late evening hours were the best. They sat on the sofa, side by side, his arm around her shoulders, while they speculated on whether their child was a boy or a girl. They discussed names, their hopes and dreams for this child and others.

Only when he was alone did Shunkaha Luta ponder what would happen after the baby was born. Would Adam Trent return to arrest him? Should he wait around and find out, or leave as soon as the child was born? Brianna was fond of the lawman. He knew it, though she had never said so.

How would she feel about her Indian if he was forced to kill the white man? And if he killed Trent, what then? He could not stay with Brianna. An Indian didn't kill a lawman and pretend it never happened. He was already wanted for killing McClain, though no one in Winslow seemed aware of the fact.

So many questions, so many things to consider, and no easy answer to any of them.

He was standing in the yard late one night, gazing into the distance and wondering what the future would hold, when Brianna came up beside him and slipped her arm around his waist.

"Pretty night," she remarked after a while.

"Yes."

"I woke up and you were gone."

"I could not sleep."

"It scared me when I woke up and you weren't there."

Shunkaha Luta draped his arm around her shoulders protectively. "I would not leave you, little one." He rested his free hand on her swollen belly. "Not with my son still unborn."

"And when your son is here, what then?" She asked the question that had been haunting her day and night ever since Adam Trent had left the ranch.

"I will never willingly leave you, Ishna Wi. You are my heart, my life."

"But?"

"I may have no other choice if the man Trent comes after me. I cannot go back to jail, Ishna Wi. If he tries to take me, I will kill him."

"Or he'll kill you."

"Perhaps."

Brianna rested her head in the hollow of Shunkaha Luta's shoulder. There had to be some way to convince Adam to change his mind about arresting Shunkaha, but how? What could she say that would persuade him to go back to Bismarck alone?

She felt Shunkaha Luta's hand moving through her hair and she lifted her face for his kiss, her eyelids fluttering down as his mouth slanted over hers. He kissed her for a long while, and then he scooped her into his arms and carried her into the house. In their room, he placed her gently on the bed, deftly removed her long cotton gown and tossed it on the floor.

"How can you bear to look at me?" Brianna asked. "I'm as fat as a heifer."

"You are not fat. You are pregnant with our son. Never have you looked more beautiful than you do now."

"Flatterer," Brianna accused. "What do you hope to gain by your sweet words?"

"Only the chance to look at you," Shunkaha replied. He sat next to her on the bed, his eyes moving over her face and figure. Her breasts were heavy and full, her stomach high and round, her legs long and slim, though the ankles were puffy. Her golden hair spread over the pillow like sunshine. "The chance to touch you." His hands curved around her breasts, slid down her sides and rested on her belly. He felt their child stir beneath his hands, and his heart swelled with love for the woman who sheltered his unborn child within her body, and for the new life that rested in her womb.

He stretched out beside her and Brianna turned in his arms. "I wish we could make love," she murmured.

"Soon," Shunkaha Luta promised, though he wondered how he could wait even one more day when he longed to bury himself in her warmth now, to possess her, to be a part of her.

"It won't be soon enough," Brianna pouted. "The baby isn't due for another two weeks, and then we have to wait at least six weeks after that."

"Only six weeks?" Shunkaha Luta remarked. "Among the

Lakota a woman does not receive her man until the child is
weaned."

"But that could take over a year!" Brianna exclaimed.

"Sometimes two," Shunkaha muttered glumly.

"Is that a custom you feel strongly about?" Brianna asked,
blushing a little because it must be obvious that she could
not wait until they could be intimate again.

Shunkaha Luta's laughter rumbled deep in his throat. "I
think this is one time when the white man may have the
right idea."

"I think so, too." Brianna's hand slid across the flat wall of
his chest, over his shoulder, down the length of his arm, and
came to rest on his flat belly. For a moment she pondered
the unfairness of it all. He was responsible for her being
pregnant; it wasn't fair that his belly was still hard and flat
while she looked as if she had swallowed a watermelon!

Shunkaha Luta nuzzled her neck, and her hand slid to his
trousers, tugging at the waistband. He quickly shrugged
them off and they lay face to face, bodies touching, their
breath mingling as they gazed into each other's eyes. Brianna laughed softly as the evidence of Shunkaha's need rose
against her thigh.

"Soon," she said, laughing harder at his agitated expression.

"Now I know why so many men take a second wife," he
groaned.

Brianna slapped his arm playfully. "Do you mean to lie
there and tell me you would sleep with another woman
while I'm as big as a house with your child?"

"Not another woman," Shunkaha Luta corrected. "Another wife."

"Well, you just put that idea out of your head right now.
There's not going to be any second wife in *this* family."

"I was only making a joke," Shunkaha Luta said, captur-
ing both of Brianna's hands in one of his. "You are woman
enough for me."

"I love you," Brianna whispered fervently. "I love you so much. Promise you'll never leave me."

"Do not ask me to make a promise I may not be able to keep, little one," Shunkaha chided softly. "My word is my life. I cannot break it."

"Promise me."

"I cannot promise I will never leave you, but I promise that I will stay with you as long as I can."

As Brianna's time drew near, Luke and Margie Croft began dropping by almost nightly. Margie Croft was like a mother hen, clucking and cooing over Brianna, insisting the girl rest while she prepared their meals and washed and dried the dishes.

Shunkaha Luta was a little put off by Margie Croft's intrusion in their life, but the woman had a cheerful disposition and it was obvious that Brianna enjoyed the older woman's company. Luke Croft was steady and reliable. He didn't say much, and Shunkaha Luta thought that was a blessing, since his wife was rarely quiet. The two men often went outside, leaving the women to chatter about babies and recipes and the outrageous price of yard goods.

Luke Croft introduced Shunkaha Luta to the game of checkers, and the two men spent many an evening hunched over the kitchen table, hardly saying a word as they tried to out maneuver each other.

It was on one such night when Luke Croft and Shunkaha Luta were playing checkers that Brianna's water broke.

Margie Croft helped Brianna change out of her dress into a clean nightgown, got her settled into bed, and then went into the kitchen to inform Shunkaha Luta that he was about to become a father. Luke was instructed to go into town for the doctor, and Shunkaha Luta was directed into the bedroom to sit with Brianna while Margie rounded up the items the doctor would need when he arrived.

Brianna smiled at Shunkaha as he entered the room. "You don't look so good," she remarked.

"I have never been this close to being a father before," he replied with a wry grin. "Are you in pain?"

"No," she answered, and then gasped as a contraction caught her unawares.

Shunkaha Luta watched helplessly as she endured the brief contraction, knowing they would only get worse before the child was born—knowing there was nothing he could do to help. Indeed, he felt hopelessly out of place in this room. Lakota men did not participate in childbirth. Such things were best left to women. But Brianna was reaching out for his hand. He moved quickly to her side, taking her hand in both of his. Her hand was small and pale, so delicate and white when compared to his own big brown one. She sucked in a deep breath, her hand grasping his, as another pain knifed through her.

"Ishna Wi." He murmured her name, his voice filled with anguish.

"I'm all right," Brianna assured him when the contraction had passed.

Shunkaha nodded, though his expression was doubtful.

Margie Croft bustled into the room carrying a bowl of cool water and a clean cloth, which she placed on the table beside the bed. Helping Brianna to sit up, she braided the girl's hair, secured it on top of her head, then bathed her face and neck.

"How long does it usually take?" Brianna asked.

"Land sakes, child, there's no way to tell with a first baby. They usually take their time, but you never know." She glanced at Shunkaha's worried face and patted his arm reassuringly. "Don't fret none. She'll be fine."

Shunkaha nodded, but during the next two hours he began to doubt that Margie Croft knew what she was talking about. Brianna's pains came harder and faster, and he was amazed at Brianna's strength as she endured one pain after another. She clung to his hands, squeezing them with incredible strength as their child struggled to be born.

It was near midnight when Luke Croft arrived with the doctor. Adam Trent was with them.

"What took you so long?" Margie Croft scolded her husband as the doctor examined Brianna. "You've been gone for hours!"

"There was an emergency at the jail. Prisoner got shot trying to escape. Doc worked on him for a long time, but the man died anyway."

"What's he doing here?" Margie Croft asked, nodding in Trent's direction.

"I don't know. He was at the jail, and he insisted on coming along."

"There's trouble brewing," Margie Croft predicted.

Luke Croft nodded. The tension between the Indian and the lawman was so thick you could have cut it with a knife.

Margie and Luke went into the kitchen to brew a pot of coffee, leaving Shunkaha Luta and Adam Trent alone in the parlor.

The lawman waited until the kitchen door closed, and then he drew his gun and leveled it at Shunkaha Luta.

"Put your hands behind your back," he ordered gruffly.

Shunkaha Luta did not move. His dark eyes bored into Trent, daring the lawman to pull the trigger.

Adam Trent cocked the gun. "Put your hands behind your back," he repeated tersely. "Or that baby won't have a father."

A muscle worked in Shunkaha Luta's jaw as he slowly obeyed the lawman's instructions.

"Now turn around."

Shunkaha Luta hesitated, and then did as bidden. Now was not the time to fight. It would cause Brianna too much stress if she knew there was anything amiss. And he could not take a chance on getting killed, not now, when his child was about to be born.

His body went rigid as he felt Trent handcuff his hands behind his back.

"Well," Margie Croft said as she pushed her way through the kitchen door into the parlor, "it shouldn't be much longer. I've made coffee . . ." Her voice trailed off as she saw the gun in Adam Trent's hand.

"What the hell's goin' on here?" Luke Croft demanded.

"The Indian is wanted by the law," Adam Trent answered curtly.

Margie Croft set the tray down on the table near the sofa. "Wanted? For what, I'd like to know."

"Murder."

Margie Croft's hand flew to her breast. "Murder? Oh, my."

"Who'd he kill?" Luke Croft wanted to know.

"One of the road bosses."

"Oh, yeah, McClain," Luke Croft murmured. "I recollect hearing some talk that he'd been killed by an Injun."

Shunkaha Luta turned around, his eyes moving from Margie Croft's face to her husband's. These people had been his friends. Had that changed, now that they knew he had killed a white man? He was surprised to find that he cared what they thought, that he had come to value their friendship, their opinion of him.

A heavy silence hung over the room, and then, sounding as soft and sweet as the song of a lark on the first day of spring, came the first lilting cry of a newborn child.

Shunkaha Luta swung toward the sound, his heart lifting with anticipation. At last, his child was here.

Margie Croft rushed toward the bedroom door and opened it so that the new father might see his wife and child. Shunkaha Luta flashed her a grateful smile, and then he hurried into the room, all else forgotten as he gazed at Brianna and the small, blanket-wrapped bundle cradled in her arms.

"Here, now," the doctor admonished. "I'm not finished in here yet."

But Shunkaha Luta ignored the man. Going to the bed, he dropped to one knee and smiled at his woman. Her face was pale and damp with sweat, but her smile was radiant.

"It's a boy." She drew the blanket back so Shunkaha could see the child's face. Tiny fists flailed the air.

"You have done well, Ishna Wi," Shunkaha Luta murmured, his voice thick with emotion.

"Isn't he beautiful? Perhaps he'll have a sister next year."

"Perhaps."

"Would you like to hold him?" Brianna asked, thinking it strange that Shunkaha had not touched his son.

"Ishna Wi . . ."

"What is it?" she asked, alarmed by the grave tone of his voice. She peered at him intently, and then she noticed that his arms were drawn behind his back.

"Adam Trent is here."

A lead weight settled over Brianna's heart. Her child was not even an hour old and already Trent had come to take her son's father away. Two large tears welled in her eyes and slid slowly down her cheeks.

"Do not weep, little one," Shunkaha Luta begged softly. "I cannot bear your tears."

Brianna nodded, then groaned as the doctor expelled the afterbirth. Shunkaha Luta rocked back on his heels, his eyes intent on Brianna's face, as the doctor finished cleaning her up.

After assuring the couple that everything was fine, he took up his satchel and left the room. A moment later, Margie Croft peeked into the room.

"Come in," Brianna called.

"Shall I take the baby?" Margie Croft asked. "He needs a bit of a bath, and I think you two might like to be alone."

"Yes," Brianna said, handing her son to the woman. "Thank you."

When they were alone, Shunkaha sat on the edge of the bed and Brianna put her arms around him, holding him as tight as she could. Bending, Shunkaha kissed the top of her head, then let his lips trail over her forehead and nose to her mouth. He kissed her hungrily, desperately, suddenly afraid that he might never see her again.

Margie Croft washed the baby quickly and efficiently, then dressed him in a clean sacque and laid him in the cradle his father had made for him. Then, squaring her shoulders, she marched into the parlor and confronted Adam Trent.

"It's shameful," she declared. "Arresting a man the day his child is born. What can you be thinking of?"

Adam Trent took a step back, feeling like a rooster being attacked by a banty hen. "He's a wanted man," he said defensively. "I'm only doing my job, and doing it the best way I know how. Any other time, there would have been bloodshed, his or mine, and I didn't aim for that to happen if I could prevent it."

"The law, the law! There's more to life than the law. That man needs to hold his wife in his arms, and she needs to be held. And he needs to hold his young'un, as well. You ought to be ashamed of yourself."

Adam Trent looked over Margie Croft's head to her husband for help.

Luke Croft shrugged elaborately. "She does rattle on sometimes," he admitted. "But this time she's right."

Adam Trent felt his anger rise. "You two are almighty interested in what's right and what's wrong," he retorted. "What about Jim McClain's rights? That Indian killed him. Killed him in cold blood so far as I know. The fact that his . . . his wife just had a baby doesn't change that."

Luke and Margie Croft exchanged glances. Trent was right, of course. A man had been killed and his murderer had been apprehended. If it hadn't been for their love for Brianna and their affection for Shunkaha, they would have been incensed to think that a known criminal was running loose in their midst.

"I'd best go look in on Brianna," Margie Croft said. "She's likely tired. Maybe a little hungry."

"I'll go with you," Trent said.

Shunkaha stood up as Margie Croft and Adam Trent entered the room. Brianna had fallen asleep, and Margie Croft clucked softly as she saw the dark shadows under the girl's eyes, the tear stains on her cheeks.

"Poor lamb," the woman murmured. "She's all done in."

Adam Trent grunted softly. Then he drew his gun and waved it in Shunkaha Luta's direction. "Get over here," he ordered. "Sit down with your back to the bed."

Shunkaha Luta did as bidden and Trent unlocked the handcuffs and handcuffed Shunkaha's right hand to the brass bed frame.

"That should hold you for the night," the lawman mused, holstering his gun. He turned to Margie Croft. "We'll be leaving at first light."

"Leaving?" Margie Croft echoed. "Who's going to look after Brianna and the baby when you're gone?"

"Why, I assumed you'd be here."

Margie Croft shook her head. Perhaps if Trent thought Brianna would be all alone, he would stay for a few days, thereby giving Shunkaha Luta and Brianna more time together.

"We have to get back to town," Margie Croft said. "We have a business to run, you know." She looked over her shoulder at her husband, who was standing in the doorway. "In fact, we'd best be getting on home. It's late, and we have to open the store first thing in the morning. Goodnight, Mr.

Trent, Shunkaha. We'll be by to look in on Brianna in a couple of days."

Adam Trent swore softly as the Crofts left the house. He had intended to head out for Bismarck at first light. Now he'd have to hang around here until Brianna was on her feet again. He scowled at Shunkaha Luta. How long did it take for a woman to recover from childbirth, he wondered irritably.

Tossing his hat on the bureau, he sat down in the rocking chair near the window, took off his boots, and settled back to try and get some sleep.

The sound of a baby crying aroused Brianna from a deep sleep. Frowning, she snuggled deeper into her blankets, wondering what a baby was doing in the house, and then her eyes flew open. It was *her* baby, of course, hers and Shunkaha's.

She sat up as Adam Trent stepped into the room, a tiny blanket-wrapped bundle held awkwardly in his arms, his face wearing a look bordering on fear.

"Here," Trent said, thrusting the baby into Brianna's arms. "I think he's hungry."

"Yes," Brianna agreed. She looked past Trent to the foot of the bed where Shunkaha Luta sat glaring at the lawman. "Would you mind leaving the room while I . . ." Brianna blushed prettily. ". . . while I feed my son."

Now it was Adam Trent's turn to blush. "No, of course not," he said quickly. "I'll go out and look after your stock."

When they were alone, Shunkaha Luta stood up, stretching, and then he sat on the foot of the bed. Brianna smiled radiantly as she joined him there and they spent a moment admiring their son before she put the baby to her breast.

Shunkaha Luta felt a lump rise in his throat as he watched Brianna nurse their child. Surely he had never seen anything more lovely. Brianna had never looked more beautiful. A wealth of sun-gold hair fell around her shoulders like a

halo, and her eyes were warm with love for the child suck-
ling at her breast. And the child—he was a study in perfection from the top of his black-thatched head to the soles of
his tiny pink feet. He reached out to stroke a chubby little
hand and the baby's fingers curled around his, holding tight.

"Are you pleased with your son, my husband?" Brianna
asked.

Shunkaha Luta nodded, not trusting his voice.

"How do you say father in Lakota?"

"*Ate.*"

"And mother?"

"*Ina.*"

"Well, *ate*, what shall we call him?"

"Do you wish him to have a Lakota name, or a white
name?"

"Could he not have both?"

Shunkaha Luta nodded. "If you wish. Though it might be
better if you raise him as a white child."

"Why do you say that? He is half Lakota, and I want him
to know it and be proud of it."

A look of great sadness passed over Shunkaha's face. "I
will not be here to help you raise him, or to teach him the
ways of the People. It will be better for him, and for you, to
pretend that he is white."

Brianna bit down on her lower lip. She had pushed all
thought of Adam Trent aside for the moment, wanting only
to take joy in her son, to bask in her husband's love. Now, too
soon, Shunkaha Luta's words had brought her back to reality.

"Shunkaha, what will I do without you?"

"You will do the best you can, as always, little one. I will
have no worries for my son, for I know his mother will raise
him well."

His words brought tears to Brianna's eyes, and she pressed
her head against his shoulder. How could she go on without
him? Each day of their lives together she had grown to love

him more, to need him more. How could she face the responsibility of rearing a son without a husband to help her? How could she face the future without the man whose hand was stroking her hair, whose love and strength and goodness she had come to rely on?

Shunkaha Luta gazed out the window as he stroked Brianna's hair. How could he leave her alone? A woman needed a man; a son needed a father. He thought he would rather cut off his right arm than leave her, and yet he had no choice. Adam Trent was determined to take his prisoner back to Bismarck. His only hope was that he would be able to escape, and yet, even that would solve nothing. He was a wanted man. He could not ask Brianna to spend her life hiding out in the hills because of him. What kind of life would that be for the woman he loved, for his son? Truly, she would be better off without him.

"Have you thought of a name yet?" Brianna asked, her voice muffled against his arm.

"No. You decide."

"I've always liked the name David," Brianna mused. "It was my father's name. What would you think of calling our son David Red Wolf?"

Shunkaha Luta repeated the name, and then he nodded. "It is a good name, Ishna Wi." He drew away as the door opened and Adam Trent entered the room bearing a tray.

"I'm not much of a cook," the lawman remarked, placing the tray on the table beside the bed, "but I did my best."

"Thank you, Adam," Brianna said. "It looks fine."

Trent handed a plate of bacon and eggs to Shunkaha. "You want some coffee?"

Shunkaha Luta nodded. He offered no thanks when Trent handed him a cup. The man was an intruder in his house, the enemy. He deserved no thanks.

"Leave us," Shunkaha Luta said. "I wish to be alone with my woman."

Adam Trent frowned. It was on the tip of his tongue to tell the Indian to go to hell, and then he shrugged. The man deserved to spend some time with his wife and child. He threw Shunkaha a wry grin, plucked the butter knife from the tray, and left the room.

Adam Trent cooled his heels for three days. In that time, he did the cooking, tended the stock, tried not to be jealous of the fond looks that passed between Brianna and the Indian. Brianna looked radiant whenever she held her son, cooing to him, softly stroking his downy cheek, rocking him to sleep. He felt a twinge of guilt at the thought that he was taking away the man she loved, that he was depriving a child of its father, but it wasn't his fault that the Indian was a murderer. A man committed a crime, he had to pay the price. That was the way of the world.

He was a little surprised at Brianna. He had expected her to beg him not to take Shunkaha Luta back to Bismarck. He had thought she might even resort to tears, but she never mentioned their imminent leave-taking, and Trent was grateful. It proved she was resigned to the inevitable, that she had accepted it. She was unfailingly kind and polite, apparently harboring no ill will, and he was grateful for that, too, because he had not given up the hope that she would be his once the Indian was out of the way.

Brianna recovered her strength quickly, and on the morning of the fifth day after the child had been born, Trent informed her that he was leaving that afternoon.

"So soon?" Brianna said.

"I'm afraid so. Is there anything that needs doing before I leave? I think you've got enough wood to last a couple of months."

"Thank you, Adam. You've been very kind."

Her words cut into Adam Trent's heart. *Kind, indeed,* he thought guiltily.

"I'll go out and feed the stock and make sure everything's in good shape," Trent said, not meeting her eyes. "Would you mind packing us a lunch?"

"Of course not."

"Thanks."

Brianna prepared a huge lunch and packed it in a sack, then went in to sit with Shunkaha Luta. He took her in his arms and held her close, his face buried in her hair, and she felt the tension in him and knew that he was dying inside because he was being taken away from her, away from their son.

They sat quietly close for an hour, not saying a word. It was enough that they were together. Later, Shunkaha watched as she nursed their son, and then she placed the boy in his father's arms, felt the tears burn in her throat as she gazed at the two people she loved most in all the world.

Too soon, Adam Trent came to get Shunkaha Luta. Brianna clung to her husband, showering his face with kisses, whispering that she loved him.

"*Ohinniyan,*" she murmured as he pressed one last kiss to her lips. "Forever."

"*Ohinniyan,*" Shunkaha Luta murmured, and then she was standing on the porch, alone, watching Adam Trent and Shunkaha ride away.

She watched them until they were out of sight, and then she turned and went into the house. Moving quickly, she prepared a sack of food and set it aside. Going into the bedroom, she packed her child's diapers and clothing, added a change of underwear and clothing for herself, as well as her hairbrush and her personal toilet items.

Laying the baby in his cradle, she went out to the barn and saddled her horse, then turned all the stock loose.

Back at the house, she whisked about, making certain everything was locked up. She washed the breakfast dishes, made the bed, took up her provisions in one hand and the baby in the other, and left the house, carefully locking the door behind her. Adam Trent might think he was taking Shunkaha Luta away from her without a fight, but he had another think coming!

It was near dusk when she came upon the lawman's night camp. Shunkaha Luta was handcuffed to a tree; Trent was frying up a mess of beans and bacon when Brianna rode up.

"Got enough for one more?" she asked.

"What the hell are you doing here?" Trent asked brusquely.

"I'm going to Bismarck."

Adam Trent stared at Brianna, at a loss for words. He glanced at his prisoner, saw that the Indian was grinning openly.

"Did you have anything to do with this?" Trent demanded.

Shunkaha Luta shook his head, his eyes on Brianna's face. They had been separated for only a few hours, yet he had missed her dreadfully. The thought that he might never see her again had filled him with despair, and now she was here, her sky-blue eyes alight with mischief.

"Well, Mr. Trent, are you going to stand there staring at me all night, or are you going to help me down?"

"What? Oh." Trent moved forward and lifted Brianna to the ground. *Women*, he thought irritably. *They were more unpredictable than flash floods and summer storms.*

The baby was asleep and Brianna placed him beside Shunkaha, then went to the fire and began stirring the beans.

Adam Trent watched helplessly, and then he sat down on his saddle, his chin cupped in the palms of his hands, his elbows resting on his knees. *Women*, he thought again, and let his eyes rest on her face.

Brianna chatted amiably through dinner, her conversation including both men. Shunkaha Luta said little, and Adam Trent said less. Brianna seemed not to notice.

After dinner, she washed up the dishes, nursed the baby, then sat beside the fire, inviting Adam to join her.

"All right," Trent said, letting out a long breath. "What's this all about?"

"I want you to let Shunkaha go free."

"I can't do that," Trent retorted, surprised she would even ask such a thing. "He's wanted by the law for killing a man."

"It was self-defense."

"Was it? Not the way I heard it."

"And what did you hear?"

"I read the report McClain's partner filed. It said the Indian escaped and bashed McClain's brains in."

"It wasn't like that. McClain had shot Shunkaha and would have finished him off. There was a struggle and Shunkaha killed him in self-defense."

Trent snorted. "Is that what he told you?"

"Yes, and I believe him."

Trent shrugged. "I guess you can believe what you want, but it doesn't change anything."

"You don't believe it was self-defense," Brianna accused, "and neither will anyone else."

"He'll get a trial."

"Sure," Brianna said. "And who'll be sitting on that jury? Twelve white men who think just like you do."

"Dammit, Brianna, I don't make the laws!"

"Isn't there anything I can say to make you change your mind?"

"No, so you might as well go on back home in the morning."

"Oh, no," Brianna said, playing her ace in the hole. "You're very stubborn about upholding the law. You see only black and white. Very well, Mr. Trent, then I insist you arrest me for helping Shunkaha escape from jail."

"Don't be ridiculous."

"I'm perfectly serious. And if you won't arrest me, then I'll turn myself in when we get to Bismarck."

Adam Trent swore under his breath. Women! He raked his fingers through his hair, then scowled at Brianna. Was she serious? Would she really turn herself in?

"Fine, turn yourself in," he said, calling her bluff. "But if they arrest you and send you to prison, they'll take your baby and put it in a foster home. Is that what you want?"

"No," Brianna said in a small voice. "I want you to let Shunkaha go free. Please, Adam. He saved your life, you know. Doesn't that mean anything to you?"

"Of course it does, and I'm grateful. But I can't compromise the law. I took an oath when I pinned on this badge. I swore to uphold the law."

"Then I'm under arrest, too!"

Adam Trent let out a long sigh. What was he going to do with her?

Before he had quite made up his mind, a gunshot rang out in the stillness. Trent swore as the bullet plowed a deep furrow near his bootheel. Pushing Brianna to the ground, he drew his gun and fired at the muzzle flash as a second gunshot nicked his left arm.

There was a wild war cry, and an arrow swished through the air to land in the tree just above Shunkaha Luta's head.

There followed a heavy silence, and then a voice called out of the darkness. "Throw down your weapons, *wasicu,* or you will all die."

Shunkaha Luta grinned into the darkness. "*Hou, colapi,*" he called. "Hello, friends."

"Shut up!" Trent hissed.

"*Hou, cola,*" called the voice from the darkness. "What are you doing with the *wasicu?*"

"I am his prisoner. My wife and child, also."

"Shut up," Trent warned, "or I'll kill you now."

"That would be a mistake," Shunkaha Luta remarked.
"The Lakota will not look fondly on one who kills a brother."
"Perhaps you should surrender," Brianna suggested.
"Surrender!" Adam Trent exclaimed. "Are you crazy? Besides, there can't be very many of them or they'd rush us."

There was a movement in the underbrush, the sound of a gunshot and a high-pitched yelp as a bullet found its mark in Trent's right shoulder. His Colt fell from a hand gone numb, and before he could retrieve it, he was surrounded by three Lakota warriors.

Two of them jerked the lawman to his feet and bound his hands behind his back while the third warrior unlocked the cuffs and freed Shunkaha.

No one was paying any attention to Brianna, and she hurried toward her son, picked him up, and held him to her breast. He made a sleepy sound and snuggled against her, his thumb in his mouth.

Shunkaha and the Lakota warriors were talking rapidly among themselves. After a short while, the three warriors sat down and began rummaging through Trent's packs for something to eat.

Brianna came to stand beside her husband. "Who are they?"

"Renegades. They have left the reservation and now they are on the run because they killed a white soldier." Shunkaha Luta glanced at Adam Trent, who was squatting on the ground. His right shirt sleeve was soaked with blood, and his face was pale. A fine layer of sweat sheened his brow.

Brianna followed Shunkaha's gaze. "What are they going to do to us?"

"Nothing."

"And Adam?"

"They mean to kill him, a little at a time."

"Why?"

"He killed one of them when he fired into the brush."

"But that was self-defense."

Shunkaha Luta shrugged as if it were of no importance. "These warriors are renegades, Ishna Wi. They have no families. They cannot go back to the reservation. They are angry and confused and they feel the need to shed blood."

Brianna laid her hand on Shunkaha Luta's arm. "You can't let them kill Adam," she said urgently. "You must stop them."

Shunkaha Luta gazed down at Brianna, his dark eyes glittering fiercely. "You must not interfere in this, Ishna Wi. No matter what happens this night, you must not interfere. The blood lust is strong within these men. I do not know how much honor they have left."

Brianna held her child closer as a cold chill crept down her spine. She realized suddenly what Shunkaha was trying to tell her. These men had nothing to lose and nowhere to go. If they turned on Shunkaha, there would be no one to protect her and the baby.

It was going to be a very long night.

Chapter Twenty-three

Brianna sat in the shadows several yards from the roaring fire, her son pressed to her breast, her face drawn and pale as she watched Shunkaha and the other three warriors dance around their prisoner. Shunkaha Luta had shed his shirt, and the bright orange shadows cast by the flames flickered across his chest and face, touching his skin with a hellish cast. Fear for her own life and for that of her child and Adam Trent grew with each passing moment, for this was a side of Shunkaha Luta she had never seen.

Adam Trent had been stripped naked and spread-eagled near the fire. Sweat ran freely from his body, caused by the nearness of the flames and the gut-wrenching fear that twisted his insides, filling his mouth with the brassy taste of terror.

The Lakota warriors danced for three-quarters of an hour, then they sank down on their haunches and regarded the white man through fathomless black eyes.

The lawman's mouth went dry as one of the warriors drew a knife from a beaded sheath on his belt. A low murmur of barely contained excitement rose from the throats of the other warriors. The fun was about to begin.

A cold grin spread over Shunkaha Luta's face as he took the knife from the warrior's hand. "White man," he said, his voice hard and merciless, "how much pain can you bear without weeping?"

Trent swallowed hard. "What do you mean?" It was hard to speak, his throat was so dry.

"My brothers mean to cut the flesh from your body an

inch at a time." Slowly, Shunkaha Luta laid the blade against Trent's chest. A slight increase in pressure drew blood. "You know how it is when you cut yourself, how it hurts when the air hits the wound? Your whole body will feel like that. You will wish for death, white man, but it will be a long time coming."

"Go to hell," Trent rasped.

Shunkaha Luta grinned. "Perhaps you are braver than I thought." He nodded. "We will soon know."

Trent's whole body went rigid as Shunkaha Luta tossed the knife to its owner. In desperation, he twisted his head around, his eyes fixed on Brianna. *I will not scream,* he vowed. *No matter what they do to me, I will not scream.*

Brianna had laid her son on the ground beside her. Now she rose to her knees, her hand pressed to her heart, as she gazed at Adam Trent. Oh, why hadn't he stayed in Bismarck, she thought helplessly. If he died, it would be partly her fault.

She lifted her gaze to her husband's face, unable to believe that this was the same man who had loved her so tenderly, who had treated her with unfailing kindness. Never had he looked more savage. Never had she feared him more.

The Indian with the knife bent forward and she could see his hand moving across Trent's chest as he made a shallow square cut and drew away a strip of flesh.

Gagging, she turned away, unable to watch.

Shunkaha Luta threw a brief glance in Brianna's direction, silently praying that she would not interfere. He was playing a dangerous game, and all their lives hung in the balance.

Adam Trent sucked in a deep breath as the knife-wielding warrior cut into his flesh a second time. The pain was intense, yet worse than the pain was the fear that he would not be able to hold back the cry that would brand him a coward. From someplace deep in the back of his mind came a reminder that the Indians hated a weakling, that white men who had behaved badly while being tortured were made to suffer more, while those who laughed in the face of pain and fear were often granted a quick death.

A sudden sense of loss, of sadness, filled Adam Trent's heart. Was that all he had to look forward to now, just a quick death?

"White man."

He heard Shunkaha's voice as if from far away. With an effort, he drew his gaze from Brianna's trembling form and met the Lakota warrior's eyes. He was surprised to see that they were alone. The other three warriors had gone into the bushes to relieve themselves.

"What do you want?" Adam Trent forced the question through trembling lips. He was shivering convulsively now.

"I am going to offer you a life, white man. Your life in exchange for mine."

"What do you mean?"

"My brothers have agreed to release you if you will let me return to Winslow with Brianna, and bother us no more. In addition, you will take the body of my dead warrior brother and tell your people it is mine so that no one else will come hunting me."

Adam Trent stared at Shunkaha Luta, unable to speak. Relief went through him like sand held too tightly in a hand.

Shunkaha Luta mistook his silence for doubt and his face grew hard. "I will not ask you again, white man. I said once that I would not spare your life a second time, but I do so now because Brianna thinks highly of you. Whether you live or die makes no difference. I will return to Winslow with my woman. You will never have her."

"I accept your offer," Trent said quickly, and then he gazed at Shunkaha Luta intently. "Do you think me a coward?"

Laughter erased the harsh lines from the warrior's face as

he picked up a knife and cut the white man free. "I think you are a wise man," he allowed. "Wise and brave. And if you are smart, you will leave this place tonight, before my brothers change their mind."

"Smart's my middle name," Trent said. Rising to his feet, he pulled on his pants, then held out his hand. "I'm much obliged for your help, both here and back in Winslow."

Shunkaha Luta nodded gravely as they shook hands. "I hope that someday you find a woman to please you as my woman pleases me."

Adam Trent glanced at Brianna, who was standing across the fire. "I hope so, too," he said softly, and collecting the rest of his gear, and the body lying dead in the brush, he rode away from the camp. He never saw Brianna again.

Brianna and Shunkaha Luta did not have much time to talk that night. The three Lakota warriors curled up near the fire and were soon snoring softly. Brianna was certain she would never be able to sleep after all that had happened, but she had barely closed her eyes when sleep claimed her.

The warriors were gone the following morning. Brianna felt strangely ill at ease with Shunkaha. As she nursed her son, she kept remembering how Shunkaha had looked dancing around the fire, the way his eyes had glittered when he held the knife. She could not help wondering what would have happened if the warriors had refused to release Adam. Would Shunkaha have taken part in torturing the lawman? Twice she started to ask Shunkaha what he would have done, and twice she swallowed the words, not certain she really wanted to know the answer.

When she finished nursing the baby, she prepared breakfast. Shunkaha Luta saddled their horses. They ate a silent meal, and then Brianna washed the dishes while Shunkaha packed their gear.

And then it was time to go.

Brianna was reaching for the baby when Shunkaha Luta caught her by the arm and turned her around to face him. "What is it?" he asked. "What is troubling you?"

"Troubling me? What could possibly be troubling me?"

"Ishna Wi, do not build walls between us."

Brianna gazed into his eyes, her own looking lost and confused. "I watched you last night and I didn't know you."

Shunkaha Luta frowned. "I do not understand."

"Would you have used that knife on Adam?"

Shunkaha Luta drew a deep breath and let it out in a long sigh. "What do you think?"

"I don't know. I would like to believe that you wouldn't, that you could not be so cruel. So . . ."

"Savage?"

"Yes," she admitted shamefully.

"I would have, at one time," Shunkaha Luta told her. "But no more."

"Because of me?"

"Yes." Shunkaha Luta smiled at her. "The warriors intended to kill Trent, but I told them that I needed him alive, and they agreed."

"Then all that business about skinning him alive was a farce?"

"Yes, once I had convinced them to let me have the white man for my own purposes."

"That was cruel, letting Adam think he was going to die when you knew all along he wasn't."

Shunkaha Luta shrugged. "It was the only way I could think of to make him see things my way." He drew her close and kissed her forehead. "Trent is alive and well, and Shunkaha Luta is dead as far as the white man's law is concerned. Are you not pleased?"

"Of course I am."

Shunkaha Luta took Brianna's face in his hands, his

thumbs tracing the line of her cheekbones. "I have often thought that I would return to my people, but I know now that you are my people. I listened to my brothers talk last night, heard the anger and the bitterness in their voices, the sense of hopelessness. They are lost, without homes, without family, without purpose. They are seeking the old way of life, but it is gone. I know that now."

His hands dropped to her shoulders and he drew her close, savoring the sweet softness of her, the way she pressed herself against him, her arms twining about his neck.

They stood together for a long moment, listening to their son gurgle contentedly. And then Brianna drew back a little, her eyes seeking her husband's. "Where are we going from here?"

"Home," Shunkaha Luta replied simply.

Brianna's heart skipped a beat. "To Winslow?"

Shunkaha Luta nodded. "The farm will be our home now. We will start a new life together, you and I. And our little one."

"Will you truly be happy there?"

"I am happy wherever you are," he replied, and drawing her into his arms, he kissed her, his lips moving over hers in a long possessive kiss filled with passion and promise for the future.

Brianna was breathless when he released her.

"Are you ready to go home, *mitawin*?" he asked.

"Yes," Brianna answered softly. Her heart was filled with joy as Shunkaha Luta lifted her to the back of her horse and placed their son in her arms.

She watched Shunkaha swing effortlessly aboard his own mount, her eyes admiring his easy strength, the spread of his shoulders, the love shining in his eyes.

And then she touched her heels to her horse's flanks and followed Shunkaha Luta home.

Epilogue

Brianna sat on the top rail of the fence, watching as Shunkaha Luta instructed their three-year-old son in the art of horseback riding. David Red Wolf was the image of his father, from the color of his hair and eyes to the way he walked and talked. He was listening attentively now as his father explained that he must hold the reins lightly but firmly, never letting them go slack so that he lost contact with the horse's mouth, never jerking on the reins.

Brianna's heart swelled with pride as she watched father and son. How quickly the time had gone, and how happy they were together. The farm was thriving. They had several hundred head of white-faced cattle, a half dozen well-bred horses, as well as the usual number of pigs and chickens. They had a dozen rabbits to please Davey, a sheep for Brianna, a huge yellow hound for Shunkaha. Brianna's garden flourished under her loving care, and their vegetables were eagerly bought by many of the people who lived in town.

Her eyes strayed to her husband. It had not been easy for him, learning to be a farmer, adjusting to spending both summer and winter in the same place. During the first year he had often been restless and she had harbored a secret fear that she would wake one day to find him gone, back to the mountains and valleys of the Black Hills. But, gradually, he had come to love the land as she did, to think of it as his, at least while he lived. Most of the townspeople had come to accept him, though some remained standoffish. A few refused to speak to either of them, but Brianna had learned to live with it, believing that, with time, everyone would come to appreciate Shunkaha Luta for the fine, decent man that he was.

Margie and Luke Croft had become their dearest friends. They spent Thanksgiving and Christmas together, went to the church dances and socials together, visited during the week. It was the Crofts who were truly instrumental in getting the other townspeople to accept the idea that Shunkaha was not a heathen savage. Luke and Margie were well liked and respected, and if they found no fault in Shunkaha, then perhaps there was nothing to find.

Shunkaha had given up buckskins for dungarees and a cotton shirt, had traded his moccasins for boots, at least when they went to town. Only his long hair remained unchanged.

Once, she had suggested that he cut his hair, but he had refused. "I cannot cut it," he had said with a wry smile. "I may live like a white man, I may dress like a white man, but I am not a white man. I am Lakota and proud of it."

It was the only request he had ever denied her and she accepted it without complaint. In truth, she liked his long hair, ancient symbol of a true Lakota warrior.

She sat there, basking in the sun, content to watch her husband and son as they circled the corral. Davey sat erect, his legs dangling at the horse's sides, his hands holding the reins as his father had taught him. He grinned and waved as they passed by her, and she waved back, but it was Shunkaha who held her attention. She never tired of looking at him.

Shunkaha Luta felt her gaze and his eyes found hers. A slow smile spread over his face, and Brianna felt her insides grow warm as his love crossed the distance between them, caressing her.

I love you. Brianna mouthed the words as she dropped her hand over her abdomen. A new life rested there, just beneath her heart.

Shunkaha Luta led the horse around the corral one more

time and then he lifted his son from the mare's back and Davey ran off toward the barn and the new kittens that were sleeping there.

With long easy strides Shunkaha Luta crossed the corral to stand beside Brianna, his arm circling her waist. Their eyes met and held and the love they shared passed quietly between them, as strong as the mountains, as sure as the sunrise.

Shunkaha Luta felt a tug at his heart as he gazed at Brianna. Much in his life had changed, but his love for her remained ever the same, and though he no longer hunted the buffalo in the shadow of the Pa Sapa, and though he no longer rode the war trail with the Lakota, he knew that, in the eyes of his woman, he would always be a warrior.

He placed his hands around her waist, lifting her from the fence into his arms. She smelled of sunshine and soap and freshly baked bread.

Gently he put her on her feet, his eyes never straying from her face. She was his woman, his wife, more precious, more beautiful, with each passing day.

"*Ohinniyan, wastelakapi,*" he murmured.

A wave of love washed over Brianna as she returned her husband's gaze, and she thought she would never ask for more out of life than the riches she already had: a lovely home, a healthy child, and a man who loved her with all his heart, as she loved him.

"Forever, beloved," she replied, and lifted her face for his kiss.

Manufactured by Amazon.ca
Bolton, ON

22349102R00168